LOVE (LITERALLY) BITES

CORINA BAIR

Cover art by @little_alfard

First edition, January, 2026
Copyright © 2025 Corina Bair

Paperback ISBN: 979-8-9909467-5-0
EPUB/ebook ISBN: 979-8-9909467-4-3

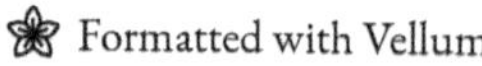 Formatted with Vellum

For everyone who hides who they truly are, even from themselves.

Let your inner freak shine!

Author Note

Hello lovely romance readers,

I have two important things to share with you before you read Love (Literally) Bites.

First, this story takes place in a queer-normative world. There are multiple characters who are part of the LGBTQ+ community, but they do not experience discrimination, prejudice, fear of coming out, or any of the atrocities we experience in the real world by being part of this community. I understand that the characters' experiences are not representative of the world we live in, and I have done this intentionally. I hope you find relief in not only the lack of conflict and hate, but the unconditional love and acceptance this book brings.

Second, although this is a feel-good contemporary romance with significant paranormal elements, please review these content notes:
   - Physical assault
   - Estranged parents/family
   - History of unhealthy/mentally abusive parents (not referenced directly but implied through memories/dialogue about the past)
   - Workplace harassment, fired from job
   - Drinking blood (because vampires)

Thank you, and happy reading!
   Corina

1

SHIFT HAPPENS

RAYA

I DO NOT HAVE the energy or mental fortitude I need to deal with ill-mannered, entitled old men today. If he interrupts me one more time... well, I won't do much because I need this job, but I will do my best to send bad karma after him, that's for sure. I plaster something that hopefully resembles a polite smile on my face and unclench my jaw.

"As I was explaining, Mr. Bartholomew, Henry has all of the data points prepared and will send them over to you as soon as he is back in the office." I do my best to explain patiently—again—why I'm giving this presentation at the last minute instead of Henry, my coworker who has been collaborating with this client for the last six months. Mr. Bartholomew, however, doesn't think highly of these circumstances, and based on the increasing scowl on his face, he's determined to remain unhappy.

"For now," I continue, "these are the statistics I was provided—"

"I don't have time for this incompetence," he says, pounding a hand on the table in emphasis. I wish I were surprised that none of the other men in the room intervene on my behalf, and it doesn't escape my notice that I'm the only woman present. "I demand to speak with your supervisor."

At this final insult, my patience snaps, and I can feel it happening. My skin tingles for a split second before it starts to reshape.

Oh no, no, no. Not now, not now!

I whip my body around, giving my back to the room as long, white whiskers sprout on my cheeks and my nose shrinks. The pain is fleeting, thankfully, though the circumstances could certainly be better. Wondering what animal it is this time, I hesitantly reach up to my face, fluttering my fingers over my cheekbones and meeting soft, short fur surrounding a flat, twitching nose.

Rabbit. Awesome.

I squeeze my eyes shut, willing myself not to let the frustrated tears fall. Not where any of the men in this room can see. As subtly as I can, I run a hand up and over my hair, sighing in relief when I find no floppy rabbit ears to go with the nose and whiskers already adorning my face.

Belatedly, I realize multiple voices have risen around the room, including the increasingly loud voice of Mr. Bartholomew demanding my attention.

Taking a deep breath, I straighten my shoulders, tip my chin up, and slowly turn back to the conference room, balling my hands into fists at my sides. I latch my eyes onto the wall above the heads of those in attendance for this disaster of a presentation, and attempt to close my ears to the stifled gasps that ricochet around the room.

Mr. Bartholomew, unsurprisingly, has not even one polite bone in his body and therefore no problem shattering the haunting silence. "What is this?" he bellows. "In all my days, never have I been met with such ineptitude. An out of control shifter, acting like an animal on top of everything else that has gone wrong in this meeting? Absolutely not. I will not stand for it—"

The door to the conference room flies open and my boss strides in. All it takes is one look at me for his lips to pinch, flattening into a thin line as he turns to the outraged clients.

"I apologize for my employee's behavior," my boss begins, and I have to hold in my squeak of protest at his assessment of the situation. "Please, let me see what I can do," he says, gesturing for Mr. Bartholomew to take his seat again.

As everyone settles back into their chairs, he turns to the front of the room where I'm still frozen, the clicker clenched in my fist. "Raya. You're dismissed."

Just like that, I no longer exist to any of them. Not even Mr. Bartholomew graces me with so much as a sneer as I rush from the room. Eager to be away from the excess of toxic energy, I slip into the bathroom down the hall, lock the door behind me, then slowly walk over to the sink, avoiding my reflection in the mirror.

My knuckles turn white as I clench the sides of the sink in front of me, holding my breath to prevent a scream of frustration. I squeeze my eyes closed, then take a quick breath and brace myself to look in the mirror.

There it is. White whiskers, as I suspected, on either side of where my nose should be. Instead of a human nose though, the flattened, triangular shape of a rabbit nose covered in silvery white fur twitches at me. I gently run my fingers over the part of my face that has shifted. I look ridiculous.

At least it's soft.

If I had the nose to do so, I would have snorted. Some-times I hate that my brain always provides a positive. Some-times I don't want to see the silver lining, but that's not how my mind works.

Shaking my head, I turn away from the mirror and stretch my arms wide, rolling my shoulders to loosen the tension that crept into my neck and back throughout that meeting. There's not much else to be done; in my experience, once I shift, it's simply a waiting game. Whatever part of me took on animal features could go back to normal in thirty seconds, or it could take thirty minutes. Luckily, it never lasts much longer than that.

Not yet, at least.

As I force the meeting from my mind, I lean back against the closed door, propping one foot up on it as I wait, and trying not to let my thoughts spiral. I rush back to the mirror when I feel tingling again, just as the lightning flash of pain crosses my face and the fur recedes, my normal features returning to me. I blow out a breath, puffing my cheeks out and scrunching up my very normal, human-looking nose to test its durability.

I waste no time as I leave the bathroom, dashing through the hallway back to my cubicle and flinging myself into my chair. I promptly bury my face in my hands, pressing the heels of my palms into my eyes until I see spots behind my eyelids.

That. Was. Awful.

I can finally admit to myself how truly terrible the entire experience was now that I have a little space from the incident —and don't have fur sprouting from my face. I'm gearing up for an internal pep talk work when a curly-haired redhead appears in the opening of my cubicle, knocking twice on the faux-doorframe.

"Hey Raya, boss wants to see you," she says with a slight cringe, which I return. We both know this won't be good.

When I get to his office, I wait for him to speak first, offering a polite smile that he does not return. My boss is an average looking man, and he sits at an average looking desk, doing what I consider to be an average sort of job. All in all, not the best boss, but not too terrible either.

"I'll cut right to the chase," he says, slicing through the silence. "You're fired."

"I'm..." My mouth is hanging open. "What?"

"I'm sorry, Raya. I don't know what sort of... condition," he stumbles over the wording before rushing through the rest, "you are dealing with, and it's not my business, but it's obviously getting worse and you clearly can't control it. The shifting. Whatever is happening with you, I mean." He pauses for a breath, and I snap my mouth closed. "Ultimately, it's become a problem to the point that it's making many of us humans in the office uncomfortable, and it's risking our client relationships. Your performance today nearly cost us one of our biggest contracts, and we can't afford that."

"Right..." My voice is quiet, barely more than a whisper as I attempt to process how unfair this is.

"You understand. Of course you know you need to figure out whatever this is." He vaguely waves his hand around the space in front of me, then waits like he expects me to agree with him. When I continue to blink in his direction, he clears his throat roughly before continuing. "Alright then, that'll be all. Have your desk cleared out by the end of the day. We'll mail your last check."

I stand on shaky legs and walk in a fog back to my cubicle. Someone left an empty box on my desk. My face flames in embarrassment and I do my best to prevent myself from reacting any further as I pack up the few possessions I have in my work space.

The past twelve months since I graduated have been rough. I'm tired of bouncing from one consulting agency to the next, only staying for a few months at a time before leaving for one reason or another. I'm especially tired of not feeling financially secure, and my thoughts immediately go to what my parents will think of yet another failure, and my heart sinks. I don't want them worrying about me any more than they already do.

Lugging the box into my arms, I straighten and take one last glance at my bare cubicle before I turn around to leave. It's only then that I notice the uneasy quiet around me, the lack of talking or typing. Faces peeking over cubicle walls and around corners, eyes that quickly slide away from me when I notice them.

Their last chance to get a look at the shifter freak.

It brings all the embarrassment, fear, and unfairness rushing back in. Pinching my lips together, I avert my eyes, fixing them on the floor. Only one person acknowledges or speaks to me as I leave—my boss's assistant—who whispers a soft, "I'm sorry, Raya" as I pass her desk.

This seems to be the final straw, as that tell-tale tingle is back, and before I know it, whiskers adorn my face again. I heave a sigh, heft the box a little higher in my arms, and trudge toward the elevator.

It's not until the doors have slid closed that my brain starts spinning back to the meeting. When I was constantly being interrupted and belittled, talked to like I was an idiot. I can't believe how rude those men were, and I hate that there was no one on my side, especially because I didn't do anything wrong.

It's this that angers me the most, as embarrassment morphs into defiant frustration. I did not do anything wrong. With that thought, I exit the elevator and push my way through the doors outside. Anger swirls in my chest as I fumble with my phone, intending to call a ride share so I don't have to walk the mile back to my apartment with this stupid box, when the tell-tale tingling prickles my skin again.

2

____

PESKY LITTLE TRUTH-TELLING SPRITE

RAYA

My frantic gaze scours the street, hoping some miracle can stop it, but in the blink of an eye, my hands and forearms sprout coarse fur, turning into wolf paws: pads, claws and all. Of course, this means the box I was carrying is now on the ground, with my possessions scattered across the sidewalk.

I hate this day. I am not a hateful person, but this day, I *hate.*

As my eyes flick between my hands—*paws*—and my belongings scattered around me, time slows. Everything seems to stop, the sounds of the cars driving by lengthen and stretch, the chatter of people quiets to a low buzz, and the sidewalk and buildings around me tunnel out of my vision. It's almost as though I have ceased to be, until a light touch brushes my elbow, there and then gone, and reality snaps back in a rush.

"Hello? Are you okay?" A low, smooth voice pulls me back to my senses, grounding me.

I blink, my eyes sharpening on the man standing before me. A man with dark brown hair and piercing blue eyes who towers over my five foot, three inches.

Hellooooo, hotness, my brain happily supplies, while the rest of me remains immobile, blinking at the disorienting world around me.

"Do you need help?" That voice pulls at me. He's bent at the waist so he can look directly into my eyes, and my brain takes far too long to stumble back into motion. I scrunch my eyes shut, count to five, then open them again, hoping against hope I imagined this whole scenario.

"I was stepping out for a coffee," the stranger says, crouching down further to pick up my belongings and place them back in the box, "when I saw you drop everything." He glances at my paws, then up to my eyes. My face heats, likely turning red around the fur and whiskers. "Lucky timing, I guess."

My brows draw together. "Lucky timing?"

"Well, it doesn't look like anyone else was going to help you."

I can't tell what that detached tone of voice means, but I suppose he's right. He straightens, box tucked under one arm, and reaches into his back pocket. "Looks like you might need a ride?"

"Oh, no, that's okay, I was just going to call a ride share," I say, not wanting to get into a car with this bizarre, semi-kind stranger.

He flips his phone around without a word, showing me that he had the exact app already open that I was planning to use, and I shuffle my feet, chewing the inside of my lip as I debate the situation. He raises one eyebrow while his lips flatten into a scowl. I could wait it out, but there's no telling how long it'll be until my hands are usable again, and the last thing I want is any of my now former coworkers to see me sporting wolf paws in addition to the furry face.

"I imagine it may be hard to call one on your own with..." he cocks his head, looking intently at the ends of my sleeves where my hands should be, "paws?"

"Yeah..." I sigh, shoulders slumping, and hold them up in front of me. The mustard yellow sleeves of my cropped sweater slip down my furry forearms, exposing the wolfy appendages to the crisp, Portland air. "Embarrassing, right?"

He shrugs and starts typing. "Address?"

Although confounded by his lack of response to my very unusual partial-shifts, I suppose I have no better options, so I give him an intersection near my apartment.

"Three minutes," he says, and I offer a nod of thanks.

I can't help glancing at him from the corner of my eye, my head bobbing in an awkward nod while darting my gaze along everything around us except him. The quiet becomes unbearable after only a few seconds.

"You don't have to wait with me," I say.

He looks down, pinning me with vibrant blue eyes. "It's fine. I'd rather not leave you standing out here alone after that spectacle."

I pull back, weirdly thankful, but also affronted. I'm not expecting the rough tone or the backhanded nature of that statement, but he doesn't seem to notice, and a black sedan pulls up not long after.

He opens the back door, sticking his head in to converse with the driver before stepping back and gesturing me inside. I sit down and attempt to grab the seatbelt, forgetting for a moment that I don't currently have thumbs. My eyes turn up to the sky as my lips pinch, resigned to hoping I don't die in a car wreck today, when the box is settled onto my knees and the stranger grabs the seatbelt, pulling it out and leaning across my body to buckle me in. My eyes flare and I suck in a breath, pushing back into the seat as far as I can and trying to ignore how incredible he smells as he invades my space. Something woodsy and warm, a stark contrast to his abrupt demeanor.

"All set," he says as he pulls away, though I'm unsure if he's talking to me or the driver. He steps back from the car, nods once, and then closes the door. No warning or goodbye, not even a wish for good luck.

My attention snaps to the driver when he asks me to confirm the destination. By the time I look back out the window, we're already moving and my confusingly gruff rescuer is nowhere in sight.

I TRUDGE up the steps to my apartment, thankful my shift back to all human features happened after only a few minutes of awkwardness during the ride share. I let the box thud to the hallway floor outside my apartment so I can search for my keys, when Reverie shrieks from the other side of the door.

"Zuri, it's Raya. She's home early!" The little creature bellows at the top of her lungs, which comes out like a tinny, high pitched screech as she's only about seven inches tall and weighs less than the light scarf around my neck. She's a cute little sprite, regardless of how piercing her excitement can be.

I give up on finding my keys, knowing Zuri will let me in, and sure enough, the door flies open only a few seconds later. I nudge the box inside with my foot and push my way past my roommate, then flop onto the couch in the living room. Reverie is flitting around in front of my face, sparkling pink wings flickering behind her and muttering under her breath about how my forehead wrinkles are on full display this afternoon, which is just fantastic considering sprites aren't able to lie.

Moon above, I'm only twenty-two. I shouldn't even have forehead wrinkles yet.

I rub my fingers across my forehead before waving my hand at Reverie to back off. She flits to the back of the couch, choosing to pace back and forth across the top of the cushion, which is at least better than flying around my face. My fingers move from my forehead to my temples, rubbing little circles for a moment before I cover my eyes with both hands, wishing I could hide from reality for a little while.

A finger taps on the back of one hand a moment later, and I remove them slowly, cracking one eye open to see Zuri hovering over me. Her box braids create a curtain around us as her eyes dart between mine, eyebrows pinched together.

"Careful, Reverie will come after your wrinkles next if you keep that up," I mutter.

"Why are you home? With all your work stuff? Did you quit?" Z fires questions at me, her warm brown eyes wide with concern and I groan, but there's no avoiding it.

I sit up and address my two best friends, the ones who know everything about me. I tell them about the meeting, how I was fired, and the confusing signals from the helpful stranger that allowed me to get home safely. I'm thankful for their gasps of shock and outrage on my behalf, and soon I'm smiling at Reverie's threats to "show them who they're messing with" and Zuri's assertions that it's their loss and I will come out on top and find something better suited where I'm appreciated anyway.

I unfold my legs and lean back, finally feeling like I'm able to relax after getting it all out. This is a disaster, but it's not irredeemable.

"So..." Zuri's voice is tentative, and I cautiously fix my gaze on her, eyebrows raised. "Well, I mean, I know it's not your favorite subject, but..."

"Just spit it out!" Reverie has little patience when it comes to speaking your mind. It's both a blessing and a curse, often at the same time.

Zuri shoots a glare at our tiny sprite friend, but secretly I agree with the sentiment.

"I only wanted to check in on the whole shifting thing,"

she says in a quick rush, and I figure I should have known that's what the stammering was about.

"It's fine," I reply.

"It's not fine. You were fired today because of it, it's been getting worse, so clearly it's not fine." We exchange equally heated glares, but I soon deflate, because Z is right.

"Okay, it's not fine, but I'm working on it."

"Are you? How?" Zuri's shoulders relax, and I feel a little bad at the white lie, but not bad enough to tell the truth—that I'm employing the timeless strategy of avoidance by distraction.

"Don't worry, I know it's serious, okay? But I've got it covered and bringing it up doesn't help." I try to soften my voice so the words don't come out as harsh as they sound, and Zuri nods. I flick my eyes to Reverie, who is now standing with her arms crossed on the knitted pillow next to me, wings pressed tight together and sapphire blue eyes narrowed in suspicion. She's also tapping one foot. I quickly look away.

"I just want you to be okay. It used to only happen once a month and now it's up to, what, pretty much every day? That's serious, Raya. What if it keeps getting worse?" Zuri says.

"Yeah, I know..." I trail off, looking down at my hands and remembering the wolf paws they turned into earlier. I don't like hearing one of my worst fears spoken aloud.

"Well, you'll land on your feet, and until then, you've got us," she says with a decisive nod, and I dredge up a smile.

I appreciate the sentiment, but I'm tired of being stuck in this same loop. I haven't been able to hold a steady job since graduating last year, and it's starting to make me seriously question what's wrong with me. Shaking my head in an attempt to rid myself of the thought, I come back to reality to hear Zuri asking what I'm going to tell my parents.

"I'm not going to tell them anything," I say.

Reverie and Zuri both give me questioning, slightly disapproving looks. I frown back at them.

"They already worry about me enough, as you just pointed out with the unexplained shifting, and I don't want to put any more stress on their shoulders. They've seen me fail enough times already." Not to mention the fact that if I don't find a new job soon, I won't be able to afford my portion of rent and will have to move back home with them.

"I'll start job hunting tomorrow and hopefully have a new one in no time. They don't even need to know anything happened." I infuse as much confidence into my voice as I can, hoping it will convince all three of us.

3

THANK GOODNESS FOR ANNOYING LITTLE BROTHERS

RAYA

It's been a few days since The Incident, as I've been calling it in my head, and that's given me enough time to come to terms with the situation so I don't feel like I'm drowning anymore. More like... floundering. In the waves. Where my feet can't touch, and I don't know where the shore is... But hey, my head's above water and I can breathe. That's pretty important, so I've got one good thing going, at least.

"HAPPY BIRTHDAY!" Two eager voices slap my ears as I round the corner into the kitchen.

I can't help but smile as I roll my eyes at the two of them. Reverie lives for birthdays. Well, what she lives for is sugar—it has a similar effect on sprites as alcohol does for humans, and birthdays are one of the times she lets herself cut loose. Currently, she's hopping up and down on the counter, bronze skin gleaming and sparkly wing dust flying everywhere.

As I watch, the excited hopping starts to transform. A couple wing flaps at the top of each jump flutter her higher into the air before she barely touches her toes to the counter and repeats the increasingly exuberant jumping-turned-flying, holding herself aloft for a couple seconds each time.

"Stars above. You're so stinking cute," I say to her. Reverie wrinkles her nose at the endearment, landing a little more roughly on the counter in response, but then clasps her hands to her chest and shimmies her body back and forth.

"What…" I narrow my eyes, gaze bouncing between Reverie and Zuri, who is sipping her coffee with innocently wide doe eyes and a much too casual pose leaning against the counter. I point between them. "What's going on? You didn't plan a surprise party, did you? You know I hate them."

Zuri snorts. "No, chill, we would never."

My shoulders drop from where I had apparently hiked them all the way up to my ears in the last four seconds. Surprise parties are one of my worst nightmares.

"Besides," Zuri continues, "I figured you wouldn't want to go out on account of all the shifty shifting lately, so we figured you'd like an afternoon in, just us. After you're done with family brunch, of course." Z smirks at her own pun, which is what makes me crack a smile too. I love when others think their own jokes are funny, especially when they're not.

"What's with the weirdness then?" I ask.

"We're just really excited!" Reverie yells as she shoots into the air again, executing a mildly impressive mid-air backflip, considering it didn't look intentional. "We have all your favorite things planned!"

"Ooooookay, and that's enough sugar for you." Zuri snags the frosting bowl and tray of cupcakes Reverie has been hovering around and sets them on the opposite side of the kitchen before turning an empty plastic container over on top of them.

"Good luck with that," I grin at Zuri, tipping my chin toward Reverie and her ongoing aerial acrobatics as I head toward the front door. Zuri tips her eyes to the sky in response, folding her hands in mock prayer for salvation.

"Have fun with your fam!" Reverie shouts from the kitchen. "Love you!"

"Love you too, you little chaos monster." I raise my voice as I aim my head toward the kitchen in reply to Reverie. "And you too," I say, turning to Zuri and exchanging a quick hug before I head out to meet my other favorite people.

CUTE DOESN'T EVEN BEGIN to describe this place. It's sickeningly adorable, with pastel colored walls and tables, crisp white chairs, cloth napkins folded like swans, and fresh flowers in vintage vases centered on each table. It's basically begging to be posted all over social media, and since I'm the first of our group to arrive, who am I to deny such a clear sign from the universe?

Right as I finish snapping a couple pictures, familiar rambunctious voices that can only belong to my family rico-chet through the door. My mother comes striding in like she owns the place, long silky hair flowing behind her and arms already outstretched. Her heels click across the floor, and I inhale her cool, fresh scent as she leans in for a hug, then strokes my hair and arm as I pull away, wishing me a happy birthday. My dad is next, smiling softly as he waits his turn. He's a portly man, shorter than my mom with a gentle, relaxed nature, and he gives the best cozy hugs.

My siblings have already rounded the table, waiting their turn for hugs while engaging in some sort of intense discussion about beaches, or the ocean. I'm not quite following, but whatever it is, they are very invested. Our mom clears her throat pointedly in their direction and they snap to attention; I don't suppress my grin, relishing that I'm not the one in trouble this time.

My older sister, Josephine, waves a hand in our mother's direction as she saunters around the table to embrace me.

"Happy birthday, little sis," she says, then pats me on the head like a child before running her fingers through my hair. I roll my eyes; I've tried to break Josephine of this habit, but it must be a protective older sister thing.

Wesley, my younger teenage brother, gives me a bro hug with a chest bump that sends me staggering into the table.

"Oh shit, sorry!" he says, gripping my shoulders to steady me, his face caught in a grimace.

"Wesley! Language, please," our mother admonishes as she flips a napkin into her lap.

I sit down between my dad and sister, and beam around at my family. It's not often we manage to all gather together like this, and I'm so glad they were able to meet up on my birthday. This one is already turning out better than the last.

My family are all feline shifters, and their animals are strikingly appropriate for each of their personalities. My dad shifts into a large house-cat, with long, fluffy fur and a penchant for naps. My older sister's animal is a sleek black panther. She's fiercely loyal, always looking out for others. Wesley shifts into a bobcat; when he was younger he was super cute, but now that he's in his last year of high school, his bobcat's sneaky demeanor definitely compliments his often snarky attitude. Thankfully, today he seems to be in a good mood, likely due to the massive stack of pancakes he'll be devouring.

Lastly, my mom, strong and regal, undoubtedly the matriarch of the family, shifts into a beautiful Siberian Tiger. As a child, I always loved petting her thick striped fur when the family all shifted together.

Well, all except for me, of course. My shifts didn't start happening within the normal age range of five to ten like every other shifter we know, and instead began long after I had given up hope of ever shifting at all, exactly one year ago.

Despite being my "golden birthday" as they say—turning twenty-two on June twenty-second—my last birthday was *not* a favorite, and I blink away the memories of that awkwardly embarrassing day. Between my first ever shift, an awkward half-shift at that, plus it being in public, in front of both friends and family, it was one of the worst days of my life. Not only was it physically painful, but the mental stress it's brought to my life has been unbearable. I'm constantly anxious now, worried about shifting, wondering when it's going to happen, and how long it'll last, and if I'll ever have control of my life again.

Here's to hoping twenty-three goes better, I think, mentally crossing my fingers for extra luck.

"So, darling." My mother pauses for a sip of water as she looks over the rim of the glass in my direction. "Any new lovers of late?"

"MOM." Wesley's wide eyes convey his horror, but I'm not surprised. Mom loves to make a statement and I've gotten used to the nosy nature of her questions.

"What? I'm only asking because I care," she says to Wesley, then turns back to me. "No cute girls or boys at work you might be interested in?"

"Ew, Mom," Josephine cuts in this time. "First off, girls or boys? She's turning twenty-three, not thirteen. Secondly, lay off! It's her birthday."

While she pouts at the rebuke, my dad pats her arm to comfort her, then turns to me as well.

"How's work, sweetie?" he asks, and I do my best to hold in the cringe. I hoped to avoid directly lying to them, but here it is.

"Oh, you know," I say, eyes directed at the menu in my hands. "Work is work. How's everything with you all?"

I can feel my sister's inscrutable gaze drilling into me, but I ignore it, and when no one responds quickly enough, I fill the silence.

"These maple donuts sound amazing. Should we get some for the table?" I look to my brother, who is always ready for more food, and he unknowingly jumps to my rescue.

"I'm always down for donuts, I'll split with you," he says, and I chuckle at his ambition. There's no way I'm eating half of that donut plate, but he can think what he wants.

The conversation picks up around me, ebbing and flowing, and I enjoy listening to my siblings poke at each other, my mother playing mediator while my dad relaxes next to me. Thankfully, no one brings up my shifting, and I know the only reason they refrain is so they don't add strain to my birthday or bring down the mood. The last thing anyone wants is a reminder of my breakdown last year.

As the food disappears and the meal winds down, I tap my glass lightly with my fingernail.

"I wanted to say thank you for making the effort to be here. I know you're all busy and it's tough to make all our schedules align, but after the last year," my voice hitches and my dad squeezes my arm as they wait for me to continue. I clear my throat, "After last year, having your support means a lot. So. Yeah, that's it. Love you all."

My face heats, but I don't regret the awkward, bumbling speech. Dad gives me a sideways hug from his seat on one side as my sister does the same from the other. My mom reaches across and pats my hand with a smile on her face, and when I glance at my brother, he's making a gagging face into his elbow.

"You're the worst," I say with a laugh as Mom pretends to swat at him, cracking a smile at his antics. My heart balloons in my chest when he smirks back at me, his intention to distract everyone and lighten the moment having been wildly successful.

4

HOW MANY TABS IS TOO MANY?

RAYA

ZURI SAUNTERS in one evening with two glasses of wine and a tall glass bottle. It looks like one of those fermentation-type bottles that restaurants use for water when they leave it at the table, only instead of being clear, the liquid inside is a deep, rich red.

"Wine?" She holds out one of the glasses and I accept it with a sigh, setting it on the counter next to my laptop.

"That's new?" I tilt my head, not recognizing the bottle she's holding, but assuming it's blood all the same. Zuri is a vampire, but she was raised in an extremely progressive family —they only believe in drinking blood that has been ethically sourced with the donor being well compensated for their time and contribution, and they never, ever, drink directly from humans or animals. The "traditionalists" AKA old-school vampires, on the other hand, don't abide by current legal or ethical guidelines, and many drink only from humans, whether the victims are willing or not.

"Yeah, you know that new place I've been going to for the last couple months?" Zuri asks.

"Mhm." I nod, then take a sip of my wine.

"Right, so they started this new sustainability initiative where you pay an initial fee to start using glass bottles, but then every time you return an empty one, you get a slight discount on the next one. It's cheaper after only five bottles, and there's basically zero waste. Awesome, right?"

"Actually, yeah. That is pretty cool." I blink in surprise; I had no idea vampires, or humans, or whoever runs these blood clinics, were so innovative or invested in... the environment? Shrugging, I return my attention to Z, who has uncapped the bottle and is now adding it to her wine. It doesn't change the color, but my shifter senses pick up on the slight coppery scent, so I bring my own glass closer to my face to cover it, then take a long sip.

"No luck yet?" Zuri says.

I shake my head, eyes blurring across the computer screen, and she squeezes my shoulder.

"I'll let you keep at it. Let me know when you need a break."

My web browser has thirteen different tabs left open and I refresh each page with the saved job searches I've been using. My search filters have been getting significantly less related to my actual degree while my fingers have become slightly more frantic with each application I submit, but I know it will eventually pay off. One week of job searching is not very long, and I expect it will take at least a couple before I start to hear back about interviews, but moon and stars, this is draining.

When I finally attend an interview the following week for a project management position I'm only mildly qualified for at a tech consulting firm, I'm understandably nervous. I only partially shift once during the whole thing, but manage to continue the interview and explain that the shifting does not impact my functioning or ability to complete my job. Luckily, it was only my ears that shifted into twitching bunny ears, and it lasted only a few minutes. The interviewer didn't seem offended or put-off by it, thankfully.

Regardless, my spirits are more upbeat the next few days, now that my hard work of applying day in and day out is paying off. But I'm still facing the fact that I won't have enough income from my last paycheck to cover my portion of rent this month, whether I get the project manager position or not, and I refuse to ask my parents or sister for financial help.

Zuri had suggested the blood bank she uses as a backup option for a quick payout, so I text her for the address and plug it into my GPS.

It's raining when I step outside, the beat of the drops relaxing as they tap, then streak down my umbrella. It's clear with yellow trim around the edges, and a bright yellow, smiling sun in the middle—perfect for brightening a rainy Portland day. The few blocks to the blood clinic take no time at all.

I'm the only one in the waiting room when I get there, which helps calm my nerves somewhat. It's set up similar to a pharmacy, with a secure area behind the counter and another section off to the side with doors where, presumably, I'll go when it's my turn to give blood.

No biggie, just like getting a flu shot.

The lady behind the desk has fabulous bright red glasses and is wearing a vintage dress.

"Raya?" she calls, and I stand, striding up to the tall desk.

She gets me set up with the proper documents and I verify that payment is sent within twenty-four hours directly to my bank account. The payment is based on how much blood I want to give, taking into consideration the maximum is for my weight and how much money I need.

"And don't worry," she continues, offering an encouraging smile after dumping a load of information on me. "The clinic is run entirely by humans, so there's never a concern about vampires going rogue around so much blood."

I blink as my hand pauses over a signature line. That's a worry that hadn't yet crossed my mind, but I'm glad it's already been thought of and addressed.

After signing the final consent and confidentiality forms, I'm led into one of the side rooms. I expect a standard doctor's office, but am surprised to see the vibe is much more relaxed. While still sterile and clean, I'm sitting on an adjustable seat similar to a dentist chair, and instead of intimidating anatomical posters on the walls, there are motivational quotes. "Give the gift of life; share your blood" and "Your blood saves lives" and "You don't have to be a doctor to be a hero." It reminds me a bit of a middle school classroom if it were combined with a dentist office, with a heavy focus on blood, obviously.

Shaking my head at the wandering thoughts, I refocus on the phlebotomist who knocks and swiftly enters the room. They're wearing bright purple scrubs with straight brown hair pulled back into a ponytail. They check my vitals, then we talk through how much blood I would like to give based on my BMI.

I decide to only give two units for now, which equates to what an average vampire might drink for four light meals, two average meals, or one big meal, which can last them up to a week. If I dip into my meager savings, that will give me the last bit of money I need to cover rent, and hopefully by the end of next month I'll be fully employed again.

The phlebotomist offers an encouraging smile as they prick my vein and attach the tubing. I wasn't sure how I'd respond; turns out I'm not squeamish about it at all. I figure it's because I'm used to living with a vampire and having blood in our fridge.

"We're halfway there already, how are you feeling?" they ask when they switch out the collection bag for a second one.

"Fine, actually," I reply, shrugging my opposite shoulder.

"You're doing great, we'll be done in no time."

I lean my head back against the padded seat, watching as the blood bag next to me slowly fills up and imagining the dollar signs filling my bank account at the same time. It almost feels like the pent up anxiety is flowing out of my veins right alongside the blood, making me feel light headed in more than one way.

When the needle is replaced with a little cotton ball and teal sticky wrap, they smile and tell me I'm all set.

I hop up from the seat and immediately sway to the side, the floor tilting up to meet me before warm hands wrap around my upper arms.

"Whoa there," they say, "let's take it easy for a few minutes. Was this your first time giving blood?"

I nod as they help me sit back down.

"Hang tight, I'll be right back with some juice."

I blink up at the ceiling until they return with a familiar purple juice box. I hold in a chuckle when I recognize it's one of Reverie's favorites, which means it's full of sugar.

They stick the straw in and pass it over.

"Take your time, it's best to drink it slowly and relax. You'll be on a fifteen minute watch timer now anyways," they say.

I have nowhere to be anyway, so I let myself sit back and enjoy the juice while the phlebotomist putters around the room until I've finished it.

When I step back outside and unfold my umbrella for the walk home, I smile up at the sky through it, thankful for a resourceful roommate and healthy body that have allowed me to continue living my best independent life for the next month.

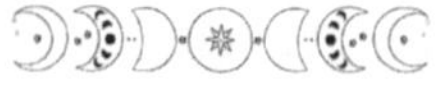

UNFORTUNATELY, I find myself still unemployed and more antsy than ever when another couple weeks crawl by without any further call backs. It's safe to assume I didn't get the project management job I interviewed for, and although bummed, I'm doing my best not to let it get me down. I was able to pay rent for July, and if I need to I can sell some blood again in two weeks to help cover August expenses. Talking myself through the positives has always helped me feel better when a situation starts to feel dire, and today is no exception to that rule.

I'm still sticking to the same routine—breakfast, avoid talking to family, put real clothes on, and apply for jobs—when a couple hours into the endless cycle, I get a call from a vaguely familiar number.

"Hello, this is Raya." I use my most pleasant professional voice when I answer, just in case.

"Hi Raya, this is Noemi with Pacific Northwest Consulting Group, we interviewed you recently for the project manager position?"

"Oh yes, Noemi, hi! Thanks for calling." My heart rate must be in the 200 range all of a sudden, and I hope Noemi can't hear it through the phone.

"Of course. I wanted to let you know the position you applied for has been filled, but we actually had another open up quite suddenly that I think you're a perfect fit for, a Training Lead. If you're interested, is now an okay time to go over it with you?"

I blink a few times, trying to catch up with the words I'm hearing.

"Yes! Yeah, now is a great time!" I say, cringing when I realize how desperately enthusiastic that came out.

"Perfect. So here's what you need to know..." Noemi breaks down the job description, expectations, salary, responsibilities, and emphasizes that this position includes frequent traveling and collaborating with others, while also training employees at other companies on how to effectively use the implemented software. I confirm my willingness and ability to follow through on everything Noemi mentions, marveling that what sounds like the perfect job seems to have fallen into my lap.

"There's one catch," Noemi says. "We need you to start immediately."

WALKING into Pacific Northwest Consulting Group, or PNCG, I still can't believe my good luck. I wore a brand new thrifted outfit today in the hopes it'll bring me good luck. A flowy floral top in deep reds and blues is tucked into a matching red high-waisted cordoroy skirt. It has carved wooden buttons down the front that I simply couldn't pass up, not to mention the texture is divine. I've paired the outfit with dark blue flats that have a dainty strap around the ankle, and pulled my hair back into a loose french braid that hangs over my shoulder.

I pinched myself after the call yesterday, then had Reverie tug on my hair to be double sure it was real. I take the elevator to the sixth floor where Noemi greets me with a warm smile.

We take the first part of the day to go through the intake paperwork, all the boring stuff you have to do every time you start a new job that I have become far too competent at given my young age. I don't know why I've had such trouble finding a place I fit in, but I'm hopeful this one will be a good match.

When I'm shown to my work station, which is not a soul sucking cubicle or in a long row of identically sterile desks, but is part of a semi-open work space with what looks like three other desks clustered together with mine, my eyebrows shoot up in surprise.

"Not what you're used to?" Noemi laughs as I shake my head. "It works well for us. Looks like everyone is at lunch, so you'll have to wait until they're back to meet them, but you're grouped with Asher, Alex and Kendall. Asher is the Technology Specialist you'll be working closely with, and Alex and Kendall are both in client services."

Noemi helps set up the work laptop that was waiting on the desk, and right as she's readying to leave, my new coworkers come wandering in.

"Oh, perfect. I was about to step out, but let me introduce everyone first." Noemi takes a step back, turning so she can gesture to me. "This is Raya, our new Training Lead. Raya, this is Asher, Alex and Kendall."

With that, Noemi strides out of the shared workspace, heading back to her office without a backward glance and completely oblivious to the mortification sluicing down my spine.

5

NOT AS IT SEEMS

RAYA

MY EYES ARE ABOUT to pop out of my head and my tongue is in danger of falling out of my mouth at the impossible coincidence I'm faced with.

"Huh. Didn't expect to see you here," Asher says, sauntering over to his desk and eyeing me up and down. "No paws this time?"

My anger at his accompanying smirk quickly morphs into further embarrassment when I realize the situation I'm in. I hadn't expected to see that helpful stranger again, but here he is, sitting kitty-corner from me and exposing my biggest insecurity to my new coworkers.

Stars, this is not ideal.

I suck in a breath and try to keep the polite smile pasted on my face. Not that I was expecting to be best friends with my coworkers, but I had been hoping for a warmer welcome.

"You two know each other?" Alex asks, their brows furrowed as they sit at the desk next to mine.

"Not really, we ran into each other once and I helped her with a little... rodent problem," Asher replies as he opens up his laptop, blue eyes flicking to mine for a moment before returning to his computer screen, dismissing me.

"Riiiiight," Alex draws out the word as their eyes bounce between Asher and me.

I clear my throat, trying to regain any small grasp on this situation that I can.

"Thank you, again," I say, throwing a bright smile his way to prove everything's fine and I'm all good now.

His only reply is a single grunt, not even looking in my direction as he does so, which does not help the apprehension coursing through my veins. I turn my attention to Alex and Kendall, doing my best to give the appropriate responses as they both welcome me before excusing themselves for a meeting. I'm left with the sticky silence between me and Asher in their wake.

I fidget with my laptop again, then jump in my seat when the shared desk phone rings. Asher throws a judgmental frown at me as he pushes the button to answer it.

"Asher, hey. I didn't get a chance to show Raya around the office and I'm tied up the rest of the afternoon. Can you give her a quick tour for me?" Noemi says, apparently not realizing she's on speaker-phone.

His eyes catch mine as he rumbles an affirmative and hangs up. Sparks shoot up and down my spine, though I'm not sure if they're in warning or excited anticipation.

"Let's do it then," he says, voice gruff with displeasure as he stands and brushes a hand down the front of his buttoned shirt, drawing my attention to the way it stretches across his broad chest.

I quickly avert my gaze and trot after him as he points out different work areas, spouting names of who sits where and what projects they're working on. He's curt, direct, and I have no chance of keeping any of it straight, but I pretend I'm following along all the same.

He shows me where the printer/copier and office supplies are, telling me I can take what I need for my desk. I nod in confirmation and he moves on to the bright white kitchen with an adjacent break room that has windows overlooking the Willamette River. It's peaceful, and I pause to take in the view.

"That's basically it. Management and HR are in the same hallway as Noemi's office, and bathrooms are near reception. Anything else you need?" he asks, clearly ready to be done babysitting me.

"Nope, thanks. I'm all set." I beam my brightest smile at him again, which he apparently hates, as he abruptly turns and stalks away.

I sigh and slump into one of the armchairs. I need a few minutes to wrap my mind around this situation. I cannot believe I'm working with Asher—the mystery man who helped me when I needed it, and now clearly can't stand being in my presence.

I pull my phone out to text Zuri, knowing she'll commiserate.

Me: You'll never guess who sits next to me at work.

Zuri: OMG who?! Is it someone I know??

As I'm about to reply, two people walk into the kitchen area behind me, mid-gossip-sesh. I freeze, not wanting to be caught, but also kind of wanting to listen in.

"I heard it's an alias. You know who he really is right?" one guy says. The other person must have shaken their head because they don't answer, but he continues. "Yeah turns out his name isn't really Asher Sullivan, it's Asher Walton."

The other guy scoffs. "No way. Who told you that?"

"It's true. I looked up pictures. He's right there standing with his parents. Same guy."

"Asher. Like, sits at the desk by the door, dark hair, always frowning, thinks he's better than everyone else?"

"That's the one."

Their voices fade and the blood drains from my face as my jaw unhinges. I blink at my reflection in the window before jerking my phone up, fingers flying.

> Me: Oh no

> Me: Please tell me Asher Walton isn't who I think he is.

> Me: Is that the evil vampire family you've talked about?

> Me: The super old school one that attacks humans and drinks from the vein and doesn't care one lick about consent? The ones causing all sorts of issues for the progressives trying to pass more ethical laws or whatever?

> Me: PLEASE tell me I have the wrong name.

> Zuri: YES you have the right name but wait

> Me: Alert alert SOS send help what do I do

> Zuri: Hold up. Is that who sits next to you?!

> Me: Yep. He's using a fake name though? He's going by Asher Sullivan

Zuri: Are you sure? His family is rich as
heck. I doubt it's him.

Me: Pretty sure

Zuri: Okay. Look. If it is Asher Walton, he's
not going to do anything at work. Or at
least, not around others. So just don't be
alone with him.

Zuri: We'll talk it over tonight

Zuri: You'll be fine.

My cheeks puff as I blow out a breath and lean my head back against the seat. I've heard horror stories about this family; they're in the news all the time, as they're something between politicians and public figures. Everyone knows they're corrupt, but money can make all sorts of problems disappear. Having to tip-toe around my new coworker is the last thing I need right now. Can't a girl just get a nice, normal, chill job?

I am determined to be fine. I'll kill him with kindness and won't be alone with him. My mystery rescuer turned work-place scorner has now turned out to also be a notoriously terrible vampire with untold wealth and power behind his name. No biggie, it could be worse.

ASHER

I toss my keys into the dish by the door and toe off my shoes while Milton meows at me from his perch on the console table. I'm never sure if that meow is a welcome home or go away. Side-eying Milton, I loosen my collar and unbutton my shirt cuffs as I stride into the kitchen. Today was not what I expected.

I didn't think they'd be able to fill the position so quickly. Obviously, I'm relieved I won't have to pick up the slack as much now that the new girl has started, but did it have to be *her?*

I yank open the fridge, glass bottles clanking at the abrupt movement, and grab one at random. I went to a new blood bank a couple weeks ago and they had some sort of sustainable initiative going on, so apparently I'm drinking blood from glass bottles instead of plastic bags now.

What a step up in the world.

I snag a glass, letting the cold liquid slosh into it before holding it up to my nose and taking a deep inhale, the scent already helping me relax. Coppery, metallic, and sharp, exactly as I like it. But then I pause, taking another slow whiff. There's a sweet undertone I haven't sensed in blood before.

I take a tentative sip, and as soon as it hits my tongue, my brows shoot up to my hairline. I pull back and hold the glass up again, swirling it around and carefully inspecting the liquid for any hint that the blood's been mixed with something else. Not finding anything suspicious, I examine the bottle, but there's nothing different about it either.

At the second careful sip, I have to hold in a moan. This blood is *decadent.* It's absolutely indecent how good it tastes. Unlike anything I've tasted before, both salty and sweet, it's a test of my self-control not to gulp it all down at once. Blood hasn't been this enticing since... Well, I prefer not to let my mind wander to those dark years.

My family has taken enough from me already. My childhood, my innocence, any hope I had of believing the best in people. They stomped that out of me before it had a chance to grow, doing their best to replace it with bloodthirsty ruthlessness. I'm glad they didn't succeed in making me the monster of their dreams, the heir apparent to their bloody empire, even if they haven't yet given up on those endeavors. I'll do what I've done since I turned eighteen.

Nothing.

I'll ignore their texts. Avoid their calls. Turn a blind eye to their very existence.

I glance at Milton where he sits in the doorway, but he only stares back, silently judging.

I swirl my glass, taking both it and the bottle to the living room with me where I flip on the TV to a random documentary. Unfortunately, it's impossible to focus. Between this blood that's making me feel slightly wild, and thoughts of the new girl at work, I haven't absorbed anything at all about... Ancient Egyptian tombs?

With a heavy sigh, I pause it and turn on some music instead, resigned to let my thoughts take whatever course they need to so they'll let me relax. Immediately, they turn to her.

Raya.

Today was such a mess. I accomplished nothing thanks to her distracting presence, and I couldn't even look at her for too long or I felt like I'd combust. I thought she was cute with her wild hair and the little rabbit nose before, but once I saw her full human form, I was hit with how stunning she is. Honey-blonde hair with loose tendrils framing her face that almost shimmered as she walked. Rich brown eyes that seemed to see right through me. All of five feet and a couple inches, she nearly knocked me on my ass the instant I saw her.

My first words to her that morning weren't exactly polite, but to be fair she did catch me off guard by showing up unannounced to my place of work. Then it felt like I was sent spinning off into a different realm when she turned her hesitant smile on me.

Huffing, I roll my eyes and take another sip, this time letting out the appreciative groan that claws up my throat.

The worst part was, she seemed genuinely happy to be there, and that warmth radiated out from her. Her smile as she settled in and organized her desk felt like a physical blow, like it would have bowled me over if I wasn't already sitting when she aimed it in my direction. Simply looking at her sends my thoughts into a tailspin, and when her heartbeat kicked up as we started the office tour, I nearly staggered at the urge to take her into my arms. Whether to comfort her or drink from her or something else entirely, I'm not sure.

Not to mention her scent. Sun-ripened strawberries and fresh coconut, a combination so delicious I can nearly taste it. I practically ran away from her at one point because I couldn't control my reaction; my mouth watered and my fangs started to lengthen without my consent. I haven't lost control like that since I was an adolescent being starved and then tortured with fresh blood by my parents.

I have no idea how I'm supposed to get any work done with her around. My reactions to her are unreasonable and unwelcome.

What's up with the random shifting though?

She's piqued my curiosity. I caught another partial shift today when Raya was setting up her new laptop that I'm pretty sure she doesn't realize I noticed. Her nails had turned to claws, without the full wolf paws this time. I didn't say anything, though. I'm not a complete asshole, despite how I reacted to her today, but I did question it.

Admittedly, I don't know much about shifters, but I do know they don't normally shift into multiple different animals —or animal parts—and they also don't normally have such poor control over it by adulthood.

Left to wonder, I turn back to my meal and finish off the last few drops, practically licking the inside of the glass clean. I hold up the bottle again and take a picture of the ID number on the label, hoping I can get more, debating how crazy it would be to call and ask.

"What do you think?" I ask Milton.

He turns his slitted green eyes on me, then saunters over, leaps into my lap, and settles into a cat loaf facing me.

Taking his attention as approval, I dial the number on the bottle and rattle off the ID. Unfortunately, the clinic informs me that was all they had from this particular donor. No, they don't know if they will get more, and they're very sorry but they can't release any information about donors.

Sighing, I hang up, reasoning that it likely tasted better due to how hungry I was, plus there was no plastic aftertaste that comes from the bags I'm used to.

I push it from my mind for now, hoping a run through Forest Park will help set me straight. I normally run at a normal, human pace, but every so often it feels good to let go, to unleash my inner vampire and run at my true, lightning-quick speed.

I pretend it's simply because I need the exercise, and not that it has anything to do with outrunning thoughts of a dazzlingly gorgeous shifter.

6

KILL HIM WITH KINDNESS
RAYA

I STRIDE into the office with my head held high, shoulders back, and a pep in my step. Alex is already seated at their desk next to mine, but Asher and Kendall aren't in yet.

"Morning," I say, smiling at my new coworker and hoping we can get some more bonding time in today. I always feel more comfortable when I know those around me a little better.

"Hey, how'd the rest of your first day go?" Alex asks, turning their attention to me.

"Oh, yeah, it was good!" I reply, perhaps laying the cheer on a bit too thick, but Alex doesn't seem to notice. They flick a lock of dark hair out of their eyes.

"Nice. Well if you have any questions, I'm happy to help. I know it can be stressful settling into a new job and trying to find your place."

"Thanks, that means a lot. Asher showed me around yesterday, but besides that I haven't gotten a chance to do much yet, so I don't even know what questions I might have."

"No worries, you'll be fine. Everyone's pretty nice here and no one will mind if it takes you a minute to catch up on things." Alex smiles in encouragement, which I return before switching focus to my laptop, reminding myself not to go anywhere with the blood sucking, evil vampire if I can avoid it.

I settle in, checking my email and clicking through the first of the onboarding documents. Kendall still hasn't shown up yet when the vampire walks in, striding through the office like he owns the place. Asher drops a sleek leather bag into the bottom drawer of his desk, then turns my direction, eyeing me up and down with an impassive expression.

"You're with me, let's go," Asher says with a chin jerk, blue eyes piercing mine as I blink up at him.

"I, sorry, what?" I stammer, trying not to feel stupid, but wondering what I missed.

"You've been assigned to shadow me today since we'll be working on the Alpha-Med account together. We have a meeting with the team to go over our plans in..." he pauses to fling his arm out then pulls his exposed wrist up in front of him, checking his watch with a frown, "two minutes. Best not to be late on your second day."

With that, he turns on his heel and starts walking out. I frantically spin to Alex, a lump in my throat at my safety plan going sideways already, but Alex shrugs and tilts their head for me to follow him. I jump up from my seat and take two steps before turning back around, stumbling into my desk as I search for a pen and notepad to take notes, then slamming the top drawer closed when I find one and rushing out after him.

I firmly believe people with long legs should be shackled when walking in public with people who have shorter legs. It's really not fair how Asher can appear to be casually strolling down the hallway toward the elevator while simultaneously moving at the speed of light. I practically sprint to catch up with him, breath puffing in and out of my lungs when I stagger into the elevator and straighten my skirt, thankful he held the door for me, but also slightly concerned about being in such a small, enclosed space with him.

"Where are we going?" I ask, trying not to show that I'm breathing hard from simply walking quickly down a hallway, and entirely certain I'm failing in the endeavor.

He arches a brow from where he leans his hips back against the opposite elevator wall, arms crossed over his chest and feet planted wide like he expects me to cause problems. I'm not sure where he might have gotten that impression of me; I spend much of my life actively avoiding being any sort of problem, especially ones that involve other people.

"Conference room," he says, then seems to realize he's being rude, and takes a slow breath before continuing with a slightly less scathing tone. "Likely the same place you had your interview."

"Right, thanks," I say, flashing a polite smile as the elevator opens and trying not to let it sting when he looks away instead of returning it. I step out to the side, allowing him to take the lead as we walk into our first meeting together and actively avoiding checking out his broad form in those fitted slacks and tight shirt.

Asher folds himself into one of the chairs along the conference table and promptly turns his attention to the overcast clouds outside the floor to ceiling windows that comprise an entire wall of the meeting room. I have my most professional smile firmly in place as I follow and sit on his left. I'm pretty sure his eyes flicker in my direction, but he doesn't otherwise acknowledge my presence next to him, so I slide my notepad and pen onto the table and cross my legs. Then uncross them. When I re-crosses them the other way, I notice his jaw clench, and while I'm not completely sure it's in reaction to my fidgeting, I do my best to sit still anyway.

The account manager starts the meeting and introduces me as the Lead Trainer for the project, asking everyone to help get me up to speed as soon as possible. We'll be heading to San Diego in a couple weeks to implement the changes and go live.

When I'm asked to step to the front to give a quick overview of my experience and what I will be bringing to the team, my fight or flight instinct kicks in. Except when it comes to my particular instincts, I don't fight or flight, I freeze. Because I only started this job *yesterday*. I'm not bringing anything to the team yet.

I stare at the Project Manager, eyes wide and unblinking, until a knee nudges mine under the table. Jolting, I jerk my gaze to Asher, who is still staring out the window like the grey clouds hold the most interesting secrets and if he watches them long enough, they'll spill. Blinking rapidly now, I suck in a breath and stand, forcing myself to walk to the front of the room. When I turn and see all the expectant eyes from coworkers I haven't formally met yet, plus a few who have video-called into the meeting, my heart starts racing again, and I feel that tell-tale tingle beneath my skin.

No, no, no, no, no!

Asher's head jerks around, a solid scowl on his face. His narrowed eyes catch mine just as I feel what I assume to be a rabbit tail pop into being.

Inside my pants.

Nestled into the top of my butt cheeks.

Stars, this is awkward.

My face flames, and I tear my gaze from Asher's when the furrow between his brow deepens. It takes every single shred of my self control to stop my hands from grabbing my butt and feeling myself up in front of my new team.

At least it's not visible. It could be worse.

I smooth my hair behind my ear in a surreptitious attempt to ensure nothing else shifted, then I remind myself I have plenty of experience talking in front of groups of people. This is literally what I went to school for. So I straighten my shoulders and introduce myself, share my previous work experience in coordinating with other teams and providing on-site training, then give a few quick ideas of how they can help me catch up to where I need to be on the current project.

When I sit back down next to Asher, I shimmy back and forth a bit, ignoring the side-eyed, questioning glare he shoots my direction. Who knew trying to sit with a fluffy rabbit tail invading my butt crack would be so awkwardly uncomfortable?

THE REMAINDER of the work week brings more of the same curt, aloof attitude from Asher, further dulling my hopes of things turning more friendly between us. I continue to randomly shift, and everything from black cat ears to cheetah spots covering my neck and hands to slitted hawk eyes and furry wolf paws decide to make themselves at home on my body. Each time it happens, I'm unable to control it, upping my frustration with myself and my inner shifter.

This, of course, only seems to make it worse.

I've had to work closely with Asher since he's the one ensuring the new program will work as expected, so he's essentially had to walk me through it as it's a new software I'm not familiar with yet. Despite how irritating I assume this has been for him, he hasn't turned me away when I've had questions, though his responses aren't always the friendliest.

He's even commented on how "quickly" I'm picking it up. Of course, this was laced with sarcasm, accompanied by a smirk, and was said right after I asked a question he had already previously answered.

'Deep breaths, you can do this. Kill him with kindness,' has become my latest mantra.

Unfortunately, my inner animal has other ideas at the

most inconvenient of times, and instead of just a toothy wolf smile, I get a whole wolf snout popping out of my face in the middle of one such "catch up the new girl" meeting. Asher rears back when it happens, eyes wide as he blinks at me in consternation. His sarcasm reaches unparalleled levels when he regains composure and his coolly controlled voice gripes, "Isn't there anything you can do about it?" while flicking his wrist in my direction—"it" of course, meaning the shifting.

"No. There's not," I snap at him, the words barely comprehensible through my snout, then slam my laptop closed and stride out of the office, snagging my coat and bag from the hook by the door as I go. This vampire is not only morally corrupt, but completely intolerable. I need a break from his relentless negative energy.

Once outside, I lean against the building in a small alcove, waiting until my shifted face tingles and reverts back to normal features. When it does, I walk a few blocks to the park along the river, noticing as I go that I apparently tucked my laptop under my arm before fleeing. I take in the fresh air, listening to the gentle lapping of the Willamette as the breeze ruffles my hair.

I'm not in the right headspace to go back into the office today, especially if I want to avoid triggering an evil vampire and keep all my blood inside my veins, so I call Noemi to ask if working from home for the afternoon would be feasible.

When Noemi agrees, my shoulders relax and fur that I hadn't noticed along my neck and arms recedes back into my skin with a light prickle.

7

___

SUBPAR BLOOD

RAYA

I STARTLE when my phone rings a few hours later, buzzing along the counter next to my laptop. Seeing that the caller ID is proudly proclaiming the best mother in the world to be calling, I smile and pick it up.

"Hey, Mom."

"Hi, honey! I've got your dad here too," Mom says, and the forced cheer in her voice immediately puts me on alert.

"Oh okay, what's up? Is everything okay?" I vacillate between worrying I'm in trouble and worrying something is wrong with someone else in the family.

"Everything's fine, we just wanted to check in on you."

So, the first option then. I wrack my brain, wondering what I could have done, or not done, to warrant a tag-team phone call from my parents.

"How have you been doing with your shifting?" Dad asks.

"It's..." I don't know what to say, and the silence is dreadful. I can practically hear a timer tick-tick-ticking down the seconds to my doom. "It's not great."

"We're worried about you." Mom takes the reins again,

and I tuck my lips into my teeth to avoid snarking back. I'm an adult, they don't need to worry about me all the time.

"We're worried about the full moon, and how it will impact you," Dad clarifies, and this pauses my defensive thoughts. "It's in the final waxing quarter, and I know your mom and I are already feeling its pull, which means you must be too."

Even though my family are feline shifters, they still feel the moon's call. Most people think only wolf shifters respond to the moon, likely due to all the fairytales about werewolves, but in reality, we all do, no matter what our inner animal is. I had forgotten about this; I haven't had to worry about or keep track of the moon for the first twenty-two years of my life, and even once I started shifting, it has always seemed random.

"Oh," I say. *Very eloquent.*

"Have you felt it?" Dad presses on, his voice gentle and deep, comforting like a heavy blanket.

"I'm not sure. I mean, it has been kind of getting worse, so... maybe?" I cringe as I say the words, knowing I'm understating it, but also knowing they won't be happy I've kept this much from them.

A tense beat follows and I can clearly picture the look my parents are exchanging.

"We think you should come over and stay with us next week for a couple days around the full moon, just until it starts waning again, then its pull over you should lessen." My mother cuts straight to the point of the call, and my initial instinct is to deny it, but I also see the value of what they're saying.

I remember how my siblings had a hard time when they first shifted and felt the moon's pull, though my brother struggled with it more than my sister. He was only eight, and the first few months when he found his animal he was unable to stop himself from shifting into the cutest little bobkitten on the days surrounding the full moon. My experience has been entirely different, obviously, but I do wonder if the moon is what is causing my increasingly erratic and uncontrollable shifts lately.

Then I realize I can't possibly stay with them, even if I wanted to.

"I can't," I say with a sigh, and I cut Mom off before she can fully form the protest I hear coming. "I won't be here. I have to travel for work next week, I'll be in San Diego."

Silence.

Neither parent speaks for what feels like ages, until finally my dad breaks it.

"Okay, we'll look into it and see if there's anything that can help you control it. I've heard CBD oil can help calm the strength of the moon's pull. I'll give some of my buddies a call, and your mom will ask around, too. It'll be okay."

I nod even though they can't see it, my throat choking up at the love and care my parents have always shown for their freak of a daughter. For most of my life, I was an outcast in the shifter community because I had no animal and couldn't shift. Despite that, my parents never treated me differently from my siblings and always included me in shifter activities if I wanted to participate.

Once I turned twenty-two and the random shifts started, they barely batted an eye, even though I know they were likely freaking out when not in my presence. No one, to my knowledge, has ever even heard of a shifter who can shift into multiple different animals, or one who didn't start shifting until they were an adult. Let alone one who partially shifts random body parts. Normally it's all or nothing, human or animal.

No matter how you look at it, I'm different, but my family never saw that as a bad thing and I love them all the more for it.

Choking out a thank you, I end the call. My mental faculties are officially fried.

I am so done with this day.

Asher

I snag a new bottle of blood from the fridge when I finally get home, Milton twining between my legs and leaving behind a smattering of fine black fur on my ankles and shins. I'm ready to relax for the weekend before flying out for San Diego on Sunday. Of course, my thoughts immediately turn to Raya and our time together, as has become my new nighty routine.

I'm still kicking myself for my lack of control and professionalism around Raya. After running away from, and avoiding, the confounding woman on her first day, I figured the best strategy for the second day would be to interact with her as little as possible. Following this logic, I arrived to work at the last minute, which already set me on edge. Even worse, I completely lost my wits as soon as I walked in.

The first thing I saw was her long, wavy hair, and I had an instant urge to bury my nose in it. The high-necked shirt with a silky bow around her neck didn't help my instincts, it was like a present wrapped up just for me. Then she turned those doe eyes on me and I practically swallowed my own tongue trying to get my suddenly dry mouth to form words properly. She turns me inside out and her mere presence makes me act like a complete idiot.

I know that isn't an excuse for how I've been treating her, but even when I see it happening, I can't stop it. It's as though I'm outside my own body, not in control. My brain isn't working properly, and what signals it does manage to send don't seem to be received by the rest of my body. I did my best throughout that meeting to be respectful of her position and role, which pretty much meant listening intently and avoiding looking at her. I didn't trust my own eyes not to devour her and make a fool of myself in front of everyone.

When I sensed her heart rate randomly spike though, I couldn't help meeting her wide-eyed gaze. I've replayed that moment over and over, but I still can't figure out what it was I saw there. Fear? Embarrassment? She hadn't even started speaking yet, so I wasn't sure what the deal was, though I have a suspicion it may have been another shift. I've come to realize she isn't able to control them, which I'm also pretty sure isn't normal for a shifter.

Despite my ongoing curiosity and desire to help, I haven't wanted to ask and inadvertently make things worse. Knowing me, it would come out all wrong, and I'd end up insulting or hurting her. That hasn't stopped my brain from circling around it. My inner vampire senses weakness, but all I see in her is strength. I can't fathom how she deals with her situation in a professional setting day in and day out, all while blinding the world around her with her smile. I suspect most people would crumble under that stress.

I managed to make it to the end of the week without making too much of an ass of myself in front of her, although she might think differently. She's picking up everything at work more quickly than I expected, especially considering she's basically onboarding herself, and I've been impressed by how much she's absorbing. I wince when I remember the confused look that had flashed across her face when I tried to hold in an impressed smile during one of our one-on-one meetings; I fear it came out as a cringe instead and probably gave her the wrong impression.

I swipe a hand down my face when my mind replays what happened shortly after that. She'd startled me with a sudden shift, unexpectedly sprouting a wolf nose in the middle of her face. My stupid, stupid brain, and even more stupid mouth, blurted out the question that's been circling in my head all week—isn't there anything she can do about it?

Her reaction was piercing. It felt like I had stabbed myself in the chest when I saw the shock and hurt etched into the lines of her face, because of course not. Obviously, if there was something she could do, she would be doing it, right?

I didn't expect her to storm out, although admittedly, I didn't think the comment through before I said it. And it was quite offensive, so I don't blame her for leaving. My face heats with embarrassment alongside the anger at myself for creating such a situation in the first place. When she didn't return after an hour, I checked in with Noemi, who informed me Raya was working from home the rest of the day. I guess she told Noemi she needed a quiet space so she could focus and get caught up on what she's been given so far.

Shaking my head at my abysmal behavior, I resolve to do better, and take a swig straight from the bottle. This upcoming trip will be a good opportunity to show her who I truly am, not the idiotic asshole I've been coming across as. Pulling up my personal laptop, I speculate that an online search to learn more about the basics of shifters is a good place to start. Mainly so I can avoid stepping in my own shit in the future.

I'm not used to being around shifters to begin with, and especially not one as unique as Raya. She's determined, hard working, and surprisingly good at her job despite being thrown into the deep end and told to swim. She's kind to everyone she meets and always has a smile at the ready, although that seems to no longer be the case when it comes to me. I'm sure my contradictory attitude helped create this icy wall between us, and I wish I could dissolve it.

Maybe spending a few days together outside of the office will give us the change of perspective needed to bridge this gap. I feel almost desperate for her warmth and radiance, and at this point all I can do is hope she will give me a second—or hundredth—chance to show her who I am.

My eyes devour every article I can find on shifter transformation. Anything that seems like it might remotely be a valid source. I take it all in and commit as much as I can to memory. I don't know what help I can be with this information, as I'm sure she knows more about her own community than I can hope to read online, but I'm desperate and don't know what else to do. I suppose it makes me feel useful, closer to her in a way that feels otherwise impossible.

When this thought crosses my mind, I figure that's my cue to stop. I'm losing sight of things and *closer* to her is not what either of us needs.

Clicking out of the shifter searches, I turn to trip planning and look up blood banks in San Diego. It doesn't feel good to not know where your next meal is coming from, so I like to be prepared and have a couple options already saved to my phone before I travel somewhere new. Finding one within walking distance of the hotel, and another a few blocks down from the convention center, I feel more prepared and close my laptop right as my phone chimes from the kitchen with an incoming text.

Having finished the current bottle of blood, which was nowhere near as good as the first one I had from this place, I take it into the kitchen. I quickly rinse it in the sink before rescuing my phone from Milton's paws which are batting it toward the edge of the counter.

I roll my eyes and mentally brace myself when I see it's a text from my cousin, Chadwick.

When the message opens to a photo, no text included, just a professional shot of said cousin side by side with my parents at a black tie event, a frown pulls at my lips and delete it. I have no desire to see his name, face, or those of my parents on my phone.

Although I ignore the message and don't reply, it still sits with me. A heavy, murky feeling in my chest. My cousin wants to take my place in the family business; he wants to be the heir my parents wish I would be, and honestly, I'm okay with that. Chadwick would be much better suited to the role anyway, but that doesn't eliminate the desire for acceptance, or the despair that my family is past redeeming.

I'm not cut out for the ruthlessness of the Walton family, and unless they change their heinous ways, give up their "traditions", I have no desire to be associated with them. There's a reason I haven't been photographed at any events with them in recent years, just as there's a reason I haven't accepted any calls, or responded to any of the many emails from my parents, either. I want nothing to do with them, their black market blood, or their dirty money.

Chadwick can have at it.

8

WHO EVEN LISTENS TO PODCASTS ANYMORE?

RAYA

Early September arrives before I know it. With it comes the work trip, and the rising full moon. I had a long chat with Zuri the other night about the Walton family. We might have taken it a step too far when we went online and did a deep dive into Asher's family and history, but what's some minor stalking if my life could be at risk? Weirdly, there wasn't much about him from the last few years, but we guessed maybe he's simply not the type to want public attention, which is at least one point in his favor, if true. One thing keeps sticking in my head, though. I can't figure out why he's working such a normal-person job at the consulting firm.

From what we read, it's assumed he has a massive trust fund, which means there's no reason for him to work. Especially not at a corporate, open workspace, shared microwave in the kitchen area job like this. Unless... consulting is his passion?

I scrunch my nose at the thought, huffing a breath with the reminder of how much is on my plate with this trip. This is why they needed someone to start so quickly; the client expects us to deliver, and I've had to push myself the last two weeks to be ready in time.

As the Training Lead, I need to fully understand the updates being made, problems that could arise, and all the ins and outs of the new software so I can teach the clients' employees how to effectively use it. An anxious part of my brain torments me with thoughts that if this doesn't go well, my future at the company will be in jeopardy.

I'm trying to stay optimistic, packing nearly every item of professional warm-weather clothing I own for the five day trip to San Diego. I would love to spend some time at the hotel pool too, so hoping for the best, I toss my favorite bikini in alongside a stack of panties, then sit on the carry-on sized suitcase in an effort to zip it closed.

The consulting firm is paying for the flights, lodging, and food, but not a checked bag, and since I'm still on a fairly tight budget, I've packed everything I can into a small suitcase and an equally small duffle bag to avoid extra fees.

Luckily, it's a short and quick Sunday evening flight without any layovers. Unfortunately, I've learned Asher will be the only one from the team accompanying me. A couple of our coworkers will be arriving later in the week and staying for a day or two, but no one else was deemed necessary for the entire week. Avoiding being alone with him is going to be significantly harder than anticipated when we're the only two team members there.

Lugging my suitcase out of my room, I call for Zuri, who agreed to give me a ride to the airport while reminding me what a good friend she is, that she likes colorful seashells and 'punny' stickers, and wouldn't turn down a fun new hat if one were presented to her.

Rolling my eyes, I give Reverie a light kiss on the top of her pretty pink head, promising to bring back treats for her as well, then follow Zuri out to her car.

"So, what's the plan for dealing with the probably dangerous douche canoe?" Zuri asks.

"Ugh. I don't even know. Can you believe I'm going to be stuck with him for nearly a week?" I lament. "I seriously don't know if I'm going to survive. I mean, besides his stupid snarky attitude, I've got the random shifting, and the full moon, *and* being thrown into this job. I hardly even know what I'm doing, yet I'm expected to train everyone else on it."

I didn't realize how much I was holding in until it all came pouring out during the twenty-five minute drive across the river to the airport. When Zuri pulls up to the drop-off zone, she puts the car in park and turns in her seat, then places both hands on my shoulders.

"I know it's a lot, but you can do this," she says, her voice earnest and eyes unblinking. "You've been through hell with this shifting stuff, and you've managed the stress of it your entire life. You're an excellent trainer, I'm not worried about that part of it at all. You're authentic, and kind, and easy going, and a great teacher. They're lucky to have you. You've got CBD oil for the full moon, so use it, and load up on caffeine in the morning if you need to."

I blink, trying to take in these solemn words from my feisty friend. She's not the type to coddle others, but this doesn't feel like coddling. This feels real, and if the look on her face is anything to go by, she means every word.

"Thank you," I say, my voice soft, offering a watery smile when Zuri pats my shoulder and then pulls me in for a hug.

"You've got this. Give him hell, stay safe, and give the others the best training they've ever had."

I laugh. "You are such a dork."

As I walk into the bustling airport, Zuri rolls the window down and yells to my retreating back, "And be careful!"

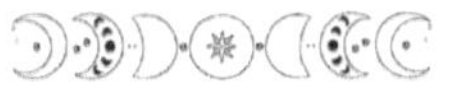

I don't seen Asher anywhere yet, and I'm starting to hope that maybe we were put on different flights. I arrived early to the gate and have staked out the area, keeping one eye peeled for Asher's dark hair and piercing stare, while doing my best to look like I'm casually reading as I wait.

After forty-five minutes of leg-bouncing anticipation, I still haven't seen him, and it's my turn to board. I let out a breath I hadn't realized I'd been holding and my shoulders slump, though I'm not sure if it's in relief or disappointment. Refusing to look at that emotional mess any further, I shuffle along in line until my boarding pass is scanned, then continue my shuffle down the jet bridge and onto the plane.

Finding my seat, I step in so others can pass and grab my water bottle, book, and headphones from my duffle, then step back into the aisle to put my bags in the overhead bin. Taking a deep breath, I grasp both handles of my suitcase and heave it up, only for it to miss the bin completely and come crashing back down, first hitting my shoulder, then landing on my foot.

With a muttered 'oof' of pain, my face flushes hot and I feel the dreaded tingle under my skin. Before I can even hide behind my hair, mouse whiskers sprout along my cheeks, surrounded by short grey fur. I take a deep breath, then peek around, hoping fruitlessly that my ordeal would have gone unnoticed.

Looking toward the back of the plane, more eyes than I can count are staring at me, and my shoulders hunch up when the tingle starts again. My throat closes, and my tongue feels thick in my mouth as the nightmare continues. My ears lengthen, and droopy, twitching rabbit ears poke out of my hair. All I want at this moment is to hide, but I need to get my bags put away.

Before I can try to heft one up again, a body steps into my space and takes hold of the handle, gently brushing my hand away and setting my bag on the seat. I let out a squeak of surprise, causing my skin to redden even further at the irony of squeaking while simultaneously looking like a mouse-rabbit. Then I glance up and fully register the presence standing next to me.

Asher.

He's here, somehow, and he's... shielding me?

He has his jacket unzipped so it's hanging loose to either side of what is already a fairly wide and muscular body, and his arms are stretched around either side of me, hands propped on the seat back and overhead bin so he's blocking most of the others on the plane from my vision.

"I've got it," he says, his voice low and gentle, and my skin tingles *again*. This time, I don't feel the shift, but my vision alters, becoming more sharp, with colors that almost seem to glow. My eyes must have changed, but Asher doesn't flinch or look away. He doesn't acknowledge in any way that there's something wrong or abnormal about me right now. He simply nudges me out of the aisle, then tosses my bags in the overhead bin with an easy flex of his muscles. I try to avoid staring as he sits down in the seat next to me, but it's even harder not to look at him when my vision is so enhanced.

I have no idea what's going on. Asher must sense my confusion, because he smiles, but this only serves to make it worse, and my brows furrow even further. I'm not sure he has ever smiled at me, and it does weird, wiggly things to my insides, like I'm full of worms.

Or butterflies.

I turn to look out the window, not speaking one word to him, and he seems content to let me have my space. I try my hardest not to roll my eyes at his performative chivalry, but can't help glancing at his arm, right next to mine. He's only wearing a fitted cotton tee under his jacket, and when he lifted those bags up, I got an eyeful of bulging biceps.

Blessed Mother Moon. How do vampires build up so much muscle? Is there a lot of protein in blood?

I squirm in my seat, uncomfortable with the physical pull I feel toward someone who has such different fundamental values from myself, and that's assuming he has any sort of values or moral compass at all.

Although, he did help me twice now when I've needed it, and he didn't give me a hard time or ask for anything in return in either situation. I'm not sure how that version of him fits with the gruff work-place version I've seen over the last couple of weeks in the office.

As my mind circles around the conundrum that is Asher Sullivan/Walton, my eyesight returns to normal, and I briefly wonder what my eyes looked like when they shifted. My ears shorten next, and I run a hand through my hair, tucking a few strands behind a normal, human ear, while I wait for my face to morph back into my typical features too.

Before that happens, I hear someone speaking to Asher next to us.

"Hey man," they say, "sorry, but I think you're in my seat? I'm in B."

"Oh, yeah, I was going to ask if you wanted to swap? I have the aisle, but we're together, so I'd prefer middle if it's all the same to you," Asher says, and I do my best not to react to those words, *we're together.*

Why would he say that? Why does he want to sit by me?

"Gotcha, no problem," the stranger says, tucking themselves into the aisle seat and fastening their seatbelt.

Asher doesn't so much as glance my way, let alone offer any sort of explanation for this change.

I try to read, but I can't focus well enough to lose myself in the story. Instead, I spend most of the flight attempting to listen to a podcast I have downloaded featuring free tourist areas in San Diego, but my thoughts keep circling back to the man sitting next to me. Legs taking up more space than they deserve, head tipped back with earbuds in, and arms loosely crossed over his chest. I wonder if there's anything in the world that manages to get under his skin.

When we touch down over two hours later, I can't recall one single thing that was mentioned on that podcast.

9

___

FROM BAD TO WORSE

RAYA

I CAN'T DECIDE how I feel about this weirdly chill version of Asher. From the airport, it was a quick drive along the harbor to the Gaslamp District downtown, and Asher was relaxed and polite to both myself and the driver the whole time. I'm trying to figure out how likely it is he has a secret twin who swapped places with him for this trip as we pull up to the hotel.

I follow Asher into the sleek hotel lobby, suitcases rattling along behind us as we step up to the counter. He gives both of our names and I lean against the tall counter next to him as we wait.

When the concierge asks for the names again, typing with a little more gusto this time, I straighten up, noticing a slight furrow between his brows. I glance at Asher, but he ignores me.

Finally, the concierge looks up from the screen, eyes bouncing between us.

"I'm so sorry, Mr. Sullivan, but it seems we only have the one room booked under your name. We don't have any reservation for a Ms. Merritt."

Then he looks at Asher expectantly, like he will have the solution to this problem. I'm starting to understand how Reverie feels half the time, like she's too small to be noticed.

"That's okay," I say. "I'll just take whatever you have available."

The concierge glances at me, and then back to Asher, then down to the computer before replying. "Unfortunately, we don't have any rooms open at the moment."

"I'm sorry, what?" I say, at the same time Asher says, "How is that possible?"

"Well," the concierge says, his voice calm and careful, "it's TwitchCon, so we are completely booked. We even have a waitlist in case of any last minute cancellations. I'm happy to add you to it, if you'd like?" The concierge is clearly trying to offer a polite smile, but I am beyond it.

"What are we going to do?" I turn to Asher now too, hating the pleading tremble in my voice. "Some of our meetings are booked here at the hotel, and the company office is across the street. There must be another option close by," I trail off, muttering to myself as I pull out my phone and step away.

A frantic search reveals that there are no current openings at any of the hotels within a five mile radius, and I don't have the funds to rent a car for anything further. Feeling tears gather in my eyes at what is turning out to be a miserable day, I blink furiously while praying to all the stars above that I don't shift right now. That would be the cherry on top.

A hand enters my vision, covering mine and easing my phone down. I already know who it is, and his gentle touch spurs on the tears, causing a few to streak down my cheeks. I spin away from him, swiping at my face furiously.

"It's fine, you'll stay with me. We'll make this work," he says.

His tone doesn't give any indication how he feels about

that arrangement, but I have no other answers or ideas, so I simply nod. Keeping my eyes glued to the floor, I grab my duffel and suitcase, then follow him into the elevator where he pushes the button for the eighth floor.

The elevator ride takes years, and when it finally spits us out, I can feel his eyes burning over every inch of me. I refuse to acknowledge it, instead setting my shoulders back and tipping my chin up with a steadying breath. Now that we aren't in such a public place, in front of others who could see if I had another embarrassing shift, I'm feeling more calm and in control again.

The room isn't anything special, with a standard king bed, small kitchenette, and decent sized bathroom next to a closet.

Wait.

My eyes fly back to the bed. The one, *single*, bed—because of course the company wouldn't have reserved a room with double queens. Not when only one person is supposed to be staying here.

Gulping at the thickness in my throat when I contemplate sharing a bed with him, I turn away and place my suitcase next to the set of drawers to begin unpacking for the week.

Neither of us speak, both metaphorically tiptoe-ing around the king-sized elephant in the room as we settle in. I retreat to the bathroom to shower off the plane ride before bed, dreading my chances of keeping myself safe from him when we're forced into such close quarters.

I slip into my silky pajama set, a pale pink button down short sleeve shirt with tiny sunflowers printed all over it and matching shorts. I bundle up my dirty clothes and steel myself as I open the door.

"It's all yours," I say, gesturing to the bathroom with steam billowing out behind me.

"Wow, leave any hot water for the rest of us?" Asher asks, and once again, I can't tell if he's mocking me in a friendly, teasing way, or if he's being mean. My lips scrunch to one side as I inch past him to the far side of the bed and sit down on the edge.

"I called down for more pillows and an extra set of blankets. They should be up any minute so if someone knocks, that's probably what it is," he says.

"Oh, okay great. Thanks," I reply, trailing off as Asher closes the bathroom door before I finish speaking.

WHEN HE COMES out bare chested in a pair of low-slung shorts twenty minutes later, my eyes nearly bug out of my head.

"What. You…" I splutter, nothing coherent coming out of my mouth because he has abs *for days*. So many ridges of muscle are staring me in the face that my mouth starts to water; I want to run my tongue along those ridges and count them.

When I manage to pull my eyes from his torso, the most infuriating smirk takes over his face, and naturally that's the moment my inner animal decides to show up. With a little tingle along my cheeks and forearms, I sprout smooth patches of short grey fur.

"Ughhhhh," I throw my head back and let out a groaning yell fit for the undead, as my frustration with this shifting nears its breaking point.

Asher's smirk disappears and a look that might be concern replaces it.

"Are you okay?" he asks, reaching out like he might touch me, but I pull away.

"What does it look like?" I snap, holding my arms out wide and turning away to hide my frustration and sadness.

"I'm sorry. Is there anything I can do?"

I'm surprised to hear that he sounds like he means it, but I'm not sure what he expects me to say. If I can't do anything, what could he possibly do?

"It'll go away on its own," I mutter, "eventually."

"It…" he trails off.

"What?" I look up at his tentative voice, trying to keep my hackles in check.

"Nothing."

Are his cheeks turning pink? Can vampires blush?

I'm fully invested now, and I perk up again.

"No, tell me. What were you going to say?" I ask.

"I was going to say that it looks…" When he stops again, I purse my lips and prepare for the worst. He must see or sense me closing up, because his eyes widen and he rushes to finish. "No, it's not bad. I was just thinking that it looks soft."

My head tilts at this, and my hand rises to my cheek. I've never even considered how my various types of fur might feel to others. Stroking my fingers down my cheek, I shrug, and he leans forward.

"Well?" he asks, and somehow his voice is even more hushed than it was before, almost reverent. "Is it?"

I reach out to him, watching as his gaze flicks between my outstretched hand and my eyes. One side of my mouth quirks up at his hesitancy.

"I won't bite you," I say, and I'm pretty sure his lips twitch into what might almost be a smile at the implication that of the two of us, I'm not the one with lethal fangs.

Asher extends his hand and places it in mine, letting me take the lead and guide him. I run his fingers over the fur on my opposite arm, and he sucks in a breath. I raise my eyebrows in question, and he nods.

"Yeah," he says, clearing his throat, "soft."

With that, the short grey fur pulls back into my skin, and I'm left with his fingers circling my elbow. He lets them trail down my forearm to my wrist, leaving sparks and goosebumps in their wake as he pulls away, his eyes fixed on mine.

My breath stalls, a different tingle flickering over me. I break eye contact and look away.

What in the world?

I've never let anyone touch me like that before, not when I'm shifted. And even though physical touch is a necessity for shifters, it's normally comforting. Not... Whatever that was, making me all hot and bothered in the most irritating way.

Grabbing a couple pillows and the extra blanket, I stalk away from the bed and start to create a little nest on the floor.

"Absolutely not." His voice is harsh and full of command, all traces of the softer man from minutes ago are gone.

There's the asshole attitude I know and loath.

"Excuse me?" My defenses are back in place, and when I look up at the man glowering over me, my spine stiffens at the threat I sense in his stance.

"You take the bed. I'll sleep on the floor."

I scoff. "You can drop the nice act, Mr. Walton," I say. "It's just us now, you don't have to pretend anymore."

My brows draw together as what might be hurt flashes across his face, but what does he expect from me? I can sleep on the floor same as he can.

"That's not my name."

It takes me a second to catch up, not expecting him to address that part of my statement.

"What do you mean that's not your name?" I say, my tone icy.

"I had it legally changed years ago. My name is Asher Sullivan." His tone is equally frosty, and his words put a crack in my defenses.

"You... what?"

Asher grabs the pillows and blankets from me, then snags a couple more from the closet and lays them out on the floor at the foot of the bed, not answering me as he lays down with a quiet huff. I'm left standing in the middle of the room, thoughts racing circles around the inside of my head. I can't help wondering who he is, why he changed his name, what could cause someone to do that and whether it has anything to do with why he hasn't been photographed with his family in years.

"Asher? What did you mean you changed your name?"

He continues to ignore me and rolls over so all I can see is the broad expanse of his back.

Giving up on it for now, I quietly walk back to the bed and climb in, lying stiffly on my back, arms straight at my sides. I do my best to lie still, not wanting to bother Asher more than I clearly already have, but I can't sleep. I feel guilty, like I made a grave error, and I don't know how to fix it.

I toss and turn for what feels like hours before I whisper into the dark, silent room. "I'm sorry. Can we start over?"

No answer.

I roll over again, sensing that he's not sleeping either, although he lies still as stone at the foot of the bed.

"I may be the world's most broken shifter, but my ears work just fine. I know you're not sleeping," I say, my voice soft and carrying more hurt than I intend it to.

He rolls over with a sigh, then mutters, "I'm trying to."

I purse my lips as more fur sprouts out along my upper arms and back. It feels more coarse this time. Dense and bristly, it's not at all comfortable to lay on, so I roll to my stomach as he speaks again, so quietly I almost miss it.

"And you're not broken."

I huff. *What is his deal?* This man is so confusing. Before I can reply, he interrupts my thoughts.

"Go to sleep, Raya."

Why does my name on his lips make my heart flutter?

10

EAVESDROPPING IS RUDE

RAYA

OUR FIRST MORNING of meetings and presentations goes about as well as I expect it to, given the challenges of this trip so far. Thankfully no major mishaps, but certainly some close calls with the untimely shifting. I'm currently hiding at a little cafe down the street during our lunch break, hoping some extra caffeine and time away from work—and Asher—will settle my nerves.

I didn't take the CBD oil last night that my parents insisted I bring with me. I honestly forgot, what with all the only-one-bed confusion muddling me up all night. The morning was as awkward as I imagined it would be as we pretended a weird mix of politeness and ignoring each other while getting ready.

On top of the lack of sleep, I definitely feel the moon's pull today, and I know it will only continue to get stronger for the next three days. It's not until our last day here that it might start to ease up a bit as the full moon passes and begins to wane.

Heaving a sigh, I finish off my lunch and walk back out into the unrelenting heat and sun. My flowy top is sticking to my sweaty back as I walk into the clients' headquarters and aim for the elevators, relishing the chill of the air conditioning on my skin. Asher is already in the conference room when I arrive, and I stumble a step when I see him in sharp profile against the windows overlooking the harbor. His looks are striking, and I'm noticing it far more than is safe.

He turns when he hears me enter, offering what I think is supposed to be a tight smile but looks more like a grimace. Then his gaze darts to my bare legs below my skirt, before quickly refocusing on the table in front of me. I almost think I imagined his attention, until I notice his hands fisted at his sides as he clears his throat.

Twice.

I tip my head to the side, taking in his stiff posture and closed off body language. I don't understand what it is about me that makes him so uncomfortable. Deciding to ignore whatever he has going on for now, I pull out a chair and sit, tugging at my fitted, forest green skirt as I cross my legs. I keep my eyes laser focused on Asher as he joins me, rounding the table and pausing before choosing the seat directly to my right.

I quirk an eyebrow, though he doesn't see it as he's now refusing to acknowledge me—and not being subtle about it at all.

Interesting seat choice for someone who scowls at me multiple times a day.

ASHER

Those legs will be the death of me. All smooth, creamy skin. Not to mention the way that high waisted skirt makes it seem like they go on for miles. It's all I can do to keep my thoughts under control as my mind attempts to drag me into the gutter. I glue my gaze to the laptop screen in front of me as Raya completes her presentation and strides back to her seat.

Why did I sit next to her?

Being so close I can inhale her warm coconut scent, just a hint of fresh strawberries, and sense the blood rushing through her veins is sweet torture. I take a hard gulp from my water bottle, wishing it was something stronger than water and hoping the rest of todays meetings go by quick and easy. I need a cold shower to wash away the intoxicating effect of the woman sitting next to me, but I have to endure this torture for at least another few hours. This afternoon is all about coordinating the rest of the week and making sure everyone is on the same page. All I have to do is sit back and confirm I'm ready to do my part.

Unfortunately, this leaves plenty of time for my brain to wander. It's impossible not to breathe her in, not to close my eyes and imagine what her soft skin might feel like under my fingers, under my tongue, under my teeth as I bite into her neck.

Wait.

My eyes snap open.

I can't want that, for far too many reasons, but the most important of which is that she seems to despise me and would never agree to it. I have no idea how much she knows about vampires or what she thinks about us, but I wouldn't blame her if she was disgusted by my kind. Many of us are the worst this world has to offer, and I will not subject her to the monster my family tried to make me into. There's no way she would consent to me drinking from her, even if she knew how pleasurable I could make it.

Never say never. My horny brain is not helping the situation, and I startle when Raya pushes her chair back, uncrossing those devilish legs as she stands and excuses herself to the restroom. Again. For the fifth time in fewer hours.

I narrow my eyes at her back as she leaves, then notice other confused and concerned looks when I glance around the conference room. That's all I need to spur me into action; I announce I'm going to check if she's okay, then stride out the door after her.

Spying a glimpse of her honey-gold hair whipping around a corner down the hall, I jog that direction, but don't catch up before Raya slips into the restroom and locks the door behind her. I lean against the wall a few feet down the hallway, determined to wait and ensure she's alright, while trying my very best to convince myself I'd do the same for any other coworker.

If I thought Raya was actually going to use the toilet, I wouldn't have loitered, but my gut says there's something else going on. Sure enough, I hear harsh breathing as the water turns on for a moment. There's some faint splashing and then the water turns off, followed by muttering coming from behind the door when I move closer.

Without my enhanced vampiric senses, I wouldn't have been able to hear her, but as it is, I'm able to make out a few words that don't do anything to help me better understand the situation.

"...wrong with me... stars ... need ... a grip."

I glance up and down the sparse hallway to ensure I'm alone, then take the final step forward so I'm right outside the door and angle my head so my ear is closer, tuning out any other ambient sounds as much as I can.

"...ridiculous, Raya. Come on, just turn back." Her voice is full of frustration and something else I can't quite decipher.

At that point, she must turn the sink on again because I can't decipher her words underneath the sound of running water. I swipe a hand down my face to reset it, then pace a few steps up and down the austere hallway as I decide what to do. There isn't a great option here, but I don't want to leave her to deal with this alone. I cross my arms and lean against the wall opposite from the restroom as I settle in to wait for her.

Raya jumps about a foot in the air when she sees me, slapping a hand to her pounding chest and instantly gaining a cute little rabbit nose. I try to hold in my grin, I know this isn't the time for amusement, but it's hard to contain.

"Stars above, you scared me!" Raya whisper-shouts, as if that doesn't make the whole scene even cuter, until her fingertips find the bunny nose twitching on her face. "Freaking, fudging, dang it! What is wrong with you," Raya shrieks, whipping back into the restroom and slamming the door.

I blink at the empty hallway, realizing I hadn't moved a single muscle during that one-sided exchange and mentally punching myself in the face. I followed her to help, not to make it worse.

I step forward and gently knock on the door.

"Go away," Raya says, and I'm unsure what emotions her words are laden with, but they sound heavy.

"Are you okay? You keep leaving, and I wanted to see if there was anything I could do to help," I reply, keeping my voice slow and calm.

"Great. Just great. Not only do I look like a freak, but now people probably think I have a UTI or bowel issues or something." Her grumble is adorable.

I bite my lip to hold in the laugh that wants to break free. It's such a strange sensation, wanting to laugh. I can't remember the last time I felt this way, if ever. I suspect Raya didn't intend for me to hear that though, so I don't answer.

When she emerges again a couple minutes later, sans bunny nose, her eyes are blazing and her lips are pinched together. My heart stutters at the sight, wondering anew how I can get her to stop hating me.

"Are you okay?" I ask again.

Raya pins me with a fierce look, one I assume is supposed

to be a glare, then shakes her head as she pushes past me and heads back toward the meeting room.

"Raya," I say, reaching my hand out, aching to touch her but stopping before I make contact. Raya pauses to look sideways at me.

"It's your shifting, isn't it?" I say, still trying to keep my voice quiet and calm, then continue when her only response is to bite the inside of her cheek. "Look, maybe I can help."

I run a hand through my hair before I can think to stop the nervous habit, and Raya's distrustful eyes track the movement. I get lost for a moment tracing the freckles across her nose.

"How?"

"How?" I parrot back to her, unsure what she's asking.

"You said maybe you can help." Her voice and posture are both stiff, sharp and unyielding. "How?"

"Right, yeah. I mean, I had to learn to control my emotions and urges in order to not be a completely unhinged, blood sucking vampire at all times of the day and night, and I was thinking maybe some of those lessons could help you, too."

Raya scrunches up one side of her nose and blinks at me, her face a mask of confusion, but before either of us can speak another word, a voice interrupts from down the hall.

"Hey, you two good? We've got a schedule to keep."

"Yep, be right there!" Raya's bright voice chirps back at him and she turns away from me. Her sweet strawberry and coconut scent swirls around me as she looks my way once more, a lingering, searching look that I'm too pessimistic to hope might be intrigue, before striding back to the meeting.

11

DROWNED RAT ISN'T MY BEST LOOK

RAYA

I'M SITTING at the hotel bar that evening, nursing a grapefruit mocktail and contemplating the disaster that is currently my life, when my least favorite person slides up to the bar next to me.

"Hey, sunshine. Mind if I join you?" Asher asks, and his smooth voice sends involuntary shivers down my spine.

I ignore the mocking nickname and gesture to the open stool. He sits without turning away from me, then orders "whatever she's having."

His eyebrows go up in surprise when he takes a sip and notices there's no alcohol.

"Not a drinker?" he asks.

I shrug. "Just figured now wasn't a good time."

I'll blame it on work if he asks, though the reality is that I assume alcohol won't help with the shifting situation I'm struggling with.

He simply nods, and my shoulders relax a fraction as we fall into a semi-easy silence, until he breaks it a couple minutes later.

"I was serious about what I said earlier." He glances sideways at me, blue eyes surrounded by dark lashes, while twirling the glass in slow circles on the bar. "About helping you."

I try not to scoff, remembering he had said something about controlling his urges.

"What did you mean, when you said you had to learn to control your urges?" It's not what I intended to say, but as usual, my curiosity gets the better of me.

"Well..." he trails off, giving me another sideways look, so I school my face into a neutral expression and raise my eyebrows for him to continue. He rubs his thumb and forefinger over his brow, kneading at his temples for a moment.

"Being a full-blooded vampire from a strong, ancient line can be challenging."

This time the scoff comes out in a full blown snort, because *right*. Being from one of the wealthiest, most influential families in the world must be such a hardship.

"Never mind," he says, shaking his head and turning slightly away from me.

A punch of guilt hits my chest and I frown, both at his reaction and mine. I don't treat anyone else this way, but he brings out my defensiveness like no one else has. Before I can think better of it, I'm encouraging him to continue.

"I'm sorry, that was insensitive. Please, explain."

His chest expands with a deep breath, then he slowly turns back toward me on the exhale, and his stormy blue eyes meet mine. They're piercing and soul searching, and I don't think I could move a single muscle if I wanted to, which I don't.

Slowly, he nods at whatever he finds within me, then begins to explain.

"When I said I was from a strong bloodline, what I meant is that it makes our impulses stronger. Our vampiric instincts can become overwhelming and hard to control, which my parents only encouraged, but learning to listen to my body, to be more in tune with myself and those instincts has allowed me to take charge. Even when my inner vampire would rather rip into someone's neck."

His eyes flick to the pulse now hammering in my own neck, and I shudder at the cold reminder and the mental image it brings of a bloody, horror-filled life. I take a sip of my drink to give myself a moment to take in his vicious words.

"What do you mean that your parents encouraged it?"

His eyes leave mine at this question, and I tilt my head at him as he takes another deep breath, then runs his fingers through dark, messy hair that looks like he's already done so fifty times today.

"Let's just say we don't agree on what it means to be a vampire."

I don't know what to say to that, because I'm pretty sure being a vampire means drinking blood. The concept seems clear cut to me, but he doesn't look inclined to expand on it.

"Okay," I say, "but don't you drink from humans anyway?"

He looks back at me with a smirk that I feel low in my belly, and leans teasingly into my space.

"Only if they want me to," he whispers, breath ghosting across my ear, and my nose is filled with the smoky scent of him as he pulls away.

"Why would they want that?" I match his whisper, my eyes bouncing between his, which are glimmering in the low bar lighting.

"Maybe someday you'll find out." He throws the last of his drink back as he stands. "I'd be happy to oblige, all you have to do is ask."

With that, he flashes his fangs at me as one side of his mouth tips up in a crooked smile that has no business being as sexy as it is. I shiver as his gaze dips down my body before he strides out, vehemently denying to myself that any part of me likes the look of those pointy teeth.

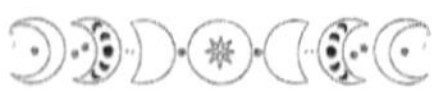

I NEED SOME SPACE. After gulping down the rest of my drink, I think about taking a walk, but don't want to deal with the oppressive heat wave happening right now. I see a sign for the pool and realize a relaxing swim sounds perfect for clearing my head; all I have to worry about is running into Asher in our room.

I feel pressing my ear to our door to see if he's inside before entering. A sigh leaves my body when I find it empty, although again, I'm confused by the conflicting feelings of relief and disappointment that waft through me.

A quick bathroom change into my bikini and a hotel-provided robe has me skipping for the pool in no time. Somehow, there's no one else here when I arrive, and I assume all the TwitchCon people must be too drained to do anything other than crash in their rooms.

Not one to look a gift horse in the mouth, I pile my towel and robe on a chair before jumping right in. I swim a couple laps back and forth, then dive to the bottom and tip my head back, looking at the water rippling above me. When I come up for air, I float on my back with my eyes closed and ears barely under the surface, relaxing with the gurgling filter and dull hum from the heaters in my ears.

I ease my eyes open with a soft, contented smile on my face, then let out an unholy screech, splashing and flailing when I accidentally inhale some water in my shock at seeing someone looming above me on the edge of the pool. Spluttering and coughing, I manage to half-swim to the shallow area and put my feet down, then round on Asher with fire in my eyes.

"You," I pant between the words as my brain tries to catch up. "Scared me!"

"I didn't mean to startle you, I thought you would have heard me come in. You know, shifter senses and all."

I'm still gasping for breath and trying to slow my racing pulse. I push a hand against my chest, the hard drum of my heart beating against my palm.

"You good?" he asks, and I look up to see him standing in the water next to me, startling me *again*, and I hiccup in response.

He pats me gently on the back to help clear my lungs, and the zing of his large hand and warm skin against mine causes a certain, unwelcome tingle to shoot through me.

"Oh Mother Moon, please." I look to the sky, drawing out the last word in desperation, but it does no good. Before I even finish speaking, my ears have shifted. Lowering my chin back down, I reach up with both hands to feel them, trying to figure out what sort of animal has graced me this time, but I wrinkle my nose in confusion when I feel narrow, pointed ears with thick fur sticking out of the top of my head. Kind of like one of those cat-ear headbands I saw a cosplayer sporting on their way to the Con earlier.

Asher angles his head, eyes flickering over my hair and ears, and whatever I was feeling earlier instantly turns to mortification.

This, of course, only seems to encourage my inner shifter. Next thing I know, I'm covered in sopping wet grey fur, and I feel exactly how I imagine I look—like a soaking wet rat.

When I look back at Asher though, his lips are tilted, curving up into a small smile.

"I look like a drowned rat, don't I?" I say, my voice clearly conveying how miserable I am about it.

"Nah," he says, but at my skeptical look, he turns course. "Okay, maybe a little."

Then he has the audacity to chuckle. I fume, feeling my skin heat with anger instead of embarrassment.

How dare he laugh at me? Make light of my situation, humiliate me.

"Stars and teeth! You are the worst!" I feel ready to combust, and I hardly notice when my fingernails sharpen into what might be cat claws.

Covering his mouth with one hand, Asher appears flabbergasted when he repeats, "Stars and… teeth?"

"It's a phrase! People say it." My emotions are going haywire. Is this the moon? I've always been a 'big feeler', as my mom says, but my emotions aren't normally this chaotic. I can't tell if I'm annoyed or angry or amused by his reactions to me. The water sluicing down his sculpted chest certainly isn't helping.

"Riiiight." He draws the word out, nodding seriously to make it clear he doesn't believe me, before cracking up again.

"Why are you laughing?"

He tries to reign in his chuckling, but he can't erase the mirth from his eyes.

"You're just so cute, I can't help it," he says, gliding closer.

"I'm.. what?" There's no way he thinks this soggy mouse look with… whatever ears are on my head, is *cute.*

"I mean, the red fox ears, and that little scowl you keep trying on. I don't know how else to describe it."

"Cute," I deadpan.

He seems to realize that I think's he's making fun of me, so he wades even closer, following as I back into the wall, then pauses right before our bodies meet. With his hand barely under the surface, centimeters from the fur covering my arm, he meets my gaze again with that intense stare.

"Yes, sunshine," he says, his voice more quiet and serious than it was before.

I stare at him, unable to decode what I see in his eyes, or untangle the confusing knot of emotions swirling inside myself. My body makes the decision for me as I move slightly, just enough for his fingertips to graze my upper arm. As he traces his fingers down to my wrist, it's like he erases the fur from my skin. It recedes in the wake of his touch, the cat claws disappearing too, and I shudder as I watch it happen.

My eyes travel up his roped forearm, taking in the strength in his form, his broad chest with a dusting of dark hair, the lines of his throat bobbing as my gaze moves over it, and my ears twitch on top of my head. My eyes latch onto his lips, then I flash my gaze up to his, only to see a burning heat reflected back at me.

I gasp, eyes flaring, but have nowhere to go. My back is already pushed up against the edge of the pool, and my hands fly to his chest. Whether to push him away or to feel more of his skin against mine, I can't say. Maybe a little of both.

Asher's eyes cut to my neck, where my pulse is pounding through me, and I clench my thighs beneath the water. He notices the movement, and his lips part. His tongue licks over the fangs that have extended in his mouth, and it's my turn to gulp a hard swallow.

He takes a shuddering breath as he jerks away from me, dragging a hand through his hair again before dunking his entire body under the water. I'm still frozen against the wall when he emerges a few feet further away and straightens in the waist deep water, facing slightly away from me. It runs down his shoulders and back in tantalizing rivulets and I cross my arms over my chest to hide my reaction to him.

He pauses at the movement, but then clenches his jaw as he strides up the steps out of the pool. Throwing a "see you in the room" back at me, he slips his feet into sandals and wraps a towel around his waist as he leaves.

I wait a few minutes, then slowly glide to the steps, feeling like I'm following a ghost when I take the same path he did. I towel off and pull on the robe, my mind spinning and unable to make sense of what just happened between us as I head back to the room.

12

BREATHING IS HARDER
THAN IT SOUNDS

RAYA

ASHER IS in the shower when sneak into the room a few minutes later, and I breathe a sigh of relief at not having to confront him right away. I turn on the TV so I don't have to hear him showering and think about how he's naked in there, especially now that I know what he looks like with glistening skin.

"Oh my stars, get it together," I mutter to myself, then pull out my silky pajamas.

Thankfully, my phone has a message from Zuri to distract me.

> Zuri: How's it going? You doing okay?

I cringe when I think about telling her that not only did things not go to plan, and that I'm not avoiding Asher at all, but in fact I'm sharing a room with him. Pretty much the opposite of the intended plan to keep my distance and not be alone with him. I decide to keep it vague in the interest of avoiding a lecture.

> Me: It's going, no issues so far. How's everything at home?

> Zuri: All good over here, somebody really misses you tho

> Me: I know, we haven't been apart much. Tell her I miss her and let her play with your hair to make up for it

> Zuri: Great, thanks for that. She was reading over my shoulder so I can't even get out of it now.

I grin when I imagine their corresponding faces of horror (Zuri) and delight (Reverie) at that request.

> Me: Have a great night!

> Zuri: MISS U LUV U COME BACK SOON

> Me:

Obviously, that last one was Reverie. Zuri must have given in to her pleading puppy-dog eyes, or maybe traded sending a message to get out of having her hair done. I'm smiling when I hear the bathroom doorknob click as Asher turns the handle.

I avoid eye contact and slip past him into the bathroom as soon as he exits, taking my turn for a shower and some extra space to mentally prepare myself for coming face to face with him again. What I do not intend is for my mind to wander back to his lips and what they might feel like on mine. I have to constantly redirect my thoughts and end up taking twice as long as I normally would to shampoo and soap the chlorine from my skin.

He is a questionable, immoral vampire from an evil, corrupt family. Internally scolding myself, I turn the water off and steel my spine for what I hope is not the most awkward encounter of my entire life.

When I open the bathroom door, he's lounging in the desk chair watching TV. Legs sprawled out in front of him with a worn t-shirt hugging all the right places, he dominates the space, and I feel tiny in his presence.

He looks over at me as I walk toward the bed and doesn't even try to hide the appreciation in his eyes. I ignore it as I complete my bedtime routine, then perch on the edge of the mattress near the foot where his blankets are piled from the previous night.

Before the words register in my brain, I'm speaking.

"Do you want to share the bed? We can make a pillow wall." As soon as the words leave my mouth, I clap a hand over it, eyes flaring wide.

Have I completely lost my wits?! Then again...

I drop my hand and school my face into what I hope is a neutral, unaffected expression. He searches my eyes as he stands, his flitting back and forth between mine, before one corner of his lips barely turns up, and he slowly shakes his head. I scan his face, but can't decipher the look on it. It's one I haven't seen before, and I don't know what to make of it or his rejection.

He sits down on his pile of blankets at the foot of the bed, same place as the night before, and looks up at me perched above him.

"Thank you, but not this time," Asher says, and a tiny ember flares to life in my chest.

I remember to drop some CBD oil under my tongue so I don't answer the moon's call in my sleep, and before I know it, I'm out like a light.

I SHOULD BE USED to having a rabbit face and ears by now, but somehow, I'm not. Today is the first day of real work, where I will be training the client's employees on implementing and utilizing the new software. Naturally, I've shifted three minutes before my presentation is supposed to start.

My hands grip the edges of the sink and I hear it creak under my weight. Letting go, I shake my head. I can't wait any longer. Twitching bunny nose or not, I need to go.

As I walk back into the conference room where the first slide of my presentation is already projected on the screen at the front, I decide to make light of it. Filling my lungs and pasting a smile on my face, I walk in, and heads immediately turn in my direction.

I step to the front, then look around and my smile turns intentionally rueful as I circle a hand around the air in front of my face.

"I know. Ridiculous, right?" I force a chuckle and a couple people smile in response, while many shoulders relax. "It's a new thing. Just ignore it, that's what I do."

With this, I wave my hand, gesturing toward the screen. "Shall we begin?"

Nods and shuffling follow as people pull out notepads or laptops, and I'm pleased to find I don't hear one snicker or whisper from the group in front of me. I begin to relax as I start the first of many training presentations this week, and as I move to the second slide, my face tingles back to its incredibly normal, blissfully boring human shape.

ASHER WALKS into the hotel room later that afternoon to find me sprawled out on the bed with black cat ears (not the fake headband kind, unfortunately) and a black cat tail sticking out of my gym shorts, the end flicking back and forth.

His face cycles through an amusing carousel of expressions in a matter of seconds. I'm pretty sure I catch shock, confusion, amusement, and what I think might be concern. I refuse to acknowledge my brain telling me that I also saw a flicker of interest in his eyes when we both realized I'm only wearing running shorts and a sports bra. I had been planning to go to the gym, until my black cat features made an abrupt appearance and I flopped onto the bed instead.

I sit up and watch as he slowly walks into the room and sets his leather bag down on the desk, then unbuttons the top of his shirt. My mind spins into overdrive, silently begging those fingers to keep going, and internally crying when they don't. Instead, he practically stalks over to me, eyes narrowing as I straighten up in his presence.

"What?" I say, my voice wary as I lean slightly away from him.

He stops his advance and blinks, clearing some of the predatory aura he had going on, and while that does wonders for the tension in my shoulders, I'm mortified to feel my lower stomach and thighs unclench too.

It doesn't mean anything.

"Let me help, sunshine," he says, and I'm shocked to hear that he almost sounds... pleading.

"Please," he adds.

Past pleading then—begging.

I smother the smirk trying to break out on my lips, and pull up the rational part of my brain. Nothing I've done seems to have helped. If I'm being brutally honest with myself, I haven't tried much to begin with. At this point, I doubt anything he has to teach me could make it worse, so I meet his eyes and nod my assent.

"Okay," I say.

"Yeah?" His eyes are wary, so I confirm again, a slight smile crooking the corners of my mouth.

"Yeah."

Asher snags a throw blanket from his makeshift bed and snaps his wrists to spread it out across the floor. Then he grabs two pillows and sets them down, sitting on one and waving me over to sit on the other.

I curl my legs under me on the pillow, facing him with only a couple of feet between us. My breath catches at the detail I can see on his face, realizing I never paid much attention to these smaller parts of him before. The way his eyebrows have a natural arch, how thick and dark his lashes are. The streaks of silvery-blue and gray that crackle out from his pupil, creating a striking effect in his blue eyes.

"So I don't suggest anything you've already tried, what has and hasn't worked in the past?" he asks.

I shrug, and he quirks an eyebrow.

"I don't know," I say. "I haven't really tried anything."

"What about in the bathroom?" He references the previous day when I was hiding, then yelled at him and slammed the door in his face. I flush at the memory.

"I mean, I tried to tell myself to shift back, but that didn't work. Obviously," I grumble the last word as I pout at my lap.

"What else?"

I think back to all the times I've hidden in various bathrooms over the last few months.

"I guess... I've tried washing my face. Pacing, does that count?" I let out a self-deprecating chuckle, and he frowns.

"What about breathing?" he asks.

"What, like meditation? Never been my thing." I've never been good at remaining still, especially not when I was a child. Always bouncing around from one thing to the next.

"Not necessarily," he says. "Let's start with some slow, deep breaths. Follow my movements, and breathe with your stomach."

At my confused expression, he holds out a hand for mine,

then places my palm against his abs as he takes a deep breath. I startle and yank my hand back, feeling like it's on fire. Now I know what the phrase "rock-hard abs" truly means.

His eyebrows pull together at my reaction.

"I was just trying to show you what I meant, how to breathe with your diaphragm."

"Oh." My cheeks heat and I extend my hand, letting him take it in his and place my palm against his stomach again.

I have to use every ounce of self control I possess not to claw into him. My fingers twitch and my palm itches with the urge to run my hands up under his shirt, to feel his skin against my own and count every muscular ridge I can find.

"You're not following," he says, and I jolt out of what was starting to become a vivid daydream when he places my other hand on my own stomach.

"Sorry, go again." I flash him one of my brightest smiles to prove I'm on board this time, and his stomach rises beneath my palm as he breathes in. My brow scrunches when I take an answering breath and don't feel the same rise on my own.

I look down at my hand and breathe in again, but it doesn't move.

"What? How are you doing that?" I say with an incredulous laugh.

His answering smile is crooked, and swooping in my lower belly, right below my hand.

"It's weird, I know. Most people don't breathe properly. Here," Asher says, adjusting his position so he's next to me and placing his hand on top of mine. His fingers splay between my own, his touch searing. He stills for a moment, eyes flicking to mine before he looks back down at his fingertips where they press into the bare skin of my ribs, right below my sports bra.

Asher clears his throat, but his voice still comes out a bit hoarse.

"Fill the top of your lungs first, like this." He demonstrates with exaggerated motions, his shoulders and chest rising. "Then fill the bottom of your lungs, like this." His other hand covers mine on his own stomach as he again breathes in, muscles stretching and ribs expanding beneath our joined hands.

"You try," he says, as he slowly releases the breath.

I breathe in with my chest, and he nods, then averts his gaze when he notices where he was staring. His fingertips tap my stomach muscles as he says, "now here" with the rest of my in-breath.

Our hands rise, a practically minuscule amount, but I smile in triumph nonetheless. His answering smile is warm, proud, and I really, *really* like it.

13

WHEN YOU HAVE TO TEACH
A VAMPIRE HOW TO HUG

RAYA

I WAKE on day three to Asher groaning as he stretches to silence his alarm. I yawn and roll to my back as he stands, then stretch my hands over my head with a contented moan of my own, reveling in the feeling of finally getting a good night's rest. I freeze when I notice him staring at me, then yank my arms down and snatch the blankets to my chest.

"Sorry," he mutters, swiping a hand down his face before shuffling into the bathroom. His voice is low and scratchy from sleep, and my stomach tightens at the sound.

He's dangerous, you absolute heathen. Get your head in the game.

We switch places, and the TV is on when I exit the bathroom, Asher's face locked in a rigid mask. It's showing a couple arm in arm posing for pictures while a third man stands off to the side. The sound is muted, but his family name rolls across the bottom of the screen and he immediately flicks it off and turns to the kitchenette when he notices my attention.

"You can leave it on, if you want," I say.

He grunts in reply, and I eye him warily. My curiosity is slowly getting the better of me.

"So..." I trail off, not sure how to ask in a polite way what the deal is with his family. "Are you close with them? Your family?"

His look of disgust could freeze the stars right out of the sky.

"No."

I take that as the end of the conversation, and I sneak around him into the kitchen.

I had been surprised to see bags of blood in the mini-fridge the first night here. He's stabbing a straw into one now, Capri-Sun style, as I tuck a mug under the coffee machine.

"Ugh," Asher cringes as he looks at the bag of blood like it personally offended him.

"Expired?" I ask, doing my best to be polite, even though I have about a million accusations swirling through my head.

"No, I just forgot what it tastes like from a bag."

I scoff. "Right, you're used to the fresh stuff."

So much for polite.

"What?" His brows scrunch in an expression that is way too innocent for a big, bad vampire. Part of me wants to reach over and smooth my finger over the groove between them. The other part wants to punch him in the throat.

"I guess only straight from the vein is good enough for you?" My tone is scathing.

"I don't... No." He stammers, and I roll my eyes. "No, this place I go to in Portland started using glass bottles a few weeks ago. I got used to not having that stale, plastic taste anymore, but I couldn't find anywhere like that here. So..." he holds up the plastic bag, "back to plastic it is."

"Huh," I say. It's my turn to scrunch up my face, and I try to make all the different things I know about him make sense.

It's like piecing together a puzzle when half of them are missing the picture.

"Ready to practice? We've got some time before we need to head out." He crinkles up the empty bag and drops it in the trash can under the sink, then takes a swig of mouthwash before returning to my side.

"Sure, yeah." I attempt to clear my head as we settle on the floor pillows, mirroring each other.

We fall into an easy rhythm, with me following the breathing pace he sets, and it takes enough focus to use the proper muscles that my mind doesn't wander.

Well, not at first anyway.

After a couple minutes, I start to notice him. His intensity, and the way he focuses on this task, this moment, as though it is the only thing in the world right now. The dark lashes that sweep against his cheekbones every time he lowers his gaze. The muscles cording his forearms.

"You're getting it," he says, interrupting my thoughts and I blink back into reality. "Let's add in some grounding."

He instructs me to stand and copy his movements, as we did before. He plants his feet shoulder width apart, and I copy him. He stomps each foot, and I startle, my wide eyes darting from his feet up to his face, and that sideways smile invites mine out to join it. Without a word, he deliberately stomps one foot, followed by the other, then looks pointedly at my feet.

I stomp and my stomach tenses in an effort not to laugh.

This is so weird.

He raises his arms up above his head, spreading his hands wide, and tips his head back with his eyes closed. I don't mind this form of teaching; staring at him is turning out not to be a hardship at all. In fact, I wonder if maybe we should add a lunch session to our routine, too. Before I can follow his movements, my skin tingles and fluffy, perked ears twitch into being on my head.

I sigh and drop my arms; the sound bringing Asher's attention back to me, and his arms fall too as he opens his eyes.

"Ah, well, now we can see if this helps," he says. "Again, from the beginning."

He puts his hand on his stomach, jutting his chin at me to do the same, then closes his eyes and breathes. I follow for three breaths before he adjusts his position, planting his feet and then taking a deep inhale as he reaches for the sky.

I mimic his movements, breathing in and noticing how the air fills my lungs as I reach as high as I can. I close my eyes and tilt my head back as I exhale, pulling my hands into my chest. I take another breath, not caring if I'm going off script; I'm doing what feels right, what my instincts are telling me to do.

When I open my eyes a couple breaths later, there's a new expression on his face.

"You did it," he says, his intense eyes sparkling with triumph.

I suck in a quick breath. My hands dart to my ears, and a smile blooms across my face. I feel lit up from the inside. Invincible.

"I did it!" I squeal. My first time having any sort of control over the shift. I'm about to burst, so I throw my arms out and leap into him.

Physical touch is natural for shifters; apparently, it's foreign to evil vampires. Asher stumbles back a step before his entire body goes rigid. My arms are wrapped around his waist, my face smashed into his chest, when I feel his hands tentatively curl around each of my upper arms.

"Haven't you ever hugged someone before?" I say. "You're supposed to put your arms around me."

Asher clears his throat, then slowly circles his arms around my back.

"Now squeeze a little," I prompt, trying not to laugh at the weirdness of having to give instructions on how to hug.

When I pull my face back to look up at him though, my smile drops and my stomach falls to my feet. His face is stone, completely blank and unreadable in a way I've never seen before.

"Oh, I'm so sorry." I stumble a little as I pull back, and his hand darts out to catch my arm, steadying me. "I didn't mean, if you don't like to be touched, I should have asked—"

"It's fine," he says.

My hands twist in the hem of my shirt as my eyes dart around the room, looking at anything but him.

"Right, well. Um, thank you. For the tips, they worked. Obviously. So uh, I'll just finish getting ready then."

I ignore the tingles as I grab my clothes and sprint into the bathroom.

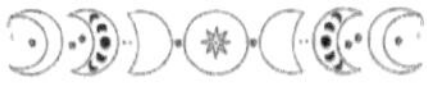

AFTER WORK, I buy some tacos and horchata on my walk back to the hotel. Asher isn't around, so I settle into the sole chair at the desk-turned-table. I send him a quick "where are you" text before unwrapping a potato taco and taking a deliciously massive bite.

I groan at the flavors exploding on my tongue.

"Should I give you a moment alone with your taco?"

I catapult out of the seat as I splutter bits of potato and cheese onto the desk.

"Stars, what is wrong with you?" I shriek. "Why do you always have to sneak up on me like that?"

His chuckle is infuriating, yet it somehow melts the irritation straight out of me until I feel like a soft puddle of goo, waiting to be squished.

It doesn't take him long.

"Seriously, you should really get your ears checked. I've never met a shifter so oblivious to the world around them," he says, and there goes the sweet, melty feeling. Anger surges back in until fire is burning behind my eyes. There's plenty wrong with me, I already know I'm the most messed up shifter in the universe—he doesn't have to point it out.

"You're a jerk." I turn my back on him and grab a handful of napkins from the to-go bag. My movements are jerky as I wipe down the table and pick up pieces of half-chewed tortilla from the floor.

"Hey," he says, a trashcan moving into view as he places it closer. "I'm sorry, I didn't mean to be a jerk."

I huff. I consistently remind myself he's not a good guy, and despite that, I still nearly forgot. He's been getting under my skin lately, and I don't want him there.

Liar.

"Honestly." He reaches a hand toward me, but stops before making contact. "I'm not sure what about that upset you, but I didn't mean anything by it. I was joking."

"Well, it wasn't funny," I say.

"I can see that now. I won't say it again."

I narrow my eyes as I turn to look at him, searching for any hint of a lie, but he seems earnest.

"Okay." I slump back into the chair. "You want a taco? I've got potato and shrimp."

"I'm good, but we should practice again when you're done," he says, then settles onto the floor in his blanket nest, scrolling through his phone while I finish my meal.

I can't stop my eyes from flickering over him. He's got this intense aura that pulls my attention, and the more I try to ignore it, the harder it gets to do so. Finally, I ball up my wrappers and toss them into the trash, then stand and take the two steps necessary to get to our make-shift practice area still set up from this morning.

"Start with breathing," he says, "then we can try some muscle relaxation."

I follow his lead again, first breathing together, then tensing and relaxing various muscles throughout my body. I feel more relaxed than I have in ages afterwards, but it's too early to reasonably go to bed yet.

I meander that direction anyway and pile up a bunch of pillows against the headboard before flopping down.

"You wanna watch something?" I ask, then mentally kick myself for opening the door to him again.

His head pops up from the foot of the bed, a million questions in his eyes.

I roll mine and pat the bed next to me.

"Come on. You can at least sit up here, there's plenty of space. Your butt has to be numb from the floor by now."

One side of Asher's mouth curves up as he stands and rounds the opposite side of the bed. I hate how his predatory movements create a different, but equally unwelcome, tingle low in my belly.

"I didn't realize you cared about my ass."

"What! I don't! I was just saying—" My cheeks flame and my emotions can't decide whether to settle on embarrassed or angry or... something else I've been avoiding when it comes to Asher.

He chuckles and talks over me before I can dig myself an even bigger hole. "I'm kidding. What do you want to watch?"

Flicking on the TV, he scrolls through the guide, stopping when he gets to a FRIENDS rerun and quirking an eyebrow at me.

"Uh. YES." I snatch the remote and hit enter. My love of this show borders on obsession.

I STARTLE AWAKE when Asher shifts on the bed next to me. I hadn't meant to fall asleep, but FRIENDS is my comfort show, so I should have realized it was likely to happen. Especially after that muscle relaxation exercise we did earlier.

"Sorry sunshine," Asher whispers. "I was just going to get ready for bed."

"You're good," I whisper back. "I don't want to sleep in these clothes anyway."

We end up brushing our teeth side by side, and I try to ignore the buzzing sensation of bees on my skin every time I feel his eyes on me. I close up my toiletry bag, avoiding eye contact as I squeeze past him out of the bathroom. Somehow, I'm wide awake and full of tension again.

Sighing, I scoot under the covers after dropping some CBD oil under my tongue and forcing my eyes closed. Unfortunately, they don't stay that way for long, that restless buzzing is incessant and my body doesn't listen to my mind when I tell my eyeballs *not to look*.

As soon as Asher steps back into the room, my eyes squint open to take in the low slung shorts and broad, shirtless chest I've been trying not to stare at every night this week. It's a lost cause, but I don't have long to berate myself before he sinks to the floor, out of sight.

In an effort to distract myself, I send Zuri a text.

> Me: You up?

> Zuri: It's a bit far for a bootie call

> Me: Hilarious 🙄

> Zuri: What's up?

> Me: Nothing, just can't sleep

> Zuri: You're on your own then, I'm busy 💀

Thinking about sex is exactly what I was trying to avoid, and here Zuri goes throwing it straight back into my brain. She's obviously not a good distraction. I drop my phone next to me and stare at the dark ceiling.

Being kept up by thoughts of an annoying man when all you want to do is snuggle into a cozy, deep sleep is the absolute worst.

14

PILLOW WALL, SHMILLOW WALL
ASHER

I CAN'T STOP TOSSING and turning, unable to get comfortable on the floor despite how many blankets I have piled under me. I also can't help being hyperaware of every little sound Raya makes. The memory of her pulse thrumming beneath her skin when I trapped her in the pool the other night is on repeat in my brain, torturing my vampiric senses. She takes deep, slow breaths, like she's willing her body to succumb to sleep, although I can tell it's not working.

When I roll over again, she huffs, and my eyes fly open.

"Ugh. Just get up here," Raya's voice carries an edge of exasperation, the whisper-yell sounding like a canon in the otherwise quiet room. The silence reverberates around us and ricochets through my head as I try to comprehend what she's implying.

"Can you elaborate?"

"I'm sick of feeling guilty for having the bed and you're clearly not comfortable and we both need to be our best which means getting a good night's sleep at least once this week so just... sleep up here." She word vomits, then grabs a pillow and shoves it over her face before quickly emerging again to set some ground rules. "No touching, we'll build a pillow wall and stay on our own sides, but I don't want your floor blankets in the bed."

I let out a soft chuckle into the safety of the darkened room, but her point is valid. I wouldn't want 'floor blankets' in the bed either.

I raise my head to look at her, but can barely make out her features in the darkened room.

"You sure?" I ask, but she's already re-arranging the pillows in a line down the middle of the mattress. I think she attempts to glare at me before pulling back the blankets on what will be my side of the bed and then flopping dramatically back down, facing away from the pillow wall and curling up with another huff.

I tuck myself in as quickly and quietly as I can, then proceed to not fall asleep for hours as I strain my self control, refusing to even glance in her direction. It's much harder said than done, but I manage for the most part. Unfortunately, I can't turn my ears or nose off, so I'm forced listen to her resting peacefully next to me as her sweet scent surrounds us until I finally drift off, wondering if I'll see her in my dreams again.

RAYA IS on my side of the bed, wrapped around me like a koala with her legs entwined with mine, an arm flung over my chest, and her face nuzzled right into my neck. I both love and hate this moment. I've been dreaming of her body flush against mine ever since The Hug. The Hug, when she smashed through all the walls and boundaries I've spent my entire life building around my body, mind, and heart, taking everything I have and claiming it as her own. The Hug that taught me how to hug. The Hug that made me feel things I've never truly felt before, things I used to dream of feeling, but gave up on long ago. The Hug that felt like it twined our souls together.

I squeeze my eyes shut, and it's then that I realize this isn't like those other dreams. This moment has that ethereal quality in between dreaming and waking where you still have one foot in each realm.

I tip one eye open the smallest sliver so I can peek down at her. Raya has somehow completely obliterated the pillow wall. It's nowhere to be found, and my brain is clearly not functioning yet because the only thought I have is *how can someone with such terrible morning breath possibly be so beautiful?*

The obvious answer is that it's impossible. I'm still in that dream world imagining her warmth against me, with all her soft curves perfectly fitting into my hard planes. Her plush lips barely brushing against my neck every few seconds. Her honey-blonde hair boldly fanned across my shoulder and pillow as though it has every right to be there. The toned muscle of her leg snug against mine with the sheets tangled around them, tying us together.

Maybe if I close my eyes I'll go back to sleep fully, and then when I wake up things will be back to normal, pillow wall and all.

I close both eyes again, focusing on falling asleep, breathing deep and slow.

It doesn't work.

I can't focus on anything other than *her*.

Her sweet, strawberry coconut scent. Her petal-soft skin.

Her beautiful brown eyes, hazy with sleep, blinking up at me.

Wait.

I startle, a small jump in my muscles that causes her eyes to fly open. Raya practically leaps away from me, though the tangled sheets make it impossible, so she ends up flopping around like a fish out of water.

I try to hold in my mirth. I really do, but it's such an unbelievable situation, and the uncoordinated, flailing limbs next to me are a sight to behold.

The laugh bubbles up from deep in my chest, a full, joyous feeling overcoming me as it releases into the world.

Raya freezes, wavy hair falling into her face, a cluster of limbs and sheets, and stares at me with her jaw hanging open. It's such a comical scene that it only encourages my laughter. A fleeting worry that she'll be offended by my outburst passes through my mind, but before I can even acknowledge it, she's cracking up right along with me.

Her eyes crinkle at the corners and a belly laugh like I've never heard bursts out of her. She howls with laughter, then wraps her arms around her stomach as she leans forward. My sides are starting to hurt with the force of my own laughter.

"What is happening?! " she manages to croak out, and we both wipe tears from our eyes.

"I think we're laughing, sunshine," I reply.

I've never laughed until I cried before, and I'm not sure whether I like it, what with the stomach cramp and aching cheeks and all. It feels too open, too vulnerable, like I'm exposing my soft heart to a potentially deadly flame, unsure how close I can get before it starts to burn. The light reverberating out of her is worth it though.

I haven't had much joy or happiness in my life, but it's one of those things you don't realize you're missing until it shows up. Now, I look back and see my life in shades of grey. Loneliness, depression, rejection... I grew up never being enough for my parents. Not ruthless enough, not hungry enough, not smart enough or big enough or ambitious enough, and all of it is still true. I've never fit into their world, and even when I accepted that and did my best to cut ties, *my* world stayed relatively grey.

A lighter shade maybe, but still grey.

Until Raya. She struck me like a laser beam of undiluted euphoria. At first, she scalded me with her brightness; I'm not used to color or light in my world, so being in close proximity to it—to her—was blinding.

Now, I can't look away. I've become addicted to everything about her, from her strange little shifts, to her kindness and warmth, to her competency and resilience. She never gives up, never quits, and never seems to lose that inner spark.

She's radiant in her joy, and I want to soak in every single drop.

THERE'S a strange sense of hesitant camaraderie between us now. We go about our normal morning routines, but the quiet isn't uptight. It's more... a comfortable tension. A soft, shimmering thread pulled taut between us.

I'm not sure what to make of it. Raya no longer appears to despise me, if our morning koala situation and ensuing laughing fit is anything to go by, and she's gifted me a couple easy smiles since then too.

I have a working theory that her smaller smiles are more genuine, compared to the beaming, blinding things she tends to throw out to strangers and coworkers. I've seen the quieter ones when she's talking on the phone, I assume with either family or friends, and they're stunning.

I want them for myself.

Just like I want everything else about her.

We complete an informal breathing and grounding session together after eating and brushing our teeth, then the two of us head down the elevator and across the street. As my job is mainly behind the scenes, it's likely to be another boring day for me. I'm looking forward to the meetings with Raya though, if only so I have a reason to stay present and engaged.

Can't be caught daydreaming like a fool if I want a chance with her.

... since when do I want a chance with her?

Telling my fangs to simmer down, I figure I must be low on blood intake. I refocus on the morning of endless meetings, wondering why it feels like ten years have gone by, yet every time I check my watch it's only been a few minutes.

Finally, the last meeting before the lunch break starts, which is also the first meeting we're both attending today. I arrive first, and I nudge the chair next to me with my knee, pulling it out for Raya as soon as I see her walk in. My insides glow when she smiles her thanks, the grin turning softer as she sits down next to me and crosses one graceful leg over the other.

I try my best not to leer, but it's impossible not to notice her. She's wearing another of those fitted, textured skirts she seems to like that barely reach her lower thighs. This one is navy blue with brass buttons running from the outside of her left thigh up to her inner left hip. Her usual flowy top is tucked in, and the low neckline has ruffles that tie into a bow right between her breasts. It's somehow professional while also being sexy and cute at the same time.

Now that I'm in her presence again, my mind keeps replaying the feel of her wrapped around me this morning. An increasingly hard situation to deal with.

Raya keeps glancing at me from the corner of her eye, and I wonder if she knows how wound up I am over her. Never have I been the kind of person who can't sit still, but apparently she brings out the most juvenile responses in me, barely controlled fangs at the top of that ever-expanding list.

Eager to take her to lunch (hopefully she agrees), I don't even realize I'm drumming my fingers on the table until she taps my knuckles with her pen. I immediately flatten my hand before balling it into a fist and hiding both hands in my lap.

Raya's lips tip up the slightest bit at my reaction, and I immediately feel antsy again.

This is ridiculous; how can one person affect me in such a way? I'm not acting remotely like myself anymore.

I practically jump out of my own skin at the feel of her hand on my thigh a few minutes later, stalling the bouncing I must have been doing.

"Stop it, you're shaking the whole table," she whispers out the side of her mouth, completely oblivious to the effect she's having on me as she pulls her hand away, leaving sparks of heat in its wake.

I scrub a hand over my face and adjust in my seat. Checking my watch again, I thank whatever deity might be listening that this meeting is nearly over.

"Lunch?" I ask as soon as everyone starts moving and packing up. My voice comes out more gruff than I intended, and I wince at the look on her face.

But then Raya tilts her head; the feline motion is smooth and graceful, something I've noticed she does frequently. She blinks, deliberately, I think.

I clear my throat and try again.

"Sorry, I meant, would you like to go grab some food?"

"I certainly planned too." Her lips are pursed, her best attempt to hide a mischievous grin if the twinkle in her eye is any indication, and it loosens something in my chest.

I roll my eyes as she stands.

"I meant with me."

"Ah, why didn't you say so?" Raya is already flouncing her way toward the door before she finishes speaking, and she spins around, walking backward for a couple steps as she scrunches her nose at me playfully. I don't miss the glimmer of amusement in her gaze as she turns forward again with a cheerful, "Let's go then!"

My lonely heart shudders to life in my chest.

Raya chatters as we walk toward Little Italy. She also chatters throughout lunch.

I can only try to keep up. This is a new side of her; I've seen her act this way with others, but she's always been reserved and cautious around me. If anyone else talked to me this much, I'd be out the door in two minutes flat, but Raya's voice is like music to my ears. She soothes me in a way I didn't know I needed, and I want to hear every word she has to say. It seems like she's finally letting down her walls, and I'm terrified of messing up.

If this is my chance, I don't want to lose it, so I do what I can to match her, letting my walls down a bit too.

I hold doors open and flag down a waiter when her water needs refilled. I lightly tug her arm so she doesn't step in a suspicious looking substance on the sidewalk. I offer comments here and there, ask questions and hoard every small piece of her she shares with me, all while doing my best not to sigh in contentment at the warmth I feel being near her.

I can't tell if she's exceptionally good at ignoring it, or if she's oblivious to my infatuation—because yes, I've decided to face the music and accept the truth. I'm mildly obsessed with her, and I'm already planning some new stretches I can teach her tonight to go with the breathing we've been doing. I should probably be worried at the lengths I'd go to in order to get my hands on her, to feel her skin against mine again, and to bask in her sweet scent.

15

DEFINITELY DO RILE THE VAMPIRE

RAYA

WITH THE FULL MOON OVERHEAD, I expected to be shifting on and off at least every hour, and although I've felt the tingles that often or more, it's only resulted in a partial shift a few times today.

So, pretty much like any other day, but at least it isn't worse.

As I'm packing up from the last breakout group of the day, I realize I'm excited to see Asher. Not only that, but I think we've been flirting. I'm avoiding inspecting it too closely, afraid of what it might mean for my mental health that I'm having feelings—giddy, bubbly feelings—for a semi-evil vampire.

I consider calling Zuri about it, but discard that idea as quickly as it comes. The guilt is heavy on my shoulders for keeping this secret from her, but I know how Zuri feels about him, and there's no way she would understand. If I do talk to anyone about it, whatever "it" might be, I would need someone much less biased. Since I don't have anyone like that in my life, it's basically me going in blind and hoping for the best.

Always a good strategy.

Sighing, I loop my work bag over my shoulder and meander down the hallway to the exit. Maybe I'll find him at the bar, or he might already be back up in the hotel room.

"Oof." I run straight into a brick wall as I round a corner. My nose bounces off said wall, which smells suspiciously delicious, and I pinwheel my arms as my balance is thrown backwards.

An arm encircles my waist, and my balance alters again. This time, when my nose catches that cedar-smoke scent, I recognize that it is not a wall, and is in fact a muscled chest. A very solid, very broad, very defined *vampire* chest.

"Why are you made of rock?" I groan, voice muffled and nasally due to my hand covering my smarting nose.

"I'm... sorry?" Asher's baritone voice is hesitant but amused, and I narrow my eyes when I look up at him.

"You should be. I'm surprised my nose isn't broken."

I'm only half joking, and his lips twitch up in response as we turn and head to the exit together.

"That sounds terrible. How can I make it up to you?"

"Tacos," I say, no hesitation.

"Haven't you had tacos, like, every day of this trip so far?"

I stop walking and simply blink at him, eyebrows raised.

"Right. Tacos it is," he says, and I grin at the 'why did I even ask' look on his face.

His eyes immediately latch onto my mouth, and my smile turns a little crooked with mischief. I open the door and turn back to him.

"Soooo, now? Or..."

"Seriously?"

When I don't relent, he rolls his eyes. "Fine, let's just drop our bags off first."

I give him my most disapproving look, then twirl on my

toes, striding off down the sidewalk in the opposite direction of the hotel.

"It'll only take two minutes—" he starts to say, then exclaims in my wake. "For real? You ran into me on purpose, didn't you? It was all a set up. I'm being played and I fell right into it."

I bite my lip to hold in a laugh. I didn't, but the nose ache is worth it. I'm going to remember how fun it is to rile him up.

Asher grumbles under his breath as I devour a Chile Relleño burrito, and I quirk a brow at him when he re-adjusts in his seat for the millionth time.

"What's your deal today?" I ask, and you might think he was the shifter if you didn't know better. His impression of a deer in headlights is spot on.

I swallow and lick my lips; his eyes drop to my mouth again, then skim my neck, then lower before quickly averting to the metal high-top table between us.

He clears his throat before a mumbled "M'fine" is aimed at the floor.

Very convincing.

I crumple up the aluminum wrapper and hop up off the tall stool.

"Ready to head back?" I ask.

He pins me with a glare as he pointedly grabs his cross-body leather bag from the table, and I pinch my lips between my teeth.

This is so fun.

I'm pretty sure he's not actually mad. His lips keep inching up at the corners and I'm determined to get him to break at some point. I will get another laugh out of him if it's the last thing I do.

WE'RE both relaxing back at the hotel when I send a text to the family chat, checking in and letting them know I'm doing alright with the full moon. I don't get a reply, but I didn't expect one.

I check in with Zuri too, asking if her and Reverie want to FaceTime, but apparently Rev is out of commission—crashed on the couch after a sugar high with evidence sent in the form of a very unflattering picture, and Zuri is about to get in the shower after a run.

Asher is on his laptop at the desk and I can see the screen from where I'm propped on our practice-area floor pillows. A low note of disapproval rumbles from his throat, and I catch sight of a new email at the top of his inbox.

> From: Claude Walton
>> Subject: Urgent
>> Son, this has gone on long enough. We have important news...

Asher deletes it without opening the message, then snaps his laptop closed. My brows furrow, but his family is a sensitive subject and we aren't that close yet, so I don't pry.

"How did today go?" Asher's voice breaks into my doomscrolling a short while later, and I struggle to pull myself out of the social media zombie brain I've fallen into.

"Fine?"

"I mean with the shifting and the full moon and all that."

"Oh, right. Yeah, pretty normal actually." I shrug.

"Cool."

"How'd your day go?"

"Great, zero unexpected animal parts popping up on my body," he replies.

"Hilarious," I deadpan as I pin him with a mock glare.

He smirks in response and leans back in the desk chair as he watches me.

The silence between us is palpable, and after a few moments I look intently at his shoulder, just below his left ear. I squint my eyes as I lean forward, then I widen them dramatically.

"What? What is it!" He's twisting and turning, trying to see whatever it is I see, and I burst out laughing.

Asher freezes with one hand fisted in his shirt, stretching the collar and sleeve as he looks over at me. He drops his hand with a glare and then slowly stands. It's like a switch flips and the predator has suddenly awoken.

My senses spark with the danger.

He takes a single, deliberate step toward me, and I shriek as I jump to my feet and dive across the room. I'm aiming for the bed, but don't get there before he intercepts me. He snags my waist and yanks me back into his hard chest.

I wasn't sure what I was expecting with this little game, but tickling was not it. His fingers somehow find every ticklish spot I wish didn't exist. I'm laughing and kicking out at him, but I can't find purchase and somehow he evades every swipe. Distantly, my skin tingles, but I can't process in the moment what shift is happening or where.

"You dare play tricks on me, little shifter?" He growls at me, and his fingers dance along my ribs.

"Never!" I twist in his hold as I shriek another laugh, but it cuts off when a thudding sound booms from the wall next to us.

We both freeze for a split second before I turn in his grasp and split into giggles, hiding in his arms and pressing my face into his shirt with both hands covering my mouth.

"Oh my stars, the neighbors! What do you think they thought was happening?"

He doesn't answer me though, and I peer up at him as my

hands drop from my mouth. I vaguely notice cheetah spots fading back into my skin, but my attention isn't on myself. Asher looks thunderstruck, frozen, and his hands around my waist clench tight.

"Oh, no, it's okay. I'm sure it's fine, it's not like they're going to kick us out for one noise complaint." I try to soothe him, gently placing a hand on his chest, but nothing I say changes his demeanor.

"Asher?"

I wait a moment, my head angling to the side, and when his gaze doesn't follow me, I reach up and boop his nose.

His head jerks back, and he snaps back into the present moment.

"What was that?" he asks, his voice gravelly.

"*Me* what was that? More like *you*, what was that!" This is ridiculous. I'm starting to think he might want to get his head checked. I mean yeah, everyone zones out sometimes, but he seems to be doing it a lot this week.

He shakes his head in consternation.

"You good?" I ask, more seriously this time, and he nods as our gazes lock.

"Yeah, I'm good." His eyes soften as he looks down at me. "Should we try some stretching while we're here?" He gestures to the blanket under our feet, and I shrug.

"Sure, might as well. You think stretching will help too?"

"I do," he says, and that's that.

We start with tandem breathing, and I revel in the opportunity to ogle him. Obviously, I need to stare at his chest in order to follow his breathing, and if his t-shirt is a little stretched, who am I to complain when it clings to his muscles like that?

He has to clear his throat multiple times to remind me to do the stretch with him when I stare at his lean muscles for too long without mimicking the movements. I'm beyond feeling abashed for it at this point, so I smirk or shrug before leaning into the stretch.

After he demonstrates a few basic ones, he stands and moves around behind me.

"Keep going," he says, "I'll help deepen them a bit."

I'm surrounded by him as I pull in a deep breath, and when I exhale, his hands urge me a little further into it. We do this in a few different poses, with him adjusting his position around me, and my skin has been tingling for far too many uncomfortable minutes at this point.

"Have I shifted?" I finally ask, blinking up at him from where I'm stretched out on my back and straightening my legs as he pulls away.

His eyes flick along my body. "Not that I can see."

"Huh. It's felt like I was going to for a while now."

His eyebrows jump up.

"Maybe you should try to shift on purpose. If it's already close to the surface, this could be a good chance to gain some more control."

I'm kind of annoyed I hadn't thought of that myself, but to be fair, he's quite distracting. Especially braced above me with his hands on my skin, pushing my bent leg into my chest. Anyone would be distracted in that kind of situation.

I sit up and curl my feet beneath me. My eyes close as I take a deep inhale, noting how our combined scents fill the room. I look inward, hunting for that inner animal, the ball of essence my family have all referenced in the past. I think I feel it, but it's different for me. It's all encompassing; rather than sitting low in my chest, it fills me entirely from my toes to the tips of my ears. I focus on the tingles right below my skin, pulling on that essence as I do so.

"Raya," Asher whispers, his voice soft, almost reverent.

My eyes pop open and he takes my hands, guiding them up to fuzzy ears.

"Black cat," he says, and pride blooms in my chest.

"I did it," I whisper back to him, and he nods.

Beneath my fingers, I feel my ears shift again. This time, they double in size, with the fur turning thicker. My eyes widen in alarm, as this is not something I've noticed happen before.

Asher tilts his head as he eyes my changing ears.

"Wolf." He smiles at me, his eyes lit up in a way I've never seen from him. "You did it."

"That second one wasn't on purpose, so really I did it only once, and for barely a few seconds." My shoulders slump, and my ears drop back into my head, becoming human once more.

"Once is infinitely more than you've done previously. Once is a foundation. Once is amazing," he says, and my eyes dart up to his, a small smile already forming on my lips.

Who could have guessed a questionable vampire would be the one to help me learn how to shift?

16

A FULL MOON RUINS EVERYTHING… OR DOES IT?

RAYA

I GATHER up the pillows strewn across the bed and begin lining them up.

"You might as well not even try," Asher interjects. "It's not like they stopped you last time."

I don't have the courage to meet his eyes as a mortification ices down my spine. Instead, of course, a tingling shift flits over my body, but it's not a partial shift this time. The air crackles around me and before I know what's happening, I'm enveloped in clothes, and I'm *tiny*.

With a terrified squeak, I start thrashing around, trying to find a way out of the suffocating pile of fabric when a massive hand pulls me out. I'm sitting flat in the palm of none other than the devilish vampire.

My heart rate skyrockets and my entire mouse body trembles. My equilibrium is thrown off when the hand moves, and I scramble on my newly formed miniature paws to keep myself upright.

Asher arranges the shirt I had been wearing into a round nest, then carefully settles my mouse body into the middle of it. He slides off the bed onto the floor, where he looks much less like a real life giant and more like just a very large head.

I burrow into the shirt, inhaling the sense of safety that comes with it, which is quickly followed by horror.

I am a mouse.

Not only a mouse nose, or whiskers, or fur, but an entire freaking full-bodied *mouse* and this is quite possibly the worst thing that has ever happened to me. I wasn't sure if I would ever fully shift into an animal, and if I did, I didn't know what it would be like. I can't say I like it. Maybe if I go outside, a hawk will swoop down and save me from this misery. Before I can further contemplate the merits of this plan, a shushing sound comes from the large head a few feet away from me.

"Shhhh, Raya, it's okay. You're safe," he whispers. "Raya, sunshine, I'm sorry."

My ears perk up at that. *Sorry?*

"You're okay. I won't hurt you." He speaks quiet and slow. It's the same way I'd talk to a terrified child. "You can have the bed, I'll sleep on the floor."

Well that's not what I want.

With another wave of tingles, my body rapidly expands and reforms itself. I get a glimpse of Asher's eyes widening before he whirls around.

I don't blame him. I've seen my parents shift, and it isn't pretty. At best, it looks weird, with the bulging muscles and reforming limbs, skin and fur trading places. Kinda gross, honestly.

Still, his rejection stings a bit.

I scramble into my clothes, then let loose a full body shudder.

"Are you decent?" Asher's muffled voice comes from the other side of the bed.

"Yeah," I sigh, resigned to my fate. "I'm dressed."

I flop down on the bed, burying my face in a pillow and

deciding to never be around another living creature during the full moon ever again.

The bed dips as he tentatively perches on the opposite edge, safely across the pathetic pillow wall.

"I..." he swallows hard, then clears his throat. Apparently he's too appalled to speak. Again, I don't blame him, but the sting is getting sharper.

He sighs and scrubs a hand over his face.

"Shit, Raya, I'm so, so sorry." He sounds devastated, and when my head pops up to try to figure out what the heck is going on now, his eyes look devastated too.

"What?" My voice is a little high pitched and squeaky, but I push the humiliation back.

"I didn't mean to embarrass you. I'm really sorry, I was teasing, but I shouldn't have."

How did he know he embarrassed me? I do my best to wave it off.

"Nah, you're fine, it's the full moon. It's making everything a hundred times harder than it needs to be this week."

"Even so, I apologize." He sounds so earnest as his eyes blink sincerity at me.

"Thanks." My voice is soft, and I offer a tentative smile.

"Maybe you didn't notice earlier, what with the whole shifting thing, but I wasn't complaining," he says.

"What does that mean?"

"It means I liked it, sunshine," he says, and my eyes widen as the meaning of his words sinks in. "I liked having you pressed up against me this morning. I like the feel of you in my arms."

My eyes flare. That is not the direction I saw this going. I rest a palm on my forehead, staring straight up at the ceiling. When he doesn't move, I shift my eyes to where he's still barely sitting on the bed.

"You can sleep here. I won't freak out again."

"I don't want to make you uncomfortable," he says, then adds, "or hurt you if you shift again while sleeping."

I ignore his concerns, pursing my lips and patting the bed next to me. Asher sighs, and I can't tell what the meaning of it is, but he pulls back the covers and slides in next to me regardless.

Feeling the sheets move against my skin and knowing it's due to his proximity is enough to light up my nerves. I try to relax, but my entire body is tense as I pinch my eyes shut. It's like his presence next to me has the weight of a bomb; I'm waiting for it to go off at any second, and I don't know if I'll survive the fallout.

After an eternity of sharp silence in which I barely dare to breathe, Asher grumbles something under his breath, then rolls onto his side. His arm snakes around my waist and pulls my body into his, my back to his front, no consideration at all for the meager pillow wall I attempted to put between us.

Somehow, I stiffen even more, confusion swirling through me when he nuzzles his nose into my hair. I don't protest though; I can't deny this is what I've been wanting. His body relaxes against me with a contented sigh, and I focus on matching my breaths to his—instead of on the panic threatening the edges of my mind.

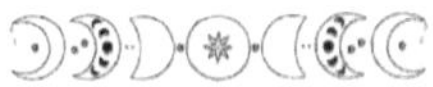

THE FIRST THING I notice when I wake up is the hard rod pressing into my backside. My whole body flushes and I involuntarily arch into him. My heart rate picks up and starts to pound, throbbing through me. Asher must sense it because as soon as it spikes, he begins to stir. He runs his nose up along my neck, stopping right above my racing pulse, his breath ghosting over my skin.

"Don't tempt me like that first thing in the morning, little shifter." Asher's voice is rough with sleep, deeper and more gravelly than normal.

"What? I'm not doing anything," I whisper, not trusting that my voice won't come out breathless with want.

"Your heart is racing. It's calling to me." He drags his teeth along the tender skin where my neck meets my shoulder, sending a shiver down my spine. "Tempting me."

His last words rumble through me as his lips move against my neck.

I try to tell myself that my pounding heart and goosebumps are a result of fear of this terrifying vampire who has me at his mercy, but my sleep addled brain doesn't agree, and I speak before I can think better of it.

"What does it feel like?" I whisper again.

"What?" he whispers back this time, and I bite my lip. His mouth is still millimeters from my neck.

"If you... you know..." I angle my neck the tiniest bit, but it's enough for him to catch the movement, and his chest rises against my back with a sharp inhale.

"If I bit you?" He pretends to bite me, lightly pinching the skin at the base of my neck between his teeth, causing me to suck in a quick breath and freeze.

My emotions are all over the place now; there's definitely some fear mixed in at this point as my shifter instincts respond to the threat of a vampire at my neck, but there's also undeniable lust threading through me as my insides turn molten with the feel of his body pressed against mine.

I offer a hesitant nod in response, and his lips ghost over the indents his teeth leave in my skin as he releases me.

"It feels however I want it to feel. It can hurt." At this he lightly drags his teeth from my outer shoulder to the base of my neck.

"It can be numbing." This time his elongating fangs scrape up my neck and behind my ear.

"It can bring pleasure..." His words flutter over my skin and his fangs graze the shell of my ear before he sucks my earlobe into his mouth.

It's at this moment that I realize the full effect he has on me. My thighs are clenched together with my ass pushing back into him, and I'm straight up panting. Like a dog in heat.

Or a turned on shifter during the full moon.

I gulp in air and swallow some of it on accident while trying to wrestle control of my senses back from him, causing me to choke as my earlobe pops out of his mouth.

His lips curve against my ear into what I'm sure must be the smuggest smirk to ever grace this plane of existence. I choose not to give him the satisfaction of confirming it by looking.

It takes me a few seconds to compose myself before speaking again, and I ignore the breathiness of my voice when I finally respond.

"I didn't know any of that was possible."

"It's all about intention." His nose is in my hair again, his fingers tracing patterns over my lower stomach. "I told you all you have to do is ask, and I'll happily make you feel the best you've ever felt."

I don't respond—don't know how to respond—but I don't pull away either, and he takes that for the yes that I mean it to be. Asher kisses lightly along my ear and neck, and as he nips at the sensitive skin, he tightens his hold around my waist.

I'm forced to let out the involuntary whimper that's been hiding behind my lips this whole time, and he loosens his hold when he hears it.

Pulling back from me, Asher raises himself on one elbow, angling his body over mine as he admires me quivering beneath him.

"Later, little shifter," he says, lightly tracing the line of my neck with one finger and following the path with his eyes.

When my throat bobs under his touch, his gaze flicks back up to mine. "Now, we practice."

"Wait, what?" I scramble up, my body chasing after his without my permission, but he's already across the room and closing the bathroom door behind him.

Stupid, horrible, evil vampire.

I slap a hand to my forehead, then swipe it down my face.

"What just happened?" I whisper, voice muffled by the hand covering my mouth in what I'm absolutely, positively sure must be one hundred percent horror, with no hints of desire to be found. Besides, if there were any, they'd obviously be due to the full moon and not the sinful vampire I've been sharing a room and bed with.

THE SHIFTING practice that morning doesn't go as well as the day before. I'm not able to shift on purpose, but I do feel more centered and stable, and I focus on my inner animal presence again. It's getting easier to differentiate it from myself.

I attribute the mediocre progress to my emotions going haywire from Asher's bedroom antics this morning. Despite sharing a bed with him, I've been getting better sleep than I have since this random shifting started over a year ago. It makes no sense, as I should be more anxious and uncomfortable in such close proximity to him, but I'm responding opposite to that. Not to mention, it's becoming incredibly difficult to focus when he's anywhere near me.

I still can't wrap my head around it; it feels like we've been dancing around each other forever, even though we've only known each other for a matter of weeks.

It could be that weird phenomenon that happens when you're in a new place so everything feels different but normal at the same time. That's how I've been feeling, and it makes me dread returning to Portland. I'll have to come clean to Zuri about Asher, which is sure to be a disaster. There's no way I can tell her everything though; what would Zuri think about me wanting to be bitten? I shudder.

Insane. That's what she'd think.

There's no way I can deal with that right now. I'll be as honest as I can, without revealing too much about how close we've gotten.

On top of that, I'm not sure how to handle our work relationship back in the office. Are we allowed to date? I need to look into the corporate policy on office relationships. Not to mention that I suspect I've been wrong about him. He doesn't seem like the horrible person I've been led to believe he is, although I remind myself that I don't know him well yet and it could be an act.

I file these thoughts away for later and focus on my phone, scrolling through my itinerary. It's our last day of meetings before we fly out tomorrow, and it's looking pretty boring. On the bright side, we're being treated to a nice dinner tonight, so I have that to look forward to.

17

———

DESPERATION

ASHER

HER ENTIRE BEING lights up when she sees me in the lobby that evening and it's a punch of the brightest sunshine straight to my withered heart. It knocks the breath out of me, and I have to take a second to compose myself before I melt into the floor and start panting after her like a lovesick puppy. It's ridiculous how quickly this woman has wrapped me around her finger, though luckily she seems to have no idea.

I inwardly chastise my aching gums—now is not the time for fangs—as she walks over, and I take a deep breath to calm the urges hounding me.

Mistake.

All it does is pull her coconut scent in so it's in my nose and on my tongue and all I want is to let my fangs drop and ravish her. I give her a closed-lip smile instead, and she tilts her head in response.

"Why are you being weird?" she asks, amusement clear in her sparkling eyes.

"Shouldn't you go get ready?" I change the subject, not willing to get into the many things about her that make me feel slightly unhinged while we're standing in a hotel lobby.

She rolls her eyes. "Okay then. Are you waiting down here?"

"We can meet at the bar if you want. Then walk over together," I suggest, and she nods.

Turning away, she tosses a quick "Give me thirty," over her shoulder as she strides to the elevator.

I sidle up to the bar, ordering my usual, which the bartender already knows as I've been here every day since we arrived. I'm not normally a big drinker—well, not alcohol anyway—but it's been nearly impossible to be in our hotel room without my fangs dropping. Raya's scent is everywhere, coconut with a hint of strawberry, and it becomes more enticing by the hour. So, instead of torturing myself in her space, I'm torturing myself by not being in her space instead.

Honestly, I'm not sure which is worse.

When she steps out of the elevator a half hour later, my eyes pop and I nearly drop the glass tumbler, managing to clatter it against the bar at the last second instead. I feel like a cartoon character, and I don't blame myself one bit because she is *breathtaking*.

Her cocktail dress is a sparkling emerald green, the jewel tone bringing out the rich chocolate brown of her eyes, which are further accentuated with long, dark lashes. I could easily get snared by those doe eyes, and I blink to escape their trap. Her hair is up, and my fangs ache to meet her exposed neck.

I gulp, nearly swallowing my own tongue when I force my gaze away from her neck and I catch her legs next, because they're perfection. Toned muscle and creamy skin; I immediately want them wrapped around my head with those heels stabbing into my shoulder blades.

I mutter to the bartender to close my tab for the night, and receive a confirming chuckle that the bill will go to the room. The guy could charge me triple and I'd have no idea, nor would I care.

Raya strides over, and I bask in the confidence radiating from her.

"Sunshine... you're stunning," I say, reaching out to lightly glide a hand down her arm, then mentally kicking myself because she deserves so much better than that. She's impossible to resist, and it scrambles my brain.

Raya's nose scrunches up and I hold back a cringe for whatever idiotic thing I did to cause that reaction.

"Why do you always call me that?" she asks.

"Sunshine?"

Raya nods, her eyes narrowed, and I step back, taking in her newly stiffened posture and the wariness in her gaze.

"Because you brighten the world around you." My voice softens, and I step back into her when her posture loosens slightly in response. "You're like the sun; as soon as you enter a room, it brightens. When you speak, people listen, and you offer genuine warmth and kindness to literally everyone. Your smiles radiate joy. You breathe life into everyone around you, including me." I consider stopping there, but I'm already in too deep, so why stop now? I lightly trace the shell of her ear with a finger.

"My life was grey until you burst into it, bringing color wherever you go. You've brought light to my darkness, and I've come to crave it. Crave you, little shifter, my ray of sunshine." The last few words come out a low murmur, so quiet I'm not certain she even heard them.

Raya's eyes are huge, and I suddenly worry that I've said too much. Her gaze flits back and forth between my eyes, and I feel like she's searching for more than I know how to give. I want to tell her there's nothing else to find, I've laid myself bare before her, but I don't. I stand perfectly still, keeping my barriers down and letting her search for what she needs.

When she seems to find it, her eyes drop to my mouth for a millisecond, so quick I may have imagined it if not for the way her pulse jumps at the same time, before she meets my gaze again.

"That's…" Raya stops, clears her throat. I have to tear my eyes away from it when she swallows; I haven't been this tempted in well over a decade.

"That's the nicest thing anyone has ever said to me." She reaches up and cups one palm on my jaw. "Thank you, Ash."

"Ash?"

"Ash," she shrugs, "feels like it suits you for some reason."

It does feel like it suits me, but only from her. If she's a ray of sunshine, she's effectively burning my demons into ash with only her presence. I'll take all of it—all of her—that I can get.

I offer an elbow for her to take, if she wants.

"Shall we?" I ask.

Her smile is a soft one, nearly heartrending in its tenderness. It fills my chest until I'm worried it'll burst.

"We shall," she says, and tucks herself right in against my side, both hands wrapped around my biceps as we walk back out to the lobby.

Her heels click a staccato beat against the floor, and I can't help glancing down at them. I force my thoughts away from the pictures forming in my head; pictures of her without the dress, pictures of the dress pooled on the floor around her shoes, pictures of my hands gripping those incredible thighs, and what her face might look like when she comes. I've actively avoided getting involved with a coworkers in the past, but here I am, falling head over heels for this ridiculous shifter.

I suck on my teeth as we walk across the street to the seafood restaurant, tonguing my fangs in an attempt to lessen the ache, but it does no good. As I knew it wouldn't.

It's her. She's under my skin and irritatingly stuck there.

When we follow the hostess into the reserved section in the back, heads turn toward us and I do my best not to glare at the eyes running up and down Raya's body. If I had hackles, they'd be up in arms, and as it is I have to pinch my mouth shut to stop the growl threatening to emerge.

She isn't mine, and I have no right to be so territorial or possessive. That thought is unbearable, and everything in me rebels at the idea of not having her. I want her to be mine, and I want to be hers. The idea that we aren't anything close to that starts an irritating headache behind my eyes. I dig my fingers into my temple, only now realizing what trouble I'm in.

"Are you okay?" Raya asks, her voice quiet as she squeezes my arm.

I look down at her, and although she's still smiling, there's concern in her gaze.

"I'm fine," I say, doing my best to look reassuring. Based on her pinched eyebrows, I'm not doing a good job.

I pull her chair out for her to sit, doing my best to prevent my gaze from lingering on Raya's legs as she gracefully lowers herself and smoothes her short dress over her thighs. It feels like tearing my own eyeballs out, but I manage it somehow. I take the seat next to hers, accidentally-on-purpose brushing my knuckles down her thigh when I drape my napkin over my lap, satisfaction floating through me when goosebumps break out across her skin.

We sip on our drinks, making small talk with the others seated at our table as we wait for the meals to be served. I don't participate much, which isn't out of character for me, but I am much more invested and attentive than usual. Of course, my attention is solely focused on the enchanting creature next to me.

Raya is animated, polite and friendly to everyone, and fully engaged in each conversation she's drawn into—which is basically every single one. I meant what I said earlier; she radiates light and it draws people to her. Everyone wants to speak with her, make her smile, hear her laugh, be graced with her attention. I can't blame them for it, because I feel the same way.

When the servers come around with our orders, I tug at my shirt cuffs and sigh at how slowly this dinner is progressing. I've been holding myself back as best I can, but I can't help tracing my fingers along her leg, brushing her arm with mine, nudging my knee into hers at every chance I get.

All I want to do is sprint back up to our room where I can have Raya and all of her attention to myself. I don't eat much; vampires can eat human food, but it doesn't do anything for us and I prefer not to as it doesn't always sit well. I pick at the fresh seafood, pushing it around so it looks like I ate more than I did, and keep an eye on Raya's plate.

When it looks like she's done and has carefully crossed her utensils over the remaining scraps of food, I stand and offer my hand.

Raya's eyes bounce up to mine in surprise, a question in her gaze.

"I thought you might want to turn in early, since we have an early flight tomorrow. I'll walk you back to the hotel, if you're ready to go?" I offer in explanation, not feeling one iota of guilt for the lie. We don't fly out until mid-afternoon, but no one else needs to know that.

A rosy flush creeps up her neck as she places her hand in mine, and one side of my mouth tilts up at the corner.

"Right, probably best to call it a night. It was great chatting with all of you!" Raya waves as we leave, tucking her hand against my upper arm again. It takes all of my concentration not to flex my muscles in response to her light touch.

18

___

THIS ISN'T EVEN OUR FLOOR

RAYA

THE HAIR on my arms stands on end as we walk arm in arm out of the bustling restaurant, down the sidewalk and back to our hotel. My heels tap too loud on the lobby floor, the only sound between us as we head toward the elevator bay. Asher is in predator mode, he has been all night, and my inner shifter isn't helping the situation. Every time I think about him, sense his gaze on me, feel his light touches, hear his whispered words, my mind instantly wonders what else he could do with that filthy tongue or what it would be like to have his scent wrapped all around me.

The way he murmured "ray of sunshine" earlier... it almost sounded like my name, said with reverence, and a hint of something even deeper.

Raya sunshine.

We step into the elevator and I feel primed to run, like at any moment he might attack and I need to be ready to escape. Which is nonsense, of course. I'm pretty certain at this point that he isn't a danger to me, but that instinctual response, the dichotomy of our races being in close proximity urging me to move, won't let up. Instead of that instinct instilling fear, I'm feeling more and more turned on, with a sense of excited anticipation threading through my muscles. My heart rate has been slowly rising, adrenaline trickling through my body, and if I've noticed it, I'm certain Ash has too.

I wonder what he would do if I ran; would he chase me? Would he catch me, and what would he do when he did?

As the elevator doors close, Asher turns toward me, his gaze alight with predatory intent. An inhuman glint gives his normally bright blue eyes a dark, sinful look that causes my breath to catch in my throat. Without even realizing it, I've allowed him to back me into a wall, and his arms come up to cage me in. He rests his elbows on either side of my head against the mirrored elevator, and as I lean my shoulders and head back, my hips angle forward, brushing against his.

Asher sucks in a breath and presses his entire body into mine so my back is flat against the mirror, and now I do know what it's like to be surrounded by his scent. It's as devastating as I was afraid it would be. My eyes nearly roll to the back of my head as I breathe him in.

His breath on my neck sends shivers down my spine, and his gravelly voice elicits a following tremor.

"Do you have any idea what you've been doing to me all night?" he rasps, both of our gazes pinned to each other's lips.

I lick mine and then bite my bottom lip, not bothering to respond because he has no right to talk—he's been doing worse to me.

His thumb tugs it out from my teeth and then glides across it. My eyes dart up to his, but he's still intent on my mouth. As I'm about to go up in flames, we move at the same time. I lean forward, tilting my mouth up as he leans down, crashing his lips against mine.

His kiss is hard, intense and demanding as his tongue swipes out, and I gasp when sparks shoot through me. Asher doesn't hesitate. His tongue sweeps into my mouth as he cups my jaw with one hand, angling both of us in a way that makes me think he's trying to kiss all the way to my heart. I quickly run out of oxygen, but I don't care to breathe, not when this is the alternative.

I feel the tell-tale tingling, but I focus on the present moment, and by grounding myself I manage to hold back the ears that I sense wanting to transform on my head. A distant part of myself is proud that I'm able to prevent the shift, but the present part of me doesn't care one bit.

My fingers thread into his dark, silky hair, tugging him closer. I whimper when he pulls back for a breath, and his lips curve into a satisfied smirk against mine at the sound. Our mouths are already melding together again though, his lips firm but molding to mine, and I feel drunk, despite only having had a virgin strawberry daiquiri with dinner.

More than drunk, this feels like an out of body experience. I've never been this attracted to anyone before, and never have I practically dry humped someone while making out with them in an elevator.

Right as that thought passes through my head, the elevator doors ding and someone pointedly clears their throat. Asher tastes my bottom lip once more, then pulls back so his hands are braced on either side of me.

I don't think, don't spare a moment for it. I act on instinct, and my instincts tell me I have just enough room to escape.

So I do.

I duck beneath his arm in the brief moment when he's looking over his shoulder at the person with their hand on the door, and I run. I risk a glance behind me, eyes widening as I see Asher step off the elevator, exchanging places with the other man. I turn forward again, a thrill running down my spine as a low chuckle echoes down the hallway behind me.

"Are you running from me, little shifter? This isn't even

our floor. Where do you think you'll go that I won't catch you?"

My hair is a mess, my dress is disheveled, and wildness surges through my veins. With a giddy laugh, I tip my head back and fling my arms out, letting my shoes fall from my feet as I sprint down the hallway. The carpet is thick under my bare soles, and doors fly past on either side as the air rushes over my skin. I don't care that I probably look—and sound—insane. The hem of my dress flutters against my thighs, a tease of what's to come.

As I round a corner, I glance back again, and the sight nearly sends me careening into the wall. Somehow, Asher looks to be calmly jogging along behind me, his long legs easily eating up the carpet and a confident smirk on his stupidly perfect face with my heels dangling from one hand.

He stopped to pick up my shoes?

I'm sprinting like my life depends on it, and he's not even breaking a sweat. I narrow my eyes and aim for the stairwell. The door slams open when I shove through it, and I stall in surprise. This is the nicest stairwell I've ever seen, with plush carpeted stairs and a black wrought iron handrail.

I have no idea what floor we're currently on, but I know I still need to go up, so that's what I do. Unfortunately, I only make it one flight before an arm snags my waist, yanking my back into a hard chest as teeth clamp onto my lower neck, just shy of drawing blood.

My body goes limp. I involuntarily angle my head for him to have easier access to my neck, all the while silently berating my inner shifter for the submissive response, in denial of the satisfaction swirling through my blood. The chase was fun, and I relish the feeling of powerlessness that overcomes me in his presence, especially when my animal practically purrs now that he's proven himself.

Asher whips me around and crushes me into the wall,

caging my body with his again. I'm panting, and my heartbeat is a rush of blood pounding through me, diluting any other sounds I might hear. At first glance, Asher doesn't even look like he took a brisk walk. When I look closer though, I see the muscles flexing in his jaw, the tight shoulders and mussed hair, his dark blue eyes fully dilated and lips clamped shut over the fangs he had on my neck moments ago. He pauses, entire body rigid with restraint as he looks down at me.

I meet his eyes and tip my chin up in challenge. My lips twitch up, silently daring him to take it a step further.

Not needing any further encouragement, he does. Asher rakes my dress to my hips as he drops to his knees before me and hikes my leg up, slinging it over his shoulder, then inhales my scent with a groan.

My hands fly to his hair; this isn't what I was expecting. I thought he'd attack my mouth again, not... this.

"What..." I'm still breathless, overwhelmed with the sensation and presence of him as he presses his nose to the crease of my hip and nips at my black satin thong.

"I need you," his voice rumbles against me.

My grip in his hair tightens as he runs his nose down my inner thigh and grazes his teeth over my tender skin.

"Not here." He pulls away with another groan, this one sounding almost painful, then sweeps me into his arms. My shoes somehow end up in my lap, then he blurs us up the stairs. It's the only way I can describe it.

I blink, realizing I never had any chance of escaping him. Shifters can run faster than humans, but apparently vampires beat all. He moves so fast my eyes can't even track where we're going, and in a matter of seconds, I'm back on my feet in front of our hotel room door, one of his hands still gripping my waist while the other searches his pocket for the keycard.

When he finally pushes the door open, we crash through and I take the opportunity to turn the tables on him. I push my body against his, backing him into the wall this time as I rake my fingers through his hair, pulling his lips back to mine.

The groan he lets out is swallowed by my mouth and I revel in the power of making this stoic man *feel*. I angle us toward the bed, our mouths still hungry as we lick and suck and taste each other. He stumbles and mutters something about "practice pillows" under his breath. My laugh is more like a breathy sigh between his lips; neither of us is willing to let anything interrupt this moment.

It feels like we've been building toward this since he first walked up to me on the sidewalk, before I knew who he was. We've been circling each other for weeks; me wary and distrustful, Asher apparently unsure what to make of me. But in such close proximity, it was bound to happen. The tension snapped, and we can't resist the force of it bringing us together.

Nor do either of us want to anymore.

When we part for air again, both panting this time after having landed horizontally on the bed, I have to tear my eyes away from the fangs peeking out from his kiss-swollen lips. I'm sure mine are equally red and puffy, but I'm also sure we need to have a quick conversation before we go any further.

"Wait." I raise a hand to his chest as he leans over me again.

Asher backs off, settling on his side facing me.

"We can stop," he says, and I smile at how tortured he sounds as he says it.

He swipes a hand down his face, and I take pity on him.

"No, I don't want to stop. We do need to check in real quick tho. I'm not on birth control, but I'm clean, got tested a couple weeks before this trip. You?"

"Also not on birth control, and also clean," he replies.

I roll my eyes.

"Really? Now is when you want to make jokes?"

He growls and buries his face in my neck, sucking on that

tender spot right behind my ear. I nearly get lost in him again, before I manage to squeak out.

"Ash... condom?"

"Don't have one, don't care. There's plenty else I want to do with you." His voice is deep and gravelly, and my toes curl as I give in to the haze of lust taking over every ounce of my body.

19

CURSES

RAYA

TIME FILTERS through in flickers of awareness. All I know is Asher.

His smoky, cedar scent with a teasing hint of bergamot, his sensual touch trailing over every inch of my skin, his wicked taste on my tongue. One second we're making out and dry humping over our clothes like the horniest of teenagers, and the next I'm naked and he's swiping his tongue down my neck.

His mouth circles my nipple, grazing it with his fangs and I suck in a sharp breath. His lips smirk against my pebbled skin before he sucks the tender bud into his mouth, laving it with his tongue while pinching the other and rolling it between his fingers.

I moan and close my eyes, tilting my head back as I fall into the sensations. I lose time again, lost in the pleasure, when I surface to his teeth scraping up my inner thigh. I spear my hands into his hair, eyes flying open when I register where he's going.

Asher pulls back to look at me, but instead of meeting my eyes, he gazes down between my legs. His rumble of approval vibrates through my thighs draped over his shoulders.

"So wet for me, sunshine."

I gasp when he blows cool air against my hot center, then swipes a tongue up my pussy. He doesn't hesitate, licking and sucking, teasing my clit while being careful not to nick me with his fangs, but it's too soft. It's not enough.

I want more.

I tighten my hold in his hair, gripping and pulling. My eyes squeeze closed as my hips lurch with desperation, and a whimper escapes my lips when I don't get what I want.

"Use your words, little shifter." His lips move against me, and I open my eyes again to see him staring up my body, eyes vibrant when they meet mine.

"More," I gasp, "your fingers."

My back arches when he slides two fingers into me, curling them against my inner walls as he finds my clit with his mouth again and sucks. I throw my head back at the sensation, eyes rolling as my focus narrows to the feel of him.

Everything blurs together, a haze of pleasure as the tidal wave of sensation builds inside me. Each stroke of his fingers, the suction from his mouth, his grip on my hips. Even the pressure from his nose nudging my mound as he sucks and licks adds to the incredible feelings he's eliciting. My legs tremble, my entire body tightens, the pleasure is overwhelming and more intense than anything I've felt before.

As it peaks, my breath catches, and I stay there, hanging for eternity, a shooting star burning through the night sky. I'm right on the precipice for timeless moments before the orgasm crests and crashes over me, pulsing through my body and clenching his fingers inside me.

"That's my good girl." His mouth gentles and slows as he stays with me, prolonging the sensations and sending after-shocks rippling through me.

Finally, I fall limp.

My hands drop from his hair. My back flattens to the

mattress. The breath punches out of me, and my legs turn to noodles.

"Holy shit."

His responding chuckle sounds satisfied as he pulls back and gently traces one finger around my pussy, almost like he's committing it to memory. Then he swipes his hand across his jaw, cleaning the wetness from his face as he crawls up the bed next to me. His fingers don't leave me though. He trails them over my skin, up and down my arm closest to him. I close my eyes, inhaling a deep breath. It smells like sex in our room now.

Sex and *him.*

"Good?" he asks.

"So good," I gasp, still trying to catch my breath.

"I don't think I've heard you swear before."

"Worth it." My face stretches into a content smile as I blink my eyes open. When I turn toward him, his gaze snags on my bitten bottom lip, and his mouth parts as he pushes his tongue against one fang.

I'm surprised to feel completely at ease with him. No discomfort or awkwardness after the best orgasm of my life. No fear of the evil vampire and his exposed fangs. No worry about what the future holds. I'm here, in this moment, with him.

As my brain clicks back into reality, his eyes briefly flick to the top of my head before meeting my gaze. He quirks one side of his lips up when I catch him.

"What am I this time?" I ask, resigned to my fate. Even after days of practicing morning and night, there's no way I can pull in a shift right now.

"Fox ears," he says.

I search his face, trying to figure out where his head is at. He soothes any concern I might have before I even get a chance to think it.

"Kinda sexy, to be honest." Asher rubs his chin, looking almost embarrassed as he says it, but I'm too caught off guard to hold my reaction in.

"Really?" I say, and my hesitant smile turns into a grin. "You like?"

He nods, looking at my fox ears again. I reach up, feeling the tufted ears peeking out of my sex-mussed hair. I tilt my head, thinking about it.

"I guess it's not that different from those sexy black cat costumes people wear at Halloween. Just... real ears, instead of a headband?" I search inside myself, trying to sort out the tangled emotions swirling in my chest. Surprise, definitely. Pride? Or something like it, similar to confidence or a new feeling of attractiveness.

I feel seen, accepted, kind of confused but also pleased that he likes every part of me he's been privy to so far. I set it aside for now, satisfied with the good outweighing what might not actually be so bad. I'm ready to move on to more fun topics.

I roll onto Asher's chest and his hands immediately find my waist. I shiver as they span much more of me than I thought they would, then sit up to straddle him, licking my lips when his eyes dilate.

"My turn." I purr the words, my voice turning husky as I drink in the sight of him stretched out below me.

His entire body hardens under mine as I lean down to kiss his neck. His hands lower to grip my hips, and I copy his movements from earlier. I lick and kiss, nibble and suck my way from one ear up and down his neck to the other, then trail my lips down his chest. His nipples tighten as my mouth skims over them, and I let out a breathy, satisfied laugh as I make my way down his body.

I trace the ridges of his muscles with my fingers, then do it again with my lips when they tense and shift under my touch. I lift my gaze as I move lower, looking up at him through my lashes to see his jaw clenched and eyes fixed to me, on fire with need.

Not breaking eye contact, I flatten my tongue and lick a stripe from the base of his shaft to the tip. His groan is obscene, and my answering smile is full of triumph.

When I wrap one hand around his cock and cup his balls in the other, his throat bobs in a swallow and he props himself up on his elbows, watching with anticipation for what I'll do next. I don't have the patience for teasing today, and I don't think he'll mind.

I straddle one of his legs, resting my wet pussy on his shin as I get into position. Asher groans at the sensation. The pressure feels good on my still swollen clit, and I wiggle back and forth a bit as I settle in. His groan turns almost tortured when I lean down and swirl my tongue around the head of his cock, then suck it into my mouth.

I ease my way down the shaft, getting used to the feel of him in my mouth, then hollow my cheeks and get to work. He throws his head back, neck taught and forearms bunching as his fists clench.

"Fuck," he grinds out as I pull back, and when I suck him in again, one hand flies to the back of my head. His fingers tangle in my hair as he grabs a fistful and yanks me off him.

We stare at each other, both of us panting, me with challenge in my eyes and Asher with desperate need in his.

"I'm not gonna last if you don't go easy on me, sunshine."

"Don't want you to last," I say. I tug my head toward his bobbing cock, a sting in my scalp as I pull against his grip. I bite my lip at the zing it sends through me, and he groans again, sensing the uptick in my heart rate.

"You're going to kill me," he growls as he relents, allowing me to take him into my mouth again. His hand stays in my hair this time, and I find I like it there. I like the give and take of power, feeling both in control and not.

I let loose and explore his pleasure, using different speeds and pressures, twisting and swirling to find what he likes. I take note of every time his muscles tense, each hitched breath and clenched fist, until I can read him easier than an open book. He's shuddering under me, and I hum when he gets impossibly harder in my mouth.

"I..." he groans, "I'm going to—"

He tries to warn me, but I've been waiting for it, and I act as soon as I sense he's close. I take him as deep as I can, tears pricking my eyes when he hits the back of my throat, but I don't let up until he's done. I watch his face, feeling a warmth in my chest that I get this moment when no one else does, and I keep my mouth closed around him until he's spent, pulsing and coming straight down my throat.

I gently release him from my mouth, and his elbows slide out, dropping him flat to the bed. I bite my lip as I slide off his leg to sit next to him and my gaze roams up his heaving chest to his flushed cheeks and sex mussed hair.

Asher's eyes are closed, and it's his turn to try to catch his breath.

"I agree," he finally says. "Holy shit."

I throw myself down next to him and laugh. It's a full bodied, heartfelt laugh, and when I turn my head to look at him, the matching smile on his face is nearly enough to stop my heart.

20

———

TWENTY QUESTIONS

RAYA

I WAKE to the smell of coffee the next morning. While it's a pleasant surprise, after the activities of the night before I was kind of hoping for a different wake up call.

Rolling over, I spot Asher moving quietly around the room. There's a pile of clothes on the desk that he must have picked up from where we discarded them last night, and he's now setting the "practice pillows" on top of the floor blanket which is folded and placed on the desk chair. He notices I'm awake when he turns back around to sweep his eyes over the room.

"Morning, sunshine," he murmurs with a lopsided smile. His voice is soft and tender, unlike his previously gruff exterior. My heart feels like it might burst, and there's no holding in the answering grin that blooms across my face.

"Good morning," my voice is still thick with sleep, and as I start to sit up, he holds out a mug of coffee.

"Thanks," I say, looking around again. My face must be full of questions because he answers them before I ask.

"I figured you needed it, so I let you sleep in. It's 11am, we need to head to the airport in about an hour so I started cleaning up the room a bit. Your clothes are there." He points to one of the folded piles on the desk, and I blink a few times in response. My brain is still sleepy.

When what he's saying finally clicks, I'm not proud of the velociraptor screech that comes from my mouth, but it is what it is.

"Eleven?!" I scramble off the bed, forgetting that I'm completely naked until it's too late. Although my entire body flushes under his heated gaze, the Cheshire-cat smirk on his face causes me to snap into action.

"No time!" I say, pointing a finger at his face. There's a robe hanging in the bathroom and I decide that's good enough fo rnow. I shut the door and jump in the shower, berating myself for not setting an alarm the night before, and then wondering what even happened the rest of the night. I must have passed out after our sexcapades because I don't remember anything else until I woke up this morning.

I rush through my morning routine, not bothering with makeup or styling my hair. I throw it into a messy braid so I'll be comfortable on the plane and turn to packing my bag, all the while grumbling to myself under my breath. I'm normally fairly even tempered, but being woken up and told I need to hurry is not the way to get on my good side, no matter how excellent someone might be at giving orgasms.

My cheeks flush and my skin tingles at the thought. I pause my folding to take some deep breaths, slowing my heart and causing the tingling sensation to recede.

That alone is enough to turn my entire mood around. I straighten with a smile on my face only to see Asher watching me, a knowing look in his eye.

"Nicely done," he says, and I don't have time to wonder how he can read me so well.

"Thank you," I reply, my pride shining through.

We make it to the airport with plenty of time to spare, and

I can admit my earlier grumpiness was mostly unwarranted. Like PDX, the San Diego airport is easy to navigate, and it takes less than twenty minutes to get through security. I grab some snacks, then we settle in at our gate where I pull out my book, quickly getting lost in the adventures of a badass female former-pirate overcoming magic and mayhem on the high seas as she takes on one last quest.

I barely take my nose from the pages, even as we board and find our seats. I allow Asher to guide me with a hand on my elbow or lower back, nudging me gently one way or the other as I somehow manage to survive treacherous waters, pulling off a daring rescue while dodging dangerous artifacts and magical attacks.

A short time later—or maybe a long time, I'm not sure—I finish the book and snap it closed with a heaving sigh. Unfortunately, the plane is still in the air and I didn't bring another book with me. Nor did I stop by the airport bookstore to pick one up, even though I knew I was almost done with this one. (Admittedly, one of my worst life decisions to date.)

I close my eyes and relive some of my favorite scenes, wondering what it would be like if I lived in that world. I would like to think I'd be on the pirate captain's crew, but realistically I'd more likely be a regular old village person. I don't feel like I have badass female main character energy, and I'm totally okay with that.

The reminiscing doesn't entertain me for long, and without realizing it, my leg starts bouncing. My eyes fly open when I feel a heavy hand on my knee, stilling the movement.

"Sorry," I offer Asher a sheepish smile as he moves his hand back to his own leg, to which he nods and leans his head back against the seat, closing his eyes. I know he's not sleeping, but he does have earbuds in. I drum my fingers against my thigh, looking out the window at the clouds swirling around the plane and wondering what he's listening to.

I jump when his hand grips my knee again. Turning to face Asher, I wrinkle my nose and bite the inside of my cheek.

"What is it?" He pulls one earbud out and turns toward me.

"Nothing, I'm just bored," I say. I hold my book up with a shrug. "Finished my book."

Asher flips his wrist to check his watch. "Only another hour, you'll be fine."

With that, he returns his earbud to his ear and tips his head back again. I chew on my lip, contemplating what I'm going to do for an hour, plus extra because landing and taxi time before we can deplane.

Before I know it, I'm tapping his biceps, and he plucks out his earbud again with a slight scowl on his face.

"Whatcha listening to?" I ask, blinking innocently up at him with a practiced smile on my face—the one that almost always gets me what I want.

"The news," he says, and I stick my lower lip out in a pout. *No thanks.*

When he sees I'm not pleased with that, he shrugs and moves to put the earbud in again. I shift in my seat, pulling my feet up and resting my chin on one knee as I go back to staring out the window. I quickly become uncomfortable, so I try to sit criss-cross, nudging his arm off the armrest so I can fold it back and have more space for my legs. Asher rolls his eyes but allows it, shaking his head. I'm pretty sure he doesn't mind.

Tapping my fingers, I start wiggling my toes in my shoes too, making a fun new beat that I nod my head along to. When my knee starts bobbing too, rhythmically bumping into his leg, Asher pulls both earbuds out and turns toward me again.

"How do I make this stop?" he says, his voice exasperated, but a twinkle of amusement dancing in his eyes, too.

I widen my eyes, looking around as if there's some other culprit that has offended him.

"Make what stop?" I ask.

"This—" he waves his hand up and down in front of me, encompassing my entire body. "The restless fidgeting."

"I'm bored."

"And?"

"And... I don't know. You could talk to me," I say, trying not to pout for real this time.

Asher's lips quirk and he pulls out the case for his earbuds, slipping them inside before he snaps it closed.

"Okay then. What do you want to talk about?"

A giddy grin lights up my face. I have so many questions. He narrows his eyes when he sees it, but I dive in before he can back out.

"How old are you?" I ask, and his eyes widen.

"Oh, so we're doing that are we? Right." Asher straightens in his seat, pushing his shoulders back like he has to brace himself for the "get to know each other" conversation. "I'm twenty-eight."

I try not to balk, but he doesn't look twenty-eight. I didn't realize he was so much older than me. I would have guessed he was only a couple years older, something around twenty-five, maybe twenty-six at most.

"Oh, cool," I say, cringing at how lame that sounds. "And your parents?"

At this, his face closes. I can practically feel the wall as it slams down between us, shutting him away from me. I frown at the reaction; I didn't think that was a particularly invasive question. Vampires can live decades longer than humans, and I was curious if his parents were older than mine, what time period they might have grown up in, that kind of thing.

"Never mind, I don't actually care how old they are," I say, waving my hand to clear the air and quickly trying to backpedal.

"What do you do for fun?"

Asher clears his throat, visibly trying to reconnect, and I soften at the effort he's putting into being present and engaged.

"I like to run," he says, and I snort a laugh. "Why is that funny?"

"It's just, I mean. Run like a human, or run like you did at the hotel? Because that can hardly be classified as running."

He smirks at this, another layer of the wall between us crumbling.

"I like to run like a human," he gives me a pointed look, "on human running trails. Though I do also like the occasional vampire-speed run. I've been enjoying Forest Park lately, northwest of the city. Have you been?" he asks.

"Oh, yeah! Only a couple times, but it has some really pretty trails. I didn't take you for the outdoorsy type."

"What type did you take me for?" he asks, and I bite my lip in response. He notices, and he leans into my space for a brief moment before sitting back again, that predatory look flitting in and out of his eyes.

I will my heart to calm. It's truly ridiculous how he can wind me up in a matter of moments. The pilot announces we'll be arriving in Portland soon, and that snaps me back into reality.

"So." I stop, looking down at my hands as I twist my fingers together, wondering if he's thought about what this is between us, especially considering we're coworkers.

Asher reaches over and takes one of my hands, threading his fingers through mine, and I freeze at the gesture. We've been incredibly intimate, but this feels different. This feels intimate in a new way. A close, affectionate way.

My eyes dart up to his serious face.

"So?" he says, prompting me to continue.

"Um," I look back down at our entwined fingers. "What are we going to do about us? When we get back."

"I already looked into PNCG policies. I'd like to talk to HR, see if we can fill out the forms that indicate we're seeing each other, if you'd be open to that."

I flash a grin and my skin tingles. "I like that idea."

"Me too." His lips quirk at the corners again, seemingly unable to resist answering whenever I smile at him.

"Sooooo." I look down at my lap again, tapping my fingers against the back of his. "Does this mean we're together then?"

Asher doesn't answer until I meet his gaze.

"Yes, if you'll have me," he says. "Raya, can I take you out on a real date?"

A smile whips across my face as I nod in agreement. I tuck one arm around his biceps and lean my head against his shoulder, snuggling in and biting my lip when he softly kisses the top of my forehead. I close my eyes, content now that I have a real life daydream to focus on for the rest of the flight.

21

NO SECRETS HERE

RAYA

WE GO our separate ways after baggage claim, and I'm fairly certain I wouldn't be able to stop smiling if my life depended on it. The joy only expands when I open my apartment door and am nearly smacked in the face by a glittering, reckless sprite.

I duck the tiny winged attacker and Reverie gets snagged in my hair instead of latching onto my nose. We both laugh as I help extricate her. I hold her up, exchanging our version of a hug before she hops up onto my shoulder and tangles her hands in my hair for stability.

"RAYA'S HOME!" Rev's shrill voice rings through the apartment and I wince for my poor eardrum as Zuri strides out of the kitchen. She wasn't supposed to be here, but her work must have finished early.

"I figured that was who was unlocking the door, seeing as no one else has a key." Zuri's smile is as wide as mine and we embrace tightly.

"What are you feeling? Food, unpacking, chill?" Zuri asks, turning to head further into the apartment as Reverie tucks herself into the crook of my neck with a contended hum.

"Might grab a snack and relax on the couch for a bit," I say as I wheel my luggage into my room.

"I can't believe you left for so long," Reverie says, wiggling a little on my shoulder.

"I know, I'm sorry." I wish I could take Reverie with me, but seeing as her race is largely thought to have died out, it's best if she stays hidden. We try to get her out into nature whenever we can, but she gets anxious at the possibility of being seen by others.

"I nearly starved to death!" Reverie whisper shouts, to which Zuri snorts in response.

"You did not. I kept plenty of sprite appropriate food out for whenever you needed it, you little menace. You're just mad I didn't have your favorite sugary treats on hand 24/7," Zuri replies.

I'm pretty sure I feel Reverie cross her arms and pout on my shoulder, and I'm also pretty sure it's pretend.

"I brought you each a little something," I say, handing over the souvenirs.

Reverie gasps and flicks her wings, sending a shower of glittery dust over my shoulder as she turns the plastic shot glass this way and that, inspecting each scenic picture wrapped around it.

"Another for my collection! I love it," Reverie says, hugging it to her chest. Turns out, shot glasses are about the perfect size for sprites, so we've got a small collection going. The glass ones are too heavy for her though, so when I spotted this plastic one in the airport, I knew I had to get it.

"Glad you like it!" I say, then turn to Zuri, who is holding up a dainty bracelet.

"Each of the crystals are supposed to help with different things," I explain. "Rose Quartz for peace, Aventurine is for patience, Amethyst for tranquility, and Moonstone for intuition." I point to each as I talk, then hold up my own wrist.

"I got one too."

Zuri grins and slips it on, tightening the strings and admiring our matching bracelets.

"Good choices. Thanks, girl," Zuri says.

Warmth settles in my chest; I'm home.

"So how'd the trip with the murderous vampire go?" Zuri asks as we all settle onto the couch.

"He's not murderous," I grumble, rolling my eyes up to the ceiling. So much for that happy, peaceful feeling I had a moment ago. I'd hoped to avoid this conversation for at least a day, but apparently not.

"Not that you know of, but that family is bad news." Zuri is oblivious to my disagreement, but not for long.

"I don't know. He's actually pretty nice, and even helped me with my shifting," I say, not surprised at the shocked silence that follows. I sneak a look at Zuri, then see Reverie hovering in the air next to my temple. I look at her from the corner of my eye as she flits around my head, poking at my skull.

"What are you doing?" I ask, leaning away from Rev's strange prodding.

"Checking for a head injury."

Zuri scoffs, "Good call."

"I'm serious! I can kind of control the shifts now. I wouldn't be able to do any of it without his help. He's not what you think."

I recognize that I sound like a petulant child, but I'm not sure how to have this conversation. I knew Zuri would be opposed no matter what, but I hoped the two of them would at least be open to hearing my side of things.

"Really?" Reverie lands on a small fluffy pillow in the middle of the coffee table that we keep there for this type of situation. It's hard to have a conversation with a sprite when they're seated on the back of the couch or someone's shoulder.

"Yeah. I mean, I had a hard time coming to terms with it too, but I really think he's a good guy."

Zuri's lips pinch into a line, but she doesn't reply, and Reverie looks thoughtful, tilting her head so her purple hair cascades over one shoulder, magenta streaks sparkling through it as she considers.

"So let's see this shifting then!" Reverie stands and claps her hands.

"I'm not a show pony. Besides, I'm still learning. I kinda have to, like, feel it first? Or be in the right mood?"

They both stare at me blankly and I throw up my hands.

"I don't know, okay? My inner animal has an attitude or something." I glower as my lips pull down.

"Well, that's okay," Reverie backpedals, "I'm sure if you keep practicing it'll get easier."

"Yeah. I hope so."

Reverie flutters her way back to my shoulder, this time nestling in for my comfort rather than her own. I tip my head and rub my cheek against Rev's soft hair, a silent thank you for always being on my side.

I HEAD over to my parents the next morning for Sunday family brunch, constantly flip flopping on whether I should tell them about Asher or not. On top of that, although I'm proud of how far I've come with my shifting, I'm nervous they'll ask for a demonstration like Reverie did. I asked if she wanted to come with me to brunch, but she wasn't feeling up for an outing.

I sigh, reminding myself to take deep breaths and grounding my body in the present moment. So far since I've been home, there have been no unexpected shifts. I've had a few instances of the tingles that prickle my skin before it happens, but with the skills Ash taught me, I've been able to prevent it.

As soon as my foot hits the porch step, the door flies open and my mom welcomes me, a massive smile on her face and her arms spread wide for a hug. I grin, happy to be back with my family who hopefully won't judge me for who I've been spending my free time with.

My dad is right behind my mom, ready to embrace me as well.

"We're so glad you're home, honey," he says, giving me a bear hug and then swinging an arm over my shoulders as he steps to my side.

"I was only gone for a few days, geez," I say, laughing at how dramatic they're both being when my mom slips an arm through mine on my other side and marches us all toward the kitchen.

"Well, it's been over a week since I've gotten to hug you, so you'll have to deal with a little extra affection to make up for it," Mom replies, no nonsense to be had.

"Sup, sis," my brother says as we walk past the living room. His back is to us and he's playing a video game, driving like a maniac on the TV screen.

"Hey, Wes. Missed you too."

"Breakfast in ten, Wesley," Mom calls out and he offers a quick head jerk in response, thumbs jabbing at the joy sticks on his controller.

"Is that our sweet, darling Raya, finally returned to us after being gone soooo long in the big city?" My sister, Josephine, smirks at me as she ups the dramatics, teasing my parents for their over the top welcome.

Mom lightly swats Jo's arm in rebuke as she passes. "You watch your tone there, missy. I'm still your mother."

Untangling myself from my parents, I give my sister a hug, too.

"What are you doing here? I didn't expect you back until Thanksgiving," I say.

Josephine shrugs. "I had a free weekend, figured I'd swing by since it's been a while." She pauses, taking in my appearance and peering into my eyes.

"You good?" she asks, voice low so our parents don't hear.

"I'm good," I assure her. Josephine doesn't look convinced, and I'm not surprised. I never could keep anything from my big sister, so of course she'd notice that I'm nervous, but she drops it for now.

We all find seats around the table, and my dad serves up french toast with maple agave syrup, fresh blackberries, apple slices sautéed in cinnamon sugar, and a maple cool whip to top it all off.

"Wow, Dad. You really didn't have to go all out like this," I say, starting to feel bad at all the extra effort from my missing one week of family brunch.

"I wanted to, and I won't hear any more about it," he replies.

My brother wastes no time diving in, and I beam around the table as my family chatters.

"So, Raya," Mom turns to me, "tell us all about your trip. How was San Diego?"

"Oh it was great!" This part I can talk about, no problem. "It was hotter than I expected, but nice to be in the sun for a few days. Honestly though, the food was the best part. There are little Mexican places all over and oh my gosh. I can't even tell you, it was so good."

My dad is likely the only one who really cares about the food, but they all nod along anyway.

"And how was the work? You had some presentations, right?" Mom asks.

"Yep, it went well. I was worried since they kind of threw me in last minute, but it wasn't anything I couldn't handle. I had some help from my coworker too, so that was nice, not to be completely alone with it all."

"Good, good. Glad to hear it, honey. How did the full moon go?" Dad asks, and I feel my face flush. Naturally, my sister pounces on it.

"What is *that*? Why are you turning red?" Jo says, planting her elbows on the table. This, of course, only causes me to redden even further, and I feel the tell-tale tingle start to zip up my spine. I close my eyes, inhaling a deep breath through my nose and letting it out slowly through my mouth as I open them again.

"Oh. My. God. Raya, spill!" my sister says, and Jo's intensity causes even my brother to start paying attention.

"It's nothing!" I try to put them off the trail, but no one is having it.

"Okay, so I have this coworker, Asher," I start, ignoring Jo's widening eyes and gleeful smile. "He's a vampire, actually, but he was able to really help me with the shifting. He taught me some ways to manage my breathing and emotions and stuff, and I was able to partially shift on purpose a couple times, and I've been getting better at holding it off too. I even did it just now."

"Just now?" Dad's eyebrows pop up.

"Yep. Like, thirty seconds ago," I say. "I felt the weird tingle that always happens before I accidentally shift, and that's why I closed my eyes. So I could focus and stop it."

"Oh, honey." Mom's eyes are a little glassy, which causes me to squirm in my seat. "We are so proud of you, that's wonderful."

"Mhmm yeah, great job being a shifter." My sister is awesome, like, ninety percent of the time. This is not one of those times. "I want to hear more about this "coworker.""

"You're seriously the worst sometimes," I grumble under my breath, but everyone, even my brother, is looking at me expectantly. "Okay, fine. We spent a lot of time together this week, and we sort of hit it off. We're going to talk to HR about our relationship on Monday, see if we can get it approved or whatever."

"Oh shit, girl. That's serious," Jo says, leaning back in her seat.

"Language, Josephine!" our mother admonishes as I reply.

"Yeah, I guess it is. He's really nice."

"Vampire, you said?" Dad asks, not one to be deterred from the important details.

"Yeah, one of the good ones, though," I assure him, hoping I'm speaking the truth and haven't completely misread Asher.

Dad gives me that classic dad look, the one with the uncompromising eyes as he replies.

"I expect we'll be meeting him soon then."

I should have expected that.

22

HAPPY DANCES SHOULD BE ILLEGAL

ASHER

THE WEEK PASSES in a blur of debriefing meetings and follow up video calls with the client when, predictably, someone decided they could "fix" a software problem on their own rather than putting in a call to the team (me) who knows it backwards and forwards and is paid to solve those exact problems. When it's ultimately made even worse by said meddling, I end up with an extra stack of work on my plate.

I came in early today, on a Friday of all days, to try to get to the bottom of it before the weekend. Especially since I have a date with Raya planned for tonight, and I don't want to have any lingering work stressors hanging over my head.

On the plus side, well, Raya.

She strolls into the office with a smile on her face, and the brief glimpse of her bouncing into the kitchen already lightens my mood. Suddenly, this issue no longer seems quite so pressing. I push back from my desk and quietly follow in Raya's footsteps; I'm unable to hold myself back from her at this point. All I want to do is be near her and soak in her presence. Thankfully the meeting with HR went well, so we don't have to worry about hiding our relationship. I stop in the kitchen doorway, leaning against the wall where I can see Raya's profile facing our coworker.

"What's got you even more cheerful than normal today?" Alex stirs a pound of sugar into their coffee as they lean against the counter next to Raya.

"Oh, nothing. I'm just looking forward to the weekend," she replies, the smile on her face stretching her cheeks, and I can't help but hope it's because of our date tonight.

I told her I wanted to surprise her, and the way her eyes lit up made me want to drop to my knees in worship. Knowing she likes surprises is another tidbit I've tucked close to my chest. I hoard information about her like a dragon guarding its treasure. Confounding as it is, I've decided not to question my reactions to this sunny shifter anymore, and just go with the flow.

I silently spin out of the doorway but wait next to it, nodding to Alex as they head back to their desk a minute later. Raya is still puttering around in the kitchen, and I wait with bated breath for her to exit too.

When she turns into the hallway and sees me, her eyes brighten in that way I live for, and I meet her grin with an irresistible smile of my own. It feels less and less foreign on my face with every passing day. I've never smiled this much in my life, and it's bewildering how easy she makes it.

"Good morning, sunshine," I say, trying to control my voice so it doesn't betray how close I am to slamming her against the wall and taking her lips with my own.

"Hi! Happy Friday." Raya's eyes flicker down my body as she takes in my fitted slacks and button down shirt, and my smile turns smug. I don't try to stop it, instead enjoying the slight flush on her cheeks as a result.

I turn and gesture for her to walk with me. She raises an eyebrow as I lead us in the opposite direction of our desks.

"It's the end of the week, I thought you might need a

restock on your office supplies," I say, throwing in a wink for good measure.

Raya throws her head back and laughs. Not exactly the reaction I was going for, but I'll take it.

"Oh, you are not subtle at all, but yes, I do believe I'm in need of some more sticky notes." She playfully wrinkles her nose at me over the rim of her mug as she sips her tea. How is it that this woman can make any face, and it's always cute? I roll my eyes at her antics, opening the door to the supply room and taking the mug from her hand.

I set it carefully on a shelf as we step inside. As soon as it's out of my hands, I snatch Raya by her waist and swing her around, using her back to close the door as I press her against it. My mouth goes straight to her neck and I inhale, relishing her surprised gasp and loving the soft scent of her. Strawberry and coconut, sweetness and sunshine.

When my nose bumps her earlobe, I whisper in her ear. "You're a radiant sunbeam today in that yellow dress, hugging your curves in all the right places. You love to drive me crazy, don't you, sunshine?" I nip her ear, earning a whimper from her pouty lips, before I continue. "I've been here for hours already. I'm starving for you."

Her breath hitches and my mind reels with the implication. I didn't mean to say that last part, but it's true and I don't take it back. I'd love to taste her blood, certain she'd be exquisite, but I won't pressure her into anything she's not comfortable with. If that was what her reaction was about though... Well, that's something to explore when we aren't hiding in a glorified closet.

I pull back to look down at her flushed cheeks, her brown eyes filled with heat and her fingers clenched in my shirt.

She's perfect.

I release her waist with one hand, bringing it up to lightly trace the line of her throat before I step back and fix her hair where it's slightly mussed after being pressed against the door. My crooked grin feels wicked as my eyes hold hers and I pick her mug back up, nudging it against her hands where they're still fisted in my shirt.

She blinks rapidly, then scowls at me as she takes her mug.

"You're... that was..." Raya is the most adorable when she's flustered, especially when it's because she's turned on—by me.

"Yes, sunshine?" I muse.

She huffs, turning her back on me and grabbing an entire box of sticky notes before flinging the door open. She gives me one last glare over her shoulder as she stomps away, and no matter what her pursed lips say, the rest of her glows with happy mischief.

THE REMAINDER of the day trickles by, slow as molasses, only made bearable by the fact that I can look up and see Raya a few feet from me—and I do so many, many times. I watch as she jabs the end of her pen into her cheek while thinking. I notice how her lips tilt up sometimes when she's typing. I'm not sure if she knows how often my eyes are drawn to her, but she certainly catches me more than I'd like.

When the workday clock finally runs out and our coworkers say their goodbyes, I turn to Raya.

"Ready to go?" I ask, and she bites her lower lip with a nod.

"Where are we going?" Raya asks, practically skipping to the elevator.

"Back to my place," I say, and Raya's steps falter. "Beyond that, it's a surprise."

Raya turns to face me as the elevator doors close.

"Your dick isn't a surprise, Ash," she deadpans, and I snort.

"I mean, my dick is always on the menu, but that's not what I had planned for tonight."

"Ooooh, there's a menu?" Raya's eyebrows waggle and I shake my head.

"Of course there's a menu. You think I'd ask you to give me your Friday night without feeding you?"

Her little happy dance should be illegal with the way it draws my eyes straight to her breasts.

She chatters nonstop as I guide her to my car and drive us out to my place in a quieter neighborhood outside the main city. I'm surprised to find, not for the first time, that I genuinely enjoy listening to her and don't have any inclination to tune her out like I would every single other person on this planet.

When we arrive, she bounces out of the car. It's the first time I've invited her here, and I'm a little bit nervous.

Attempting to discreetly wipe my hands on my dark slacks as I lead her up to the door, I place one hand on her lower back. I tell myself it's so I can touch her, but there's also a part of me that wants anyone who may see us to know she's mine. Raya smiles up at me, oblivious to my possessive thoughts.

"Oh, this place is so cute!" she says, looking around at the quaint front porch.

Unlocking the door and opening it with a flourish, I invite her inside as a few butterflies dart sideways in my stomach.

I look around, wondering what about my bachelor pad gives her the impression of cute. Meanwhile, Milton lets out a strangled sounding "mrow" from his usual place next to the key-bowl. Raya lets out an equally strangled sounding "ohstarshesocute!" as I give Milton the 'be nice or else' look. He knows there's no 'or else' though, so I'm not sure how much good it does.

To my utmost surprise, he stands with his paws on the edge of the console table and leans toward Raya. She squeezes her hands to her chest, then holds one out for him to sniff. He nuzzles his head under it and purrs, rubbing against her fingers as she holds perfectly still. I sense her pulse skyrocket as she bites her lip, wide eyes sparkling.

"He's perfect," she whispers, and Milton turns his smug green eyes on me. I should have known they'd get along, her family are feline shifters, after all. He probably likes her better than me already.

Milton drops off the table and winds between our legs.

"Can I have a tour?" Her irresistible doe eyes turn my brain to jelly and I agree before I even realize what she's asking.

A tour, right.

"Well, it's not much, but it's comfortable," I say, slipping off her raincoat and hanging it on the coat rack by the door before placing mine next to it. I like how they look hanging side by side.

"Living room." I gesture forward as the space opens around us. "Kitchen is there, as you can see."

Raya's eyes roam around, taking in the details I rarely let others see.

"Bathroom is through there." More gesturing and pointing, before I lead her down a hallway past the open kitchen and living areas.

"Bedroom is this way." I take her hand, opening the door to my bedroom, and for some reason, holding my breath.

"Did someone design this for you? It's not what I'd expect of a bachelor in his late twenties." Raya pokes at my arm with a long, delicate finger and I snatch it before bringing it to my mouth for a playful nibble. She giggles as she turns and walks further into the room. It does something to me, seeing her in my space like this. She glows, her yellow dress and cheer bringing a new light to my bedroom.

"No, I did look into some design ideas though. I didn't know where to start so I kind of copied other designs I liked."

She nods, opening the door to the adjoining bathroom. Her eyes go wide as she freezes in place, and I hear her heart skip a beat. I panic for a moment, wondering what danger could possibly be lurking in my shower or toilet.

"This tub is incredible!" Raya's eyes are sparkling as she turns back to me. "How do you not live in it all the time?"

I choke out a laugh, shoulders slumping in relief that there isn't an axe murderer or wild boar in the bathroom. Then I add "sexy bath time" to my mental list of future plans with Raya.

I lean against the wall as she explores further, opening my nightstand drawers and perusing my bookshelf. When she gets to the dresser and starts pulling those drawers open too, I realize we could be here all night if I don't put a stop to it.

"Oooookay, I think that's enough snooping for now. You can do more later." I snag her waist and pull her back to my chest, curling around her and burying my nose in her hair. "I didn't know you were such a nosy little shifter."

Raya's tinkling laugh loosens my muscles and she wiggles, turning in my hold to sling her arms over my shoulders.

"I just want to know everything about you," she says.

I can't blame her for that. I've had the exact same thought more than once, though it sounds much more innocent coming from her lips than it does when crossing my mind.

23

—————

IT TASTES BETTER THAN IT LOOKS

RAYA

I CAN'T STOP SUCKING deep lungfuls of air in through my nose. Asher's place smells amazing. Woodsy, cedar and smoke, bergamot and clean linens. Like him, but more. Not to mention how cute the outside is with a large front window and bright blue door. He has a stoop, for crying out loud, and a stars-damned flower box.

As we wander back through the living area, Asher guides me to the kitchen. Milton trails after us, his tail twitching as he eyes Asher, and I grin. I love cats, and Milton is gorgeous with his sleek black fur and pale green eyes. He almost looks like a tiny version of Jo's panther form.

"You hungry?" Asher asks, and I shrug.

"I could eat." While not a lie, it also doesn't convey how ravenous I am. I only nibbled on my lunch today, my stomach a knot of nerves mixed with excited butterflies over our date tonight.

Unfortunately, said stomach decides to tattle on me with a loud gurgle. Ash raises an eyebrow, and even as I feel my cheeks heat I narrow my eyes, daring him to comment.

He doesn't.

Instead, he turns to the fridge and opens it, then starts pulling out ingredients. Flour, sugar, a bottle of pure maple syrup, baking powder, vanilla extract, an eighteen-count carton of eggs, five lemons, turkey bacon, two containers of raspberries, a bag of chocolate chips, salt, a carton of oat milk, a box of stick butter, and a bottle of sparkling apple juice. All emerge with Asher placing each on the counter as he slowly empties what is surely his entire fridge.

"What... Why do you have everything in the fridge?" I say, tilting my head in what I know is a feline gesture, as I grew up surrounded by it.

Asher looks abashed for a moment, before asking what I mean.

"You just pulled flour, sugar, the chocolate chips... I mean, all of those things, out of the fridge."

He looks between me and the pile of groceries, then picks up the bag of chocolate chips and simply holds it. It looks smaller than normal in his large hand.

"I'm guessing this doesn't belong in the fridge?" he finally says, his tone implying this is a question rather than a statement.

"No," I chuckle, "chocolate chips can go in the cupboard. Same with all the other dry ingredients."

"Right. Well, as you may have guessed, I'm new to this whole food thing."

"That's okay. Here, let me help." I step forward with my hand out, intending to wash the lemons, when he steps directly in front of me.

Asher's massive body physically blocks me from the food and I take an unsteady step back to catch my balance.

"Nope. I'm doing this," he says, "I want to cook for you."

I hold my hands up and back away.

"Okay, okay." I'm smiling as I say it, loving that he's so

intent on taking care of me, even if he does put flour in the fridge. "No problem, tough guy."

He narrows his eyes, correctly suspecting that I'm teasing him, so I offer my most blinding smile in return. It seems to work; he turns back to the food and starts sorting things, muttering under his breath.

I could swear I see the tips of his ears turn a little pink.

I can barely make out his lips moving, though I can't hear what he's saying. I glance at Milton, but he flicks his tail as his eyes track Asher's hands, not that he could actually communicate with me, but I was kind of hoping for something. Asher washes the lemons, using much more dish soap than necessary, but I hold my tongue, pushing it into my cheek to avoid giving away my amusement.

"So what are we having anyway?" I ask as he rinses the raspberries.

"Pancakes." Asher's voice is gruff, and he drags a hand through his hair, mussing it in the most enticing way as he surveys the pile of ingredients in front of him. "And such."

"Uh huh, okay well, I can help." I try to rescue him and move to grab a large mixing bowl on the counter behind him when he intercepts me again.

"Nuh uh, little shifter," he growls, "I told you, I'm doing this."

With that, his hands circle my hips and Asher lifts me off my feet. I don't have time to do more than blink before he drops me onto the counter on the other side of the sink—where I can't reach any of the food or cooking utensils. I cross my arms over my chest, sticking my bottom lip out in an effort to cover my true heated reaction to that outrageous display of manhandling.

This backfires spectacularly when Asher sees my pouty lip and takes it as an invitation to suck it into his own mouth. I lean into him with a moan, feeling the light scrape of his fangs against my lip. My body follows as he steps away and I grin at his satisfied look.

"Alright then, chef. What's next?" I say, my stomach not letting me forget what my priority should be right now.

Asher pauses in front of his prep station, hands on his hips as he inspects the display of foods that might as well be completely foreign to him. He snags the carton of eggs, then decisively opens it and begins to pull one out, to which I start coughing dramatically as I shake my head. Milton leaps onto the counter with a meow, then sits down right next to me, emphasizing our combined disapproval.

Asher side-eyes us, then slowly puts the egg back and moves his hand away. When I straighten and stop coughing, Asher purses his lips in annoyance and sends a glare my way.

"Fine," he says, and pulls out his phone. With only a few quick taps, he has a video playing.

"What are you doing?" I ask, straining to see what he's watching.

"I saved some of the YouTubes to follow," he mutters, and my eyes nearly bug out of my head.

One, because he used "YouTube" in the plural which indicates he watched multiple videos in preparation for cooking for me, and two, because he used "YouTube" in the plural and that's not a thing.

"The YouTubes?" I cackle as my eyebrows shoot up. "Stars, how freaking old are you?"

When Asher turns his eyes on me this time, I'm reminded of the predator he keeps leashed inside at all times. Milton bails, leaping off the counter and darting through the doorway.

"Keep it up, little shifter," Asher says, his voice low and lethal. "See what happens."

I press my thighs together and bite my lip when the hint of danger sends a thrill racing down my spine. Asher freezes and turns his head the slightest bit, which makes me realize my heart rate spiked as well.

One step has him back in front of me and he tips his chin down, angling himself over me as he runs his tongue along his fangs. My breath freezes in my lungs. I slowly raise my eyes from his chest up along the line of his throat to his chin, across his lips, and finally I meet his striking blue eyes as I peek up at him through my lashes.

He raises one hand, palm skating up my arm and along the side of my throat, leaving goosebumps in its wake, only to tuck a strand of hair behind my ear. Then he steps back, and presses play on the video.

I squeak a protest as he pulls away, and I just know he's smirking.

He's such a self-satisfied prick sometimes.

With a huff, I lean back on my hands and swing my feet, the annoyance quickly draining from my body as I watch him work.

"Is it supposed to smell like that?" he asks, nose wrinkling as he pokes the lumpy mass with a spoon. "And look like that? There's no way this is normal."

I crack up. This is way too fun.

"Yes," I reply. "It's perfectly normal. A few lumps are good, actually."

Asher stares at me for a moment.

"You're lying."

I laugh again and shake my head, eyes wide with sincerity.

"And you... like it. You want to eat this?" His gaze darts skeptically between me and the lumpy batter, and I nod my head vigorously.

"I really, really do. Especially once you fold in those chocolate chips and grill it up. Mmmm, I can't wait."

Turns out, lemon chocolate chip pancakes with a raspberry compote, maple syrup, side of slightly burnt turkey bacon, and sparkling apple juice is my all time favorite meal, ever. Especially eaten in front of a roaring fire with the rain pattering lightly outside a cracked open window.

"Moon above, these are so good, I can't stop." I don't contain my moan of appreciation, and I'm pretty sure Asher doesn't mind if the heat in his eyes is any indication. I even convince him to try a couple bites, though he doesn't seem as impressed with his cooking as I am, opting to stick with his bottle of blood instead. I'm thankful I've gotten used to Zuri drinking blood all the time so it doesn't phase me anymore.

"You could open a brunch place. I'd go every day," I say around a bite of crunchy bacon. "I love brunch."

"I know," he murmurs, and I stop chewing to look at him. "That's why I went for breakfast foods. You've mentioned it a couple times."

Gulping down my mouthful, I turn my attention to him.

"That's... really thoughtful," I say. "Thank you."

"Plus, it seemed easier than real food." He lifts one shoulder in a half-hearted shrug like he's trying to play it off as no big deal, but I'm not fooled. This supposedly monstrous vampire is an honest to goodness softie on the inside. I'm ninety percent sure of it at this point.

Patting my food baby, I lean back and find his arm already around me.

"That was seriously so good."

He nuzzles his nose into my hair before kissing my temple.

"I'm glad you liked it, sunshine."

"Asher." I groan as I go to lay down on the couch. "I know you probably wanted to do more than just hang out tonight, but I ate so much. I don't think I can move for a while. I'm sorry."

"If you're apologizing for not wanting to have sex, please don't," he replies, almost seeming offended. "That's not why I invited you over."

"It's not?"

"I mean, I'd never say no to you if you wanted to, but no. I wanted to take care of you, spend time together relaxing, and it seems I've accomplished that goal. The rest of the night can be whatever you want."

"Oh, you definitely did," I say. "I haven't been so stuffed in ages."

"Okay, well..." His eyes have a spark of mischief as he holds in a sly grin. "Maybe take it easy on the innuendos, this poor old man can't handle your teasing."

I snort a laugh, then slap my hand over my mouth because that was possibly the most unattractive noise I've ever made. Also, I can't believe Asher is casually joking around with me. When he grins in delight, I let my laugh ring out again, extending my leg to poke a toe at his biceps.

Asher snatches my foot in response, pulling it onto his lap and digging his strong fingers into my calf muscle with slow circles and deep strokes. I sink back into his couch and close my eyes, reveling in the feel of his hands on me as the warm crackle of the fire lulls me into a peaceful nap.

24

EVERYBODY JUST CHILL

RAYA

AFTER SPENDING a blissful weekend wrapped up in each other, I'm not ready to re-enter the real world on Monday morning. Zuri keeps sending me skeptical looks and treating me to passive aggressive comments about safety and vampires and taking care of myself and "whatever you think is best" or "as long as you're sure" types of remarks.

I am 110% over it.

"Okay, how about I bring him around sometime?" I say with a huff. "That way you can see for yourself that Asher isn't some big, bad, evil vampire lord set on taking advantage of me and slowly sucking me dry or whatever."

Reverie shrieks with glee. "Can you take me shopping? I need to buy a new outfit to meet him! It has to be perfect."

Meanwhile, Zuri begrudgingly mumbles something that sounds as close to agreement as I'm likely to get, so I nod once at them both and grab a muffin, heading out the door for work seventeen minutes early. I opt to wait in line at the local coffee shop around the corner so I can avoid interacting with others for a little longer. I'm already people'ed out and this day has barely even started.

When I slump into the office with what I'm sure is an unconvincing smile plastered on my face, Alex immediately notices.

"What's with you?" they ask, and I shrug.

"Mondays, am I right?" I say, hoping the deflection will get them to leave me alone.

"You got that right," Kendall is the one who grumbles a reply.

I glance at Asher's empty desk as I open my laptop.

"I heard he won't be in this morning, not sure why though," Alex says, apparently noticing my question before I voice it.

I simply nod in reply, figuring that sounds about right. Of course the only good thing in my day wouldn't work out. When it rains, it pours, or whatever.

Feeling a tingle, I close my eyes and focus my breathing. Unfortunately, when I open my eyes, my eyesight has changed. Similarly to how it did on the plane when headed to San Diego, my sight seems to have sharpened with the colors all slightly warped.

I sigh. At least it's not something super obvious. I angle my face down and focus on this email, letting the shift sort itself out.

As I STEP out of the building for my lunch break, a hand snatches my wrist and I shriek as I collide with a hard chest.

"Did you miss me, sunshine?"

The familiar rumble of Asher's voice reaches my ears, and I punch my fist against his pec where both hands have landed.

"Asher, ugh. Don't do that, you scared me," I grumble as I pull away from him.

When I look up, his face morphs into concern and confusion as his eyebrows draw together, the sides of his lips turning down.

"What's wrong?" he asks, voice rough.

I fold my arms tight around myself, hugging my jacket to my chest as I walk down the sidewalk.

"Nothing. Just a stupid Monday," I say, then continue when I hear him following me. "Where were you this morning, anyway?"

"I had something to do."

I huff and quicken my stride.

Typical male response.

Asher catches up and matches my pace, then softly asks if he can walk with me. Glancing up, I see the concern lingering in the tightness of his shoulders.

I shrug.

He walks next to me in silence for a few blocks, and I appreciate the quiet support.

"Do you want to talk about it?" he asks, voice tentative.

I shrug again, and hear him sigh. Placing a gentle hand on my arm, he slows us both to a stop.

"Look, Raya." Asher swipes a hand across the back of his neck. "I'm not good at this. I don't know how to talk about emotions or, I don't know, the real things. Deep things. But I'm trying. I want to give you what you need, I just don't know what that is. Can you tell me?"

My frustration dissipates as his earnestness seeps in.

"I'm sorry. It's me, I don't get angry that often, but when I do." I shake my head. "It's hard to stop. I don't know why."

"If you want to talk about it, we can. Or we don't have to. We can keep walking."

I turn to keep walking, but then stop and hold out my hand in a peace offering. The stress visibly falls from his body as his hand envelopes mine and he tucks them both into his jacket pocket for warmth. We walk in silence for a couple more minutes until I feel ready to talk.

"Zuri is giving me a hard time," I say, "about us."

"What about us?" His voice is careful, neutral.

"She doesn't like your family, which means she doesn't like or trust you, and she doesn't want me around you." I peek up at him, but his face is set in an unreadable mask.

"You've mentioned her before, I'm assuming she comes from a progressive family."

I nod, and he silently returns it.

"I know you don't want to talk about them, but…" I trail off, and he sighs.

"They're not good people. Zuri is right, but I'm not like them, Raya."

I nod again, silent as I wait to see if he'll say more.

He doesn't.

"I was thinking maybe you could come over sometime." My heart starts to pound, and I realize this is a bigger deal to me than I anticipated. "I'm certain once she gets to know you, she won't think that anymore."

Asher immediately agrees. "Of course, Raya. Anything. I don't want to be the reason you and your friend aren't getting along."

"Okay. Maybe in a week or two. Are you still down for dinner at my parents on Thursday? It's okay if you want a break from everything, I know this is a lot to put on you all at once," I say, my eyes on my feet as we walk back toward the office building.

He stops again and ducks his head to meet my gaze.

"Sunshine, listen to me. You are not too much. Your family is not too much. Your friends are not too much. I want to meet all of them, and if I didn't, I would tell you. Okay?"

I blink as my eyes turn glassy, unable to turn away.

"Okay," I whisper.

A FEW DAYS LATER, my week having much improved, Asher drives us over to my parents' house for dinner. I'm pretty sure I'm more nervous than he is based on how my skin keeps tingling in random places. I can't stop bouncing my leg, while he's all calm control with one hand propped on top of the steering wheel as he drives.

The front door opens as we pull into the driveway so I don't even have time for a quick pep talk before we head inside. My smiling mother gives us both hugs as I introduce them, and the men do that man handshake back slap thing that guys do.

We shrug off our coats and my dad starts right in.

"So, I hear you work with my daughter."

"Dad, come on, we haven't even taken our shoes off yet." I protest the interrogation that's about to start.

"I'm only making small talk, honey," he says, squeezing me in a one armed hug.

I shake my head and grab Asher's hand.

"Come on. I'll show you around."

I pull him into the living room, where Wesley is playing video games, as usual.

"Wes, this is Asher."

"Hey, man," my brother at least meets his eyes and gives him one of those dude bro chin jerks as he says it. That's more than I normally get.

"Hey, nice to meet you," Asher replies.

"You too." He's already turned back to his game, so we move on.

"Kitchen is through here." We follow the sounds of soft jazz into the brightly lit room.

"Jo!" I stop in the doorway, beyond surprised to see my sister. "Why are you here on a work night?"

She's already pulling me into a hug, and her voice is low in my ear, though not quiet enough that Asher doesn't hear too.

"I couldn't miss a chance to scope out the new guy," she says, eyeing him as we pull back from each other.

She holds out a hand to Asher and he meets her with a twinkle of amusement in his eye.

"Jo. Raya's older sister," she says. Then, narrowing her eyes with her hand still white knuckling Asher's, she adds, "Panther shifter."

He nods once, holding her gaze.

"Asher. Vampire."

Their hands finally unclasp and I shake mine out in sympathy. Too many over protective cats in this house, that's for sure. I snag Asher's elbow as I turn out the door.

"That's enough of that," I say, throwing a glare over my shoulder at Josephine, who smirks at my back. I point up the stairs to the bedrooms, then point out the bathroom, home office, laundry, and back patio.

"Nice place." Asher comments as we walk back into the kitchen and my dad looks up from the stove.

"Can I help you cook, Mr. Merritt?" Asher asks.

My stomach flutters and I bite my lip at how cute he is, especially since I know he has next to no clue how to cook.

"You cook?" my dad asks with obvious surprise while waving him over.

"Not at all," Asher replies with a wince, "but I'd love to learn. You mind teaching me?"

"Let's see what you've got." Dad slaps him on the back and hands him a knife. "We're making fajitas. Slice the bell peppers into half inch strips. You know how to sauté veggies?"

"Honestly? I have no idea what you just said." Asher grins sheepishly as my father lets out a deep belly laugh.

"You're not half bad, are you, son?"

I sit at the table as I watch them work together, a smile

stuck on my face. My stocky dad is a good head shorter than Asher, but he's clearly the one in charge as he shows Asher what to do and watches closely as he follows directions.

I jump in my seat when Jo plops onto the chair next me.

"Stars, Josephine. You need to chill," I say, hand on my chest.

"Uh, I was not being stealthy. You're just so lovesick you have no idea what else is happening around you."

Is that true? It very well could be. Regardless, the dopey-feeling smile is already back on my face at the thought of how well things are going so far. Jo watches me for a few moments until I self-consciously smooth my hair behind my ear and tuck my lips into my teeth.

"What?" I say.

"You really like this guy, don't you?" Jo asks after another moment of staring straight into my soul, her voice thoughtful.

My eyes drift across the kitchen again, watching Ash's muscles ripple when he attempts to flip the veggies and chicken in the pan like my dad does.

"I think I really do," I say.

When we settle around the table to eat, I nudge my knee up against Asher's, seeking contact. He nudges mine in return, and a couple minutes later places his hand on my leg under the table. Soon enough, as I knew it would, the conversation turns to us.

25

ANSWERS LEADING TO MORE QUESTIONS IS THE WORST

RAYA

"So TELL us about your family, Asher," Mom says, eyebrows politely lifted as she steps directly into the pile of shit I had been most hoping to avoid. My face pales, and Jo notices immediately, eyes shifting between the two of us as I clench my hand onto his.

He clears his throat and takes a sip of water before answering.

"Truthfully, I'd rather not talk about them," he says. His voice is slow and careful as he attempts to navigate a topic full of landmines. "We don't exactly see eye to eye."

It's clear no one in my family likes this answer, and my sister has no qualms about poking the beast.

"Why not?" she demands.

Asher clears his throat, and I interrupt.

"Jo, don't." I turn to Asher, "You don't have to talk about them if you don't want to."

"Are they dangerous?" my dad asks, and when I avert my eyes, Jo pounces.

"Oh, we most definitely do need to talk about this."

My eyes dart to each member of my family, noticing how

even Wesley has stopped eating to eye Asher. I open my mouth again, ready to deflect, but Asher squeezes my knee. A blank wall coming down over his eyes gives him a look of resolved detachment.

"I was born Asher Walton, son of Claude and Estelle Walton," he says, and my sister's fork slams to her plate while my mother's knuckles turn white around hers. He nods and rolls his lips between his teeth before continuing. "I see you've heard of them. I changed my last name to Sullivan when I moved out at eighteen, and did everything I could to cut myself off from them. I don't agree with their way of life."

"And they let you go?" Mom asks, suspicion coloring her tone.

Asher drops his eyes from hers.

"Not exactly. They're still trying to convince me to rejoin the family. Or at least, I assume they are. Anytime they find a new way to contact me, I delete without reading it. They have been reaching out more lately, but nothing has come of it."

"How will you ensure that our Raya stays safe?" my dad asks. He puts a hand on Josephine's arm when she clenches her fists on the table.

"Her safety is my top priority, followed closely by her happiness. I would never put Raya in danger. I haven't seen my family in years, and if I thought for even a moment that they'd harm her because of me, I'd end them." His voice is laced with steel, his eyes are cold and hard on my dad's, and the rigid line of his body demonstrates exactly how serious he is.

My dad nods once, slowly, letting the silence stretch with his eyes locked onto Asher's, then nods again at whatever he sees in Asher's gaze. He leans back in his chair, and the release of tension ripples around the table as everyone relaxes. Jo remains suspicious, but Wesley returns to his food. I exhale a sigh of relief as tingles rush down my arms, trailing light grey fur in their wake.

"Raya?" my mom's hawklike attention is on me now. "I thought you had your shifting under control, dear."

"I mean," I gulp, "I do, mostly. It's just every so often it gets the better of me still." My face heats with embarrassment and shame.

Asher leans in, his hand on my thigh again and his lips close to my ear so my family can't overhear, even with their enhanced shifter hearing.

"Deep breaths, sunshine. You've got this," he says, and I lock my eyes onto his as I take a steadying breath. Then another.

With a slow exhale, the fur pulls back into my skin and I look back to the table to see my parents both with slight smiles on their faces, my mom nodding in approval. My sister is indecipherable at this moment, whereas my brother looks downright confounded.

"What type of shifter even are you? Are you adopted?" He turns to our parents. "Is Raya adopted?"

"Stars above, Wesley. What is wrong with you?" Josephine explodes at him, and I sit back in my seat, astonished. That never occurred to me, but before it can even settle into my thoughts, Dad is already shaking his head.

"No, she's not adopted," he says. "She's special."

Special, when all I've wanted was to be normal, to fit in, to belong. I hoped that by gaining my ability to shift, I'd finally be accepted, but if my brother's reaction is anything to go by, that isn't any more likely to happen now than it was before. Now, instead of being the shifter freak who can't shift, I'm the shifter freak who shifts too much.

My parents exchange a significant look.

"What is it? What's that look?" I say, voice urgent.

When they don't answer, my sister pipes up.

"Well? We all know you're hiding something now, so you might as well come clean."

My dad folds his hands on the table and looks down at them as my mom shakes her head, then takes a deep breath and straightens her spine.

"Are you sure you want to do this now?" Mom asks, eyes going to Asher sitting next to me.

"Yes," I say, taking his hand in mine, not caring if he overhears my business. I've wanted answers my whole life, and I'm not about to wait any longer if they're finally within my grasp.

"We don't know anything for sure. All we have are guesses," she says, and I lean forward.

"You were born on the summer solstice, Raya," Dad says. "Not only that, but it was also at the height of the new moon."

"Ooookay. So what?" Jo voices my exact thoughts.

"We looked into it once you started shifting," he continues, "and not only was it the day of the solstice and new moon, but somehow you were born at the exact height of both events, while they were in eclipse."

"Wait, what?" This time it's my brother who voices my thoughts.

"We checked your official time of birth, then looked into the astronomical records of both events. It's well documented that shifters respond to the moon and other celestial anomalies in unique ways. I thought I remembered there was an eclipse that day, and I was right. When you started shifting after your birthday last year... Well, we were trying to find any explanation we could, and this is where it led. We don't know what it means, but it does seem significant."

"Okay, but..." I trail off. "Sorry, what? I mean, solstice and new moon, eclipse. Sure. But what does the "height of events" or whatever mean?"

Mom takes another slow breath before beginning again.

"Alright. You've all heard of the summer solstice." As her eyes circle the table to see everyone nodding, she continues.

"We normally consider it to be a full day, but in reality, it's a moment. In the summer, it is the moment in which our specific location on Earth is most tilted toward the sun, recorded down to the minute. The exact minute you were born, Raya, was on the summer solstice for our location that year."

My skin starts to pebble and the hair on my arms stands on end. That's a wild coincidence already, and my parents aren't done yet.

"When we checked further, it turns out the new moon was at its zenith at that exact moment in time too, creating a perfect eclipse. We all know the moon is essential to shifters; we respond to its call no matter our animal, and celestial events have always been important to our kind. It makes sense that this could be why your animal is different."

"Does that mean there could be others like her?" Jo asks.

Dad nods slowly, his eyes full of concern as he takes in my baffled expression.

"We think so. We found a few historical records of shifters with otherwise unheard of abilities—invisibility, partial shifting, communicating with animals—but not much information is out there. They also seem to be linked to astronomical events, but just as we haven't gone around proclaiming your struggles, it's doubtful others would either."

I can't do more than blink. This is impossible. For a shifter, out of everyone on earth, to be born, down to the minute, during an eclipse on the solstice... what are the chances? I can't even fathom doing that math, but the probability must be astronomically low.

I snort, and everyone's eyes lock onto me in astonishment.

"Sorry, bad pun," I say, pointing to my temple. "In my head."

Even Wesley looks concerned for my mental welfare now.

I stare at my reflection in the window across from me. I

have no idea what any of this truly means, or what additional impacts there could be, or if there's anything to be done about any of it at all. Everything is still up in the air, and while I have some possible answers, I also have more unknowns.

Fantastic.

Asher's hand squeezes mine, bringing me back to reality. I blink my eyes to refocus, noting the increased concern on everyone's faces as they stare at me.

"Okay, well," I say, then stop when I don't know what else to say.

My sister swoops in, coming to my rescue as usual. "That's enough of that, I think. Let's give Raya some time to let it all sink in. Dessert, anyone?"

I offer a shaky smile, hoping it's enough to reassure them for now.

WHILE ASHER DRIVES ME HOME, my reflection stares back at me from the window. Average brown eyes, blonde hair in relaxed waves, no outward signs to hint at the confusing information that has rocked the foundation of who I am. It seems like there should be something to show how unmoored, how detached I feel. I'm unsure who I am or what any of this weird phenomena means about me.

When we pull up to my building, my body is on a slight delay. I open my car door after Asher has already closed his and is rounding to my side of the vehicle. It takes me an extra moment to remember to move my body to step out of the car.

I wait as Asher punches in my code to open the door, grateful he remembers it because I'm pretty sure I wouldn't be able to. His hand is light on my lower back as he guides me inside, waiting for the elevator to take us up to my floor.

As the doors close in slow motion, I turn my body toward

Asher. His lips are moving, and sound trickles into my ears like it's coming through a long tunnel.

"Raya?" he says, and I notice the deep lines etched around his eyes and mouth. "Raya, sunshine. Can you hear me?"

I nod, and my head feels a little less muddled, but still slow.

Am I nodding correctly?

"Are you okay?"

"Mm'kay," I mumble. My lips don't want to move properly.

"Shit." His curse is low, and I'm pretty sure it's not aimed at me, but I try to frown anyway. I feel my head tilt as I contemplate it.

"Where's your key?" he asks, and I fumble with my purse, but manage to pull my keys out. The world is starting to come back to me now, as we walk slowly down the hall toward my apartment.

"I'm okay," I say, partly to Asher, but also in an attempt to convince myself. I can feel my feet hitting the ground and time speeds up in a rush, coming back to me all at once and bringing me to a sudden halt.

"That was weird. So weird. I felt, I don't know, fuzzy all over inside my head. I think it was shock or something."

Asher's hand hasn't left my body, whether supporting my arm or back or holding my hand, he's not left my side for a single moment. We step up to my door and he looks down at me, then speaks softly.

"I know your roommate doesn't like me, but can I come in and make sure you're okay? I won't stay if you don't want me to."

I'm already shaking my head. That's a terrible idea, and not only because Zuri would probably accuse him of drugging me or something, but because Reverie will be there too. I have to warn him first, make sure he'll keep our secret before I trust him with such precious information.

"No, I don't think that's a good idea. Zuri should be home, she'll make sure I'm okay," I say, cringing at the hurt that flashes through his eyes.

His lips thin, but he doesn't push the issue.

"Text me when you're in bed?" he asks.

I raise my eyebrows and his ears turn pink. It's adorable, I love it when I manage to needle him a bit.

"That's, no." Asher rakes a hand through his hair and I giggle. "That's not what I meant. Just so I can make sure you're okay. That's all."

"I know." I grin up at him so he knows I'm not mad, then sigh as he gathers me into a hug against his chest.

"You sure you're okay?"

"I'm sure. Thank you for taking care of me. I'm glad you were there for all of that tonight," I say, and his body softens at the vulnerability in my voice.

"I'll always be here for you, sunshine. Always," he says.

Unlocking the door, I turn back to him one last time as I step inside.

"See you tomorrow."

26

NEEDY, NOSY VAMPIRE

ASHER

I HAVE my head bowed with both hands resting on the smooth doorframe as I stand outside Raya's apartment door, trying my best not to press my ear to it as I listen to her walk inside and hang her keys while her shoes hit the floor. Raya said she was fine, but something was definitely off on the way up to her apartment, and I'm worried something bad will happen as soon as I leave.

Which is ridiculous. What could possibly happen inside her own apartment? I'm being irrational, but I feel compelled to protect her.

Shaking my head at myself, I drop my hands and step away from the door right as I hear voices inside. Raya's is easy to identify, but the other is high pitched, almost like a child's voice. My body stills and I angle my head toward the door.

Does she have a kid?

No way. She would have told me, and she'd have called or video chatted with them during the trip, which I definitely would have noticed. Right?

"Rev, please. You are so nosy! I'll tell you everything tomorrow, okay? I need some peace for now."

Raya's voice goes in and out as she walks around inside, close enough to the entrance for me to make out most of what she's saying if I strain to listen. Her tone of voice and the way she's talking certainly don't sound like how most people talk to children.

"If you don't cut that out, I'm locking you out of my room tonight and you'll have to sleep with the living room plants instead." Raya's voice is muffled through the door, decreasing in volume as she walks deeper into the apartment and I hear an answering, high pitched shriek in response.

My eyebrows furrow as my lips turn down. *Sleep with the plants?*

Shaking my head again, this time in an attempt to clear it, I walk away, assuming I must have misheard because that conversation made absolutely no sense, no matter how I look at it.

RAYA IS busy most of the weekend with family, chores, "girls day" and other adult things that I should probably be doing too, but I don't because all I can think about is her. It's a bit much, if I'm being honest with myself. I've never fallen this hard or fast before, let alone felt so obsessed, and it's bewildering.

The only positive is that she doesn't seem to mind me texting her all the time. I've never had to charge my phone daily before, and it's a new routine I'm still getting used to since I'm using it all the time now.

> Me: Morning, sunshine. How are you feeling after last night?

> Raya: Eh. So so. Mostly okay but still a bit overwhelmed I guess. 🖐

Me: It's definitely a lot to take in.

Me: What about physically?

Raya: Physically? Fine... Why?

Me: You seemed a little off last night so I wanted to make sure.

Raya: Oh, yeah. Idk I think I was in shock or something? I feel a lot better today and I think a cozy girls day in will help too.

Me: Glad to hear it.

When lunch rolls around, I order food to be sent to her apartment. I debate what to get, not having paid much attention to human restaurants over the years. I'm not sure how many friends she has over or what they all like, but I've heard good things about pizza so I figure it's a safe bet. I send two large pizzas, one meat lovers (whatever that means) and one veggie, with a side of breadsticks, and hope that's enough.

I pace the apartment, ignoring Milton's judgmental stare as I wait to hear from her when I see it's out for delivery. Finally, ten years later, my phone buzzes.

Raya: Did you send us pizza?!

Me: Didn't want you going hungry. I hope the toppings are okay, wasn't sure how much or what to send.

Raya: This is way too much for a roomies hang haha we're going to have leftovers all week!

> Raya: OMG it's so good tho. Thank you, this definitely makes my day so much better

> Me: Good.

> Raya: 🤍

I frown at my phone. I could have sworn she mentioned having "a day in with the girls" in the plural, and the way she talked had made it seem like there would be more than only her and Zuri there. Her text definitely says roomies though, and I don't think she has more than one, so I must have misunderstood. Maybe Zuri has a kid? My mind drifts back to the mystery voice, but I shrug it off. I'll ask her about it later.

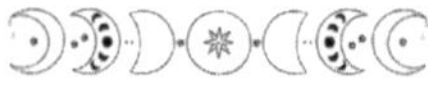

THE NEXT DAY starts the same as the last. I putter around my apartment, opening empty cupboards for no reason and imagining what they might look like if they were stocked with food for Raya.

Milton picks up on my restlessness, and he's not pleased about it. Every time I pace by him, he swipes at my ankles with his claws, then darts to a new spot from which to glare in my direction. When I start rapping my knuckles on the counter, he straight up hisses at me.

I can't blame him. I'd be irritated with me too. Scratch that, I *am* irritated with me.

I dig out a catnip toy, then toss it into the other room to keep him entertained—and so he stops yelling at me every time I disturb his peace. I puff a breath out and contemplate a run at Forest Park, but my body protests the idea of being that far away from Raya.

Ridiculous.

I stomp into the living room and turn on the TV, then zone out and don't watch it.

I attempt to play a game on my phone, but the screen times out and turns black. Four times.

I go for a walk and find myself hoping to run into her at every corner. So I force myself to turn around and walk home before I end up trying to walk all the way to her place.

I finally give up and pull out my phone again. I type "I miss you, what are you up to?" and then delete it, because that sounds pathetic. I talked to her yesterday, saw her two days ago, and will see her again tomorrow. Tapping my phone against my chin, I wrack my brain to come up with another option, something less pitiful, but that will also satisfy my craving for her.

Before anything brilliant comes to me, my phone lights up and buzzes in my hand. I fumble it in my excitement to answer, not even checking the screen first because my obsessive brain assumes it's Raya.

"Hi," I say, immediately cringing at the low, breathy need in my voice.

"Hey, cuz," the slimy voice of my cousin slithers into my ear, and I recoil in disgust. I stare at my phone screen, struggling to register the fact that not only did Raya *not* call me, but for the first time in years I'm talking to a member of my family.

On accident, but still.

"Didn't expect you to pick up," Chadwick says, and I can still hear his awful drawl even though the phone isn't pressed to my ear anymore.

I stab the red "end call" button, my heart in my throat.

Not two seconds later, it starts ringing again. I hit the red button to decline the call, then shove it across the counter away from me. I start pacing again, my head so jumbled after hearing his voice that I can't even think straight.

Why would he call me?

Normally Chadwick sends a gloating text or picture, or a link to an article praising his business acumen and the massive amounts of money he's made. I'm never impressed, but it is annoying to see how successful he is.

My phone lights up with a notification. He left a voicemail.

I stare at it across the counter until it goes dark again, then resume my pacing. I fist my hands in my hair and tug until I feel a sting on my scalp, wishing I could get away from them once and for all. Every time I'm reminded of my cousin, my mom or dad, it triggers the memories.

Memories of being blood-starved because I refused to drink from unwilling victims, and my parents locking me up. Not being allowed off the property to feed from other sources, and ultimately not being strong enough to resist. Memories of ripping into those victims when the hunger became too much. The deep red haze that would take over my vision and encroach on my mind when I couldn't hold the hunger at bay anymore, when I became desperate and deranged, out of my mind with starvation and blood-lust.

The dry husks that I'd leave in my wake.

I always vomited when I came to and was faced with the reality of what I did. I was never strong enough to resist; there was always a point where I caved to my inner vampire, unable to stop the instinctual urge to feed, even though I would have rather died myself than take from an unwilling victim. Especially because I was starved to the point of losing control, so they rarely survived.

The phone lights up again with a reminder that I have a new voicemail, and it snaps me out of the dark spiral I've fallen into. When I reach across the counter to grab it, my hand is shaking.

I open my phone and press the play button, deciding I'm already in a terrible place mentally, so I might as well see what the bastard has to say. Still, I cringe when I hear his laughter.

"Hahaha, ohhhh Asher, Asher, Asher. I was so looking forward to having a little chat with you! No matter, but I wanted to make sure you knew—you made a mistake trying to leave this family. We're making big moves, your parents and I, and everything I've been working toward is about to fall into place. Thought you might want to know, but I guess not. See you soon, baby cousin."

I slam my phone down so hard the screen cracks, a single diagonal bolt from one corner to the opposite side. I don't care. Chadwick has always had it out for me, wanting my place as heir to the family empire, and for all I care, he can have it.

This sounds different, though. This sounds like he's planning something, and the fact he said he'll see me soon...

My blood runs cold. I can't go back to them. I can't get stuck on that estate again, being forced to live like an animal, being tortured and torturing others in turn. I can't, I won't, but I don't know how to prevent them from getting to me if I don't know what's coming.

27

─────────

NOT ALL SUNSHINE AND RAINBOWS
RAYA

"So, I was thinking..." Asher glances at me during our lunch break walk later that week, and I raise my eyebrows for him to continue. "Well, you mentioned wanting me to meet your roommate. We could do that tonight, maybe? Or this weekend?"

I stumble, unsure if I'm tripping over my own two feet. That is certainly not what I expected him to say. It's been a pretty chill week, though Asher has been a little distant at times. While I can acknowledge it's probably a good idea, my brain rebels at the same time. There are so many factors to consider; what will we all do, where would be best, do I include Reverie, and if so, that brings up a whole slew of other concerns.

"Raya? We don't have to, I'm in no rush. But I know it's been weighing on you, her not liking me."

I shake the thoughts away at the concern in his voice.

"Yeah, you're right. It's a good idea, it just took me off guard."

I'm quiet for a bit as I think it over, and he runs a hand along my back in silent support. Before I can make a decision, we loop around the block and are already heading back toward the office building.

"Okay." I nod decisively. "Let's do it. You can come over Saturday. I'll talk to Zuri tonight, give her a heads up. Maybe we do a game day or something, that way it's more light-hearted and chill."

"Makes sense."

"Okay, great. Cool. Perfect. So good. No worries at all."

"Raya?"

"Mhm?" I look up at him with wide, innocent eyes.

"Talk to me, sunshine. What's going on in that brain of yours?"

"Oh, no. Nothing. Well, I mean."

I snap my mouth closed and take a deep breath through my nose, then glance around to ensure there isn't anyone nearby. I tug Asher into an alcove to give us a little extra privacy.

"Okay. But... there's something you need to know first," I say, glancing up at him as I twist my fingers together. He squeezes one of my hands in his to still the nervous movement.

"And what's that?"

"I'll tell you, but first you have to promise you won't tell anyone."

"Okay, promise."

"No, Asher. I mean it." I meet his gaze and hold it, steeling my spine. "You can't breathe a single word to anyone. Not your friends, not your family, literally no one. Swear it."

His eyebrows draw together as his eyes ping between mine.

"I swear it. I don't have anything sacred to swear by, so I swear it on you, Raya. My sunshine, I promise I won't disclose your secrets to anyone."

My cheeks pink at the notion that I'm the most important thing in his world right now, but I don't let myself get side-tracked. His eyes are clear and serious, with no hint of deception, so I take the leap and decide to trust him with my biggest secret.

"Technically, I live with two others. Zuri, as you know, is a vampire."

Asher slowly nods once, his eyes not leaving mine.

"The other... is a sprite."

Silence. I could hear a pin drop, but as it is all I hear is my heart pounding. Finally, Asher replies.

"A sprite? Raya, those have been extinct for... I don't even know how long."

I slowly shake my head, still holding his gaze so he knows I'm serious.

"Not all of them. There's at least one, and her name is Reverie. She lives with us, and we take care of her. We keep her safe and secret from the world, to avoid putting her in danger."

He stares at me. His face is blank and he doesn't react, not one single muscle twitch.

"Ash?" I lightly touch his cheek with my fingertips.

"Is this supposed to be some kind of joke?"

I pinch my lips together. This is not going well. I reach up with both hands to cup his face, brushing my thumbs along the stubble of his jaw before I pull him down until he's eye level with me. I ensure my voice is strong, quiet, calm, and clear as I speak.

"Hear me, Asher. She's real. She's alive. And she's mine to protect. By sharing this secret with you, she's becoming yours to protect, too. Please don't tell me I've put my trust in the wrong person."

My eyes flit back and forth between his, and I watch as the realization dawns on him, his face transforming. His lips part, but no sound comes out, and his eyebrows can't seem to decide if they want to furrow or chase his hairline. Blinking rapidly, he pulls out of my grasp and turns around, shoving his hands into his hair. Asher takes two steps away before spinning around to face me again.

"You're serious."

"I'm serious."

He turns away again and bends over, resting his hands on his knees as he stares across the street. I chew on my cheek as I wait for him to come to terms with this information. It's unbelievable; I know it is, and if I were in his shoes I probably wouldn't believe it either.

Finally, Asher swipes a hand down his face and turns back to me.

"I won't tell a soul," he says.

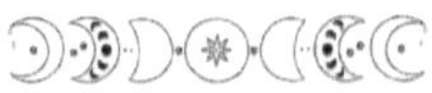

ZURI IS LESS than thrilled when I broach the subject that evening.

"You want him to come here." Her voice is flat as she stares at me in disbelief. "Where Reverie lives. In secret."

"I..." I cringe. "I kind of already told him about her."

"Uh, hello? I'm right here! And I think that's great, I want to meet him!" Rev doesn't have as many qualms about this as Zuri, as I expected. I probably should have checked with her first, though.

Zuri throws a glare at the excited sprite. "I know you're here. That's the whole problem."

"Wh-what?" Reverie's eyes fill with tears and she flies a few inches back at the verbal strike.

"Zuri." My voice is harsh with ire, and wolf claws snap out of my fingertips.

Zuri throws her hands in the air. "That's not what I meant and you know it!"

Reverie has already zipped out of the room and is likely hiding under a blanket in her little jungle in my room. I pinch my lips as I shake my head at my roommate. She has a temper, and she means well, but it often comes out wrong.

"You can't say things like that," I drop the words in a low voice over my shoulder as I stalk out of the kitchen, heading to my bedroom to find my childhood best friend.

Reverie and I grew up together, ever since we found each other one day when my family was camping in Olympic National Park. I was five years old at the time, and Reverie appeared only a couple years older than me. It's unclear where she came from or how she came to be, though. She has vague memories of living in the forest alone before I stumbled across her. I had wandered away from the campsite and was following a trail of moss. I remember it being incredibly soft, and it led me to a hollowed out tree with glowing flowers, which is where Reverie had been living. Her bright sapphire eyes peeked out and as soon as we made eye contact, it's like our souls clicked together.

Best friends, immediately.

It was meant to be, and neither of us could stand the thought of leaving the other.

Naturally, I hid her in my backpack and took her home with me. As children ourselves, neither of us knew she was such a rare creature, that all of her kind was thought to have died out, but we did know my parents wouldn't want another person staying with us. We figured she had to stay a secret, or my mom would say no, that she couldn't come home with me.

So I snuck her in. She stayed in my room, and we would hide under my blanket at night, playing make believe and whispering for hours until we both fell asleep. She craved nature, so I would pick pretty flowers and leaves from outside and bring them to her, and she'd weave them into my hair or create little fairy gardens under my bed.

My parents caught on after a few weeks when they noticed me sneaking food and plants up to my room. They couldn't believe it when they saw a real life sprite, and neither of us understood the significance of it at the time. We were simply overjoyed that my parents agreed to let her stay, and from that moment on, we became inseparable. The only time we were apart in the years following was when I had to go to school, but then I'd come straight home and teach Reverie everything I had learned that day, and so we grew up together.

Me, a broken shifter with no friends.

Rev, the last of her kind, who didn't know anything about what she was.

We're everything to each other, and our bond is unbreakable. Which means when she's hurt, it breaks my heart.

I find Reverie exactly where I expected to, hiding under a massive leaf in her indoor jungle with a blanket wrapped tight around her.

"Hey, Rev," I say softly, crouching down outside the ring of plants. "Can I pick you up?"

She sniffles, wipes her nose, then nods.

I scoop her up, blanket and all, and lay down on my bed with her.

Reverie tugs her blanket closer and peeks watery blue eyes up at me.

"She didn't mean it, love," I whisper, and Rev nods.

"I know, but still." She swipes a hand under her eyes.

"Yeah. Still hurts," I say. "I'm sorry. And I'm sorry I didn't talk to you about meeting Ash before telling him about you."

Reverie tucks herself in closer and I carefully curl around her, pulling my blanket up over both of us and hiding us away from the world, like when we were little.

When Zuri knocks on the door later, I look to Reverie to decide if she's ready to face her or not. Reverie scrunches her lips, then nods. I pull the blanket down and allow us both a moment to compose ourselves a little, then tell Zuri she can come in.

She cracks the door and peeks an eye through, seeing us cuddled on the bed together. When I wave her in, she opens the door further and steps through. Her eyes are red and puffy, and my heart hurts for them both.

"I'm so sorry, Rev," Zuri says, her voice cracking. "That came out so, so wrong. I love you, I didn't mean to hurt you and I didn't mean what I said."

"I know," Reverie whispers, but doesn't move from her spot.

"Can I lay with you?" Zuri is crouched by the bed, and Reverie nods, so she gently drapes herself on the side opposite me. Not touching either of us, but still close enough that we can all take comfort in each other.

"I hate being small. I hate being unseen, treated like I don't matter, that I can't have friends," Reverie whispers. My heart cracks again.

"I can't believe I did that. Reverie, I'm so sorry. I wish I could take it back. Can I explain what I meant? Because what I said..." she shakes her head, "it was all wrong."

"Okay."

"I meant that he shouldn't come here because it wouldn't be safe for you. I care about you so much, the problem isn't you, it's him. I don't trust that family, and having both of you here is dangerous. You are perfect, you belong here, with us, but I'm not willing to put your safety at risk like that," Zuri says, her voice strained.

Reverie and I are both quiet after she finishes speaking, and I wait for Rev to decide if she wants to say something for herself before I do.

"That's not your decision to make," Reverie replies, her voice small but mighty.

Zuri draws back, and I worry she'll get defensive again, but then she slumps against the bed.

"It's not. You're right." She pinches her lips as she stares up at the ceiling.

"I trust him, Z. He's not like his family, and I know you don't trust him, but do you trust me? I would never, *never* put Reverie at risk. I think you know that," I say.

She nods, her eyes glassy. "I do, Raya. I do know that. It's just hard, I've hated him and his family my whole life. It's hard to set that aside."

"I get that, but please. You have to try," I say.

Reverie reaches out and snags a lock of Zuri's hair, stroking it, and Zuri turns her head to look at us.

"I will. I'll do better, I promise," she says.

28

THERE'S MORE?

RAYA

I DECIDE to give Zuri some space to come to terms with our arrangement, so Asher and I go for a quick hike at one of my favorite local trails this morning. It gives me some extra time to think things over, and I decide low key card games are probably the safest route for our 'get to know and hope the vampires don't kill each other' game day.

I text Zuri a two hour heads up when we get back to the car, having already planned to shower back at Asher's place. I've still got my head in the clouds, thinking through plans and backup scenarios, when we walk through his front door and he tugs me toward the bathroom.

"What—" I start to question what he's doing when his lips cut me off.

His soft lips are warm on mine, and he pulls me against him. I instantly melt into his embrace, parting my lips when his tongue brushes over them, and letting out a soft whimper when his hand squeezes my backside.

"Your ass in those leggings. Were you trying to murder me with that hike, little shifter? Because you nearly succeeded."

He groans out the words, still kissing me in between speaking them.

I don't have the mental capacity to answer, though some part of me preens smugly at the compliment because yes, I did pick these specific leggings because of how they accentuate my curves.

His strong hands grip under my thighs and he lifts me onto the bathroom counter, stepping between my legs and parting them further as he continues to devour my mouth with his. I fist my hands in his shirt when leans us both to the side, lips not leaving mine as he turns the shower on, then his hands return to me.

Asher cups my jaw, tilting my face with his thumb under my chin, then sliding his fingers to tangle in my hair as he pulls my head back and angles me the way he wants. Tingles start shooting up and down my spine, and I focus on the cool counter beneath me for a moment to hold back the shift.

When Asher's mouth moves down my neck, my pulse jumps under his lips and he nips at it with a tortured groan, then pulls away. His breathing is heavy, chest rising and falling inches in front of me, fangs on full display. My breath catches at the sight and my heart skips a beat; his eyes fall to my pulse point before he wrenches them away and focuses on my clothing instead.

"Up," he demands, pulling my shirt and sports bra off before yanking his own shirt over his head with one hand.

The other pulls me off the counter and before I know it, he's sucked my nipple into his mouth while his hands roll the leggings down my legs until I clumsily slip my feet out. Ash's fangs graze my hardened nipple as he lets go of one and switches to the other, and I gulp in lungfuls of air, certain I'm the one in danger of perishing now.

"Off," I demand in return, pulling at his zippered pants and tugging them down his thighs.

He kicks them off and we both strip away our underwear as we stumble into the shower and he clicks the glass door closed behind him. The water is already steaming hot, and I groan at how good it feels on my tired muscles.

Asher picks me up again and I automatically wrap my legs around his waist, feeling his thick cock between us as he pushes my back against the wall.

I gasp at the shock of cold, but quickly forget about it when his hands start roaming my body. He tweaks my nipples and massages my breasts, sucking a mark into my skin above one before trailing his fangs across my neck and shoulders, leaving faint pink streaks in their wake and raising goosebumps across my entire body.

My hands roam too. I want to touch every part of him, so I do. I trace the lines of his abs, then flatten my hands over his hard pecs, trailing water across his shoulders to where I squeeze his glistening biceps. My hands don't even make it halfway around and he flexes for me, showing off.

I love it. My eyes flare and dart up to his, and he does it again with a smirk. I lick my lips before leaning forward and tracing my tongue over his rounded shoulder muscles and up his neck to his ear.

"Stop teasing me," I whisper, then nip at his earlobe. "I want you inside me."

His body shudders against mine. His hands tighten, one on my ass and one fisted in my hair, and I know I almost have him. I spot a condom packet on the shower ledge over his shoulder, and I'm beyond thankful for his optimism when planning ahead. He must have been hoping this would happen, just as I was.

I snag it and rip it open, then reach between us to roll it on his hard length. I squeeze the base of his cock before running my hands back up his muscular body, my fingers teasingly light as I lean into his ear again.

"Fuck me, Ash" I say, and he loses it.

His pupils blow wide and he pulls back just enough to line himself up with my pussy before thrusting forward and filling me in one brutal stroke. I cry out and my head jerks back, his hand in my hair the only thing protecting me from smashing it against the tiled wall. My entire body tightens and strains to accommodate him, and he grunts as he pulls out an inch, then thrusts forward again.

Somehow, it feels like he goes deeper this time.

"Almost there, little shifter," he groans into my ear, and my eyes widen.

"There's more?" My voice is breathy and incredulous; I knew he was big, but I didn't expect it to feel like *this.*

The chuckle he releases is dark, almost sinister, and I'm again reminded of the predator he keeps locked inside.

"Yes, there's more, but you can take it."

"I—"

Whatever words I was going to say are knocked right out of me as he thrusts a third time, this time burying himself entirely, his balls slapping against me as our hips meet. I'm also pretty sure I can feel him in my throat, he's filling me so deep, and I choke as I try to breathe.

"Eyes on me," he growls, and although I don't recall closing them, my eyes pop open to see him staring down at me. His eyes are fathomless, a dark blue full of heat and longing and possessive attention. It lights a corresponding fire in me, and I grind my hips against him, digging my nails into his back in an attempt to get him to move again.

He does, and it is fiery bliss. Asher works my body like he knows it better than I do, and before I fully grasp what's happening, I'm cresting the edge of an orgasm that might ruin me for all others.

"Give it to me, Raya." He grits the words out between his teeth, jaw clenched as he roughly drives into me, my back scraping against the tile. His hands clench my hips, holding me exactly where he wants as he drags the orgasm out of me.

"Come for me, little shifter."

The rasp of need in his voice sets me off. I come hard and long, pulsing around him as my mind leaves my body and shoots into the stars. Vaguely, in another realm, I hear him curse as his hips stutter, then he's coming too.

"Mine." His face is buried in my neck and he places gentle kisses along my throat as we both try to catch our breath. "Say it, little shifter."

"Yours," I breathe.

After a whirlwind shower, pulling on the spare clothes I brought, a couple scratches for Milton, and then sending Asher into the grocery store for snacks, we finally pull up to my apartment building. I text Z to confirm they're ready, and next thing I know I'm opening the door and letting Asher into my place.

His eyes explore, taking in the limited details of our entryway until Reverie comes careening in, trailing glittery dust in her wake. She halts about two feet in front of Asher's face and stares at him. Her sapphire eyes are wide, and her hair is a mess of purple and pink tangles thanks to her wild flight from the other room. Her wings flit behind her as she hovers in the air.

"Hi," Asher clears his throat. "You must be Reverie. It's nice to meet you."

Reverie darts over to me and lands on my shoulder. She's standing on her tiptoes and holding onto the shell of my ear, partially hiding in my hair. It's a strange sensation, having a tiny creature holding onto my ear for support, and I can only imagine what Reverie looks like peeking out from my still-damp hair at Asher.

I give my head a little nuzzle-like twitch, lightly pushing it into Reverie in a show of support as I shoot Asher a half smile and wink. I wasn't sure how Rev would react, as she hasn't met anyone new since Zuri and that was over four years ago now, so I warned Asher she might attack him out of excitement, or she might hide. Looks like it's leaning toward the hiding, but I have no doubt she'll be covering him in fairy dust within a few hours.

We wander into the kitchen, with Reverie angling herself on my shoulder so she can keep an eye on Asher, and I find Zuri prepping a charcuterie board.

"Hey," I walk over and give her a hug, which Zuri returns a little more stiffly than normal.

"Hey," Zuri says, then turns her attention to Asher.

"Zuri, Asher." I gesture between them for a quick introduction, then cross my fingers and mutter under my breath, "please get along."

Asher's hand brushes across my back as he steps up to the counter and starts unpacking the bag of snacks we brought.

"We figured bribes might help," he says, shooting Zuri a crooked smile, which she begrudgingly returns with narrowed eyes.

The last thing he pulls out is a glass bottle of blood that I don't remember seeing him pack. He takes it out of an insulated bag and offers it to Zuri. She accepts it, again with narrowed eyes, but her eyebrows shoot up when she reads the label.

"This is the same place I go to," she says, her voice laced with suspicion and surprise. "She told you, didn't she?"

"Actually," Asher draws the word out as he turns to face me, "she didn't. I had no idea."

They both look at me, but I shrug, causing Reverie to

flutter her wings for a moment to maintain her balance. What do I care where they get their blood from, as long as it's not some poor human or other unwilling victim?

"Hmm." Zuri purses her lips and turns to pour two glasses before placing the bottle in the fridge.

We all head to the living room, and I set up the snack station before grabbing a deck of cards.

"Alright, what does everyone know how to play?" I ask.

"Poker?" Zuri suggests, but I shake my head.

"You know I hate poker. What about Rummy?"

"Eh," Zuri says.

"Asher? Any preferences?" I turn to him in hopes he'll have something good.

"How about a classic game of Go Fish?"

"Oooooh," the squeal of excitement comes from my hair, and Zuri cracks a genuine smile for the first time since we arrived.

"Go Fish it is," I say.

We settle around the coffee table, with Asher and me on floor pillows, Zuri on the couch, and Reverie settled on the table with a custom-made wooden card holder in front of her. She practically disappears behind them once the cards are all slotted into place, but we've learned how to make it work over the years.

Zuri quickly builds up a pile of matches, and I turn accusing eyes on her as she claims another pair from me.

"You're cheating," I say.

Zuri gasps, "I would never!"

Asher looks between the two of us, his brows furrowed.

"How do you cheat at Go Fish?" he asks.

Surprisingly, Reverie is the one who answers him. I'm glad to see her starting to come out of her shell.

"She's probably listening to our heartbeats. That's how

she normally cheats, anyway," Reverie says with a giggle, then ducks down behind her cards.

"Huh," Asher says, eyeing Zuri. "Clever."

Zuri's lips start to curve up on one side, but she quickly corrects it.

"I'm simply using the skills I have at my disposal," she says, and I roll my eyes.

The game ends with Zuri taking over half the matches, and Reverie coming in second. So far, things are... going. I wouldn't necessarily say everyone's getting along, but they're not outwardly hating each other, so it's something at least.

29

VAMPIRE VIBES (NOT LOVING IT)

RAYA

"Alright, anyone need a refill?" I ask, standing up and stretching my arms. "I'll grab waters all around. Zuri? Give me a hand?"

She shoots a warning glare at Asher before sulking into the kitchen after me.

"Okay, seriously. Can you please give him a chance?" I turn on Zuri as soon as we're in the other room. "He's incredible and I won't have you glaring at him and treating him like some sort of criminal!"

Zuri scoffs, folding her arms across her chest and popping a hip out as she faces me.

"You're dick whipped. That *vampire* comes from one of the most evil families in existence. I still can't believe you brought him here and introduced him to Reverie, knowing who he's related to! That's so irresponsible and dangerous, Raya."

"Stop. Moon above, Z. We've talked about this. I brought him so you could get to know him. He's not like his family, he doesn't even talk to them. He's kind, and generous, and a little funny underneath that gruff exterior."

"I'm going to puke. I can't listen to you gush about someone like that." Zuri scrunches her nose.

"He's met my family," I say, and Zuri's eyebrows shoot up. "Yeah, I didn't tell you because I knew you'd say it was a bad idea. But I took him over for family dinner and he met everyone, even Jo was there. And you know what?"

Zuri's attitude doesn't dissipate in the slightest as she raises an eyebrow for me to continue.

"They all loved him."

She scoffs again. "Right, Josephine loved him, not to mention your mom. Likely story."

"They did. Asher walked right in and asked Dad to teach him how to cook."

Zuri jerks her head back at that, blinking as her mind attempts to fit this new information into the picture she's painted of him.

"Mhm," I continue, "Jo grilled him and he answered every single question, didn't balk or flinch once."

"Even when they asked about his family?"

I school my face so as not to give away the awkwardness of that moment.

"He handled it like a pro," I say, which he kind of did, looking back on it. It could have gone any number of ways, and none of them better.

"Hmm." Zuri taps her fingers on the counter and her eyes flick beyond me, back toward the living area where we left Asher and Reverie.

"You know I'd never put Rev in danger. I wouldn't have brought him here if I didn't trust him," I say, my voice softening. "Please, give him a chance. You said you trusted me."

Zuri sniffs once, then nods her compliance. "One chance."

My shoulders relax and we refill the empty glasses before returning to the other room.

When we walk in, I grin with glee. Reverie is on top of

Asher's head with her hands buried in his dark hair, sparkling laughter tinkling out of her.

"Uhhh, what's going on guys?" I ask, biting my bottom lip to hold in a laugh at Asher's face.

He looks slightly terrified, like he's trying hard not to move a single muscle for fear of scaring off the flighty sprite in his hair.

"He's so hot," Reverie says, looking directly at me as her tiny hands trail through his hair. "And look, he's letting me play with his hair! You hardly ever let me play with your hair."

"That's because you turn it into a bird's nest," Zuri says, snorting when she sees Reverie sitting criss-cross on Asher's head like it's the most normal thing in the world.

"Not my fault your chubby fingers are too big for my braids," Reverie says, primly straightening her spine as she continues to thread her hands through the hair around her, fluffing it into a nice little nest.

"You're going to have glitter in your hair for days now," I warn, and Asher holds in a grimace.

"I don't mind," he says, and though it's clearly a lie, he doesn't make any move to change his fate, instead opting to let Reverie continue her antics. I fall for him all the harder for it, watching how careful he is with her and doing everything in his power to ensure she's comfortable in his presence.

After another round of 'Go Fish' in which Zuri plays with a noticeably different attitude and Asher has channeled his own vampiric hearing into a skill he can abuse, I put on some music in an attempt to curb the competitive cheating. The third round ends in a draw between the two of them. Zuri grins wickedly at the tied count and promptly challenges him to a game of Speed, her favorite.

Asher matches her grin with one of his own, and his eyes sparkle at the challenge.

"Fastest vampire wins," Zuri says, shuffling the cards and

then handing them to me to cut and deal without breaking eye contact with Asher. "Good luck, lover boy."

Asher's eyes flash at the taunt. "Hope you're ready to lose in about eight seconds flat."

I count down from three, and their hands are such a blur I can't even follow the movements. I gasp and Reverie screeches, neither of us having seen Zuri truly unleash herself like this. Zuri cackles as her hands fly back and forth, while Asher's eyes are narrowed in concentration.

"SPEED!" Zuri shouts in triumph as she throws her empty hands in the air, and Asher purses his lips.

His jaw ticks once as my wide eyes turn to him; he has two cards left in his hand. For a second, I'm worried he might be a sore loser, but he simply tosses the cards down and licks a fang, angling his head for a moment before a rueful smile emerges.

"You got me, you're a quick one," he says, and Zuri strikes a pose while Reverie flits around pretending to take her picture.

I'm thankful I'm sitting on the floor when the vampires exchange a grin, else I'd have fallen straight out of my seat. Reverie catches it too and she hoots a cheer.

Deciding this is a good time to call it quits while they're all still in good moods, I stand with a stretch.

"Well, I'm gamed out for today," I say. "I hate to kick you out, Ash, but I've got some chores and things to finish up."

He nods with a soft smile, and I'm grateful for his understanding. I want some time without him around to talk to Zuri and Reverie, and hopefully since things ended up going well we can all get together again soon.

Asher neatly packs up the cards and sets the box back on the coffee table, then grabs the empty glasses and cheese board and strides into the kitchen. Zuri watches all of this with a raised brow, turning her skeptical look on me.

"I told you," I whisper. "He's a good one."

A few minutes later, after he finishes taking care of our dirty dishes because somehow he's turning out to be absolutely perfect, I walk Asher down the corridor to the elevator.

"Thank you," I say, my voice earnest as I meet his gaze.

"Anything for you, sunshine," he replies. "I think it ended up going well?"

"You let her win, didn't you?" I say, pinching my lips between my teeth to hold in a smile.

Asher chuckles and shakes his head. "I didn't, actually. That was all her."

"Really?" I'm surprised. From what I've heard, the old-blood vampire families are supposed to be the strongest when it comes to vampiric abilities, and that includes speed. He should have beat her easily, but maybe her experience with the game gave her the edge. He shrugs.

"She won, fair and square."

I narrow my eyes, not sure if I believe him, but ultimately deciding it doesn't matter.

"And you won't tell anyone about Reverie?" I whisper, a bit of anxiety leaking into my words.

"I won't." Asher cups my jaw. "Raya, I won't ever speak of her with anyone but you, and even then, only in person. I won't even speak about her with Zuri if you aren't there."

That's taking it a couple steps further than I would have, and my heart blooms with warmth at his consideration. Tipping up on my toes, I pull him down for a lingering kiss, reveling in the feel of his stubble as it scrapes against my palm before he steps into the elevator.

I practically soar through clouds of joy as I walk back down the hall to my apartment, which is only accentuated when I open the door and am promptly attacked by Reverie.

"OhmygoshRaya, he is so perfect," Reverie gushes, her hands clasped in front of her and a dreamy look in her eyes.

"Please tell me everything! Is he a good kisser? What's he like in bed?"

Shaking my head with a happy laugh, I sidestep the winged menace in search of Zuri.

"Can you at least tell me how many abs he has?" Reverie yells after me and I snort.

"A lot!" I call over my shoulder, then flop down on the couch next to Zuri while Rev flies into the kitchen, likely in search of a sugary treat.

"So," I say, glancing at her from the corner of my eye.

Zuri sighs, and I wring my hands together.

"Okay, fine!" Zuri throws her hands in the air with a huff. "You're right. He seems great."

I grin.

"He doesn't seem great, he is great," I reply, and Zuri rolls her eyes.

"We'll see, but he gets a pass for today."

Zuri nudges her shoulder into mine, and I lean into her. Shifters are tactile creatures, and Zuri has gotten used to me constantly wanting to snuggle. She angles herself on the couch, and I cozy up next to her, snagging a blanket and tucking my feet up under it too.

"He let me win, didn't he?" Zuri says.

"He didn't, actually," I laugh. "I asked him the same thing."

Zuri snags a pillow and smacks me in the chest with it.

"Thanks for the vote of confidence, traitor!"

I giggle and hug the fluffy pillow to my chest, sighing in contentment when Zuri tilts her head and rests it on top of mine for a moment. Before long, Reverie zooms in to join us, arranging the blanket folds to her liking and curling up in my lap as Zuri puts on an episode of Gilmore Girls. I hadn't been lying about wanting to get some chores done, but this is important too, and I'm too content to move.

Cheeks aching from smiling so much, I tuck the pillow up under my chin and hum a happy sigh. Everything in my life is turning out perfectly.

Unfortunately, my bliss doesn't last.

30

BIG NOPE

RAYA

ALL ANYONE CAN TALK about at work the following week is the annual company party this weekend. I'm wracked with nerves at what sounds to be an opulent event on a scale that I've never experienced.

"Do you have pictures from any of the previous events?" I ask Alex during lunch a couple days before it.

"Hmm, probably somewhere. It's different every year though, you'll love it," they reply, not catching on to my nerves.

"I heard it's always fancy though, right?"

"Oh yeah, definitely a 'dress your best' type of event. You can't be too dressed up for this one, that's for sure," Alex says, finally looking up and seeing my distress. "Girl chill, you'll be fine! Just wear a nice dress and some heels, no biggie."

I wish I could have that attitude, but it feels like a big deal to me. I really like it here, and I want to do everything I can to ensure this job sticks. I've made awesome workplace friends, I enjoy my team and projects. I want nothing more than to make a good impression on all the higher ups.

"Did you hear the news?" Alex lowers their voice and leans over.

"What news?"

"I mean, no one knows for sure," they say, glancing around. "Supposedly, it's a pretty big deal though, there are whispers of a huge announcement. Like, really big, but the thing is that no one has any idea what it might be."

They widen their eyes dramatically as they straighten and pull away. I chew on my lip, my mind spinning with possibilities.

"And that's not normal for this kind of thing? For there to be big announcements?"

"Nope." They pop the 'p' as they lean back in their chair. "Never heard this type of rumor before, normally it's just if they'll have gifts or bonuses or a live band, stuff like that."

"Huh." For some reason this information settles like a stone in my stomach. I glance at Asher's empty desk, wishing he were here to offer his input. We've been spending a couple nights a week together at his place lately and I've become addicted to his presence.

I lose patience with waiting and decide to text him.

> Me: Hey, you coming back to the office today?

> Asher: I hoped to but this meeting is taking longer than expected, some issues came up.

I chew on my abused lip again, debating if it's worth bringing up the party. Before I can decide, my phone buzzes again.

Asher: Btw, I assumed we'd go together but just in case - would you like to go to the company party with me?

Me: 😊 I'd love that

Me: Any tips on what I should wear?

Asher: Formal, it's always a nice event.

Me: Ok. What are you going to wear?

I stare at my phone as three dots appear and then disappear.

Asher: Charcoal suit and tie probably. Why?

Me: Oh, no reason

Asher: What about you?

Me: Not sure

Asher: What's wrong? You've only sent one emoji this whole conversation.

Me: Nothing! Just a little nervous I guess...

Asher: Ah, about the event? It is a little intimidating if you're not used to it. Send me pics later and I'll try to help if you want.

I start flinging clothes out of my closet as soon as I get home.

"Why does it look like a tornado in here?" Zuri walks in and comes to an abrupt halt when she sees the chaos.

"I don't have anything to wear!"

"She's been freaking out since she got home," Reverie calmly tattles.

"Uhh, looks to me like you have plenty to wear," Zuri says, staring pointedly at the clothes strewn about the room.

"No, I mean for the company event. It's *black tie*, Zuri. Formal! I don't have anything formal!"

I thrust my hands into my hair as I turn back to my closet.

"You absolutely do. Scoot." Zuri hip checks me to the side as she strides to my closet and shoves everything to the left. Hangers screech, clothes fall, my shoe rack goes tumbling.

I groan.

Meanwhile, Zuri sticks her head in and peers to the right, all the way to the end of the hanging bar hidden by the wall, then rummages around.

"Ah-ha! Knew this beauty would come in handy one day." Zuri pulls out a sparkling gold, floor length dress. "Aren't you glad now that I insisted you buy it?"

"Stars above, I forgot all about that." I scramble over and run the fabric through my hands. "Geez that was what, three years ago?"

I shed my clothes and Zuri helps me wiggle into the shimmering fabric. The bodice is tight, hugging my curves with thin straps over my shoulders and a loose neckline showing the tops of my breasts. The straps cross over the back, attaching to the sides mid-rib and leaving the rest of my back open down to the base of my spine. The skirt is floor length and flowing, with a slit up one side allowing a flash of thigh as I walk.

"Oooooooh." Reverie emerges from her houseplant den with a gasp. "Raya," she whispers. "You look magical."

I could cry, I'm so relieved to have something to wear. After pulling out a pair of classic black heels and deciding to go without a clutch since I have none to match, I grab a quick snack for dinner before cleaning up the dress.

I borrow Zuri's garment steamer, going over it multiple times until all the wrinkles have dropped, and then hang it on the back of my door until tomorrow night.

Pushing the sweaty hair from my face, I check my phone for the first time all night.

Asher: Did you figure out what you're going to wear?

Asher: Send me a picture when you decide

Asher: Raya?

I grin and bite my lip, a giddy excitement bubbling in my chest when I think about Asher seeing my in this dress.

Me: I did find something, but it's going to be a surprise!

Asher: I suppose I can't begrudge you that. At least tell me what color it is?

Me: Shimmery gold

Asher: Of course.

Asher: I'll pick you up tomorrow after work. The event starts at 7, I'll swing by at 6:30?

Me: That'd be great! Thanks 😌

One more day of work, then I'll hopefully have Asher picking his jaw up off the ground when he sees me.

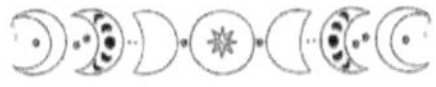

ZURI, perfect vampire that she is, left work early to help me with my hair and makeup. Her smoky eye is killer, and she somehow manages to combine it with a shimmery gold eyeshadow for an ethereal look I could never hope to recreate.

My hair is in a loose, partial updo exposing my long neck and back, and I've added some delicate gold jewelry to accent the dress.

Zuri helps me into the shimmering fabric and then Reverie dusts gold mica powder on my hair and shoulders. I twist and turn in front of the mirror, ensuring my boobs won't fall out and that everything is settled in the right place. I slip my heels on as a knock sounds on the front door.

"It's him!" Reverie whisper-yells.

Butterflies take flight in my stomach as I force myself not to rush.

When I open the door, I barely manage to keep my jaw closed. Asher looks delicious. The suit is fitted perfectly to his muscular frame and the dark charcoal color accentuates his looks, making his dark hair more devastating, and his blue eyes more striking. Then I notice his tie. His satin gold tie that somehow perfectly compliments my glittery dress.

My focus breaks when he clears his throat. My eyes fly to his, and I catch him sweeping his gaze from my feet up to my face.

"Sunshine..." His voice is a bit hoarse. "You look..."

Ash clears his throat again and lifts a hand, gently tracing a finger from one shoulder strap down along the line of my dress to my cleavage. He barely grazes my breasts, raising goosebumps across my chest and collarbones, before his finger sweeps up the opposite strap. His eyes follow the trail, stirring liquid heat between my thighs.

"You're stunning. You look like a goddess come down from the heavens," he says, and I have to strain to hear him when he continues under his breath. "You are my most unbelievable fantasy come to life."

I blink as those words sink into my skin, then say the first thing that pops into my head.

"You don't look so bad yourself," I say with a cheeky grin, deflecting with humor as usual, but thankfully he chuckles. Meanwhile, I'm resisting the urge to face-palm.

"Glad to hear I pass the test."

"Really though. Wow." I run my hand down the front of his suit, then the other over his shoulder and biceps, relishing the hard muscles beneath. Now that I know what he looks like under those fine clothes, it's a tough call to decide which view I prefer.

"Oh yeah?" Asher's eyes darken as my hands roam and he takes a small step toward me, crowding my space.

"Mhm—"

"Okay you two! Pretty sure you have to be leaving now. Like, ASAP, before you start groping each other in the hallway." Zuri's unwelcome voice cuts through the lust-filled haze.

Asher quirks a smile at my expression.

"She's right. My lady?" He holds his arm out and I snort.

"Since when are you such a gentleman?"

He makes a good impression of being affronted, but I know better.

"Bye!" Zuri pushes me out and closes the door on us.

"Don't wait up!" I call through the door, hearing an answering call from Reverie who then shrieks at Zuri for closing the door before she got to talk to Asher.

THE EVENT IS HELD at a local ballroom, which I didn't even know was a thing. I gasp when we walk in and are surrounded with opulence. The hardwood floor gleams, there are gilded crown moldings, floor to ceiling windows along one wall and a mirrored bar along the other, with two massive chandeliers glittering overhead. There's also a small stage on one side, and round tables set for a meal fill the floor.

"Wow," I say, and Asher hums in response.

I glance up to see his brow scrunched.

"What is it?"

"Oh, nothing." Asher looks down at me and clears his face. "It's always a nice event, but they've never gone this all out before."

We wander around the room as we make our way to the open bar, running into some friends along the way.

"How amazing is this?" Alex says, their eyes alight with excitement.

"Bit much, I'd say," Kendall replies, seemingly unimpressed with the grandeur.

I laugh. "It's really something. I've never seen anything like it before. I mean, look at those chandeliers!"

"Right? I wonder if they're real crystal," Alex says.

"Probably." Kendall's voice is a low drawl.

"We're making our way over to the bar, but save us seats!" I tell them and Alex raises their glass in response.

Asher's palm is warm and strong on my lower back as he keeps me tucked close to his body while we order drinks and then find our seats.

The event proceeds as expected, with plenty of networking and catching up between colleagues and friends. The emcee provides an outline of the evening's itinerary, and a catered dinner is served, complete with appetizers and dessert.

When I've eaten my fill and have to resist finishing off Asher's serving of lava cake, the emcee takes to the stage again.

"And now, ladies and gentlemen, I'm pleased to welcome to the stage your CEO, Mark Trowlen." With a wave, the emcee gestures as he backs off the stage and the PNCG CEO takes the spotlight as everyone applauds.

"Good evening, everyone," he says. "I know you've all been looking forward to this event for some time, and we are so pleased to have you all here tonight. As I'm sure you've heard, we have a big announcement to share, which is why we've gone a little over the top with this year's company event."

There are some scattered chuckles as everyone waits for him to continue.

"It's been in the works for over a year now, and I'm pleased to finally be able to share this good news with you all. In discussion with the board, we've decided to undergo a change of ownership within the company. I'll be relinquishing my role as CEO and retiring early, but never fear. You'll be in very capable hands!"

Confused muttering now fills the crowd. I get the sense this is not the direction anyone expected this evening to go.

"Known throughout the world for their business acumen and as a long-standing, highly respected family in our society, I'm pleased to welcome tonight's esteemed guests. Without further ado, please raise your glasses in welcome. I'd like to introduce you to the family who will be running the ship in the coming years, your new co-CEOs, Claude and Estelle Walton."

Clapping enthusiastically, Mr. Trowlen holds his hands up in front of him and turns to the side as an elegant couple steps onto the stage. The names register in my brain a millisecond later and I whip my head to the left where Asher sits rigid in his chair. His eyes are hard, his spine is locked and fists clenched as the couple walk to the podium.

"What the *fuck*," he whispers under his breath, my enhanced shifter hearing the only reason I pick it up.

Confused, I place my hand on his thigh under the table, and he turns his hard eyes on me.

"I thought you said you didn't associate with them anymore," I say, keeping my voice low so only he can hear.

"I don't."

"So..." I look back at the stage where the woman is mid-toast to the former CEO. "Then what are they doing here?"

"I don't know. But I'm sure it's nothing good," he growls, throwing his drink back.

31

LIVING NIGHTMARE
ASHER

MY PARENTS TAKE turns reciting a speech in which they assure everyone present that they have all the best things planned for the future of the company, and they are so very pleased to be welcomed as the new leaders. A few people are casting surreptitious looks my way. When the despicable couple waves another man on stage to introduce him, I swear again.

"That little shit."

I grab Raya's drink and down that too, forgetting she doesn't drink alcohol.

"Who is that?" she asks.

"My cousin, Chadwick. Still riding on their coattails, no surprise there."

Many in the crowd seem to recognize him or his name, and there's some genuine cheering when he steps up next to my parents. They spend way too long sharing a list of Chadwick's accomplishments, how much money he's made for other businesses, various companies he's propelled into the multi-billion dollar profit range, and proclaiming that he already has a plan to help them do the same here. Which means raises, vacation days, and better employee benefits for everyone—supposedly.

This, of course, gets the loudest cheer of all.

Raya and I sit through the remainder of the speeches, listening to my cousin prattle on while my parents pretend to be good, decent people. I'm not sure about Raya, but none of the words stick in my mind. I'm left floundering, wondering how this happened and stunned at the effort they're willing to go to entrap me again. I'm also paranoid about what this means for Raya; is she in danger because of me? They'll have access to our files, all her information, they'll know we're dating even if we try to hide it.

The emcee comes back on stage a short while later and announces that the bar will be open for another hour, and a DJ starts playing in the background.

I lean back in my seat and swipe a hand through my hair. My entire body is tense, my muscles rigid with strain.

"What do you want to do?" Raya asks. "Should we stay? Do you want to talk to them?"

"No," I growl, then sigh. "But we can stay if you want to."

"That's okay. I'd rather spend time with you than all these people anyway."

We stand to leave, and I envelope her hand in mine. As we start to weave our way through the many bodies milling about and socializing, a man steps deliberately into our path.

My father is standing directly in front of me, feet planted wide and a look on his face daring me to try to push past him. My mother and cousin are standing on either side of Claude; Estelle's expression hungry as she eyes me, and Chadwick looking smug, like he won the lottery and I didn't.

"Son," my father says, and it takes all of my power to hold in the grimace his voice triggers.

"Claude," I reply. Distantly, I hear my own voice as

though it's someone else's. Void and cold, detached. I also sense Raya's heart rate kick up a notch.

Not good.

"Asher, it's been too long," my mother coos. She attempts to reach forward to smooth my lapel, but my hand flies up and traps her wrist before she can make contact.

She drops her hand with a sniff and tilts her nose into the air, doing her best to look down on me despite her shorter stature. Chadwick is still smirking, thinking he's won the imaginary competition between us, until Raya adjusts her weight on her feet.

All three sets of eyes snap to where I have her tucked slightly behind me, and I stiffen. I know I can't do anything here in public. I can't cause a scene or attack them, and it would be best if they didn't realize how much Raya means to me. Despite knowing this, it's nearly impossible to feign nonchalance, to force myself to step aside and introduce her.

Chadwick's gaze rakes her from head to toe with a smarmy thirst in his eyes, and it's all I can do not to bare my fangs at him. My father's glare could melt iron, and my mother sneers down at her with another pointed sniff.

"What is a *shifter* doing here, Asher?" she asks, turning her attention back to me with disapproval and disgust lining her eyes. "I was under the impression this was a human agency."

Raya butts in before I can respond.

"Apparently, I work for you now," she says, tipping her chin up and holding my mother's gaze.

My heart flutters with pride at her bravery before it turns to anger. The look my parents exchange says they'll be doing something about that. Much as I don't want her fired, that would be the least of her concerns when it comes to this family.

"She's here with me," I say, putting my arm around Raya and pulling her protectively into my side.

My mother's nose wrinkles like she smells something foul.

"Now, son," my dad starts, and I already know where this lecture is going. I heard it so many times as a teenager: how important it is that I make a good match with an old-blooded, "respectable" vampire family.

Before he can continue, I raise a hand between us and interrupt.

"No, I don't want to hear it."

My father glowers at the interruption, but Raya is the one who speaks next. She extricates herself from my hold and turns to speak to me, apparently having had enough of my family already. I don't blame her.

"I'm going to go freshen up. Meet you by the entrance?" she says, and I nod, watching her walk away toward the side exit leading to the restrooms.

"Now, Asher," my dad reclaims my attention. "You've had your fun, but you've been playing around for long enough—"

I snort, interrupting again, and relishing my father's darkening complexion. Sure, I can't start anything here, but neither can he.

"That is enough," he hisses, leaning into my space. "Behave yourself, son."

"I'm not your son." I cross my arms over my chest.

My mother takes over, and my eyes meet her icy gaze.

"You've had your freedom, it's time to take your place by our side."

At that, my eyes dart to my cousin on the other side of my father, curious how he'll take that declaration... only he's not there. I narrow my eyes as my mother continues.

"We have a good match lined up for you, and now that this deal has gone through, we're ready to promote you to the top of the company. You need to sign a few things, rejoin the family, and everything will be as it should be."

My eyes flick between my parents, taking in their stone

faces. For some reason, my heart is pounding, and a sense of dread is filling my chest. What my parents are saying is nothing new. I've gotten used to tuning them out and ignoring their demands, so why is it hitting me harder this time?

I absentmindedly rub the heel of my palm into my chest, pursing my lips as my mother keeps talking even though I'm no longer listening.

I scan the crowd, looking past my parents at the exit to see if Raya is ready for me yet. She's not there, and I don't see her among any of the groups of coworkers I'd expect her to chat with. My eyes flick back to my parents.

"Are you even listening to your mother?" My father's voice is dangerously low, and I know I'm pushing my luck.

"Yes," I say, "I'll think about it."

I can't ignore the fear and adrenaline crawling up my spine. Something's wrong, and I'll say anything I need to say to get away from them right now.

"Very good," my mother preens, stepping back and slipping her hand around my father's elbow.

I take that as a sign I'm dismissed, so I give them a quick nod and stride away. My eyes scan the crowd around me, but there's no sign of Raya. Alex is chatting with a few others near the hallway to the restrooms, so I veer in their direction.

"Hey, have you seen Raya come this way?" I ask.

They nod and gesture with their drink to the hallway. "Yeah, saw her head through there a while ago, not sure if she came back through yet. There might be a line at the bathroom or something."

"Thanks."

I'm already moving before the word fully leaves my lips. I'm pushing through the doorway in seconds, looking both directions and seeing only empty hallway. Following a calligraphy sign on the wall pointing to the restrooms, I turn right and stride down the hallway. I can still hear the music from the event back here, and it makes it difficult to listen for anything else.

Coming to a stop outside one of the restrooms, I knock but get no reply. After twisting the knob, it opens easily, and I glance inside to see a very elegant, very empty bathroom. Pursing my lips, I turn around and knock on the next door. A feminine voice calls out "one minute" and it's clearly not Raya, so I move on to the third, and last, restroom. As with the first, it's empty.

My heart is pounding and I'm starting to sweat.

Where is she?

Deciding I must have missed her, or maybe she's been waiting outside for me this whole time, I stride back down the hallway toward the event room. As I'm about to pull the door open to go back in, my ears catch a scuffle from further down the hall.

I tilt my head to listen, and there it is again. My eyebrows pull down and my heart starts to pound in my chest, my instincts hounding me to hunt.

Picking my pace up to a jog, I round the corner at the end of the hallway to see a flash of gold disappearing behind another door. With a snarl, I tap into my vampiric speed and am at the door in a flash, ripping the knob completely off and throwing the door wide as I fling it open.

The door slams into the wall and bounces back, but I'm already through, and it slams closed on the rebound. I've entered a meeting room with a set of chairs, a bookcase, and a desk. Scattered on the floor are two black stilettos that my eyes quickly track. Against the far wall is my little shifter, and pinning her to that wall is my cousin.

Chadwick's hand is over Raya's mouth and his nose is trailing up her neck. His other hand has her left wrist pinned against the wall by her head, his hips are pressed to hers, and his fangs are fully bared as he scents her skin. Her body is effectively trapped and immobilized by his much larger and stronger stature, and although her free hand is scrabbling at the one covering her mouth, it's doing her little good.

I take in all these details in less than a second, and Raya's eyes find me immediately. They're filled with pain and fear, a hint of rage simmering underneath, and that's all it takes for me to snap. My sight bleeds red and I slam into Chadwick from the side. The surroundings are a blur as I let my inner vampire take full control; I'm fairly certain I've never moved so fast in my life. Even at my full strength though, Chadwick isn't easy to beat.

One of the reasons old school vampires—mainly composed of the traditionalist, old-blooded families—still choose to feed straight from the vein is because the more fresh the blood is, the more power it grants. My family, Chadwick included, adheres to the barbaric practices of old and they exclusively drink fresh blood. Whether the victim is willing or not is of no consequence to them.

I, on the other hand, have not had a drop of fresh blood since I moved out of my parent's manor at age eighteen, and that was over a decade ago. All this to say, we're much more evenly matched than I would prefer. Fortunately for me, my protective instincts seem to be giving me an edge.

We trade blow for blow, neither getting the upper hand until I dodge a punch aimed for my head, then use Chadwick's momentum to fling him across the room. He flies through the air and slams into the far wall, leaving a body-sized dent and sliding to the floor. I'm on him before he can so much as twitch. My fists pound into Chadwick's throat, face, and abdomen, then I flip him onto his stomach, wrench an arm behind his back and bare my teeth against his neck, ready to rip his throat out.

"STOP!" Raya's scream freezes me in place as Chadwick shouts at the same time.

"I submit!"

The words are garbled. Likely his throat is crushed, and he may be missing a few teeth. My eyes find Raya's and the red haze recedes. She's trembling, but standing tall with her shoulders back.

My brave little shifter.

I force my fangs back and stand, hauling my cousin with me and hopefully dislocating his shoulder at the same time, if his pained yelp is anything to go by.

"Stop," Raya says again, quieter this time, but no less determined.

32

NO MORE VAMPIRE
SURPRISES PLEASE

RAYA

NAVIGATING the wreckage strewn about the room, I cross to the two vampires as my eyes flit between Asher's. I thought I lost him for a bit there; he seemed almost feral, completely lost to the fight. The predator was fully in control and he didn't hear a word I was saying.

I can see now that he's come back to me. His eyes are still dark, still full of rage and pain, but he's there too.

"Stay away," Asher growls, jerking Chadwick's wrenched arm where it's still clamped in his grasp.

Chadwick whimpers. A pathetic sound from a pathetic excuse for a man. My eyes light with fire and I clench my jaw as my lip curls in disgust. This awful creature put his hands on me, threatened me and my Asher, was going to take from me without my consent. He deserves all the pain Asher has rained down on him and more.

I gather all the tattered scraps of my courage and take the remaining two steps forward to close the distance between us.

I clench my fist and pull it back, then slam my knuckles straight into Chadwick's sneering face, knocking his head to the side and eliciting a scream of pain as it jars his shoulder further.

I hiss, not having expected that to hurt so much, and next thing I know Asher has dropped Chadwick, snatched me around the waist, and blurred me to the other side of the room. I gasp, but he sets me down gently and then takes my hand in his, inspecting it.

His jaw ticks as his nostrils flare.

"You're bleeding." His eyes meet mine and I shrug.

I must have caught a fang when I punched Chadwick. Even though it hurts like hell now, it was worth it. My strength is flagging though; I fought him every step of the way even though he easily overpowered me. The adrenaline high is crashing, and I'm not likely to stay on my feet much longer.

"Can we go?" I say, wincing when my voice trembles.

"Of course."

Asher shrugs out of his suit jack and drapes it around my shoulders. Looking down, I see one of my dress straps is broken and hanging loose, leaving one of my breasts near completely exposed. My stomach drops and I pull the jacket tight around my body. Asher cups my jaw and I tilt my face into his palm.

"You'll be okay. I'm here, and I'm not leaving your side," he says, his voice soft.

Tears fill my eyes, and I will them not to fall; I didn't realize how much I needed to hear that.

I nod and Asher straightens, wrapping an arm around me for support. I lean into him as we walk around the overturned chairs. Asher stops in front of Chadwick and nudges him with his shoe until he looks up.

"You do not look at her. You do not speak to her. You do not touch her." Asher's voice is steel, so low and menacing it sends chills down my spine. "You do not come within a hundred feet of her. Understood?"

Chadwick drops his head, and Asher kicks him, eliciting a grunt of pain.

"Yes," he wheezes.

Asher turns us to the door and directs me through the back hallways until we find a staff member. He explains the situation and leaves his name and number. They exchange a few more words and gestures, but I don't hear them.

I zone out. My eyesight blurs.

My body begins to shake, and I can't control the trembles. Before I even register the tingling along my skin, I've fully shifted into a small, nondescript tabby cat, and my dress and Asher's suit jacket are tumbling on top of me.

I let out a surprised yelp, which comes out somewhere between a hiss and a shriek. The clothes rustle above me, and Ash's familiar hands pull the clothes away from my furry body.

"My sweet shifter, you're alright," he whispers and rubs a soothing hand over my head and down my back. "I'm going to pick you up, okay? We're going to call the car around and then head back to my place. The employee gave me directions for another exit, so we shouldn't be passing by anyone. If you want, I can carry you as you are, or I can wrap you in your dress if you'll feel safer that way."

He holds the dress out so I can crawl into it if I want, but I shake my head. I want his hands on me, even if I'm currently a cat.

Asher folds the dress and sticks it into one of the arms of his suit jacket, then lays that over his arm and gently picks me up, allowing me to get comfortable in his hold. My body is still tense, with random tremors running through me. Asher keeps up a litany of soothing murmurs, telling me I'm safe, that I'll be okay, that he's there.

When the valet pulls the car up, Asher places me in the

backseat and then unfolds my dress to lay it next to me along with the jacket.

"We'll be home soon," he says, then slides into the driver's seat and carefully eases the car into traffic.

A few minutes later, I'm able to pull myself back together, and I embrace the tingles as my body shifts back into human form. I hunch down in the backseat, managing to pull my dress up to my waist and drawing Asher's jacket around my upper body. His gaze meets mine in the rearview mirror, and although he gives me a soft smile, it doesn't reach his worry-filled eyes.

"I'm okay," I say, unsure whether it's for my benefit or his.

A glance in the mirror locks my eyes with his, but then he returns his focus to the street ahead. I slump back in the seat. Chadwick's words ring through my head as I catch random hints of his cloying smell lingering on my skin and dress.

Gold digging shifter whore, spreading your legs for my cousin in hopes of making it big.

I can feel his hands where he first grabbed me around my throat and dragged me into that room.

I bet you're wet right now thinking about his inheritance. Well, sorry to tell you slut, but he's nothing and neither are you.

The memory of his nose and mouth on my neck sends a shudder of revulsion down my spine.

You're weak, worthless, and I'll prove it.

I want to slam my fist into him again, and I also want to cry. I can't help but wonder why I didn't shift. It normally comes when I'm feeling strong emotions, and I've never been more scared in my entire life, yet there were no tingles, and the thought to reach for my animal never even crossed my mind.

It's like I was frozen by fear, mind and body, and I hate it. I hate that he's right, that I was weak and unable to defend myself.

I tug the jacket tighter around my body, pulling in Asher's

comforting, cedar-smoke scent. I try to remind myself I'm safe now, but every time I move, the smell of his cousin seeps back into my nose. I need to get it off my skin.

Thirty minutes later, Asher pulls up to his house and leaps out of the driver's seat. Opening the back door, he pauses, eyes trailing over my face.

"Are you," he pauses, finding the right words. "Can I carry you?"

I nod, grateful for his help, and unsure if I can stand on my own. Not to mention, I have no idea where my shoes are. I didn't even notice until now that I wasn't wearing them, and the temperature dropped significantly after the sun went down.

Asher's strong arms loop under my knees and around my back, and he carefully lifts me out of the car. I hold his jacket tight as he turns and knees the door shut, then strides up to his front door.

"Put your feet on mine," he instructs.

As he eases my legs down, my toes find the tops of his shoes, but he doesn't fully let go. His other arm is still clasped around my waist, taking most of my weight as he unlocks the door. Scooping me back up, he walks inside and pushes the door closed with his foot, then heads straight to his bedroom.

My mind has pretty much turned off at this point. It feels like I'm observing everything from outside my body. I feel no pain, have no cares or worries, and hardly process anything happening around me.

Asher sets me on the bathroom counter, then turns on the tap for the beautiful tub I admired the first time I was here. That seems like a lifetime ago now, even though it was only a few weeks.

"Do you want help getting in?" Asher is in front of me again, and I hear his words, but don't know how to respond.

Do I?

I must have shrugged or nodded, because he pulls me off the counter, steadying me as my weight lands on my feet, then gently tugs his jacket and the remains of my dress from my body.

I step into the tub with his help, and he sets a washcloth and soap next to me as I settle into the water. My aching muscles instantly start to loosen and I sigh in relief, beginning to come back to myself already.

Asher turns away and walks out the door. When he starts to pull it closed on his way out, my panic comes screaming back. I don't want to be alone, even here, where logically I know I'm safe.

"No." I think I murmur it, but he somehow hears and leans back in, a look of concern on his face.

"Raya?"

"I don't want to be alone," I whisper.

His eyes soften and he comes back in, closing the door behind him. Asher folds a towel and sets it next to the tub, then sits down on it, facing me.

"Do you want help washing?"

I nod, and my eyes turn glassy again.

"I can still smell him. Feel him."

Asher's jaw clenches, the muscles ticking rhythmically, but his hands are gentle when he soaps up the washcloth and brings it to my skin.

"Show me everywhere he touched you, so I can wash it off."

I point to my throat, and he leaves trails of soap suds across my neck and shoulders as the cloth drags over my skin, erasing the scent and feel of Chadwick. He cups water in his hands and uses his own skin to wash the suds away, leaving his scent on me instead.

"Where else?"

I indicate my upper arms, and he takes my left arm in one hand while swiping over the area with the washcloth, applying the perfect amount of pressure so I feel clean without hurting. I point to my wrist next, and the cloth sweeps down my arm to circle my wrist, then he takes my hand in his and washes between every finger, massaging his thumbs into my palm before placing my hand back in the water and doing the same for my other arm.

When he gets to the hand I punched his cousin with, he pauses. Nostrils flaring, he carefully washes my cut knuckles, and his eyes lift to mine.

"We can wait, but I can heal these wounds for you," he says, his voice tentative.

I angle my head in question.

"Vampire saliva..." He takes a deep breath. "It can heal, or it can harm. Based on our intent, our saliva can feel good and heal wounds, or it can hurt and be used to keep wounds open."

His eyes dart from my still bleeding knuckles up to scan my face, but I look back down at my hand, inspecting it with this new information.

As a shifter, I should have healed already.

"He..." Asher clears his throat and his jaw clenches again. "He must have intended you great harm, since you're still not healing, even after washing the wounds."

My eyes meet his again and I see the question in them.

I'm not ready for that yet. I trust Asher with my life, but I also know the attack is too fresh, and I need to let myself relax and feel safe first.

"Can we... Would it be okay if we took care of it later?" I ask.

"Of course. If you want to let it heal naturally, you can do that too. I hate to see you hurt and in pain though, so if you'll let me, I'd like to help when you're ready."

I nod and slip my hand back under the bubbles, preferring it out of sight even if it continues to sting.

Asher sets the washcloth down for now and brings a hand up to run through my hair. I lean into his ministrations, closing my eyes and tilting my head back when his nails scrape my scalp. Safe in his hands, my mind and body finally relax.

33

—————

BURN IT ALL AWAY

RAYA

ASHER ASKS if he can wash my hair, and at my nod, his strong fingers massage shampoo into my roots. I sigh into the sensation, leaving my eyes closed as I focus on the scent of him surrounding me. His shampoo and conditioner, his soap, his hands and no one else's. After helping me rinse it out, he rests his forearms on the edge of the tub, trailing one hand in the water.

"If you're feeling okay to be on your own for a bit, I'd like to go grab you some food and water. I have some snacks in the kitchen, should be good enough for now," he says.

I nod and he leans forward to press a kiss to my forehead as he stands.

"Can you leave the door cracked, though?" I ask. "So I can hear you."

"Of course, give me a few minutes, I'll be right back up."

I grab the bar of soap and run it over my skin again. I can't smell Chadwick anymore, but his touch and scent linger in my brain, tricking me into thinking it's still there. Tipping my head against the padded towel Asher placed on the back of the tub, I close my eyes, only to open them moments later when he comes back in with a plate of food and glass of water.

"Sorry to wake you, but it's probably best not to nap in a tub full of water," he says, quirking a hesitant smile.

I try to answer with one of my own.

"You're probably right."

Asher holds out a wide, fluffy towel for me when I stand and step from the bath, then wraps me up and starts to dry me off.

"I don't have any clothes," I say.

"I snagged some of mine you can wear for now."

Asher wraps the towel around me and I take it from him, drying the rest of my body off as he turns and grabs a folded t-shirt, boxers, and sweatpants. There's no way any of them will fit me, but I put them on anyway.

His clothes swamp my body, and I revel in it. I feel cozy and comfortable, surrounded by him; it's everything I've been wanting to feel safe again. He doesn't have any bandages for my still bleeding knuckles, being a vampire who can heal wounds and all, so he rips up an old t-shirt and wraps the length of cloth around my hand instead, tying it in a small knot over my palm and placing a gentle kiss on it. We move to his bed and sit on top of the comforter across from each other, eating the snacks he brought while I take careful sips of water. The silence lingers, and I take a breath to break it.

"I know you're probably wondering..." I trail off, not sure how to tell him what happened.

"We don't have to talk about it if you don't want to," he replies. His eyes are soft on mine, filled with worry and tenderness.

"I do, though. I want someone else to know. I don't want to be alone with this in my head. It's just," I stop again, fidgeting my hands in my lap.

"Just what?" he prompts after a few moments of quiet.

"I don't know how." I pull my arms tight around myself, feeling alone again all of a sudden.

Asher reaches over and pulls me in front of him. He spreads his legs around me and my back meets his front as he tucks me in tight against him. My body instantly relaxes.

"Could you, maybe, I don't know. Ask me what you want to know?"

I feel his deep inhale against my back, then his cheek is against the top of my head as he nods.

"Are you okay?" he asks, and tears come to my eyes that that's the first thing he chose to ask.

"I don't know. I think so."

"Where did he hurt you?"

"He didn't really," I say, and Asher cuts off a growl.

"Sunshine, I can see bruises all over your body. If you don't want to talk about it, that's okay, but please don't lie to me."

I hadn't meant to lie, but then again I hardly feel the pain. My body must be in shock, dissociated or something.

"Oh. Um, well he grabbed my arms, and my neck, and kind of dragged me around a bit," I say. "After I came out of the restroom, he was right there and it all happened so fast. Next thing I knew we were around the corner, and then in that room, and then you were there."

Asher's arms are tight around me and I snuggle further back into his embrace. He nuzzles his nose into my hair and breathes deep again.

"Did he drink from you?" His voice is quiet with restrained menace again, and I quickly shake my head.

"No. He threatened to. He... threatened a lot of things." I shudder, trying to get his voice out of my head again.

"Let me prove his words are lies. Can you tell me what he said?"

My heart jumps and I gulp a swallow.

"He said... he called me names. Accused me of using you for your money and connections. That I was worthless and weak and he'd prove it."

Asher turns me in his arms so I'm curled up sideways, then his hand cups my jaw and tips my face to his. I meet his eyes, seeing fierce loyalty and determination as he speaks.

"Listen to me, little shifter. You are one of the strongest people I know. Everything you've been through, you've kept your head high and spread joy and kindness wherever you go. Despite the hardships life has thrown your way, you've met every obstacle with courage and intelligence. That is not the mark of a worthless, weak person. That is the mark of an incredible individual, someone I respect and admire. Whatever names he called you are a reflection of him, not you."

I blink, tears filling my eyes again.

"Do you believe my words?" His eyes bore into me, and I know he meant every single one.

"I do," I whisper. I believe he meant them, and I also believe they're true.

"As far as the money goes," he scoffs. "Did you even know I have money?"

"I... what?" I'm confused now. Of course he has money.

"How rich do you think I am?"

"That's a weird question." I squirm in his arms, uncomfortable with the direction this is going. "I'm not with you for your money."

"I know that, but I'm proving to you that his words aren't true. So, my sweet shifter, how much do you think I'm worth?"

"I don't know. I mean, I can guess your salary. And I know your family is rich, so like. A lot?"

He raises his eyebrows and I wrinkle my nose.

"Half a million?"

"Higher."

"A million?"

"Much higher."

My eyes go round and threaten to pop out of my head. Okay, I knew he was wealthy, but more than a million I would not have guessed.

"I..." I shake my head. "I don't think I want to know."

"There. Exactly that. None of what that despicable man-child said is true, and I won't have you considering any of it for one more second. I always want you to know that I know it's not true, and I don't share any of his very misinformed, frankly idiotic opinions."

"It's just that I can't get his smell from his nose. It feels like he's still on my skin even after washing over and over, and I can't get his words out of my head." My breath hitches and I close my eyes against the onslaught of memories again.

"I have an idea," he says, squeezing my shoulder once. "I'll be right back."

Asher jumps off the bed, and I hear him rummaging around somewhere else in the house. He comes back with a big, oven safe bowl, a pitcher of water, matches, and a notebook and pen.

"Write down what he said, whatever you can't get out of your head. Put it here instead. I won't look if you don't want me to, but then it'll be out of your head and when you're done, we'll burn it."

A genuine smile tilts my lips up and I lean forward, pressing them to his before taking the notebook and pen. I bend my head and write, letting each and every one of the vile, nasty, hurtful words fill the page until they're all out of my brain and in front of me instead. When I'm done, I tear it from the notebook.

"Hold it over the bowl," Asher says. He lights a match, then holds it to the bottom corner of the page.

I watch as the flames catch, as they eat up his words,

erasing them from my life. When the flame nears my fingers, I drop the paper into the bowl, and soon all that's left is ash.

Taking the bowl to the bathroom, Asher pours some of the water into it, then puts the lid on and sets it in the sink to cool.

"As for his smell and touch on you, would you stay with me tonight?" he asks, then quickly continues. "Not for sex, I don't have any expectations, I only want to hold you. And I think, maybe, that would help you too?"

My shoulders slump in relief.

"Yes. Yes, please. I really want that."

We brush our teeth together, me using a new brush he had in the cupboard, and I feel the weirdest sense of normal domesticity after an evening of absolute horror. It already feels like a lifetime ago, yet the marks still cover my body. Shaking my head, I refill my water glass and set it on the nightstand as I slip under the covers.

Asher tugs me against him, spooning behind me and cocooning me in warmth.

"Is it okay if I touch you? Kiss you? I don't want anything more than that for tonight," he says, and I nod, agreeing with his need for nonsexual intimacy right now.

My head rests on his biceps, and his hand slips under my shirt and presses to the bare skin of my stomach, holding me tight against him. His other brushes gently down my arm, my hip, my upper leg, then comes back up to wrap around between my breasts and squeeze me tightly into him. Our legs tangle together, and he presses chaste kisses to my shoulder, cheek, and hair. Seemingly everywhere he can reach in our current position.

I bask in the affection, letting it wash over me and breathing him in as I succumb to exhaustion and drift off to sleep.

34

THIS SHIFTER BITES TOO

RAYA

THE NEXT MORNING dawns far too early, and I groan at the aches and pains wracking my body. I'm smiling at the same time though, relaxed and warm where I'm still held tightly in Ash's strong arms and surrounded by everything that is him.

"Morning, sunshine," he says, his voice hoarse with sleep as he stirs behind me.

"Morning," I whisper.

Asher's hand on my hip clenches and he nuzzles his nose into my hair. It's impossible to miss the morning wood he's sporting when it presses into my backside. I wiggle my hips into him, eliciting a barely there moan low in his throat. The sound arrows straight between my legs and I clench my thighs in response.

His mouth finds the shell of my ear and he skates his lips across it, sending shivers down my spine. I arch into him, adjusting my position so the arm circling under my neck and over my shoulder lines his hand up with my breast, and he squeezes appreciatively. Asher nibbles my earlobe and moves to the spot right behind it, sucking gently, then his fangs scrape along my neck and my entire body stiffens.

Asher freezes, muscles going rigid, and he pulls back suddenly.

"Shit, Raya," Asher says. "I'm so sorry, that was thoughtless. I'm not fully awake yet and I shouldn't have—"

I cut him off with a kiss, twisting in his arms to reach a hand into his hair and pull him down. I know he's worried he triggered me, and I'm honestly surprised by my reaction, because I *liked* it. Not only do I like the feel of his fangs, but I think I want him to go further, though I might not be ready for that yet.

"Shh," I say, lips still touching his as I whisper, "I liked it."

Asher pulls back and his eyes dart between mine, searching for my truth. I let him see it all. My desire pulses through me, and my heartbeat picks up even more knowing he can sense it. His eyes glance to the pulse in my neck, then scan down my body where I'm still covered head to toe in his clothes. He rumbles a sound that somehow sounds both satisfied and irritated at the same time.

I reach between us to bunch up the hem of the shirt I'm wearing, wiggling it up to bare my chest, and finally tugging it over my head. It's harder than I anticipated to get it off while still lying on my side next to him, but he doesn't seem to mind my awkward maneuvering, if the heat in his eyes is any indication.

Asher meets my gaze again and I suck in a breath at the barely leashed hunger. Biting my lip, I nod, and his hands are instantly on me again, roaming and squeezing my curves, rolling my nipples, sending warmth and goosebumps up and down my skin.

I tug on his hair, pulling his mouth back to mine, and he meets my tongue stroke for stroke, working me into a frenzy with barely there touches and caresses that leave me wanting so much more.

"Ash, make me feel good," I say. "I want you."

Asher sits up and strips the borrowed sweats and boxers down my legs, somehow shedding his own at the same time, then climbs over me. His heavy weight presses me into the mattress, and I wonder if this is nirvana. This feeling of being wanted and held, cherished and desired with a fierceness that astounds me.

Instead of following my request though, he continues teasing. His hands wander, and his soft lips follow. They cover every inch of my skin. He licks and nibbles in some areas, and places gentle kisses in others. My heart jolts when I realize he's kissing all of my injuries and lingering bruises, but I refuse to let tears be part of this moment.

"Now, Ash," I plead. "Take me."

I writhe beneath him, his touch turning me to madness. My fingers tangle in his already messy hair and I yank on it, trying to convince him to give me more. I feel the hint of a smile as his morning stubble scrapes along the crease of my hip to my inner thigh, almost where I want him.

"I need you," I whimper, not caring how breathy and needy the words sound. "Please."

"There's my good girl," he rasps, and his mouth finally meets my center.

Asher licks the flat of his tongue straight up my slit, pressing into my folds and finding his way directly to my clit. My hips launch up into his mouth, my back curving off the bed, and his dark chuckle vibrates through me. He devours me like I'm his favorite meal, nipping and sucking, licking and swirling his tongue exactly where I want it.

I can't possibly hold in my moans and cries, so I don't even try. When he slides two fingers inside me and curls them against my inner walls, my orgasm hits like a freight train. It rushes through me, and he bands one forearm across my lower stomach, pining my rolling hips to the mattress, but his tongue doesn't stop. He rides me through it, stroking me both inside and out, prolonging my pleasure as it pulses through me.

When my tremors start to subside, Asher rolls on a condom, then braces his body over mine, notching his cock against me. He brings my lust roaring to the surface again with one long, slow thrust. His eyes are fixed to my pussy, and he watches with predatory, possessive satisfaction as his cock splits me open and he slides in. Inch by inch, I feel every moment of his claiming, because that's what this is. I want to claim him too, but my moment will come. Right now, I revel in the sensations Asher is creating as he drags against my inner walls with each thrust, hitting every pleasure point as he changes the angle until I'm writhing beneath him again.

"Stars, Ash, you feel so good."

I'm losing my mind, I want more. I want all of him, unrestrained, giving all of himself to me. I clench around him and he growls, spearing a hand into my hair. With a quick pull, he slants my head, angling it to the side so I'm baring my throat to him.

His fangs clamp on my neck and my mind blanks. I'm consumed by white hot fire, but they don't pierce my skin, and although part of me wants to scream at him to do it, the other part holds back, not sure what to expect. His tongue laves my skin and he sucks a mark right over my pulse point.

"*Mine.*" His voice is dark, barely leashed, and it brings out my own feral animal.

Twisting my hips with a sudden shove to his shoulder, I roll us to the side, then continue the momentum. Asher's hands are tight on my hips, holding me to him while we roll, so I'm on top with my legs straddling his hips as they continue to punch up into me.

I lean down until my mouth meets his pec, then I bite. Hard.

It doesn't draw blood, but it will certainly leave a mark.

Asher sucks in a breath, and it comes back out as a raspy growl. He becomes impossibly harder inside me, and his tempo increases as he lifts and lowers me in time with his thrusts, somehow moving my body with his like I weigh nothing.

The heat builds, a wave cresting higher and higher, and I smirk with satisfaction when I see the deep grooves my teeth have left in his skin. I hope it bruises. I want to mark him permanently.

Asher sits up, one hand still holding my hips tight to his, but the other pushing my upper body backward until I have to throw my arms back or risk falling. He goes up to his knees and my arms give out, unable to hold so much of my own weight at this angle. My upper back hits the bed as he keeps my hips raised and level with his. When I meet his eyes, his are simmering pools of possessive desire, flashing with sparks of something deeper I can't quite figure out, but it speaks to me in an instictual way.

He draws himself out, oh so slowly lighting up every nerve ending I have. His eyes flick back to mine, and I fist my hands in the bed sheets, holding on to anything I can in preparation for whatever the feral gleam in his gaze means. And then he hammers into me, relentless in his pursuit of my pleasure.

My orgasm builds, that undeniable heat radiating through me, and I gasp when his hands tilt my hips so he hits a new spot deep inside.

"Oh, shit." The words are forced out before the wave catches me in its pull.

His eyes are locked on mine, watching every moment of my pleasure as I chant his name and the wave carries me higher and higher, until it finally crashes and my mind explodes with flashing white lights. My climax keeps pulsing through me, sending my body into convulsions as I helplessly ride it out and Asher continues to pound into me. My pussy is clenching around him, his hips slamming into mine, before he finally drives in one last time, sealing us together as he lets go, spilling himself into me.

We stay like that for long moments, locked together with most of my body in the air, being held up by his. I throw my arms over my head, trying to give my lungs more room to breathe. Our chests heave and we're both slick with sweat. Asher's gaze roams up and down, scorching a path over my skin as he unclenches his fingers where they've left divots in my hips. He strokes his hands over the marks, and his eyes leisurely make their way back up to mine.

I'm pretty sure I'm grinning, but I also can't feel most of my body so it's hard to tell. Based on the gentle smile he gives me though, I think that I must be. Asher lowers us both back to the bed, and I slump into the mattress.

I can barely keep my eyes open in the aftermath. Asher settles next to me and traces his fingers lightly over my skin, swirling around my shoulders and chest, up and down my arms, bringing goosebumps to the surface everywhere he touches. I sigh and roll into his side, flinging an arm and leg over him while my lungs still work to catch up.

I trace the mark my teeth left on his chest, blinking in astonishment.

Who am I? I acted like a deranged animal, completely unlike myself.

Looking up into his eyes though, all I see is pride and satisfaction.

"Don't even think about apologizing," he says, a rare twinkle in his eye. "I want to get it tattooed so it's marked there permanently."

My eyes flare in alarm at the answering heat that rushes through me.

Seriously, what in the world is this man doing to me?

Smirking, he kisses my temple, then traces a finger over my

neck, and his eyes darken for a moment again, but I'm pretty sure it's not from lust this time. I suspect I still have the yellow remnants of bruising there that my shifter healing hasn't fully taken care of yet. I don't want to look though, preferring not to have that image in my brain.

Asher slowly sits up, raising his arms above his head in a frankly indecent stretch that threatens to send my mind straight back to the gutter. Before I get any fresh ideas, he's hauling me up with him as he shuffles up the bed to rest against the headboard, then settles me against him again.

"Can I see your hand? I'd like to check if it's started healing yet."

I hold my bandaged hand out for him and he unwraps it gently. The wounds have started to scab, and the dried blood sticks to the soft cotton as he unwraps it. Wincing, he removes it as carefully as he can, but there's no avoiding the fact that it's not healed yet, and inevitably starts bleeding again.

My thoughts are flying a mile a minute, but I have no doubts when I speak.

"You can heal it for me."

My eyes dart up, seeing his gaze already on mine.

"Are you sure?" he says, voice steady.

I nod. "I know you won't hurt me."

"I'm not going to bite you, but my fangs might look a little bigger. Even more than they have when I've accidentally... well." He clears his throat. "Certain... changes happen when we have these intentions, to heal or to hurt."

I nod again, more firmly this time, understanding that his fangs are going to come out, and they might look big and scary, but he's not going to use them. I ignore the swoop of disappointment in my gut.

Asher licks his lips, then slowly raises my hand to his mouth, his eyes never leaving mine. As soon as his tongue touches the first cut, his eyes flare, and his body turns to stone.

35

HER

ASHER

"It's you."

I'm not sure if I speak out loud or not, but somehow through the blood roaring in my ears, I hear Raya's distant reply.

"It's... me?"

I have her hand clenched in mine, and I quickly loosen my grip, then push it back into her lap and let go entirely. I look away from her questioning gaze, unable to meet her beautiful eyes right now with my inner beast barely leashed. My vampiric urges are riding me hard after that fleeting taste of her, telling me to *take*, to *conquer*, to *own*. The vampire inside thinks it needs to drain her dry or risk never having another taste again, and that's a dangerous thought to even acknowledge. It's exactly the type of heinous mentality my parents tried to torture into me. The treachery I gave into too many times after weeks of starvation at their hands.

I need to get myself under control.

Immediately.

Spearing my hands through my hair, I squeeze my eyes

shut as I turn my upper body away and tilt my face to the ceiling, then employ nearly every single coping mechanism I taught Raya all those weeks ago. I focus on my breathing, the soft sheets and firm mattress pressing against my body. I fist my hands in my hair, taking note of the slight sting in my scalp as I remind myself the monster doesn't rule me, then relax my muscles with an exhale. It barely helps, but slowly I'm able to regulate myself and reign in the cursed urges.

"Ash?"

I take one last deep breath before tipping my head back down to meet her eyes.

"What's going on? Are you okay? You don't have to do this if you don't want to, or if it's, I don't know, bad. Or something."

Her cheeks turn adorably pink as she inspects the lingering cuts on her hand, avoiding my gaze. I wish I could knock some sense into myself when I realize what my reaction must have looked like to her.

"No, sunshine."

I reach a hand out, intending to turn her face back to me, but I hold back, turning it into a fist that I drop in my lap instead. I don't quite trust myself to touch her yet. Not until I'm sure my inner vampire won't break free.

"Raya, please look at me."

Her confused eyes peek up at me from beneath long, dark lashes.

"I want to heal you more than anything, please believe me, but—" I shove a hand through my hair again, wondering how to tell her I've been obsessed with her blood since before I knew her. "Your blood, it tastes incredible."

Her eyes pop wide, and I rush to explain.

"I don't know what it is. I've never tasted anything like it, except for one time. Months ago..." I trail off, eyes searching hers as her brow furrows and her head tilts a little more than is normal for most people.

"Did you give blood before we started working together?" I ask.

"I did..." Raya replies, eyes narrowed in confusion, but I'm already nodding.

"Well, somehow I ended up with it."

Raya's eyes flare again and her eyebrows shoot up. She shakes her head, but doesn't say anything. I don't blame her, it's such a wild coincidence I can hardly believe it myself.

"I drank the whole bottle in one sitting and couldn't get enough. I even called the clinic to try to get more, and then when they said they had none, I hoped to get your information. Of course, they said no, and I didn't know it was you. I don't know what it is about you..." I trail off when I see her eyes shutter.

"Just another thing that's wrong with me, I guess. The shifter freak." Raya's voice is full of self-deprecation, and she sighs, fisting her hands into her stomach.

"No, sunshine. You're not a freak, and I'll thank you for not talking about my girlfriend like that," I say, mock sternness lining my voice.

She huffs, allowing me a crooked half-smile. I'll take whatever I can get.

"I don't even know how to process this. I figured it was a fluke. The way you taste, it's what I imagine a euphoric high must be like. It's unbelievable. Honestly, now that I know, it totally fits," I quickly continue, seeing her mind going back to the freak idea. "And *not* because there's anything wrong with you. It fits because you smell so good, too. Your scent, it's like sweet coconut and ripe strawberries on a hot summer day. Now that I know, I can recognize those same undertones in your scent that I tasted in your blood."

I feel more steady now, so I reach out and pull her into my lap.

"And you smell so *freaking* good," I say, nuzzling my nose into her neck until she giggles.

"Okay, so. What now?" Raya says.

I sigh and my shoulders slump.

"Honestly, I don't know. Now that I know what to expect, I can heal you, but I'd rather we do it while fully clothed, at the very least. It can be hard to keep my urges contained, and your blood brings them out like nothing else. I can't believe I'm saying this but... less of your tantalizing skin showing might be a good idea, in this very rare circumstance."

Raya chews at the corner of her mouth, and I can practically hear her mind spinning.

"What if," she speaks slowly, "I were to tell you that I want you to bite me?"

My body goes preternaturally still. I'm not even breathing at the thought of biting her, marking her, *drinking* from her.

"I mean, you said it can feel good, right? That you can make it feel good?"

Her bottom lip is caught between her teeth now as she twists to look up at me, renewed desire and hope swirling in her gaze.

"I did say that, yes."

"So... what if you heal my hand, and then we..." She trails off, and her bedroom eyes are going to be the death of me. I can't say no to her, and I don't want to.

I clear my throat.

"Sunshine, please be sure. I need you to be absolutely positive before you agree to this. A vampire's bite can bring immense pleasure, but it's no small thing to allow me to bite you. I also, well." I pause to clear my throat again, not wanting to admit to this weakness, even though I know I must. "I don't think I'll be able to control myself if I bite you. I won't be able to stop myself from drinking."

Raya's voice lowers and she whispers her reply.

"That's exactly what I want."

Fire burns through my veins and licks up my spine, lighting me from the inside as my cock surges to attention. Raya's lips curve as she glances down and shimmies her perfect, round ass in my lap.

"I'd say that's a yes?" she teases.

I have to hand it to her. This woman knows exactly how to get what she wants from me. I'm knotted around her little finger and I don't give one shit. In fact, I'm quite happy to be there.

"Alright, little shifter," I say, adjusting her in my lap so we're facing each other. "I'll grant your wish. I need you to do one thing for me though."

"What's that?" Her grin is mischievous as she looks up at me.

"I need you to shift your arm for me. Into a paw, or really anything with claws and the strength to move me if I am unable to let go."

Her brows furrow and I want to punch myself for putting that disappointed look on her face.

"I trust you, Asher." She places her hand on my cheek. "I know you won't hurt me."

"You can't know that. This is new territory, and I nearly lost control from the smallest taste. I need to know you can get through to me if things go sideways." I'm fairly certain I can contain myself now, my vampire having settled a bit with her willing submission, but I'd rather be safe than sorry.

"How about a safe word?" Raya angles her head at me.

"We can try that, but I still want you to shift. A last resort that hopefully we won't need."

"Alright. San Diego. That's our safe word. I say San Diego, and you know I want to stop. Yes?"

"Yes. San Diego. Now, little shifter, show me those claws."

Raya scrunches up her nose and I want to kiss her. I don't yet, but I do trail my fingers over her neck. If she can't do it with this tiny distraction, she won't be able to when she really needs to.

"Ha!"

Raya laughs in triumph, holding up her hand. It's not completely transformed: instead of a paw, it's still a human hand with her long, graceful fingers, but her skin has taken on the faint spotted design of a cheetah or leopard, some sort of jungle cat with spots. What has me smiling with pride are the curled, wicked sharp claws. I nod in appreciation.

"That'll do, little shifter. Now remember, I can easily heal myself, so don't hold back."

Raya rolls her eyes.

"Oh my gosh, you're not going to hurt me. You're healing me, remember?"

She holds up her injured hand between us with the back facing me, eyebrows raised and head tilted again. That sass is going to get her a spanking one of these days.

I snatch her hand from the air, giving her a warning look to behave herself. She grins in response, of course, but quiets when I stroke my fingers around the cuts.

"Ready?" I ask, eyes flicking to hers.

Raya nods. "I'm ready."

I hold her gaze as I bring her hand to my mouth again, this time starting with a soft kiss, and she hisses in a surprised breath. My fangs lengthen and my gums ache to bite, but I push the urge away. So very slowly, I carefully run my tongue over each cut, ignoring the taste, avoiding my debauched thoughts, and focusing solely on my intent.

Heal. Heal. Heal.

As I lower her hand, the torn skin closes right in front of us. Raya sucks in a startled gasp and her eyes fly from her hand up to meet my gaze.

"That was amazing! I had no idea it would work that quickly."

I smirk.

"Well. For one, I am from a *very* powerful bloodline."

Raya gives me her most unimpressed look and I hold in an amused chuckle.

"Two, the more focus and intent, the more potent it is. Let's just say I really, *really* wanted you to be healed and out of pain."

Her eyes soften and she leans into my chest, then presses her delicious, soft lips to mine. I don't waste a second, and quickly turn it into more, delving into her mouth and nipping at her tongue.

Raya has no patience, and I smile against her skin as she tugs my face down to her neck. I pull back for a moment to roll on a condom, admiring her as I do. She has her head turned to the side and her breathing is heavy, whooshing in and out of her lungs, pressing her breasts into my chest. I take my time peppering kisses, licks, and nips up and down her silky skin, from her jaw down to her shoulder and back again as she squirms in my lap.

"Ready, little shifter?" I whisper into the curve of her throat.

"Yes." Her voice is even more breathy than mine.

I lick her neck, right over her pulse point, then my pointed fangs pierce her delicate skin, and my mouth fills with her blood.

Her exquisite, otherworldly blood.

We both moan, and I suck long and deep, eliciting another round of groans from us both. I force myself to pause for a breath, preventing my fangs from digging deeper and not allowing myself to take too much.

Raya isn't having it, though. My feisty little shifter grumbles an incoherent protest and pulls my mouth further into her neck, angling it more and working her body until her legs are on either side of my hips with my cock lined up to her pussy.

36

BUSTED

RAYA

I SLAM DOWN, driving Asher's hard cock into me with a low moan as he takes another pull from my neck. The combination of the two have me losing my mind, and my thoughts trip over the reality of Asher drinking my blood. The sensation sends fire licking up and down my nerves, igniting my skin. I'm delirious with pleasure. Pulse after pulse, it's like shots of adrenaline-infused aphrodisiac directly to my clit with each swallow he drinks from me.

Distantly, I wonder if this is what getting high feels like. If so, I can see why people are so easily addicted. I never want this to end.

Right as that thought surfaces though, Asher pulls away, delicately slipping his teeth from my skin, then licks the bite mark closed.

"No," I moan, throwing my head back in protest, hoping to tempt him with my bared neck.

"Shh, little shifter. I don't want to take too much." Asher strokes his hand up and down my spine even as I shake my head in vehement disagreement. "Besides, I can feel you're getting close."

What I feel is completely overwhelmed, and my entire focus is narrowed to two points on my body: where he's thrusting up into my pussy, and where I wish his fangs were still piercing my neck.

My wish is partly granted moments later when his lips go back to that same sinful spot, but he simply kisses and sucks, barely scraping his teeth over it in the worst sort of tease I've ever experienced. I don't have the mental capacity to be embarrassed about the needy whimper that escapes my lips, but this is Asher, so I don't need to be.

His hands grip my hips as he takes control, flipping me to my back and pounding into me with ruthless strokes. My whimper turns to a moan.

Writhing beneath him, I try to slow his pace, overwhelmed by the sensations he's sparking in me, but he's having none of it.

"I don't think so, little shifter. I know you're almost there," he says, and his husky voice devastates me. My heart swoops in my chest, stuttering before picking up its pace.

Adjusting the angle, he reaches new depths, and my orgasm looms overhead, barely out of reach.

"So tight and wet. Perfect, my perfect girl," he growls into my ear. "Give it to me, Raya. Show me how good you are."

"Oh, fuck. Asher." I'm panting, chanting, maybe even praying, I have no idea.

"Come for me, little shifter."

His fangs scrape down my neck once more and stars explode in my veins. I scream my pleasure, never having felt anything like it before as the orgasm obliterates me, and my entire body pulses. My senses are hazy, my mind in the stars as bliss smothers me. In another realm, I feel him meeting my climax with his own, hear his groan of release, sense his hands stroking my hips.

It's to that tender, affectionate touch as I start to come back to earth that my world darkens, and I black out.

"WHAT THE—"

My eyes blink open and it takes me a groggy moment to reconnect with reality. I'm lying in Asher's bed, wrapped up in his arms with a blanket covering us both.

"Welcome back," he says, and I can hear, practically *feel* the satisfaction in his voice.

"Blessed Moon, I did not just pass out from the best orgasm of my life."

I twist around to face him and am not at all surprised by his smug expression.

"Oh, you most certainly did," he says, voice playful. "And you're welcome. Also the vampire venom may have had something to do with it, some people respond more strongly than others."

I laugh and smack his chest, then hold up my perfectly healed hand.

"That's wild," I say.

He drops a kiss to my knuckles in reply and I shake my head. It's going to take some getting used to, that's for sure. I never realized how much Zuri kept from me about being a vampire. Not that I'd want my friend to be licking me or anything... Then again, maybe she doesn't know. Licking a wound would mean licking blood, and her family is vehemently against that, so perhaps it's not something she considers an option, even if she did know.

My thoughts are interrupted when my stomach rumbles. And rumbles. And rumbles some more. My cheeks, then my neck and ears heat up, until I'm fairly certain my whole body is going to be tinged pink at this rate.

"Let's get you some food," Asher says with a chuckle, sitting us both up and then tossing me a clean shirt from his dresser.

I don't want to wait for him to make anything, nor do I feel like cooking myself, so I snag some fruit and a yogurt cup from his fridge.

"So... Last night was pretty crazy," I say, then pop a raspberry in my mouth.

Asher nods and his eyes turn wary. I reach across the counter to take his hand in mine.

"I guess I see now what you meant about your family."

"Shit, Raya. I'm so sorry." Asher walks over and folds his arms around me. "So very, very sorry. That should never have happened to you. If I get my hands on that asshole again—"

"You'll do nothing," I say.

His arms tense, and I sense his protest forming.

"You already nearly beat him to death. That's enough. I don't want any more blood on my hands."

"It won't be your hands, it'll be mine." He practically snarls at me and I turn in his arms to face him.

"No. It'll be because of me, and I won't have it." I cup his jaw in my palm and lock eyes with him. "Please, Asher. No more violence on my behalf."

He sucks the fangs that have extended, then runs his tongue over the point of one as he exhales.

"Fine," he says, then adds a grumble under his breath. "Bastard better stay away, though."

"I heard that." I poke him in the side and he sends me a glare.

I beam at him, pleased he gave up his vendetta so easily.

Asher rolls his eyes, but I'm pretty sure his lips twitch before he turns away.

"Ugh, what are we going to do about work though?" I say.

Apprehension settles in my gut at the thought of going

into the office where his parents and evil cousin will be. Asher eyes me, seeming to search for something.

"What do you think about it?" he asks.

I twist my lips. "I'm not sure. I mean, I never saw the previous CEO until that party, so I can't imagine I'd run into your parents all that often, right?"

His shoulders tense as I talk and his face turns hard, unyielding.

"Besides," I say, "I'm sure they all have better things to do than talk to me."

Asher sucks in a breath, visibly trying to regain his composure.

"We should quit," he says, then nods as if it's decided.

"What? No!"

"What do you mean no? Raya, you can't work there."

My body jerks back. He did *not* say that.

"Excuse me? I most certainly can."

"No. No way. I won't let you." He's shaking his head and pacing around the kitchen now. "We'll both quit, and we'll start our own company. Together. Yes!" He snaps his fingers and spins back to me.

My eyes nearly bug out of my head.

Start a company together? He must be joking. That's huge. And absolutely insane.

"I mean, I guess that's one way to piss off your parents." I dredge up a pathetic excuse for a chuckle, but he isn't laughing. I blink at him, dumbfounded.

"Okay. Asher, listen to me." I step right in front of him. "I know you're scared. I know you don't want me to be hurt. But you also don't get to run my life. It's *my life,* not yours. I'm an adult, and I have the right to make my own choices."

I've come to love this job and my coworkers, and I don't want to give it up just because of a couple power hungry vampires who I likely won't even see. He looks away, eyes distant as he gazes past me with his fists clenched at his sides, and then he's shaking his head again, so I continue.

"Yes, I do. Even in this." My voice is steel, and he finally seems to hear what I'm saying.

The breath whooshes out of him and he deflates like a balloon.

"Raya..."

I rest a palm on his chest and soften my voice.

"I'd rather stay, see if I can make it work, but I understand if you can't." As I expected, he doesn't like that idea and is already shaking his head again.

"No, if you stay, I stay."

"Okay then. Let's go in tomorrow and see how it is. Maybe nothing will change. Maybe we won't see them, we never saw Mr. Trowlen."

I know it's unlikely that he won't see his parents or cousin. I do think that I'm beneath their notice though, or at least I hope I am. Especially after Asher beat up his cousin. I guess we'll find out soon enough.

I MAKE my way into my apartment later that day still dressed in Asher's clothes. I trashed the gold dress, never wanting to see it again. Reverie is eating a marshmallow in the kitchen when I walk by; the little miscreant stuffs her cheeks full in a guilty attempt to hide her thievery.

"Where did you even get that from?" I ask, dismayed at my friend's resourcefulness. To my knowledge, we haven't had marshmallows in the apartment in years.

Reverie gulps until her cheeks aren't bulging anymore, then shoots me a wicked smile.

"Why do you look like you were railed to within an inch of your life?"

"What?! I do no—"

"Ooooooh, you *so* do." Zuri saunters into the kitchen in time for the two of them to gang up on me. She tosses a marshmallow into her mouth with a smirk. "Spill it."

"Fine. Maybe I was." I can't help but grin at the memory. *Best sex of my life.*

Zuri's eyes turn wary as she narrows them, eyeing me up and down like she'll find evidence of a crime or something.

"What?"

"I..." Zuri starts, then pauses when she sees the warning daggers I'm shooting her way. "Be careful."

I roll my eyes as Reverie scoffs.

"You gotta relax, Z. Raya's fine! If you ask me, she knows how to pick 'em." Reverie turns to me as she continues to run her mouth. "Soooooo, was it the best you've ever had?"

My face flames, and Reverie cackles. She leaps from the counter with a flurry of wings, sending glittery dust flying as she shoots straight at me and comes to a halt in midair, hovering inches from my nose. My eyes go a little cross-eyed trying to look at her.

"It. Totally. Was." Reverie claps her hands together with each word and flicks her wings excitedly. "Tell me everything. I want all the details."

Reverie snags some of my hair and tugs on it, trying to pull me into the bedroom and away from Zuri's pursed lips.

"How big is he? What did it feel like? Did you go multiple rounds?"

The questions pour out of her, and I wonder if such tiny creatures don't need to breathe, because she doesn't seem to be stopping for air.

"Reverie," I sigh, "I know you want the details, but I'm not ready to share them. This is... different."

Reverie flutters down to my shoulder as I close my bedroom door behind us.

"Different how?"

"I mean, I really care about him. I think I might be falling for him. It feels too special to gossip about like it doesn't matter, I guess."

Reverie runs her hands through my hair in a soothing gesture.

"I think I get it. I wasn't trying to say it didn't matter."

She hops from my shoulder to one of the fuzzy pillows on my bed.

"I guess I just want to know what it's like." Reverie turns away from me, breaking eye contact as she watches her hands sweep back and forth on the pillow. "I don't know if I'll ever have anything like that."

"Oh, Rev." I crouch down next to her and cup her in my hands, bringing her up to my cheek for our version of a nuzzle-hug. "I'm so sorry. I wish we knew more about your kind, if there are others like you, or more about where you came from so we could look."

"Do you think Asher's family might know anything?" Reverie's voice is tentative, more halting than usual enthusiastic self. "I mean, they're like, super old right? So, maybe they know something."

I shake my head. "I don't know. I'll ask Ash, but no promises. His family is kinda shitty."

Reverie gasps and jumps from my hands. "You cursed! You never curse. Are you ill?"

I grin. "Oops."

Reverie scowls, but can't hold it for longer than a couple seconds, and soon she's back to her normal chaotic self, pestering me with questions and ideas as I try to mentally prepare to return to work on Monday.

37

THANK GOODNESS FOR BESTIES

RAYA

I MEET Asher for work at the entrance Monday morning, where we're stopped by a security guard.

"I'm sorry, Mr. Sullivan," he says. "I've been instructed not to let you in, but Ms. Merritt may go up."

"Absolutely not." Asher's voice is thunderous, and I set a hand on his forearm in an attempt to steady him.

"Why isn't he allowed in?" I ask.

The security guard's features pinch and his eyes dart around before he answers.

"I was told you're a danger to other staff and can't be trusted to maintain control, and if you have a problem with it, I'm to direct you to contact Mr. or Mrs. Walton, as they've agreed to meet with you to discuss the issue."

So Asher isn't allowed in after pummeling his awful cousin in my defense, and the only way forward is to meet with his parents first.

Asher snags my elbow and drags me down the block, out of sight of the security guard.

"I can't go in with you. Even if they agree to meet with me, I know their games. It won't be today, they'll make me wait, and then they'll make me jump through hoops to get what I want." He spears a hand through his hair and paces back and forth on the sidewalk next to me. "There's no good option here, Raya. I don't know what to do."

"Okay, well, why don't you use some PTO? Take today to think about it, figure out your plan, and we'll go from there."

He nods at first, then freezes and looks at me.

"What about you? You can't go in there alone."

"I'll be fine," I try to wave it off, but he's not having it.

"No, Raya. You don't get it. They are manipulative and cunning. They'll come after you and before you know it, you'll be caught up in their trap, and you won't survive it. You won't, they hate shifters, and probably you even more because I said you were with me." He turns and starts pacing again.

"Shit. *Shit.* I shouldn't have told them that. I should have pretended I didn't know you, then they wouldn't have looked twice and you wouldn't be in such danger now—"

"Hey, stop, it's okay. I'm a big girl, and Alex and Kendall are there. I'll make sure I'm not alone with any of your family, it'll be fine." I say, trying for a soothing tone despite my own chest tightening with anxiety. "Like I said, I doubt I'll even see any of them, I'm sure they have all sorts of important meetings this week."

Asher chews on his lip, his sharp fang drawing blood as his eyes flit back and forth between mine.

"I'll be okay. If anything goes wrong, I'll call you. Okay?"

I feel bad at how tormented he looks, but I hold strong. This job is important to me. I have fun here, with coworkers I care about. It's something I've never had, but desperately wanted. I don't want to lose all of that just to start over somewhere new again, and I refuse to let them intimidate me when it's unlikely I'll even see them. If worse comes to worst, I'll look for a new job, but I'm hopeful it won't come to that.

His brows are so furrowed they're almost touching.

"I promise I'll be careful," I say.

Asher's blue eyes bore into mine. Whatever he finds must be acceptable, because he lets out a world-heavy sigh, and then kisses my forehead in silent acquiescence. I squeeze him a little tighter than normal before we part ways, and I head into work on my own.

"Hey, party girl," Alex greets as I pull out my desk chair. "How'd the rest of your weekend go?"

"Pretty good, how about you?" I try to smile, but I can't tell if my facial muscles are working properly.

"Oh, good, good." Alex leans in as they lower their voice. "Crazy news though, right? How does Asher feel about it?"

I glance at his desk, clenching my jaw at the unfairness of the situation.

"He, uh," I don't know what to say.

"I mean, he didn't know, right? He would have told you at least, even if not the rest of us, but I saw your reactions. Neither of you knew?"

I shake my head, wary of airing his business.

"Holy shit. That's crazy. Kendall, did you hear that?" Alex is still whisper-yelling, and my eyes dart around the open space.

"Heard it," Kendall says, not caring in the slightest.

I spare a quick thought to wonder if there's anything Kendall does care about.

"So, what happened?" Alex asks.

"I don't know if we should talk about it," I say, doing my best to end the conversation before it goes off the rails.

"Right, right." Alex leans back over their own desk.

"Anyway, I think we should probably focus on work stuff today. Who knows what the new bosses are like, right?" I say.

I sigh at the pointed look Alex directs at Asher's deserted desk because yeah, he would know. Unfortunately, I have an impression as well.

As the day progresses, it becomes clear that ours isn't the only group feeling uncomfortable. While some people seem excited about the new names that have taken over, it's clear by the atmosphere that many others are wary. The first day under the new regime passes uneventfully, despite feeling like I'm more tense than a rubber band about to snap. I don't see any of Asher's family, and I have a tiny kernel of hope that things won't be so bad after all.

When Asher doesn't show up again on Tuesday, a couple people stop by to ask about him. Tension in the workspace mounts in the following days when he still doesn't return, and word spreads that he's taking an undetermined amount of time off.

Thursday rolls around, and I try to harness my usual cheer when I tread to the kitchen for a coffee refill, but the atmosphere is off.

"Well, well. What do we have here?" Chadwick's drawling voice fills the kitchen with an icy chill as he walks in behind me.

The coffee pot drops back into its spot with a clatter and I whip around.

Chadwick looks completely healed; arms at his sides with his hands tucked loosely in his pockets, his face is back to hard edges with menacing eyes, and his suit is cut to perfection. He exudes an air of barely restrained violence with an undercurrent of rage when he stares at me. He looks like my worst nightmare.

Correction: he *is* my worst nightmare.

My chest tightens and I'm unable to draw in air. My thoughts race and my eyes turn fuzzy as he walks toward me. Before I know it, tingles race along my skin. I try to ground myself and hold it off as long as possible as I dodge around him and sprint out of the room.

"Leaving already?" His cold voice calls out behind me. "Guess I'll catch up with you later, then."

I chant to myself as I run down the hallway, not caring if anyone sees or hears. "Almost there, just make it to the bathroom."

I slam and lock the door behind me before collapsing to the floor and letting go. I shift into a rabbit, and am promptly buried in my clothes. A sensation I wish I wasn't getting used to.

I feel like crying, but apparently I can't in this form, so I sit and wait as tremors wrack my body and a flashback to Friday night attempts to infiltrate my mind. I focus on the ground beneath my fuzzy feet, and how it felt to be wrapped up in Asher's arms all night.

When I shift back, my only goal is to get out. I punch the button for the elevator, hitting it over and over, and twisting to look over my shoulder as I wait, dreading every moment I have to stand here alone.

I leap in, then it descends slowly, but I'm finally able to pull in a deep lungful of fresh air when I exit and hit the side-walk. My feet mindlessly carry me away from the building to a park bench near the river.

It doesn't take long to realize I can't go back there today, not even to grab my stuff. Not wanting to worry Asher or interrupt his day with my near-breakdown over something he predicted happening, I call Zuri for help instead.

"Hey girl!" Zuri's cheerful voice answers after the second ring.

"Hey, um." My voice hitches, and my throat closes before I can say any more.

"Where are you?"

I sense the shift in Zuri's mood immediately.

"Um, by the river."

"Share your location, I'm on my way."

Zuri sits down next to me without a word, holding an arm out for me to lean into. I gratefully tuck myself into her side, breathing in her familiar, comforting scent.

"Thanks for coming."

Zuri nods, her cheek resting on top of my head.

"What do you need?" she asks.

"To go home, I think. I'll call Noemi and ask to work from home the rest of the day."

We take our time walking back to her car, then I buckle up in the passenger seat while she runs into the office to grab my purse and work laptop.

Zuri looks at me from the corner of her eye when we make it to our building. "Do you want to talk about what happened?"

"Not really."

"Are you okay?"

"Yeah," I say, realizing it's true. "I'm okay."

I dredge up what I hope is an encouraging smile.

"I gotta call work, let Noemi know I'm not coming back in. I can't tell you how much I appreciate you being there for me today," I say, stopping inside the door to pull Zuri into a quick hug before disappearing into my room.

Noemi clears me to work from home the rest of the day as well as tomorrow, so I don't have to worry about going back into the office until Monday. That gives me a few days to talk to Asher, see if he's spoken with his parents, or come up with any ideas for how to navigate this situation. After some couch cuddles with Reverie, I text him to meet me at the local coffee shop down the road from my apartment if he's free, which he immediately agrees to.

My foot is jiggling like mad while I wait for him to arrive. It's mid-afternoon and the place is mostly empty wooden tables, with soft jazz floating through the air.

His face is pinched in concern, hands shoved in his

pockets and steps hurried as he walks up, but the lines on his face soften when he sees me, and his exhale loosens the tension around his shoulders. Asher envelops me in a tight hug after dropping his bag onto a chair, then pulls back and cradles my face in his hands. His eyes ping between mine, thoughtful and serious and so, so beautiful.

"Hey," I say. "Thanks for coming."

"Of course. Why aren't you at work? Is everything okay?"

I break eye contact, looking down instead. He pulls me into his chest, smothering me in his woodsmoke scent.

"What happened?" he whispers.

"Um, I mean, nothing major. Just Chadwick dropped into the kitchen to say hi while I was there, and I sort of ran away and freaked out." I attempt a rueful smile, but he's back to scowling and I can't hold on to it.

"Why didn't you call me?"

"I didn't want to worry you."

"I was worried anyway, and not hearing from you all day, every day this week certainly doesn't help."

"Oh. Right." I look down at my hands, not having thought about my last few days from his point of view. Although he's been tense in the evenings, he hasn't seemed overly worried.

Asher sighs and runs a hand through his dark hair, which, now that I look at it, is incredibly messy. Like he's been doing that for hours.

"I'm sorry," we both say at the same time.

"I understand why you wouldn't want to be on your phone at work. I didn't mean to make you feel bad. I've just been out of my mind worrying, and I didn't even know you'd left, so when you called I sort of panicked."

I nod. "I get it. I definitely didn't mean to put you through all that."

"You're okay, though? He didn't hurt you?"

I shake my head. "He didn't hurt me. Just scared me a bit, and I left right after. Zuri came and picked me up, and before you protest, I called her because I wasn't in a headspace to cope with you acting like this—" I wave my hand at his furious scowl and rigid shoulders, muscles bunched like he's ready to attack. He unfists his hands, then reaches out to take mine and strokes my knuckles with his thumb.

"She's a good friend," he says after a moment, jaw unclenching.

"She is."

38

IS THIS OBSESSION?

ASHER

"So," I clear my throat, "was there something else you wanted to talk about?"

"Well…" she says, slouching in her chair. "I think we can both agree that we need to do something. You're right, I don't think I can keep working there, at least not long term. Not if Chadwick or your parents are there."

I flinch when she calls them my parents. I know technically they are, that they're my blood, but they're not my family. She's my family now, whether it's official or not.

I want to tell her what I've been working on this week, the scheme to get me out from under their thumb once and for all. I hate keeping things from her, but I'm not ready yet. I haven't fully faced what it would mean for me if it goes wrong. My tentative plan could so easily backfire, and I fear I'd be trapped with them forever, unable to protect her.

"I've been working on a plan this week, something I think could get us out of this situation entirely." I can at least share some of the background information with her, she deserves that much.

"Oh?" Her eyebrows jump and my heart thumps at the hope flooding her eyes.

"It's not set in stone yet, I've got a couple last pieces I'm putting into place." I keep going before she can ask further. "I found out Claude and Estelle bribed at least some of the board members, I'm not sure on all of them yet, but that's how they came to be the new CEO's. They bought their way in. I wouldn't be surprised if there were some threats involved as well."

Her eyes pop and I nod, pinching my lips.

"That's..." she shakes her head. "Well, really not surprising at all, I guess."

"No, it's not."

"You said you had a plan, though?"

"Raya, I need you to trust me. I'll tell you when I have something more solid, but for now, I don't want you involved. If they find out what I'm doing, if they catch wind of any of this, I don't want you or your name anywhere near it. It's too dangerous."

"If it's too dangerous for me, then it's too dangerous for you too," she whispers, her voice showing her panic.

I shake my head and squeeze her hand in mine.

"No, sunshine. They want me alive, they want me on their side. I'm not in nearly as much danger from them as you are. You, they wouldn't think twice about hurting." *Or killing, or using against me.*

Her eyes search mine, and I do my best to project calm confidence. I'm trembling on the inside thinking about what might happen if I fail, but I refuse to add any more worry or stress to her life right now. She's already carrying enough.

"You promise you'll stay safe?"

"I promise."

She nods, but is still fidgeting, anxious. I pull her onto my lap, not caring that we're in public, and she melts against me.

"Dinner? My treat," I offer, hoping to take her mind off her worries, and not wanting to let her out of my sight yet.

"Sure."

"Any place you've been wanting to go?" I ask.

"Oh my gosh, there's that new place over on Oak down by the water. I heard their desserts are to die for." Raya is practically bouncing in my lap and if she doesn't stop, we're going to have problems going anywhere respectable.

Her eyes turn to mine, wider than they were a moment ago, pleading and excited and hopeful. Does she seriously think I'd deny her anything at this point?

"Perfect. I'll call for reservations. Do you want time to change, or should we head over there now?"

"Ummm, let me change first. My place is close so we can drop our stuff there if you want, and then walk down?"

"Perfect."

I pull up the restaurant on my phone as I step outside to call, making a reservation for an hour from now. It gives us time for a leisurely stroll by the river, hot chocolate in hand, before we dump our cups and head inside.

After we're seated and our drinks arrive, Raya holds her glass up for a toast.

"To hopeful plans and good food," Raya says.

"To you, my sunshine," I reply, clinking my glass to hers and taking a sip as her cheeks turn a delicious shade of pink.

I DROP Raya off at her apartment after dinner. She tries to protest, but when she started yawning while forking chocolate cake into her mouth, I decided it was going to be an early night. We spend all day Friday working separately—me on my plan to oust Claude, Estelle, and Chadwick from PNCG, and Raya on her current client assignment—then she surprises me by showing up on my doorstep with an overnight bag. I waste no time pulling her inside and latching my lips to hers, tossing her bag to the side and relishing her giggle as it cascades through me. I ignore Milton's protest at Raya not acknowledging him, too greedy for her myself.

We drown our worries in each other's bodies, indulging in a night of slick skin on skin, lips and tongues endlessly tasting each other, and I end up sleeping better than I have all week.

Saturday morning, she invites me to her parents for family brunch the next day. It feels like things are moving forward, and thinking about what this could mean for me, that maybe I could have her, keep her—for real, forever—causes sweat to break out on my forehead and my heart to race.

Raya is all I've ever wanted, but avoided dreaming or hoping for. I never thought there'd be a day when I'd meet someone who would accept me for who I am, despite my terrible family, my horrible past, and yet here she is. Not only accepting me, but somehow burrowing her way deep into my dark heart and fractured soul so she's always on my mind. I can't stop thinking about her, obsessing over her. I carry her with me every moment of every day.

It's infuriating when I have very delicate, dangerous, specific goals I'm trying to accomplish.

"What's that scowl for?" Raya skips over to where I'm leaning back in a chair at my kitchen table, tilting her head and running her soft fingers over the crease between my eyebrows like she can erase it. I roll my eyes internally, because she basically can. One look and I'm done for.

I snake my arms around her waist and pull her into my lap, receiving a laughing shriek as she falls and burrows into me.

"What would you like to do with the rest of your Saturday?" I nip at her ear, relishing the slight uptick in her heart beat.

"Ugh," she sighs. "I should head back to my place. I need

to do laundry and it's been too long since I've spent quality time with Reverie."

My heart pangs, and helpless that I am, I almost offer to come over and do her laundry for her just so I can stay by her side and soak in her presence. I know she likes her space though, so I bite my tongue and squeeze her tighter for a moment instead before letting go.

"Alright, let's get to it then. I suppose I'll do some laundry while you're gone too."

I might as well be productive so I can ravish her when I get my hands on her again later.

Raya fidgets in the car as I drive her back to her apartment, and I glance at her from the corner of my eye, waiting for her to speak whatever is on her mind. She does, eventually.

"So, I was kind of thinking."

"Mhm?"

I keep my eyes on the road and school my face to a neutral, hopefully non-threatening expression as she glances at me.

"Well. I know I've been spending a lot more time at your place."

Poor thing, I hate seeing her nervous. I have an idea where this might be going, if she's been thinking the same as me, so I suppose I can help her out.

"Ah, you want a drawer? I'll clear out some space in my dresser and closet."

Raya does a double take, and I catch her eyes blinking rapidly.

"No? A key? I'm happy to give you the spare for my place. In fact," my brows furrow, "I should have done that already."

"No!" Raya laughs now, clearly amused by my thoughtlessness. "I mean, yes to both of those, but that's not what I was going to say."

"Alright then, hit me with it, sunshine."

"Well, I know Reverie gets lonely. So, I guess I was kind of hoping I could bring her with me sometimes?"

She has her hands clasped to her chest like she's a child asking for a unicorn or something, and again, I can't believe I hadn't already thought of that and offered.

"Of course, Raya. Of course you can bring her over, whenever you or she wants. Reverie is always welcome."

She slumps into the seat, her beautiful smile peeking out again.

"Oh my gosh, she's going to lose it when I tell her."

Her smile is beaming now, and my chest feels like it might burst. I want to bathe in the warmth of that smile every moment of every day.

"What can I get for her? What does she eat, drink? What about, like, sleeping arrangements or… I don't know. I have no idea what she might want or need."

Raya places her hand on my thigh and my muscle flexes at her touch. She circles her fingers up and down a couple times, clearly meant to be a soothing gesture that she doesn't realize is doing much more to make my jeans feel tight than helping me relax.

"I'll bring some stuff for her, don't worry. We have special cups and plates and such, mostly cute little tea sets. She'll bring clothes, and as far as sleeping, she likes to make her own little nest type thing. She has one in my room and one in the living area, so I'll bring one of them over to your place. I think she'll be happy with that."

I quirk an eyebrow as my eyes continue to scan the road and I flick on my blinker, trying to picture this nest she's talking about.

"She sleeps in the plants, so you probably haven't seen it. She likes being surrounded by them, I think it's calming? Not sure. We've made a lot of guesses and best we can figure, since she's basically a magical creature sprung into being by Mother

Nature herself, she probably finds comfort in being so close to whatever nature we can safely provide her."

"Huh. Makes sense, I guess."

I make a mental note to stop at the garden center on my way back home as I pull up to her building.

"Don't get out, Reverie won't let you leave if you come up with me."

"Doesn't sound like a problem to me." I grin, and she wrinkles her nose at me playfully.

"Maybe not for you, but I have stuff I need to do!"

"Alright, alright. I'll pick you up in the morning for brunch at your parents?"

"Yes, please." Raya pecks far too quick of a kiss on my lips, and then hops out of the car before I can snatch her back for more, throwing a smirk at me over her shoulder as she saunters away.

39

SHIFTER FREAK

RAYA

Reverie and I were long overdue for some good old couch snuggling, complete with loads of soft blankets and fluffy pillows, hot chocolate with extra marshmallows, and I even managed to rope Zuri into it for a bit last night too. I think it did all of us a world of good, and my heart is happy as I stretch out my arms and shoulders, then climb out of bed.

This morning dawns bright but cold, and I shiver as I crank up the heat in the shower. I try not to linger too long, even though the steaming water feels divine. I need to help Reverie pack a few things to take to Asher's place.

I crack a grin when I remember how excited she was last night when I invited her to come with us today. I swear I've never seen so much glitter as it clouded the air, her wings beating so hard and fast I worried they might snap. I wish we knew more about her history, her people, and my heart pangs with sympathy and loss. We've tried to do all we can without putting her in danger, but it never feels like enough.

At least I can give her this. A new space, a little more freedom and adventure.

"How many outfits should I bring?" Reverie is a whirl of chaos this morning as she decides what to take to Asher's place later.

"However many you want," I laugh. "We can always come back, too. It's not like we're going far."

"Maybe not for you, but it's far for me!" Reverie squeaks and flits away, back into our shared bedroom where I can hear her muttering to herself as I wander into the kitchen for coffee before Asher picks us up.

"Morning." I smile at Zuri.

"Hey, how's she doing?" Zuri grins and jerks her chin in Reverie's direction.

"Crazy." I chuckle and shake my head as Zuri answers with a snort.

"She's been pining over him for weeks now, you have no idea." Zuri elbows me playfully and my heart is fit to bursting with joy that Zuri seems to have accepted my relationship. "Better watch your man or she'll sneak right in and steal him from you."

"It means a lot that you both like him."

Zuri's eyes flash and I catch a hint of wariness before she smiles. I bite my lip to hold off the roiling emotions threatening to crash through me. I need the most important people in my life to get along, but beyond that, I want them to be friends too.

"Eh. I guess he's not so bad." Zuri rolls her eyes with a sniff, trying to play it off. Go Fish and Speed got them off to a good start, and his treatment of me the last few weeks has helped turn her opinion of him around. I'm thankful she's giving him a chance.

"You taking Rev to brunch too? It's been a minute since she's seen your fam."

"Yeah, I know she gets a little overwhelmed around more

than just us, but she said she didn't want to be left behind when I offered to come back for her. I think she's afraid we'd forget or something."

Zuri nods, her face pensive as she spins the mug in her hands.

"So... I guess this probably means I should start looking for a new roommate soon?"

She doesn't meet my eyes when she says it, and my heart pangs again. Things are moving so quickly all of a sudden, and I both want and dread the changes.

"We haven't talked about moving in together, but... yeah. Probably." My voice is soft, matching her tone. "He said he wanted to give me a key."

I flick my eyes up to Zuri as she does the same, and my shoulders slump. I hate the sadness I see there even as she tries to smile.

"We'll still talk all the time. And I'll come over, and you can come over too." I try not to ramble, but I'm suddenly feeling incredibly alone with all the changes happening around me.

"Come here," she says, holding an arm out.

I dart around the counter and into her hold, squeezing her tight around the waist and trying not to nuzzle into her, but failing spectacularly.

"Ooookay, that's enough," Zuri says with a laugh, pulling away from my cheek in her hair. "You shifters are too much sometimes."

"I know you secretly love it."

She rolls her eyes as a knock sounds on the front door.

"HE'S HERE!" Reverie is a streak of magenta through the air as she shoots from the back of the apartment to the front door. "RAYA!"

"Geesh, I'm coming."

I brush my hand down Zuri's hair as I pass by her, my heart already picking up at the thought of being in Asher's presence again. He's like a drug, and I am fully addicted.

My eyes light up as I pull open the door and drink in the sight of him. Tall, perfectly styled dark hair. Vibrant, slightly mischievous blue eyes. A serious expression I want to crack.

"Hey, you." I tip up on my toes so my lips can reach his as he bends down, meeting me halfway.

"Sunshine," he says, tucking a lock of hair behind my ear, then pulling back as his eyes shift past me with a smile. "Hey Reverie. You two ready to go?"

"Yep, let me grab her bag."

I turn back to the kitchen, Reverie flitting around me as her excitement dusts the air and Asher following close behind as I snag Reverie's bag from the hallway.

"I got it." His hand brushes mine as he takes it from me, then pokes his head into the kitchen. "Hey Zuri."

"Morning," she replies, allowing one side of her mouth to turn up before it falls again and a serious, not-Zuri-like expression crosses her face. "Take care of her."

I'm not sure if she's talking about me or Reverie, but I tense as I watch Asher and Zuri have a silent conversation, unsure if it's a standoff or if they're coming to some sort of understanding.

He nods a few moments later, just once, a determined dip of his chin while still holding eye contact with her as he says, "Always."

My heart thumps a beat when Zuri mimics the gesture and Asher turns to me, eyes softening when he sees Reverie bouncing from foot to foot on my shoulder.

"Let's go, don't want to be late." I give Zuri another quick squeeze and Reverie kisses her cheek before we zip her into a mini backpack, empty apart from her and a tiny blanket. I put it on backwards, hugging it to my chest as I strap in and we head out. Much as I hate hiding her from the world, and the world from her, we all know it's safer this way.

BRUNCH ENDS up being only the five of us today—myself, Asher and Rev, plus my parents—which is a relief for Reverie. She grew up with me and my family, but she still gets nervous when everyone is around. But Wesley is spending the weekend with a friend, I guess there's some sort of online gaming tournament that they wanted to participate in, and Josephine isn't going to be in town again until Thanksgiving in a couple weeks.

My mom and dad are thrilled to see Reverie, and she greets them both happily before fluttering back to my shoulder. Although we grew up in this house, it's been ages since she's been back here, so I expect it'll take her a little bit to come out of her shell.

Asher immediately steps into the kitchen with my dad, asking to help again. My heart feels so full when my dad claps him on the shoulder with a smile. They make quite the pair, with my dad barely coming up to Asher's chin, his arm slung around Asher's shoulders regardless.

I follow behind with my mom's arm looped in mine, then settle at the table. My parents have pulled out Reverie's old pillow, the one she used to sit on during family dinners. It's on the table now, set up next to my usual place with her doll-sized place setting.

I tip my head into my mom's shoulder, silently thanking her for always making those I love feel welcome.

"How's Zuri? We miss her around here," Mom says, finger-combing my hair while my dad shows Asher how to crack eggs.

"She's good. I haven't been around as much lately," I reply, my gaze flitting to Asher's back before returning to my mom. Her knowing eyes twinkle back at me.

"Ah, shoot, I broke it," Asher's disappointed voice reaches our ears as my dad claps him on the back.

"You'll get the hang of it. I don't mind a broken yolk, try the next one."

I grin, realizing he's trying to fry eggs with a runny yolk, the way I like it.

"I take it things are moving forward with you two, then?" my mom says.

"Yeah, we're going to get Rev settled into his place after this," I say. "Not permanently, just so she can go back and forth for now."

"Oh yeah? You excited?" Mom asks, turning her gaze to Reverie, who nods enthusiastically.

"He said I can bring whatever I want," she says, then quieter, "It's a little scary too, though."

"Change is always hard, even good change," my mother replies, reaching out to lightly touch a finger under Reverie's chin. "We face it with our chin up and shoulders back, yes?"

"Yes," Reverie replies, grinning.

My mom has said this to us since we were kids. Anytime we faced a challenge, she'd give us space to express our feelings, talk through our thoughts, then remind us to keep our chin up and shoulders back, to face it head on.

I think I lost sight of that, for a while. I stuck my head in the sand instead of acknowledging my shifting problems, but once Asher helped me face it, I was able to move forward.

It's a good reminder.

We all settle around the table a few minutes later with plates of eggs, toast, breakfast sausage, and fresh fruit. I place a hand on Asher's thigh as he sits next to me, smiling proudly at him.

"Thank you for breakfast," I say.

"Don't thank me yet, it might not be good. Can't seem to flip an egg to save my life," he grumbles the last bit under his breath, and I bite my lip to hold in a laugh.

I catch his narrowed gaze on me out of the corner of my eye as I cut into my egg and take a bite. I let out what is perhaps an overly dramatic moan of appreciation, partly because it really is good, but also to mess with him a little. He shifts in his seat and his throat bobs with a swallow when I lick the corner of my lips and glance at him with a smirk.

He tongues the inside of a fang, then grabs his glass of water and takes a long drink.

I turn back to my plate, a happy little smile on my lips.

"This is so good, I didn't know you could cook, Asher," Reverie says, breaking the tension between us.

He clears his throat before answering.

"I can't, but Mr. Merritt has been gracious enough to teach me a few things here and there."

"Oh, come now, son. None of that, call me Terry," my dad says. "Or I'll be starting to feel old."

"Terry," Asher says with a nod, his voice soft.

I try to catch his eye, but he looks down at his mostly empty plate, refusing to look at me as he blinks, then takes a bite of toast.

"So, you two, how are things at work?" my mom asks.

That is certainly not something I want to explain to them right now, and thankfully Asher lets me take the lead.

"A bit slower right now, I've got one project I'm working on, but not nearly as quick of a timeline as the last one," I say, sticking to truths that I feel comfortable sharing.

"It's good to slow down a bit here and there," Dad says, and we all nod in agreement.

I'm a little tense, thankful Jo isn't here to call me out on it, when Asher speaks up.

"Raya does have some news to share, though."

"I do?" I ask, turning bewildered eyes on him.

"You do." He smiles, then leans in to whisper. "Show them your shifting, little shifter. You've gotten so good at it."

My cheeks warm, and I look down at my lap as I twist my fingers together.

"Well?" Dad asks, "What is it, sweetie?"

40

SECRETS AND SURPRISES

RAYA

"OH, UM," I bite my lip, glancing at Asher.

He nods in encouragement as his hand squeezes my thigh.

"It's not that big a deal," I say, Asher interrupting me with a huff of disagreement.

My mom's eyes narrow as they flit between us, and my dad leans back in his seat with his arms crossed.

"Well in that case," Dad says. "Out with it."

I look at Asher for help, unreasonably nervous to tell my shifter parents that I, a shifter, can successfully shift.

Ridiculous.

Asher raises his eyebrows and I nod at him, my eyes pleading.

"She's gotten quite good at her shifting," he says as he turns to my parents.

My mom's chin tips up with pride, one side of her mouth curving as she winks at me. Meanwhile, my dad's eyebrows shoot up and his eyes warm, a smile stretching across his face.

"We never had any doubt," Mom says. "We knew you'd figure it out."

"You should show them!" Reverie says, then her feet start tip-tapping on her pillow. "Oh, oh! Can I pick?"

"Pick?" Dad asks.

"Her animal," Reverie says, like that should have been obvious.

I laugh, her enthusiasm combined with her acting like it's normal eases my nerves.

"Sure, Rev. You can pick."

She steps off her pillow and flies up in front of my face, then crosses one arm and props her other elbow on it, with her chin resting on her fist. She searches my eyes for some unknown sign.

I raise my eyebrows as we all wait.

She gives one decisive nod, then streaks back to her pillow and stands as tall and straight as she can.

"A wolf," she says, and Asher immediately grins, apparently agreeing with her choice. I eye the two of them, wondering what they know that I don't.

"Okay, wolf it is."

I stand and go to the bathroom, leaving the door ajar behind me, then shed my clothes and take a deep breath. I close my eyes and turn my attention inward, finding that bright, pulsing essence beneath my skin. I smile, tip my chin up and push my shoulders back, then I pull.

The shift ripples over my body, tingles race across my skin as fur sprouts in their wake and my limbs reshape, my back curls, my face elongates. I haven't fully shifted into a wolf before now, and I'm curious what I look like. Unfortunately, I'm too short to see in the mirror above the sink.

I nudge the door open and lope back into the kitchen.

Reverie leaps into the air, her wings fluttering madly as she whoops and claps.

Asher leans back in his chair, a tiny smile curving the corners of his mouth as he takes in my new, full wolf form.

My dad's eyes are glassy, and both my parents stand, round the table, and kneel in front of me.

"Oh, my beautiful girl," my mom says. "Look at you."

She reaches out a hand and runs it through my fur, and I can't help but lean into her touch. I've never had this before. It's something everyone else in my family has experienced for years, and I didn't truly know what I was missing until now. An involuntary whine comes from my throat, and I flatten my ears to my head, not having meant to let the emotion out.

I nudge the top of my head into my dad's chest, and they both wrap their arms around me, holding me tight.

"We are so proud of you," my dad whispers. "So proud."

I back up, feeling overwhelmed with so much attention focused on me, and turn toward the bathroom. I'm preparing to shift into human form again when Asher softly calls out behind me.

"You want a picture, little shifter?" he says. "So you can see your wolf?"

This man somehow knows me better than I know myself. When I stop and turn around, then sit in front of him, he quirks a smile and pulls his phone out of his pocket. I prick my ears up and look right at the camera as he takes a picture.

"Perfect."

I turn into the bathroom and he pulls the door closed behind me, then I allow myself to tingle back into my human skin, letting out a sigh filled with hope and relief, wonder and satisfaction.

WHEN WE PILE BACK into the car, mine and Reverie's bellies full to bursting, I unzip the top of the bag so Reverie can peek out and chat with us. I can feel her buzzing with anticipation through the backpack, and I suspect it's equal parts excitement and nerves.

"Got a surprise for you when we get there," Asher grins as he glances over, but instead of looking at me, he looks down at Reverie.

"For me?" she squeaks, and he nods, a pleased smile on his face as he navigates the road with one hand steady on top of the wheel.

Reverie's eyes are practically bugging out of her face as she turns them on me, and I shrug. I have no idea what it is, and he refuses to say another word about it the entire drive.

When we arrive, I turn and snap the front blinds closed so the neighbors can't see in. As soon as I turn around and unzip the bag, it becomes clear what that surprise is. What used to be an open space in front of the backyard windows is now full of houseplants—all sizes and variety, from a rack of trailing of pothos and scindapsus, to tiny African violets on the sill, to a full, leafy monstera and towering fiddle leaf fig in the corner.

Reverie shrieks with glee, diving into the mini-jungle and disappearing among the leaves.

"You..." I turn to him, heart in my throat and tears pricking behind my lids as I blink to hold them at bay.

"It smells so good in here!" Her tiny voice is muffled from the plants surrounding her as I stare into Asher's fathomless eyes.

"Me?" he asks, quirking a brow while swiping a thumb under my lower lashes, collecting the tear before it falls, then pulling me into him.

"I love you," I whisper.

His eyes widen and his fingers tighten where they rest on my waist. Asher leans down, crowding my space as his eyes search mine.

"Say it again."

His voice is low, quiet. A timbre that would be threatening

under any other circumstances, and I suddenly wonder if he's ever been told that he's loved. I sincerely doubt his family was one for such sentiments, and I don't know if any of his previous relationships got to that stage.

"Ash," I cup his jaw between my palms as I continue. "My heart beats for you. My shifter yearns for you. I'm my best self because of you. I love you so *freaking* much it's unbelievable—"

His lips crash to mine, cutting off my declaration, and I playfully smack him as I lean back.

"Hey, I wasn't done!"

He touches his forehead to mine and closes his eyes for a moment as we breathe each other in.

"Raya," his voice grates and he stops to clear his throat. "Raya, my sunshine."

He stops again, throat bobbing, and my heart thrums when I realize—he may have never felt love from others before, but he might have never felt it *for* someone else either. I have no doubt he loves me; he shows me every single day. I don't need the words if he's not ready to say them.

"It's okay," I whisper, but he shakes his head with a muttered "no" before confirming the thoughts that are flying through my head.

"My little shifter. I've never felt this way before, and I don't have all the words you deserve, but I do have these ones. I love you. I love you so much, Raya, and I'll work on it. I'll find all the words for you, but for now, this will have to do."

Asher sweeps me into his arms and kisses me like his life depends on it. I melt into him. He says he doesn't have the right words, but this is all I need. His words were perfect, and I'm full to bursting with joy.

"EW, you guys!" Reverie's voice snaps through the air and we jump apart.

I'm not sure about Asher, but I was so wrapped up in him

that I completely forgot Reverie was here, in his house, in the same room as us.

She's standing on the lip of a terracotta pot, the massive monstera a wall of green behind her, with her hip cocked, dainty arms crossed, and a scowl on her face.

"Sorry." I realize I'm panting in an effort to try to catch my breath after that kiss. "These plants, though!"

Her face instantly lights up again. "Right? They're so pretty, and lush, and perfect. And oh my gosh, they smell so good!"

Not sure what that means, maybe earthy? Regardless, I'm happy she's happy, and I'm especially touched that he went and spent... stars above. This must have cost a fortune.

Asher likely reads on my face that I'm about to ask if I can pay him back, because he presses a finger to my lips and shakes his head before I speak a word. I narrow my eyes before nipping at it, relishing when his eyes darken in response.

"Careful, little shifter," he murmurs, brushing past me as he walks over to the small jungle.

"You like it?" he asks.

"I *love* it. I love it, I love it, I love it!" Reverie shoots into the air for a birds-eye view, her hands clasped against her chest as her entire body vibrates, her special brand of glittery dust falling to the leaves below and coating them in a light shimmer.

"Good. I wasn't sure what to get, so if there's anything else you need or want that will help you feel more comfortable here, please let me know."

I groan. He has no idea what trouble he's putting himself in.

Reverie doesn't waste a second.

"Do you have marshmallows?"

"Uhh," he looks to me for help, but I quirk a brow back. He got himself into this mess with the over the top plant spree and open ended offer, he can very well learn to navigate it. "No? I don't think so."

"M&M's?"

"Um, no."

"Honey sticks?"

"I... Honey comes in a stick?"

Poor guy, he looks bewildered now and I bite my lip against the grin I can't contain. Reverie's wings droop and his eyes flare with alarm. I decide to step in before he pulls out his phone and orders a deathly amount of sugar.

"Sugar is like a drug to her. Too much can be dangerous, a little doesn't do much, but in between there is a euphoric, loopy feeling. It's been a learning curve for all of us over the years, I'll catch you up."

We settle into the kitchen and I share the notes folder Zuri and I compiled. It details everything we know about sprites. After filling a glass of ice water, I bring up the conversation we've both been avoiding.

"I'm supposed to go back into the office tomorrow," I say.

Asher nods, his lips pinched. "I know. I'm going to be at the coffee shop down the block, so if anything happens, I'll be right there."

My heart swells with affection that he's not trying to control me or take this decision away, even though we both know my safety isn't guaranteed. I assume this means he has a plan finalized.

"What are you going to do?"

Asher thumps his elbows on the table and leans forward.

"I've debated so many times if I should tell you or not."

My heart trips and his eyes flick to the pulse in my neck.

"I assume you've decided not to?" I ask, and he looks away but nods. "Can I at least know why?"

"I don't want anyone to suspect your involvement. Your reactions need to be authentic. I've got pretty much everything worked out, and after this week, I hope it'll be taken care of. They won't bother us anymore, and although I trust you, if there's any inkling that you know what's coming or are involved in any way... I can't risk that. I can't risk them thinking that."

What is he planning?

Part of my brain worries he might sacrifice himself to his family, or give in to his dark urges to protect me, but my protective instincts won't let me fully face that possibility.

"Will you be in danger?" I ask.

"Being anywhere near them is dangerous, but I won't put myself in any more danger than is necessary."

That's not the least bit encouraging or satisfactory, and in fact only increases my anxiety.

41

LOVE BITES

RAYA

MONDAY MORNING ARRIVES TOO SOON. Asher is driving me to work, while Reverie opted to stay at his place to organize a new bed-nook in the plants.

Asher parks a couple blocks away and pulls me in for an achingly sweet kiss full of tender affection and more than a hint of worry.

"I'll be okay. I'll text you and check in this time so you don't worry as much," I say as I slide out of the car.

"Be careful," he says, glowering at me as I close the door and wave.

Although there's a hefty dose of nervous apprehension running through my system, I don't let it deter me from doing my job.

"Hey, glad you're here," I say to Alex as I drop into my desk chair.

"Welcome back, you feeling okay?" they ask, apparently assuming I was out sick last Friday.

"Yeah, not bad, just a little off still," I reply, not bothering to correct them. It's the truth of how I feel, even if the implication isn't accurate.

We settle into our morning routines, and my skin prickles constantly, but it never gets far enough that I'm worried about an involuntary shift.

Hooray for small positives.

I pull out my phone every hour to text a random emoji to Asher. I try to find the most ridiculous, random ones I can, then imagine the reluctant scowly-smile on his face when he sees them.

So far, I've sent him a squid, to which he sent a string of question marks in reply, then I sent a blue bucket and he replied '...' back. He seems to catch on when I send a planet emoji, replying with an eye roll. I don't let it deter me, sending the brown swirl 'poop' emoji next, which makes me cackle when I imagine his reaction as I'm eating my lunch.

Unfortunately, that's when a most unwelcome visitor strides into the open workspace.

Chadwick steps into view, a fake smile on his smarmy face that some people seem to find charming. It makes me nauseous.

I avoid meeting his eyes, staring intently at my computer screen until he saunters away.

My shoulders slump and the breath whooshes from my chest. Just as I'm settling back into work, a new email—from Chadwick—pops into my inbox. My eyes flare with alarm when I see his name.

From: Chadwick Walton

Subject: Notice

Hello staff,

There will be a live press conference tomorrow, Tuesday, taking place on the steps at the front of the office building. The front entrance will be closed from 8:30am until 12pm, with live taping from 10am-11am.

All employees are advised to either arrive at the

office before 8:30am, or to use a side or back entrance during the above stated times to avoid any delays in the setup or taping of the press conference tomorrow.

Thank you for your understanding, and we hope you'll tune in!

Regards,

Chadwick Walton, CFO

There's also a link with instructions for how to view the live stream.

"Did you see this?" Alex says, leaning over their desk toward me.

"About the press conference?" I ask. "Yeah, I'm reading it now."

"What do you think it's about?"

"I have no idea." I frown, then say, "The only thing I can think of is the Waltons taking over. What other news is there that would warrant a press conference?"

Alex shrugs, then looks at Kendall. I eye her, already knowing she's not going to have an opinion.

"No idea," she says, barely glancing our way before continuing her work.

"Guess we'll see," Alex says, leaning back into their own space again.

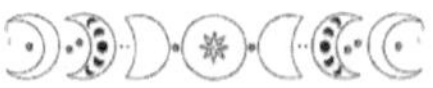

"How did today go?" Asher asks, his palm finding my thigh as soon as I plop into the passenger seat.

"Fine, actually, all things considered."

He raises an eyebrow and I shrug.

"They announced a press conference for tomorrow," I say.

Asher hums a noncommittal reply and I glance at him as

he starts the car, then look again at his carefully neutral expression.

"Do you know anything about that?" I ask him, suspicion lacing my tone.

"They've been doing their best to keep me updated," he says.

It's not truly an answer, but it's the most I'm going to get for now.

Asher's gaze flicks to my lips, alerting me that I've been chewing on them again. He leans forward and brushes his lips to mine, stopping the anxious movement and effectively distracting me. I lean into the kiss, practically melting across the center console, and he growls at the distance still between us.

"I've hated being apart from you," he says, and I huff in agreement. "Dinner at my place?"

"Your dinner or mine?" I say, my suggestive reply causing Asher's chest to hitch on a surprised inhale.

"Both." He nips at my bottom lip. "You mouthy little minx," he mutters, then he pulls away and shifts the car into drive. We're pulling up to his house before I know it.

He scoops his arm around my waist and hauls me against him as we stumble to the front door, kissing me until I'm senseless and my hands are tugging at his shirt. He fumbles the keys and huffs an irritated breath when he has to break our kiss to pick them up. Finally, we're tripping inside, our lips locked together again. Asher kicks the door closed and then we're shocked out of the moment by a high pitched shriek.

"You guys are the worst!" Reverie says, hands covering her eyes as she hovers in the hallway.

"Stars, sorry Rev," I say, having forgotten—again—that she was here.

"It's fine. I don't blame you," she says, then waves one

hand in our direction, possibly shooing us away, with the other still covering her eyes. "Carry on!"

With that, she turns and swoops away, disappearing into a leafy fern in the corner.

I turn back to Asher and grin. He takes one look and scoops me up again, then blurs us up the stairs to his bedroom. We waste no time shedding our clothes. I don't even pause when I hear a seam rip in my desperation for skin-to-skin contact.

Our movements become frantic, uncoordinated as our hands roam and grasp, but I don't care. My body is already reacting to his proximity, and my senses are heightened to the need we're both caving to. I sense a tingle as ears pop into being on my head, disrupting my loose braid, but it's a distant awareness, and it doesn't matter enough to pay attention to.

All that matters is *him*.

His strong hands sliding up my ribs, cupping my breasts, skimming over my nipples. His chest pressing into mine, forcing me to step back until my knees hit the mattress. I tip onto it with his hands cushioning my fall.

His body cages mine as he follows me down, and my fingers twist through his silky hair, dragging him closer. Asher's cedar-smoke scent surrounds me as his solid weight presses me into the mattress, his hard length heavy against my thigh.

I shudder beneath him, and he steals my breath as his lips take mine in a greedy kiss. Asher doesn't hesitate this time as he overwhelms my senses, making me dizzy with desire until there are no thoughts for anything except me, and him, and my flaming need.

The noises he's making in the back of his throat while he kisses me are turning me on even more, and it's only when he pulls back for a moment to trail his tongue and lips along my jaw to my ear that I realize he's been speaking this whole time.

Soft, possessive words that he doesn't seem to realize are coming out of his mouth, words that weren't intelligible moments ago, and only are now because my lips aren't covering his and devouring them.

"Mine," he growls, not pausing his ministrations and continuing to lick and suck his way down my neck. His hands are ravenous, tweaking my nipples and then digging into my hips to hold me in place.

"Such a pretty little shifter," he murmurs into my collarbone.

"Perfect, so perfect," he says as his lips relinquish one nipple to the swirl around the other. I'm ready to beg for more when his fangs scrape the side of my breast, and I arch into him with a throaty moan.

"Asher," I say, unable to form anything more coherent with the way he's set me on edge. I'm desperate for the euphoria of his bite, for the stretch of his cock, to feel him surrounding and owning me in every way.

"Yes, sunshine," he says. "Yes."

I reach between our bodies, finding the tip of his cock already wet with a bead of precum. It jerks when I swipe my thumb over his slit, and he sucks on my neck when I wrap my fingers around him and give him one tight pump. His hips punch forward into my hand, sending a heady combination of power and desire rushing through me.

"Fuck," he groans, and I wholeheartedly agree.

"Yes, please," I say, not caring how needy I sound.

Asher chuckles, a low, dark laugh against the shell of my ear that has the hairs on my arms rising. Before I can suck in a breath, his hands are firm on my hips as he rears back and flips me over.

My brain is spinning, trying to catch up with my body's position as my stomach hits the bedspread and my hands scrabble for purchase. I'm panting at his display of strength, struggling to catch my breath as he winds my pleasure higher with every moment.

Then his fingers dig into my hips and pull them up, raising me to my hands and knees. My legs are quivering, and I'm practically dripping for him, but instead of plunging into me, his touch leaves. I hear the crinkle of foil before sensing him step up behind me again, and my arms are trembling with expectation as I hold myself on hands and knees for him.

"Gorgeous," Asher whispers.

His fingers, so light I can barely feel them, trail up my inner thigh, then over the curve of my ass. It's the most torturous tease yet.

"Asher." I'm breathless with anticipation.

His hand pauses, cupping one ass cheek, waiting for my permission to continue, but I'm panting, unable to catch my breath.

"What do you need, little shifter?"

"You, Ash. I need you, now."

The only movement is his fingers tightening on my ass for an undefinable moment, and then both of his hands are on my hips again.

"As you wish," he says, or at least I think he does, because his cock is steadily pressing into me as he says it, thrusting in a little more each time, and nothing else matters.

I moan at the stretch, my arms giving out as he splits me open, and I land on my elbows as my head dips down to the mattress. He feels enormous from this angle, and I'm not sure how much I can take.

"All of it," he replies, and it's only then I realize I must have worried aloud.

"My perfect girl," he says. His breath ghosts across my back as his hand squeezes my ass and then traces the curve of my hip, reaching around for my center. His fingers circle my clit and I close my eyes, all of my nerves alight and buzzing. I feel myself getting even wetter, allowing him easier access as he pounds into me. The sounds we're making are obscene.

"You'll take all of me, won't you?" His voice is low, rough with a note of gravel that sends a shiver up my spine.

I nod, but he isn't happy with that. Asher tangles a fist in my braid, tugging my hair back while the other arm bands across my chest as he yanks me upright against him.

"What was that, little shifter?"

I gasp and my pussy clenches, loving this dominant side of him.

"Yes, I'll take all of you." The breathy words are barely coherent, so it must be the thought that counts.

He groans and angles my head to the side, then whispers in my ear.

"Tell me to stop, and I'll stop."

Asher's fangs scrape along my neck and I whimper, ready to start begging if he doesn't bite me soon.

"Don't stop," I say.

A pleased rumble sounds from his chest and reverberates through mine as he licks the pulse point in my neck, then sinks his fangs into me.

A bright spot of pain shocks me for a millisecond, but it's immediately followed by blinding pleasure. Somehow, it feels even better than last time as Asher groans into my neck, sucking so hard I can feel my skin bowing against his lips.

It's euphoric.

I'm delirious with bliss as I buck my hips back into him, meeting him thrust for thrust as Asher pulls from my neck and my pleasure builds impossibly high. I'm wound so tight, so taut that I'm afraid there's no way back down from here. I'm going to be stuck in this torturous pleasure forever, and that might make me cry. From joy or despair, I'm not sure, all I know is I need to come.

Asher tightens his hold on my hair, securing my bared

neck, then angles the arm across my chest so he can pinch my nipple, and that does it. My back arches, my entire body stiffens almost to the point of pain, and my pussy clenches so hard Asher can barely move inside me. He rolls my nipple and takes one last, perfectly timed pull from my neck, and my insides pulse with my orgasm.

I writhe in his arms, rapturous as pleasure sears through me, and he groans into my shoulder with his own release. From my neck to my nipple to my clit to my pussy, pulse after pulse of ecstasy races through my body until I'm spent.

I fall limp in his arms, not noticing that he's already healed my neck as I float in waves of bliss. I barely comprehend as he adjusts our positions so I'm lying on top of him with my ear to his chest, his cheek resting on top of my head, and his arms banded securely around me. Asher cradles me against him and I sigh in contentment, a serene smile gracing my lips when he places a gentle kiss on the top of my head.

I'm asleep before he has us fully tucked under the blankets.

42

BAD BLOOD

RAYA

TUESDAY MORNING DAWNS far too early. I stretch and roll over in bed, taking stock of my aching muscles, and smiling when I find I'm deliciously sore in other areas. Asher is already awake, though it seems he resents it if the grumbling groan he releases at my movement is any indication. He slings an arm around my waist and rolls me onto my side, then pulls my back flush against his chest and nuzzles his nose into the hair at the base of my neck.

Neither of our alarms have gone off yet, so I snuggle into him, letting his warmth and cedar-smoke scent surround and lull me into that sweet, quiet place between wake and sleep until we're forced to get ready for the day.

Asher and I putter around the kitchen, him grabbing a fresh bottle of blood while I pop a bagel in the toaster, maneuvering around each other with ease as Reverie sleeps in.

He's a little more distant this morning, more quiet and subdued than is usual even for his admittedly broody personality. I give him his space, taking the time to reflect on things myself as well. He said everything would be handled with his family by the end of the week, and I'm doing my best to put my faith and trust in him despite being kept in the dark. It rankles me a little to be excluded like this, but at the same time there's not anything I can do.

I have no power or control in this situation, nor do I have the resources or connections he might be able to tap into. I try not to let my mind spin with possibilities, and aim to stay in the present moment instead.

Asher drops me off at work again and I use the side entrance, eyeing the people bustling about and preparing the outdoor space for the live press conference. I get to my desk right before 9:00 am, so I have only about an hour to work on my current slide deck before Alex starts the live stream on their monitor, and Kendall and I pull our chairs up to watch together.

The Waltons step to the podium that's been set up at the top of the steps, Claude taking center as Estelle settles to his right. Chadwick steps up next, standing to Claude's left, his arrogant posture and sickening smile make me cringe.

But none of that compares to how my body reacts when Asher steps into the frame.

I blink hard, trying to clear the image, but it doesn't change and my brain can't make sense of it. Asher strides up the steps, and my heart stalls in my chest, struggling for the next beat. He nods to his parents and my airway constricts, my lungs freeze. He stands tall and straight, shoulders thrown back and hands clasped behind his back right next to his mother, and prickles flinch along my skin, up and down my arms as ice slides down my spine.

This can't be happening. How is he there with them?

Alex and Kendall are staring at me, and I stare back. Kendall shrugs and turns back to the screen, prompting Alex to do the same. I pull my phone out, but my hands are shaking and I can barely touch the correct icons as my mind spins out one disastrous scenario after the other.

Has he agreed to whatever terms they set out for him? Asher has told me about a few of the horrors his parents unleashed on him as a child, and I have no doubt he only shared the least abusive ones. Is he rejoining them now? There's no way he would do so willingly. They must have something on him. What have they done to convince him to stand up there, next to them, in support of them? And worst of all, what does that mean for his future?

I squeeze my hands into fists, then shake them out, willing my trembling fingers to steady as I click into our messages. I dial Asher, but he doesn't pick up, and my heart sinks with worry. My eyes are locked on him through the screen, and he doesn't so much as twitch as his phone rings and rings in my ear.

I hang up at his voicemail and send him a text instead. All I can think to ask is "what are you doing?" but again, he doesn't respond. Part of my brain knows his phone is on silent, that it's likely there in his pocket and he has no idea I'm trying to contact him, but the weight of betrayal still sinks down on me.

He can't be doing this.

Belatedly, I realize that confused, hushed chatter has broken out across the open workspace. Everyone seems to be wondering the same thing as me, and muted voices whisper questions back and forth. What? How? Why? Is this good or bad? After Asher's extended absence from work and the rumors that have been swirling, everyone is now wondering what he's doing there with the family he seemed to have cut ties with.

As I look closer, I see his mom is preening, her eyes glinting in the light and her mouth a tight smile, like she's trying to hold in a victorious smirk. The worry gnaws at my insides, a ravenous beast threatening to devour me. Asher's dad is standing straight and proud, tapping one finger on the podium absently as he eyes Asher standing next to them.

Chadwick, on the other hand, looks absolutely livid. He's outright glaring at Asher, having leaned forward to eye him around Claude and Estelle. Asher pays none of them any notice, ignoring everyone and maintaining a calm facade as he stands tall in his place.

Claude begins speaking, welcoming the reporters and requesting that they hold all questions to the end. I tune him out, unable to do anything other than stare at Asher, but Claude's speech is short-lived. He steps back and to the side after only a few minutes, and Estelle takes her turn in front of him at the podium. She says her piece, and we're more than halfway through the allotted time now, when her speech draws to a close and Asher reaches out with one hand, briefly making contact with her upper arm.

My heart thumps a leaden beat in my chest. Estelle angles her head and leans toward him, listening as Asher whispers in her ear, then nods and steps to the side with a smile.

That smile skewers me. My walls are crumbling, and the pretty visions of a future together are flashing to death before my eyes.

Asher steps up to the podium, and the silence on the screen as well as in the office is pointed, anticipatory. Chadwick twitches, clearly trying to restrain himself, and then Asher tips his chin up. He flicks his fingers to either side before gripping the podium, then begins speaking.

"Thank you all for coming," he says, and his voice drills a hole through my chest. "I have some news to share that it appears Claude and Estelle here are not yet aware of."

Murmurs break out around me, and a line of security walk into the frame, escalating the confusion in both myself and my coworkers. My heart trips over itself again, but for a different reason now.

"Although they were recently instated as co-CEO's, with Chadwick here as CFO, there have been some changes behind the scenes in the last couple days. It appears that some of PNCG's board members may have been bribed, some even threatened, into cooperating with the Walton's demands."

A gasp ripples through the crowd, both inside the office and out on the steps.

At this, Estelle grabs Asher's arm and attempts to pull him away from the podium. Her nails dig into his biceps and a growl rumbles from my throat, startling Alex and Kendall next to me.

"Sorry," I whisper, clearing my throat as a flush creeps up my cheeks. My emotions have gone haywire, and I have no idea what's going on anymore.

Asher removes her grip from his arm and continues speaking, even as both she and Claude try to talk over him. Their arms flail in an attempt to regain control, but security officers step up and form a barricade, sectioning the Walton's off from Asher and everyone else.

They restrain a raging Chadwick when he throws a punch at one officer in an attempt to get to Asher. When he starts yelling obscenities, security locks their arms around him and forcibly escorts him out of frame.

I breathe a touch easier with him out of the picture, but the rest of me hasn't settled one bit. Asher ignores the drama unfolding behind him as he continues.

"I have personal experience with the corrupt nature of the Walton family, therefore, I felt it was my personal duty to step up and ensure this corruption did not find a foothold in PNCG. I, Asher Sullivan, have purchased a majority share of holdings and have relieved all board members who were bribed from their positions. I will endeavor to replace them with more worthy candidates, but in the meantime, the Walton's are also relieved of their positions at PNCG."

At this, he turns to Claude and Estelle, both of whom are fuming behind him. I gasp, my hands flying up to cover my mouth.

"Claude, Estelle. You are no longer welcome on this premises."

Claude's face is nearly purple with rage, but he doesn't say a word as security forces him to the side. Estelle freezes, her features slack with shock, but recovers only a moment later.

"You can't do this," she yells. "You're one of us!"

"No, I am not," Asher says, his voice carrying the hardness of steel and the coldness of death. "I am *nothing* like you. I have not been a part of your family for a decade, and I never will be again. I reject everything you are, and everything you stand for."

Estelle's eyes look like they could shoot fire, or ice. Maybe even both at the same time, they are so full of venom and rage and hatred.

"You will pay for this," she screams as security hauls her down the steps.

The camera pans to follow both her and Claude as they're escorted away from the building, and she continues to yell threats at Asher. I tap my fingers in an anxious beat, needing eyes on him again as my thoughts swirl. The camera swings back to the podium when he speaks again.

"I will release a formal statement with additional information on the new board members in the coming weeks after they have settled in. That's all I have to say for now. I won't be taking questions at this time."

I'm already up and out of my seat, sprinting down the hall to the elevator as his last words ring from the speakers behind me.

I can't believe he did that. He went up against his parents, in *public,* and took back everything they were trying to steal from him. From us.

My heart pounds and my body trembles with adrenaline as I pace the tiny elevator. I swear, it's moving more slowly than normal as the numbers blink down.

As soon as the doors slide open, I'm running again. I can see Asher through the front doors conversing with two of the security team, nodding and then glancing up. I see the exact moment he sees me coming, as he raises a hand between the two officers and they part, making way for him to step through and meet me.

I shove through the glass doors and fling myself into his arms. He catches me against him and whirls around, blocking the cameras and sea of reporters with his body so they can't see me. Everything this man does is thoughtful, and I truly have no idea how such a beautiful person came from such an ugly family.

I tremble in his arms, overwhelmed with the noise of reporters firing questions, yelling at him to look at them, security shouting orders and talking into radios. All the while, he holds me steady against him until my legs feel more stable and my heart rate has started to slow.

"Sunshine," he murmurs into my hair. "Let's go back inside. I have a lot to tell you."

I nod, sliding my hand into his and turning back toward the doors behind me.

43

———

DEATH BY SUNSHINE

ASHER

THE MOMENT I spotted Raya running through the lobby, my mind completely blanked. I've been wavering on this decision, this plan of action, for the last week, but I knew if she had any inkling of what was coming, she'd be an anxious mess. I was fairly certain I could pull it off, but not if anyone suspected anything of me.

I push through the security team standing beside me and reach for Raya as she bursts through the doors. Camera flashes go off behind me, so I curl around her, tucking her slight body into my arms and shielding her from the reporters as best I can. She's trembling, and it nearly breaks my heart.

I never wanted to worry her, but I knew some amount of it was unavoidable. She pulls me back through the front doors, and I continue to cover and block her from view as best I can. The last thing I want is for her to get sucked into the media drama is that is sure to unfold.

We tuck ourselves into a side alcove as soon as we're out of sight and I scoop her up, needing to feel her against me. Raya's hands are nearly frantic, smoothing over my shoulders and arms, touching every inch of me she can reach.

"Are you okay?" she asks.

"Yeah, sunshine, I'm okay," I say, then clear my throat. "I'm so sorry I didn't warn you. Are you okay?"

Raya nods, but I'm not sure I believe her. Her beautiful brown eyes are glassy with unshed tears, and pain stabs in my chest.

"What is it? Talk to me, please," I say.

"I was just so scared. When I saw you up there, with them," her voice cracks and she looks away.

I tuck her head into my chest and rock us back and forth.

"You thought I was going back to them?" My heart cracks again, partly because I thought she knew me better than that, and partly because her pain is my pain.

"I know you don't want to." She sniffs and swipes at her nose. "But I thought maybe you didn't have a choice. That there was no other option. I would never want you to give up your life for mine, Asher."

My body goes preternaturally still, in the way only vampires can. So she didn't doubt my integrity, she thought I was doing it to *protect* her. In that sense, she's correct. I would do anything for her, even rejoin my family if it was the only option.

"No, love. My sweet ray of sunshine, I will never go back to them. I found another way."

She nods against my chest and I pull back, gazing down into her eyes.

"So, what did you do? I was mostly panicking, and didn't catch much of what you said." Her shoulders curl in and I swipe my thumbs along her cheekbones.

"That's okay. I'm happy to tell you everything. The quick version is that I found out they, Claude and Estelle, had bribed most of the board and that's how they acquired their positions. I decided to use that massive inheritance I haven't touched to become a majority shareholder, which allowed me to call for a vote of no confidence, nominate new board members, and basically means I was able to take control, elect a new board, and oust the Waltons."

Raya's eyes grow bigger and bigger as I talk, and the words fly from my lips. I'm ready to be done with it. I don't want to even *think* about this situation anymore. I want to move on, me and her, working together, living together, loving each other.

"Why did they seem so happy to see you then?"

My mouth tilts up. Smart little shifter.

"I have been… slowly ingratiating myself to them over the last two weeks. I replied to a couple emails they sent, made it seem like I was giving in. So when I showed up and stood next to them…"

"They thought they won," she breathes.

"They thought they won."

Raya jumps into my arms, a wide grin on her face, and my hands go to her ass, holding her against me as she wraps her legs around my hips.

"My devious vampire," she says, her eyes sparkling as I push her back against the wall.

As I lean in to kiss her, Raya shoves me away. I'm not expecting it, so I fall to the side, and a flash of beige and black catapults away from me. I catch myself with a hand against the wall and my body twists with Raya's motion as she jumps—in full jaguar form—around me.

I shake my head, having no idea what's happening.

"Ray—" my voice cuts off before I can finish calling her name, and my confusion turns to lead in my gut as my heart stops.

Raya takes one massive leap, her strong jaguar body bunching and stretching as she pushes off the floor, straight into Chadwick as he's blurring toward us. Her massive feline body collides with his, and they tumble through the air.

Their limbs tangle as they fight for dominance and control, their bodies flying one over the other with neither letting go as they swipe and growl at each other.

I have no idea how she saw him coming, how she sensed him before I did, how she shifted so quickly or got to him before I even turned around. My brain scrambles to catch up, but it's like everything is happening in slow motion as Raya's life flashes before my eyes.

Chadwick gains the upper hand, throwing Raya down underneath him and baring his fangs, ready to strike, but Raya isn't a weak human. She's the biggest cat I've ever seen, and she doesn't stay down. She uses his momentum against him and they roll one, two, three times, trading places as my heart pounds to life again.

My brain clicks into motion and I blur toward them, but their momentum has carried them too far away from me and before I reach them, it's over.

Raya's jaws are spread wide, encircling Chadwicks neck. Her massive front paws pin his shoulders down, claws shredding into his skin. Her back haunches rest on his legs, immobilizing him. Blood is dripping from them both, with a pool already forming beneath Chadwick.

I slide to my knees, skidding up to them, but unsure what to do or how to help. I don't want Raya to kill him—not because he doesn't deserve it, but because I don't want that on her conscience. Before I can decide what to do, the presence of others crowds my senses, and I look up.

"Everybody freeze!" a security officer yells, one of the ones I hired for this event.

I don't move, except for my eyes, which dart to Raya. She's breathing hard, the air gusting in and out of her, but I notice her teeth haven't pierced Chadwick's skin. She's holding him down, but hasn't done any fatal damage.

"Easy, sunshine," I whisper to her as I slowly turn toward

the wall of drawn guns and black security uniforms, placing my body between them and Raya.

My hands rise into the air as I slowly stand and compose my face.

"Explain to me," my voice is deathly cold, shaking with anger as it ripples into the air around us. "How the man I told you was the single greatest security threat, the one you were not to let out of your sight, was able to get inside this building and *threaten* my *mate*."

The last few words snap out of me and the entire line of security guards flinch back from my wrath.

"Put. The guns. Down." I snarl, razing my gaze over the line of incompetent men. "If any of you continues to point a weapon at my mate, it will be the last thing you do."

Guns clatter to the floor, and the security team leader points his down.

"I apologize, sir." His voice is shakes as his eyes dart behind me. "We weren't sure who the threat was in this situation."

I scan their faces, finding one who looks less shaken than the others. He's still holding his gun, but it's pointed at the ceiling in a position he can easily use again if needed. I point to him, then to the space next to me.

"You, over here."

"Yes, sir," he says, striding over.

I jerk my head for him to step to the side, and he stills in the position I indicated.

"The rest of you are dismissed," I say, turning away. Incompetent fools, the lot of them. I very clearly communicated who the threats were, and they failed to protect the one person I needed to be kept safe.

When I don't hear any movement, I whip back around.

"OUT. NOW," I bark, and they scatter, grabbing their guns as they dash out the doors.

I turn back to Raya and the pathetic man beneath her.

"It's okay, little shifter." I soften my voice as I approach them. "He's lost enough blood, he's no threat to us now."

Raya growls, her entire body vibrating as her glowing, golden eyes flick from Chadwick to me and back again.

It dawns on me that she wasn't worried about herself. In fact, she's never shifted to protect herself before.

Is it possible that she did this to protect me?

If that's the case, she may not be able to shift back until she feels I'm safe. I look around, but we're in a wide open, empty lobby. I think quickly, looking down at my tie. I loosen and take it off, then encourage Raya to shift her weight.

"I'll secure his hands, between that and the wounds you've inflicted, he won't be going anywhere or hurting anyone."

I run a hand down her flank, then nudge her weight to the side so I can bring Chadwick's wrists together. He's whimpering beneath Raya's jaws, and when she shifts her weight, the sharp sent of his urine strikes my nose. I make quick work of binding his hands, ensuring it's tight, even though a tie would never be enough to hold him if I truly wanted him restrained. It's more of a symbol, at this point.

"Alright, little shifter. He's not going anywhere. This security officer is going to keep an eye on him until the police arrive."

I give the man a pointed look, and he immediately dials 911, ensuring the police are on their way.

Raya slowly backs off, unlocking her jaw and releasing Chadwick's neck from her hold. He whimpers again, his bound hands reaching for his neck despite that being the only area on his body that seems unharmed. I eye the pool of blood beneath him with a sick satisfaction.

"Come on, sweet girl, let's get you cleaned up."

I lead Raya to the closest restroom and manage to flip the lock before she rumbles a warning and presses herself between me and the door, herding me to the opposite side of the restroom.

"Okay, okay," I say, backing up until I'm as far from the door, and Chadwick, as I can be. My heart is thumping an erratic rhythm in my chest, and Raya is pacing, prowling around the small space, her enormous cat form only allowing her a few steps in each direction as she continues to protect me.

What remain of her clothes are tattered rags, completely destroyed from her shift and fight. I slip off my suit jacket, then unbutton my shirt. My clothes swamp her, so it should be enough for now, at least to get her out to my car. I hang my shirt on a hook next to the sink, then I sit down with my back against the far wall.

"Raya," I say, keeping my voice as soft and calm as I can.

Her spotted head swings around, and those golden eyes pierce me.

"You're amazing," I tell her, and her ears twitch. "Thank you."

Her pacing slows and she lowers her head, looking at me from the other side of the room.

"Can you come over here? Can I pet you?"

Her head tilts and she hunches down, then shuffles over on her belly as though to make herself seem smaller. As soon as she's within reach, I tug her toward me—as much as I can when she's a nearly 200 pound cat. I pat the floor next to me and she crouches, settling on her haunches. I'm thankful this area has been closed all morning so it's still freshly cleaned.

"You magnificent woman." I card my fingers through her fur, then press my palms to her feline cheeks and gaze straight into her eyes. "Incredible. You're absolutely incredible. Thank you for protecting me. We're safe now."

She blinks one big, slow blink. I have a feeling she's not entirely in control of her animal, so I lean back and settle in, prepared to sit here with her for as long as it takes. Raya's head drops into my lap, and I continue to pet around her ears, up and down her snout, between her eyes, down her neck and along her back. As much as I can reach from this position, and soon she starts purring.

It startles me at first, the deep rumble that comes from her chest and vibrates my entire arm, but I grin when I realize what it is. Her eyes are closed, and it's not long after that, that she shivers and the spotted fur recedes. Her body contorts and transforms back into her beautiful, human skin, and I'm holding my sunshine in my arms again.

44

EMBRACING MY INNER BOSS BABE

RAYA

ASHER PULLS me into his lap before I'm even done shifting, and I huff a laugh at his impatience. I curl my legs into my chest and his arms circle around me, holding me close against him. He nuzzles his nose into my hair and inhales a deep breath. I stick mine to the bare skin at the base of his throat and breathe in his scent as well. I rub my cheeks all over his chest and shoulders, along his jaw and chin, belatedly realizing what a feline move it is to attempt to mark him as mine in that way.

When I look up, he's already gazing at me.

"You weren't afraid of me," I say.

"Why would I be?" His arms are tight around me and his fingers trace small circles in my skin.

"Because I mauled and nearly kill a man?" I say, darting my eyes to the floor next to us.

Asher stiffens for a moment before his muscles relax again.

"That is no man," he says, his voice gruff. "That is a monster, and he deserves to die."

His arms cinch tighter around me, and I snuggle into him, letting him hold me as we chase away each other's demons.

"Are you okay?" Asher asks a short time later.

I nod and tap his hands to let me go. They tighten around me for a moment before loosening, and my face flushes at my nakedness.

"Let me make sure you're not hurt," Asher says, standing and pulling me to my feet with him as he twists my body and inspects every inch of me.

My cheeks flame hotter under his scrutiny, but he doesn't seem to notice. He tugs me toward the sink and wets a paper towel, gently trailing it along one arm, then my ribs on one side, and finally around my calves, feet, and ankles.

It appears most of the blood wasn't mine, either that or I've already healed from whatever superficial wounds Chadwick managed to inflict on me. One laceration along my side still beads with fresh blood, and I eye it in the mirror before the weight of Asher's gaze settles on mine, and I turn my eyes up to him.

"May I?" he asks, eyes darting to the slice over my ribs.

I nod, and he cleans it with the paper towel before going down on one knee next to me. He ducks under my arm, and my hand curls into his hair as his circle my waist, holding me to him. Asher wets his lips, then looks up at me before swiping his tongue out and gently licking my wound. He closes his eyes and his eyebrows pinch, and I'm reminded of what he told me before. That the strength of his power is only partly due to his bloodline, more important is the conviction and intent behind the action.

As with the other time he healed me, my skin begins to knit together immediately. Asher's eyes are glued to the cut, and when it doesn't close all the way, he glares at the puffy, red skin before licking it again with a soft growl.

I smile and my ribs jump when I hold in a laugh. My poor, cranky, perfectionistic vampire, not happy with a ninety percent healed wound.

His narrowed gaze darts to mine when he feels the laugh I hold in, and I pinch my lips together, doing my best impression of an innocent doe as I beam a bright smile down at him.

He huffs and turns his attention back to my ribs, swiping a gentle finger over the healed area and only seeming satisfied when I giggle at the ticklish sensation.

Asher snags his shirt from a hook on the door and holds it out for me to slip my arms through. My heart swells with gratitude as I thread my arms through the sleeves.

"I have a spare change of clothes in my desk drawer. I left my phone up there, but if you have yours, could you text Alex and maybe they can bring them down?"

Asher nods and pulls his phone out, then holds it up to his ear. I roll my eyes. Of course he'd rather call than text.

Alex is knocking on the door moments later, and Asher cracks it open enough to snatch my clothes from their hands before slamming it shut again.

"You could be a little nicer," I say, trying to hold in a laugh when Alex yells "You're welcome!" through the door.

Asher glares at it like the door somehow offended him before turning to me with a scowl still on his face.

"You should go home," he says.

I laugh, and he draws back, blinking at me.

"Oh, were you serious?"

"Yes, I was serious. You were just injured, threatened, assaulted. You could have been killed—"

"Whoa, whoa, whoa. Slow down. First off, I was barely injured, and I'm already healed, thanks to you. Second, I wasn't threatened or assaulted. I'm pretty sure he was coming after you, and my animal sensed it. Before I knew what was happening, I was leaping, claws first. So if anyone was assaulted, it was him, not me."

I pause my tirade for a glare, and he narrows his eyes in return.

"Third," I draw out the word, and his gaze turns wary. "If anyone tries to separate me from *my mate* right now, I won't be held accountable for the destruction I leave in my wake when I do anything I can to get back to him."

Asher's eyes widen and his lips part.

"What? You thought I didn't hear that? Or did you think I wouldn't agree?" I smirk, and his lips attack me. He folds me in his arms and I melt against his chest, breathing his air and slicking my tongue against his fangs.

"My mate," he whispers against my lips, his voice reverent. "My fierce, shifter mate."

"My grumpy, protective vampire," I whisper back, earning a light swat on my ass.

I wiggle out of his hold, much to his clear displeasure, and begin dressing.

"We should go up to the office. Everyone was watching, and I'm sure they have questions," I say, buttoning my pants and straightening my shirt. I pull my hair back into a loose braid, the best I can do given the current situation.

Asher nods, a slight frown still on his face, but he takes my hand, engulfing it in his as he opens the door and steps out. His body is instantly on alert, eyes darting left and right, taking in every mote of dust floating through the air as we wait for the elevator.

When we step through the open doorway into the workspace, one person gasps, and then a cheer goes up, clapping and a couple whistles resound through the room. Asher freezes, his face an uncomfortable grimace of confusion and dislike, so I tug him forward and let my smile speak for us both. I know he doesn't like attention, but this is one instance he needs to deal with it.

I raise my hands and the room quiets.

"Thanks, everyone," I say, beaming at the coworkers I've grown to care for over the last few months. "Your support means so much. I'm so thankful to work with such incredible people every day!"

Alex wolf whistles and I grin at them.

I dart a sideways glance at Asher and he seems to have composed himself, so I step back and gesture to him.

He clears his throat, pinches his lips, then forces himself into the spotlight again.

"As Raya said, thank you. I know there have been a lot of changes lately, but know that as majority shareholder of the company, I don't intend to make any radical changes. Your jobs are safe. Your clients and projects are safe. I simply want to ensure everything is working as it should, and that there isn't any corruption in our ranks."

Everyone claps again and Asher shifts his weight. I loop my hand around his elbow and squeeze.

"I'll send out a company wide email in the next couple days with a formal statement. For now, there's no need for worry or concern. Everybody take the rest of the day off, I think we've all earned it."

Everyone cheers and claps, once again led by Alex, and although Asher scowls as he turns and strides away, I can tell he's only doing it to cover the smile that wants to break free. He isn't used to smiling. He's not very good at it, truth be told, but it's something I intend to help him practice every day from here on out.

WE PICK up Reverie from Asher's place and then head back to Zuri's apartment, as I've started calling it in my head. I suppose mentally I've already moved out, and it's probably something I should confirm with her sooner rather than later so she can find a new roommate.

Zuri scrambles to open the door as soon as she hears my

key in the lock. She swings it open and then flings herself at me. I wrap my arms around her and look sideways at Asher, but he's as bewildered as I am.

"Bloody hell, Raya, I was so damn worried!" Zuri's voice is muffled in my hair, and I pull back from her so we can walk into the apartment.

"What are you talking about?"

She gapes at me.

"What do you mean, what am I talking about?" she yells. "Last I saw before the live stream cut out was that murderous asshole Chadwick slamming through the front doors *you* had gone through only minutes before!"

Oh. Yikes.

"Ah, well, um," I turn to Asher, but he pulls his shoulders back and nods at me. Apparently, I'm on my own.

"So, I kinda turned into a massive jaguar and almost killed him?" I spit the words out as fast as I can and trail off at the end, not sure how to fully tell her what happened.

Zuri's arms drop to her sides, limp as noodles, and she stares at me.

"Wait, you what?" Reverie is the one shrieking this time as she comes streaking back into the room after checking on her bedroom plants.

"Yeah," I scratch the back of my neck, then give them a quick rundown of how Chadwick was coming for us and my animal took over.

"That's amazing, Raya! And so scary. I'm glad you're okay, holy shit," Zuri says, Reverie nodding in agreement.

"You're badass," Rev whispers, and I laugh.

"The important thing is, we're all okay. Asher did it, the company is taken care of, and we don't have to worry about the Waltons ever again."

Asher told me on the drive to his place that we can both file for restraining orders, so that should take care of the problem. With any luck, we won't have to see or hear from them again. I meet his eyes and we share a small, hopeful smile.

"Asher," Zuri starts, then stops, her eyes pinging between us.

Asher raises his brows, turning his attention to her.

"I..." she takes a deep breath, then continues. "I'm sorry. I was wrong to treat you the way I did. I shouldn't have judged you without getting to know you first. I apologize."

"Oh the contrary, vampire," Asher says, a smirk in his tone, "I wouldn't have it any other way."

Zuri's face scrunches in confusion, and Asher slings an arm around my waist, pulling me into him.

"I will never say no to Raya's friends being protective of her. For having her safety and best interests at heart."

They eye each other for a long, silent moment before sharing an understanding nod.

I clear my throat, eyes narrowed as I glance between them.

"Perhaps Raya's friends could also take into account how much they trust her to make the right decisions on her own," I say.

They both shrink a little under my sharp tone before readily agreeing with me. I grin, then pull out a deck of cards.

"Anybody up for some Go Fish?"

PLAYING WITH A VAMPIRE

ASHER

10 months later

Raya is inside the bungalow we rented on the Columbia River Gorge getting ready, while I'm outside pacing. The view is stunning, with the river down below us and mountains in the distance, the property itself is surrounded by trees. We wanted the most private space we could find so Reverie could come, and this place is perfect.

I stop to take in the view, trying to appreciate it. All I can think about is her though. I'd rather be staring into Raya's eyes, letting her blinding light radiate through me, feast my senses on her beauty, rather than the beauty of the nature around me.

She's a balm to my battered soul, and even though there are mere feet and walls between us, I feel antsy without her in my sight. I've felt broken for most of my life; a secret disappointment to Claude and Estelle for the first half of it, and then the clear black sheep with a heavy shadow when I estranged myself from them as soon as I could. Those first few years on my own were tough, especially since I refused to touch my inheritance, but looking at where it led makes me realize it's all been worth it. Everything in my life has led me here.

I've been helping Raya with her shifting still. Not so much in learning how to control it anymore, she's mostly got that down, but more along the lines of being comfortable with who she is and figuring out the ins and outs of what she can do. Turns out, many of her shifts into various animals have corresponded to whatever she's feeling in the moment, a pattern I noticed early on, but took her a while to catch on to herself.

Despite that inclination, if she focuses her attention, she can choose what she wants to shift into no matter her mood. We haven't yet found a limit on what animals she's able to shift into, but she has hit her limits on frequency and duration. Shifting takes its toll, and she's always sweaty and tired after the mental and physical toll our practices take.

Lucky for me, I quite enjoy a sweaty and loopy-with-fatigue Raya. She's even more silly in those moments, and she lets me take care of her more than she otherwise would. I love her independent streak, but I also love when she accepts my help. I'm becoming more addicted to her every moment we spend together.

Soft footsteps pad across through the grass behind me, and I recognize the tread of Raya's father. He probably saw me pacing by myself and came out to keep me company.

He's a good man.

I slow my feet and settle to a stop at the top of the ridge overlooking the river below. Terry wanders up next to me and clasps his hands in a comfortable, relaxed pose. Neither of us speaks for long moments, and I start to wonder if he doesn't approve. I've never been good enough for Claude and Estelle; what makes me think I'd be good enough in Raya's parents' eyes either?

Terry clasps a hand on my shoulder, but his eyes remain fixed on the horizon.

"Our Raya chose a good one," he says, and I blink, then glance at him from the corner of my eye. He's nodding slowly, then turns toward me. "I know you're still coming around to the idea, but we're thankful for you. I know you'd do anything for my daughter, that she means more to you than you imagined possible."

My throat bobs with a hard swallow as I fight to maintain eye contact with this short, intimidating man.

"Yes, sir," I say, and he chuckles.

"Ah, son. None of that nonsense," Terry says, turning back to the gorge. "We're glad to have you in the family."

With that bomb, he squeezes my shoulder once more before turning away and wandering into the trees. I clear my throat in an attempt to clear the emotion from my chest, but it barely dissipates, so I focus on the sky as the sun starts to lean toward the horizon in the distance, knowing the best moments of my life are coming.

Before I know it, I'm standing in a copse of trees that are strung with lights and flowers, a path of petals through the forest leading to my feet and seeming to glow in the golden light of the setting sun. Raya's parents and brother are sitting on blankets on either side of the aisle, and Reverie whizzes between the trees to her spot on a cushion in front of Raya's mom. Jo comes out next, striding toward a blanket next to Wesley, but taking a few extra steps in my direction instead of sitting down.

She walks up to me, stares into my eyes for an intimidating eternity, then clasps my biceps, giving a hard clap and a squeeze before flipping around and settling next to her brother.

Zuri is at the start of the path, right next to a massive tree that I know is hiding my bride from me. Zuri walks down the aisle, being careful not to disturb the petals, then stops and looks at the open blankets on both sides. She looks up at me, gives me a wink, and chooses the blanket on my side of the aisle.

My eyes burn and I blink to clear them, not wanting to miss a moment of what comes next.

I can't handle the emotion of today, and the important part hasn't even begun yet. Someone starts up the music, and it drifts softly through the speakers we propped up in the trees earlier. My gaze fixes on the tree that shields Raya from my desperate eyes, and finally, *finally* she steps out from behind it.

If I thought she was a radiant sunbeam before, it has nothing on the ethereal moonbeam she is now. Her hair is pulled back with a few loose tendrils dangling around her ears, and her dress is a shimmering silver with sleeves that fall off her shoulders, tempting me with the stretch of open skin around her neck. She glows in the waning light of the sun, the crisp shine of the waxing moon above, and the twinkling lights surrounding us.

Her lips are the exact color of her blood.

I forget to breathe. My chest tightens, my entire body turns rigid, and I fight my vampiric instincts with everything I have. My vampire is screaming at me to chase, to hunt, to hide her from the world and keep her as my own. My blood thrums through my veins, pounds in my temples. My fangs snap down and a low rumble builds in my chest. It is everything I can do to remain still and present in this moment.

Raya's smirk breaks me out of it. The little shifter knew exactly what she was doing with that dress, that lip stain, that hairdo. I narrow my eyes as she floats over the petals toward me, and she winks at me.

Winks.

I let out the growl that I've been fighting to keep

contained, and a laugh rings out of her, echoing through the trees and setting my bones on fire as she steps up next to me.

"Just wait until we don't have an audience, little shifter. You're playing with fire," I whisper in her ear.

She whispers back, "No, love, I'm playing with a vampire."

Her lips twitch with a grin, then settle into a soft smile as we take our places. Zuri stands from her blanket and steps up next to us, acting as the marriage officiant for the parts we can't do ourselves. I don't hear what she says, my focus is entirely on Raya, wondering if my eyes are deceiving me or if she her skin is somehow shimmering.

When Zuri steps back a few paces, it's time for our parts. I take Raya's hands in mine, her delicate fingers and soft palms are encompassed in my larger ones, but I can feel her power, even in that.

"Raya, my ray of sunshine, my moonbeam, my little shifter, my mate."

My voice is hoarse with emotion, and she squeezes my fingers as her eyes turn glassy in response. I swallow my fear, my worry, my defensive instincts that warn against such vulnerability, and my gaze never leaves her enchanting eyes as they give me the strength to continue.

"You brought light into my darkness, and life into what was a bleak and meaningless existence. I was barely surviving without you, and it was not a happy one. I didn't know what it meant to be happy until you barreled your way into my life. Your chaos broke me from the choking binds I had placed around myself, your hardships gave me new purpose and determination to do better, your joy gave me hope."

Raya blinks watery eyes and her smiling lips tremble, but I don't let any of it deter me. I can't stop now, she deserves this and so much more.

"I vow to bring all that and more to our marriage. I will endeavor to provide strength when you seek it, to brighten your glow and bring a smile to your face—and to match it with my own—at every possibility. I vow to challenge you, and to meet your challenges in return. I vow to be there for you night and day, no matter what the world may throw at us, I will always be by your side. I love you more than the earth loves the sun, or the moon loves the earth, or the stars love the sky. You are my guiding light, Raya, and I pledge my life to yours."

Raya bursts into tears, and I widen my eyes, horrified at having made her cry in such a way. Zuri pulls a tissue from somewhere and thrusts it at me, and I lean into Raya, attempting to pry her hands from her face.

"Raya, my light," I whisper. "Please."

She shakes her head and her entire body shudders with a sob. I clutch her to me, whispering my love and support for her, placing my body between hers and everyone else.

"Please, Raya, what is it? What can I do?"

"My makeup," she sniffles behind her hands, and my chest stutters with a short, quiet laugh.

She's worried about her makeup?

I bend down and pull her hands away, then swipe her tears with the tissue from Zuri and clear the black streaks running down her face.

"There," I say, dropping a kiss to her forehead. "Perfect."

Raya sniffs and turns still watery eyes up to me, pats me on the chest, and leans up on her tip-toes to kiss me.

"I don't think we're supposed to do this yet," I say, but her mouth covers mine already, and my words are muffled against her lips.

"Don't care," she murmurs into my mouth.

Zuri—very pointedly—clears her throat, and Raya breaks away with a grin. I can't help but smile back at her, and it's then I notice that pretty much everyone is crying. Zuri, both of Raya's parents, and Josephine all have tissues held to their eyes. Reverie has tears streaking down her face, but is also sporting the biggest smile I've ever seen on the tiny creature. Even Wesley seems to be affected; he has his head tilted back and is looking at the dark tree limbs above, blinking.

Raya nudges me back to my spot, takes my hands in hers, and gives me her vow.

"Ash."

My nickname on her blood-red lips, the one that is perfectly fitting for her and that she alone calls me, nearly sends me to my knees.

"Asher," she says quieter, squeezing my hands again. I squeeze hers in return, offering her the support she gave me only moments ago.

"I love you so freaking much," she says, and I smile at her reclaiming of the word *freak*. "You are stubborn, broody, and single-minded."

I start to frown, but her grin gives me pause.

"I love all of those things about you. Without your stubbornness, you would have given up on me after the first time I failed in our shifting practice. Without your broody attitude, I wouldn't have felt compelled to bring a smile to your face. Without your diligence and focus, we may not have made it through the hardships we faced over the last year."

Now I'm the one blinking watery eyes. Never have I thought those to be positive qualities, but seeing myself through Raya's eyes is... earth-shattering.

"You are the love of my life. My perfect other half," she continues.

Her warmth burrows into me, seeps into my skin, through muscle and flesh, winding through my bones and filling my heart.

"You complete me and complement me, and I vow to do all I can to return to you everything you've given to me. I will be with you always, like a barnacle you can't scrape off."

I choke out a raspy, bewildered laugh, and she beams.

"I love you, Asher. Thank you for being my mate."

Zuri jumps into action, speaking as fast as she can since I'm already reaching my hands forward to cup Raya's face in my palms.

"I now pronounce you, Mrs. and Mr. Merritt!" Zuri throws her hands up, raining flower petals down around us and everyone cheers. "KISS!"

I clasp her cheeks, holding her reverently, in awe that I get to call this incredible woman mine. My lips find hers, and she smiles against me as our mouths meet.

One of the small ones, one of her most genuine smiles, the secret ones she reserves for those she most loves.

And my soul is finally home.

THE END.

WANT MORE of Asher and Raya?

I've got a sweet and silly hiking scene, AND a bonus (spicy) ending chapter for subscribers! Sign up for my newsletter to get instant access:

Sign up at AuthorCorinaBair.com

ACKNOWLEDGMENTS

Love (Literally) Bites is the second book I wrote, even though I'm publishing it third. It was really fun to write, incorporating paranormal elements into our contemporary world and letting my chaotic shifter shine. That being said, thank you, my gorgeous reader.

Thank you for reading my book, and if you have shared this book or told anyone about it, created content or recommended it on social media, left a rating or review, thank you so very much. It means more than I can express with words on a page at the end of a book. I hope you enjoyed Love (Literally) Bites.

There are a few people I'd like to specifically thank, without which Raya and Asher's story would not have been written.

Alex. ALEX. As always, this book wouldn't have happened without you. I simply don't have the words to express how much you mean to me as person, let alone your invaluable feedback, encouragement, and consistency in pushing me to keep improving. Going on this journey together has been one of the best experiences of my life and I can't wait to see what comes next for both of us!

Thank you, AnaCena, my favorite librarian sister in law, for being an early reader and helping with editing. I am so thankful that I can always turn to you for book and writing related topics!

Shoutout to Megan of Thorns and Roses for intimacy coaching and helping me level up my spice scenes!

To my beta readers and authenticity/sensitivity readers: Hannah, Cathy, Gabriela, Nicole, Carly, Sarah, and Amanda. Thanks to all of you for your thoughtful critiques and helpful feedback in making this story what it is.

Thanks to my brother, Eric, for ensuring the astronomy related stuff was all legit, and to my sister in law, Maria, for helping me understand what the heck a consultant is. (I think I got it... but still kinda don't really know. Regardless, thanks for making Raya's job an actual job.)

Andrew. Love of my life. Thank you for helping bring this story to life. For letting me talk about my chaotic shifter and never once questioning or doubting my ideas (or my sanity.) For brainstorming and problem-solving with me when I got stuck. For bringing me water even when I said I didn't want it. I love you!

Lastly... one more thanks for the romance readers!

ABOUT THE AUTHOR

Corina writes feel-good love stories with tension-building spice, funny and relatable characters, and Happily Ever After's that feel like a hug in book form. All of her novels take place in queer-normative worlds.

When she's not reading or writing, you can find Corina forcing snuggles on her dog, rollerblading with her husband, playing cozy video games, or getting dirty in the garden.

Connect with her on socials:
@CorinaBairBooks on IG
Corina Bair, Author on FB
@AuthorCorinaBair on TikTok

www.ingramcontent.com/pod-product-compliance
Lightning Source LLC
Chambersburg PA
CBHW030756310726
48969CB00005B/1435